Dragonfly Landing

Dragonfly Landing

Helen L. O'Reilly

Illustrated by
greg herron

Dragonfly Landing

Helen L. O'Reilly

Published by:
Bug Print Press
346 Irwin Lane,
Lillington, NC 27546

In conjunction with:
Old Mountain Press, Inc.
2542 S. Edgewater Dr.
Fayetteville, NC 28303

www.OldMountainPress.com

Copyright © 2010 Helen L. O'Reilly
Illustrations by Greg Herron
Interior text design by Tom Davis
ISBN: 978-0-9829641-0-1
Library of Congress Control Number: 2010938985

First Edition
Printed and bound in the United States of America by Morris Publishing®
www.morrispublishing.com • 800-650-7888
1 2 3 4 5 6 7 8 9 10

Dedication

*T*his book is dedicated to my daughters for whom this tale was originally meant; but who grew into beautiful ladies before I could finish. Shannon: for showing me windows to the world which I would never have looked through and your generous strong spirit. Molly: for bringing sunshine into my world with your vivacious zest for life, and all the 'baby hugs'.

Also to my darling grandchildren: Scarlett and Vincent Skillman. I hope you read "Mugga's" book someday and remember me with lots of love and fond memories.

To my best friend Ryn, for showing me what courage really is.

To my sisters Hallie and Sharon, my lifetime blessings: I love you both.

For all the O'Reilly clan: Thanks for the support and encouragement – and not laughing at my little 'bug book'.

Acknowledgement

I would like to express my never ending gratitude to my wonderfully talented husband for his unflagging patience and support. I'm quite sure my little story would have remained filed in a dusty drawer without your loving "devil's advocate" editing and advice.

I also send out heartfelt thanks to Greg Herron; illustrator, brother-in-law and insect collector extraordinaire.

To my sixth grade teacher Miss Ellis for reading my short stories to the class, your encouragement was priceless.

Also: to Mary Stewart for relating the folktale of the Moonspinners in her book by the same name.

Contents

Preface

I'm sure most of my readers realize that the attributes and personas I have bestowed upon my characters are purely fictional i.e. gypsy moths who play fiddles. They come not from the pages of an entomology textbook, but from the quirky recesses of my brain. The scientific names of insects, animals and plants are to the best of my knowledge, accurate. If blatant mistakes are found by the naturalist experts among you; I apologize and wish to say that my only goal is to entertain.

Also: to my younger readers: please do not eat any of the foods my characters ate, such as wild mushrooms or berries. These could make you very sick, or even kill you.

I hope you enjoy reading the book as much as I did writing it. Perhaps it will spark that elusive part of your mind known as imagination.

Thank you
Helen L. O'Reilly

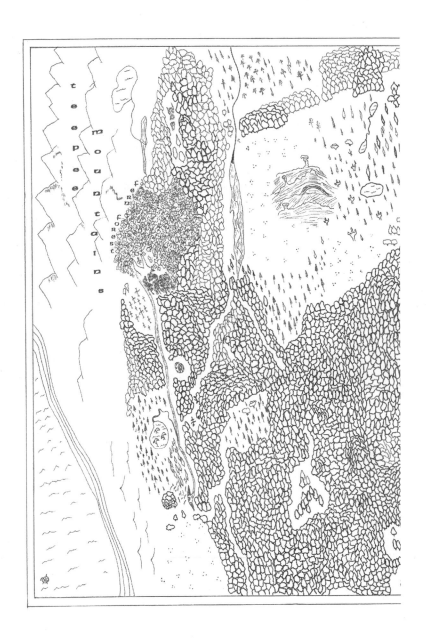

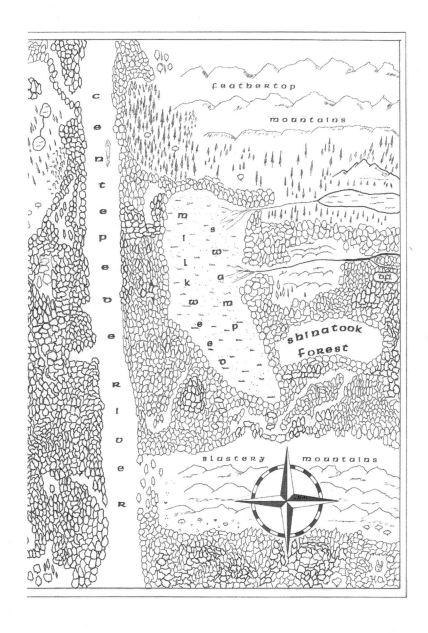

Chapter 1
The Seed Pod Festival

*T*here was a pale haloed moon suspended in an ocean of brilliant stars on what started out as a very ordinary night. For two winged creatures however, their ordinary lives were about to become extraordinarily unordinary.

SOMEWHERE IN THE darkness, a huge moth circled a field of brambles and scrub oaks searching for the tantalizing aroma its feathery feelers had been sensing since late afternoon. Finally, it spotted a moonflower vine covered in white funnel shaped blossoms, and glided in for a landing. As the moth sipped the energizing nectar a moonbeam struck its wings and a soft green iridescence flashed in the darkness.

Not far away in a glen of spice bushes and Solomon seal on the edge of an ancient oak forest, a group of young fireflies were engaged in a furious flying race. All of the fireflies blinked their tail beacons proudly as they soared over the bush tops; except for one. His remained always dark. They flew faster and higher reveling in the freedom of the open skies and when the race came to an end the group settled breathlessly on a branch.

"I won! I won," one of the fireflies called out puffing his chest.

"No you didn't," the largest racer proclaimed. "Crispin was way out in front."

"Oh no not again," a firefly with a crooked antenna groaned. "He always wins."

"Well, what do you expect," another racer added. "He doesn't have a tail light, so he's much lighter."

The larger firefly looked around quizzically, then asked, "By the way, where is Crispin?"

CRISPIN WAS SO excited about winning another race that he kept flying until he was certain none of the other racers could catch him. When he finally stopped and looked around, none of his friends was in sight. To make matters worse, he didn't recognize any of the trees or bushes around him. He circled the area for some time to get his bearings, but soon gave up. "I'll never get home if I don't get help," he mumbled to himself. "There has to be someone around who can point me in the right direction."

Just then he noticed a brilliant flash of green, flitting around a vine covered tree stump. He headed towards it and as he neared the vine, a sudden gust of wind caught his wings slamming him into the vine.

"Ahhh," the moth yelled as his perch swayed violently almost flinging him to the ground. After regaining his footing the moth searched the foliage and noticed a small firefly tightly clutching a stem. "My goodness," the moth exclaimed. "You startled me. Having a bit of a problem with our landings tonight?"

"I'm really very sorry, the wind caught me off guard," Crispin explained.

"No harm done, I'm fine," the moth replied. "My name is Tiberius. It's a pleasure to meet you young fella."

Crispin stuck out a foreleg, "I'm Crispin. It's nice to make your acquaintance."

The two insects shook, then Tiberius asked, "Are you flying alone? I thought fireflies always stayed in groups?"

"We usually do, but I'm sort of lost."

Tiberius chuckled, then rubbed a feeler. "I didn't know that someone could be - sort of - lost."

"Wellll," he said sheepishly. "Okay, I'm really lost. I was hoping you could give me directions home."

"And where's that," Tiberius asked.

"I live at Dragonfly Landing."

"Hmm," Tiberius said scrunching his face. "Can't say I've heard of the place before."

"It's in a very old oak forest and Fish Hole Creek is nearby," Crispin explained glancing nervously at the rising moon. "Oh no, it's getting late. There's a festival at my village tonight and my parents will be really worried if I'm not home soon."

"If there's a festival tonight, what are you doing way out here," Tiberius questioned.

"My friends and I decided to have a flying race before the fun started."

Tiberius grinned broadly. "And you were so far ahead that you lost everyone else; right?"

Crispin nodded; then replied, "I win all of the races."

"Really," Tiberius said cocking an eyebrow. "You must be awfully fast."

"I'm lighter than everyone else," he explained, then turned and wagged his tail. "Look, I don't have at taillight. Some of the others call me hollow tail." He frowned then went on, "I hate it. I don't want to be different."

"Sometimes being different can be a big help," Tiberius commented. "Take me for instance. I have very different eyes from butterflies. They can't see well in the dark, but I can. There are some flowers like this moonflower vine which are open only at night. The butterflies never get to taste it."

Crispin was silent for a moment then said cheerfully, "It is nice to be a champion flyer, but," his face fell a bit. "When I'm lost, no one can find me."

Tiberius inspected the slender brown yellow striped bug then asked with a perplexed frown, "Where did your light go? Did it fall out or did someone steal it?"

"Great grubs, no. I was born without one. It's a very rare condition."

"I see," Tiberius replied feeling somewhat sorry for the tiny bug. "I have a great idea," he added with a twinkle in his eye. "Hop on my back, and I'll give you a ride home. It'll be an experience you'll never forget. I'll have you home in the blink of a gnat's eye."

"Great grasshopper legs!" Crispin shouted. "I've never ridden on someone's back before. My friends will flip when they see me arrive on a giant's back."

"Hop on then, we'd best be going," Tiberius said as he lowered his body.

One big jump was all it took for Crispin to land on his target; then he sat and straddled the moth's back for support. "Now," Tiberius directed, "Grab hold of that tuft of hair behind my head and lower your body to lessen the drag."

He did as told; then Tiberius continued his coaching. "Just hold on tight and try not to wiggle too much. I'll try to fly as straight as

I can. If you spot something familiar, just tap my antenna otherwise we'll end up flying in the clouds all night."

"All right," Crispin replied excitedly, "I'm ready if you are."

"Okay, here we go," Tiberius replied flapping his wings.

With one huge bounce, the two were airborne and skimming along the ground. They climbed higher and soon the trees below were transformed into small fuzzy dots. Never having flown higher than the treetops, Crispin kept his eyes shut tight; but soon out of curiosity, he chanced a look. He watched mesmerized as Tiberius' powerful wings rose and fell in a dance of dazzling shifting green light. Later, he felt confident enough to lean over and he studied the landscape for signs of his village. To his dismay, he saw nothing familiar, so he turned his head upwards and gasped as he caught sight of the moon. "It's gigantic," he whispered, then pondered silently, 'Could we really be flying so high or is it just my imagination. Nothing seems real tonight. Maybe I hit my head and I'm dreaming all this.' He pinched a leg to see if he was awake. "Ouch, it's real all right."

He returned his gaze earthward, and noticed a thin tributary breaking free from the river and disappearing around a knobby tree covered hill. "Ah!" Crispin cried out excitedly. "There's the Roaring Springs River, and that branch must be Fish Hole Creek. We must be getting close." As they drew nearer his pulse quickened as he spotted several tiny lights twinkling through the forest canopy. He quickly tapped on Tiberius' antenna, and called out, "There's the village landing strip."

Tiberius looked down and couldn't believe his eyes. Below him; surrounded by tall stately oaks, was a long narrow strip of earth bordered by tiny glowing lights. 'That's definitely a landing strip,' Tiberius marveled to himself as he dipped lower and circled for a landing.

Suddenly Crispin tugged on Tiberius' antenna. "We can't land yet; there's a huge group of dragonflies coming. The young ones have been out practicing their take-offs and landings. They're such crazy fliers they need a place outside the village to land. You get a bunch of those guys darting and somersaulting in at once, there's always a big mess to clean up afterwards. Anybody else wanting to land here has to wait in line. Nobody minds though, it's really their runway since they take care of it."

"That's fine with me," Tiberius replied. "We'll just wait our turn."

The pair fluttered nearby and watched the aerobatic antics of the incoming dragonflies. The trainees emerged from the darkness and lined up hovering just beyond the runway. A larger dragonfly wagged its wings and the trainees took turns darting, gliding, somersaulting, and dive bombing down the runway. It didn't take long for the dragonflies to land and one by one they disappeared into the forest.

Crispin didn't see anymore incoming dragonflies so he gave Tiberius the 'okay' for their final approach.

Tiberius, never having made a landing on a real runway was a bit nervous, but held his wings steady and glided to a perfect landing. "Well now young Crispin, how was that for a free ride," he questioned as his passenger jumped from his back.

"It was the most exciting thing that every happened to me," Crispin replied hopping up and down excitedly. "I've never flown so high in all my life. I felt as though I could reach out and touch the moon. Is there something I can do for you in return?"

"It was indeed my pleasure. I've never given a ride to anyone before. It feels good to be useful."

The two new friends were shaking each others front leg to say good-bye when Crispin's eyes widened as he was struck with an idea. "Hey. Why don't you stay for the Seed Pod Festival tonight? We're celebrating the summer's end seed harvest and there's not a better show to be found anywhere in the forest."

"Hmm," Tiberius pondered scratching a feeler. "I'm not the partying type; in fact, I'm kind of a loner, and there are a lot of tasty flowers opened tonight."

"Please, please," Crispin pleaded jumping up and down on one leg.

"I...don't know," Tiberius replied skeptically, "I'm not used to being around smaller insects." He paused and eyed his huge wings. "What happens if I forget and open my wings at the wrong time?" His eyes widened with concern. "It could be disastrous. Things could get knocked over and heaven forbid I should injure some-one."

"You could sit on the edge of the clearing close to the campfire and hear some delightful music and fascinating storytelling. You wouldn't hurt anyone there, and I could bring you a cup of nectar so you wouldn't get a rumbly stomach!"

"You make it sound very inviting and perhaps it just might work," Tiberius replied with growing excitement in his voice. "Yes, I think I shall come after all. Lead the way my young friend."

Crispin leapt off the ground, made a loop in the air, and entered the oak forest with his new friend trailing close behind. Soon, the pair came to the edge of the clearing and began hiking down a smooth well maintained dirt path. They hadn't gone far when Tiberius noticed a square bark sign attached to a gnarled dead tree stump. It was illuminated by a curious golden light blazing from an acorn shell lantern. Painted on the sign in bright purple berry juice were two words with an arrow pointing straight ahead. He read the words out loud as they passed. "Dragonfly Landing."

Farther along they passed two more signs. The first stated 'Earthworms, please check in with the sentries': and the last one read 'Welcome to our Village'.

"We're almost there," Crispin gestured impatiently as he scurried faster and Tiberius quickened his pace to keep up. Suddenly, Crispin came to an abrupt halt as the trail ended and the oak branches opened up. "This is my home," he stated with a broad sweep of his forelegs. "Welcome to Dragonfly Landing."

Tiberius stood at the village entrance and gazed in astonishment at the spectacular view. The villagers had been hard at work for days, decorating for the festival and the forest of huge oak trees had been transformed into a magical wonderland. "I..I've never seen anything like this in all my life," he stammered.

"That's why I wanted you to come with me," Crispin replied proudly.

Sprawled in front of Tiberius was a huge clearing lighted with glowing orange Chinese lantern pods which had been hung from almost every tree and branch. Encircling the village was a well traveled pathway edged with brightly colored flower garlands on bamboo stakes and a roaring campfire erupted from a pit in its center.

Surrounding the campfire were clusters of mushroom tables where an odd mixture of beetles, dragonflies, bugs and small moths lounged, eating and drinking merrily. Other groups mingled amongst themselves chatting and laughing loudly. Several fat black stag beetles wove their way through the partygoers serving spongy cakes and flower topped nutshell drinks from trays balanced on their backs. Gleeful shouts announced the arrival of a gang of young camel crickets who were engaged in a boisterous game of 'kick the puff-ball'.

Suddenly panicked shouts erupted from the partygoers as the mischievous youths whizzed past the stag beetles snatching the scrumptious tidbits from their backs. One unfortunate server was knocked off his legs and his tray crashed to the ground. Several older camel crickets rushed over scolding the rambunctious youths and sent them, glum faced, to sit on a bench.

Somewhere in the shadows a band struck up a marching tune, and a line of festively dressed damselflies streamed from behind a rock and began parading around the pathway. Their heads were festooned with wreaths woven from sunny yellow dandelions and garlands of ostrich ferns which hung over their wings. Each marcher held a brightly colored flagpole which they waved with great flourish. At one point in their route, they halted to perform for the spectators.

The damselflies lined up side by side, hooked forearms and began a high kicking dance. They paused momentarily then began a whirling, rhythmic foot tapping and hand clapping routine. Afterwards, the damselflies took several flamboyant bows, and continued their march around the village.

The crowd cheered madly and flower petals began cascading from the sky. Tiberius gazed upward in curiosity and noticed the trees bordering the village were alive with activity. Insects of every description filled the canopies, sitting on tree limbs or buzzing about, hopping from leaf to leaf. Other villagers were swinging on vines demonstrating their aerobatic talents to those below. Then Tiberius spotted several families of fireflies leaning from stick built tree houses who were throwing the flower confetti. More activity in a nearby tree caught his eye and he watched fascinated as a group of katydids lowered food laden woven baskets with vine ropes. Industrious ants waiting below rushed forward, unhooked the baskets and carried them to the stag beetle servers.

Crispin who had been chatting non-stop about the festival events finally took a deep breath, paused, then asked, "Well. What do you think of our little party?"

"I can't begin to tell you how fascinating all this is," Tiberius replied.

"Great," Crispin replied clapping his forelegs. "Let's find you a comfortable place to sit."

"As long as it is out of the way," Tiberius reminded him.

He led Tiberius to a patch of fluffy moss under a hickory tree, and the two friends nestled into it with a satisfied sigh. "Oh this feels wonderful," Tiberius proclaimed. "And I will have a great view of the festivities. I can sit here and mind my own business and nobody will get hurt," he said with a determined nod.

"Good," Crispin piped up, "I will be back shortly. I need to let my parents know that I'm back safe and sound. They worry terribly when I fly alone at night."

'And with good reason,' Tiberius muttered to himself with an indulgent smile. He leaned back on his velvety wings and watched the flurry of activity and strange creatures pass by. 'I've never seen so many different insects together in one place.' Tiberius thought to himself. 'I can't believe this wonderful place was so close by and I never knew about it. Being a loner certainly has kept me cut off from the world. I definitely have to get out more!'

In the distance he could see a winding trail of tiny lights approaching the village. 'Hmm,' he pondered. 'What in the world could that be?' As the lights drew nearer, he was amazed to see that it was a band of black beetles with yellow striped heads. Tied upon their backs were acorn lanterns and a strange light shone from within.

Tiberius was fascinated, but somewhat perplexed about all the lights he had seen since arriving at Dragonfly Landing. 'Could it be some kind of beetle magic?' he pondered studying one of the nearby hanging lanterns. He scratched a feathery antenna and said out loud. "I must find out about this, it's really quite puzzling."

Suddenly, an odd mixture of musical notes floated through the air, breaking into his thoughts. He scanned the clearing and noticed that it was coming from a group of musicians sitting atop the toadstools he had seen earlier. He counted three shiny red ladybug beetles with fiddles, a gray shimmery moth strumming a spider web harp, eight fat brown junebugs with crooked reed pipes and four bright green katydids who were rubbing their legs and wings together.

A shiny black wasp came forward and climbed onto the top of a larger toadstool facing the band. He waved his front legs in the air and a hush fell on the crowd of spectators. A troop of ants streamed in with twigs on their backs and tossed them into the dying campfire. As the tinder caught and blazed, Tiberius could see hundreds of entranced creatures encircling the musicians.

"Welcome everyone to the Seed Pod Festival," the wasp announced. "Many of you have traveled for days to be here for this splendid occasion. We hope you have a jolly good time and don't forget to stay close by for the story teller after the concert. Join me now in welcoming our featured band for this evening, 'the Jumpin' Junebugs'."

A wild applause of clicks, squeaks, droning, croaks and buzzing burst from the audience. The noise finally died and the musicians began to play. The crowd swayed and tapped their legs to all their favorite songs. Some of the more popular tunes that the band played were 'Some Buggy Loves You', 'The Grasshopper Hippity Hop', 'Katy-did My Heart In', 'Mushroom Kaboom', 'Dancing with My Honeybee', 'The Potato Bug Polka', and 'Fly me to the Moon'.

Tiberius was thrilled with the sweet melodies filling the night air and began to enjoy himself more as the evening wore on. Near the end of the concert everyone was dancing to the rhythmic beat of the jitter-bug four step. It made Tiberius dizzy watching all the hopping flopping, rolling and kicking that was going on. It was all becoming a whirling blur of legs and wings. When the music came to an abrupt halt the dancers fell to the ground in an exhausted heap. After everyone caught their breath they jumped up and began cheering. A group of ladybugs came forward and presented bouquets of flowers to the musicians. They stood, bowed proudly and began sipping nectar from their flowers. The thought of nectar suddenly reminded Tiberius that he had gone quite some time without food. He was looking around for some familiar flowers to sip on when Crispin appeared with a small nut shell full of nectar.

"Oh Crispin there you are: and at the perfect time. I was beginning to feel quite famished," he announced in a grateful voice.

"Good," Crispin replied. "I brought you a cup of our best nectar, collected from the wild yellow primrose which blooms for only two weeks in the early spring."

Tiberius took a long satisfying sip, smiled at Crispin and exclaimed, "I must confess this is even better than the moonflower nectar which is my favorite drink! Thank you for bringing it to me. Now that my stomach is full I'm ready for the storytelling."

"Me too," Crispin replied as his antennas twitched excitedly.

They rested on the soft dewy moss and watched as the preparations were being made for the story teller. Another procession of ants marched from the woods carrying tinder for the fire. The sticks made the dying embers flash and blaze back to life. Crispin thought the shadows cast onto the trees by the flames reminded him of dancing ghosts. A shiver ran up his back and he buried his face in the moss.

"Crispin, are you asleep," Tiberius questioned as he glanced toward his young friend. "Wake up, or you'll miss all the excitement. Look over there. Something strange is being carried out of the roots of that tree."

The young firefly looked up slowly and saw four stag beetles carrying a chair on their backs. It was made of sticks and lined with pussy willow down. They set it down cautiously near the campfire. Trailing behind with a hobbling gait was a very old Japanese beetle, using a stout spiraling cane for support. He paused in front of the chair and slowly lowered his shiny gold and green body into it.

"It's the story teller," Crispin explained to Tiberius. "He's very old and wise. No one knows how old he is because no one can remember back that far. He knows many ancient stories passed down to him from his father and grandfather."

The larger insects fell back so the smaller ones could move forward for a better view and the babies were hoisted onto the parents' backs. The crowd grew silent as the old beetle began to speak. His voice quivered a bit at first but it soon strengthened and became strong and loud. The spectators sat spellbound as he spun one mystical story after another.

First, he told a rousing tale of how the village sentries fought off a plague of hungry locust which had flown in one hot summer day and began eating every morsel of food in sight. Next, he scared all the little ones with a frightening tale of fierce creatures in dark caves who could turn an unfortunate traveler into stone just by looking at them.

After a short break for the storyteller to rest his voice and sip a drink; he began his last tale about the journey of two fireflies and their narrow escape from a hungry hoard of frogs in the Milkweed Bog.

Finally, the ancient storyteller could talk no longer. He was tired and his old joints were stiff from sitting. He was helped up and taken back to the tree from which he had come and disappeared into a black hole near its roots. Slowly the crowd wandered off into the early morning mist. Some went into the tree canopies, some lay down in a tall thicket of grass and others disappeared into small dark holes around the roots of trees.

Crispin came over to Tiberius who was yawning and stretching his wings. "That was truly one of the most exciting nights of my life," Tiberius stated. "I shall never miss another festival again. But tell me young Crispin, where are the others disappearing to when they go down the holes."

"Home of course," Crispin replied. "There are many homes down under the ground. My family lives under that old oak tree over there," he said pointing a leg in its direction. "And it's time for me to go home too."

"I've got a great idea," he burst out excitedly. "Why don't you come with me to meet my parents, Katrina and Bertrand; and spend the night? My parents wouldn't mind at all. They love to meet my new friends and my mom is a great cook."

"I would really like that, but I'm afraid my huge wings would never make it through the tunnel," Tiberius replied with a doubtful shake of his head.

"Couldn't you at least try. It's very interesting below," Crispin begged.

"Oh all right. I'll do it for you," Tiberius replied, "but if I get stuck, you may have to get the earthworms to come dig me out, and you know what a mess they can make."

The two new friends, tired from the nights adventure traveled down a short pathway to the huge tree. Crispin brushed aside a few vines of ivy covering the black hole between two large roots. "It looks awfully dark and scary," he explained, "but once we're inside a short distance there will be light."

Crispin walked right in but his friend hesitated as he sized up the width of the hole. Tiberius decided if he were careful his wings would fit though nicely; so he crawled into the hole and crept slowly forward. It had a nice earthy smell and the ground was soft and warm. The walls of the tunnel were covered with tan and white roots which had been woven into beautiful, intricate patterns.

Tiberius reached up and traced the designs with a foreleg. The roots felt hard and knobby but had a smooth, almost slick feel to them.

"Are you coming?" Crispin called out.

"Yes. Where are you?" Tiberius answered.

"Just keep on straight and soon you'll see some light," Crispin instructed.

Tiberius crept forward cautiously, and after a short distance, he noticed a golden glow ahead, silhouetting the tiny body of his new friend. As he made his way towards Crispin, the light grew brighter and soon he could see the tunnel walls more clearly. What mystified him was that the light seemed to come from nowhere. It had to be the same light source he had seen used everywhere in the village. By the time he caught up with Crispin he could no longer contain his curiosity. "Where is the light coming from?" he blurted excitedly.

"Just a few more steps and you will find out," Crispin answered cryptically.

As they rounded a curve, Tiberius noticed two cubby holes; one on each side of the tunnel which had been carved into the walls. The bottoms were flat and each held a small lantern made from a nutshell, much like those he had seen being carried on the backs of the black beetles. The glow inside was very bright and steady; unlike the flame of a fire which leapt and flickered. The source seemed to be a small crystalline form in the center of the lamp. "Jumping grasshoppers!" Tiberius exclaimed. "I've never seen anything like this in all my life. Where do they come from, and what makes them glow so bright and steady?"

"No one really knows for sure," Crispin began. "But I bet old Mr. Icherio could answer that. He's really smart, and knows just about everything, and all I know is what I've heard in scary stories around the campfire."

"And what is that," Tiberius questioned.

"Well, that depends on who is telling the tale." Crispin began in a low voice. "Every time somebody different tells it, the story gets changed, and it's usually for the scarier; but one thing always stays the same."

"Oohhh...., and what would that be?" Tiberius said in a shaky voice.

"There's always these horrible creatures called Gorboos skulking about the cave where the crystals are found and if you're caught....weeelll, that's where the stories are different. Some say the victims are turned to stone; while others say the poor unfortunate ones are drowned in the icy cave river or roasted on a fire and eaten."

"Yikes!" Tiberius stammered. "They tell these stories to the young ones before bed time? That must make for some lovely dreams."

"Aw come on now," Crispin replied with a mocking chuckle. "Nobody reeeeallllly believes any of it!"

"But someone obviously believes just that," Tiberius said gesturing toward a glowing niche. "Because, well; here they are."

"Okay, believe what you want," Crispin stated, "But I, for one, have to sleep at night."

THE TWO FRIENDS resumed walking and soon began passing many small doors woven from ropy vines with small hazelnut doorknobs. After passing a large open room with spiders clinging overhead, Crispin and Tiberius turned down another tunnel and stopped at a door with a wreath on it made from dried goldenrod and small pink flowers. Crispin walked right in and shouted a greeting of, "Hello! I'm home," to his parents.

Tiberius, however; who could barely make it through the tunnel was much too large to fit through the small opening. He edged his way up to the door and stuck his head and antenna through it to look around. In the middle of the room was a table and three small chairs made from bark and nutshells. On it there was another small lamp like the ones he had seen in the tunnel and a bouquet of wildflowers in a vase. Crispin's mother was busy in the corner stirring something in a pot and was unaware of the visitor peering in her door. She turned around and seeing Tiberius' enormous head let out a bloodcurdling scream and collapsed into a chair. Tiberius was quite startled by her outburst and jumped backwards tumbling onto the tunnel floor.

"Crispin! Young fella, come here at once," his mother ordered after recovering from her scare. He hopped into the room and stood facing his mother with one wing over his eye. "Who is this," his mother questioned while tapping a foot impatiently as she waited for an answer.

"I'm sorry my friend scared you mother," Crispin began impishly. "He didn't mean to. I wanted him to see where I lived and to meet you and father. His name is Tiberius. He's a luna moth and he's awfully nice. He helped me find my way home when I was lost. Can he stay for a pollen cake please?"

"Yes, Yes. Of course he's welcomed, but unfortunately he must eat his cake outside. He will bust down the door if he tries to come inside. Now run along and fetch your father so he can meet your large new friend."

Crispin returned a moment later scurrying behind his father. Bertram was wearing a sensible brown work vest which fit so snug its wooden buttons threatened to pop with the slightest cough. Sticking from a small side pocket was the stem of a reed pipe and a green stained cotton drawstring dangled at its side. He put on a pair of wire rimmed spectacles and began inspecting the visitor. "Well now, who have we here? I must admit you're a beautiful creature; such shiny soft wings. Crispin's friends are always welcome. It's a shame you can't make it through the door and sit for a spell."

"He's fine right where he's at," Crispin's mother added as she handed a soft yellow cake through the door to Tiberius.

"Is this the first time you've visited anyone underground?" Crispin's father questioned.

"Yes, it's an amazing place," Tiberius replied. "Especially the crystal lights along the tunnel."

"We don't know what we would do without them," Katrina stated as she pulled nervously at a pink bow on her apron. "We would have to leave our warm safe tunnel homes if it weren't for our lights." Crispin's father took off his glasses and let out a long sigh.

"What's wrong with everyone?" Crispin asked sadly.

"Many of us older creatures in the village hoped it wasn't true, but we can't ignore it any longer. At first we thought it was our imagination or perhaps our failing eyesight but then others younger than ourselves noticed too. We don't know what to do about it."

"What's happening," Crispin inquired as he searched his parents' dark faces.

"It's the tunnel lights son. They are glowing dimmer and dimmer every day."

"You mean one day they will stop shining forever and we'll have to leave our homes?" Crispin moaned. "And where will the dragonflies land?" He added quickly.

"Yes," Bertrand stammered. "One day they might and we don't know when it will happen, but we have to be prepared. I wouldn't worry too much about the dragonflies. They can land in the dark. The landing strip lights just make it easier."

Tiberius who had been enjoying his pollen cake now stopped chewing and listened horrified at the sad turn of events. What would happen to this wonderful place and his new friends? "We can't let this happen," Tiberius blurted. "I'll do anything I can to help."

"Thank you my friend," Crispin's mother offered, "but you aren't a tunnel creature such as us. What concern is it to you?"

"It's my concern if my friends are going to be hurt," he answered sympathetically then yawning; blinked his eyes slowly and sleepily.

"I must have worn out my new friend," Crispin announced as he too was overcome by a persuasive yawn.

"Yes. It's time for bed," his mother directed, "and your friend can sleep in the tunnel. He will never make it back home in time now. The birds will see him and have a nice moth sandwich for lunch."

Tiberius agreed and laid his tired body down on the soft earth. He fell asleep in the wee morning hours and dreamed of campfires and crystal lights.

Chapter 2
The Council Chamber

Some time later a rhythmic tapping on his wings awakened Tiberius. A line of small, red ants were marching right over him. He was, after all blocking most of the tunnel. Tiberius unfolded his wings, stretched and stood up yawning. For a moment he was unsure of where he was but then the events of the preceding night came back. He knew it couldn't have been a dream because as he looked around, he saw the tunnel walls with their strangely glowing lights and the door to Crispin's house. The lights did seem to be glowing a bit dimmer to Tiberius but he hoped it was just his imagination. Crispin's door opened and the small lightning bug scurried out followed by his parents.

"Did you sleep well?" Bertrand inquired.

"Yes, very well," Tiberius answered, "although I had some very strange dreams."

"That's not unusual after a Seed Pod Festival," Katrina added with a small chuckle. "I'm surprised you didn't have a few nightmares as well."

"Fortunately, I didn't," Tiberius replied as he followed his friends who had begun walking down the tunnel. "Where are we going?" Tiberius questioned.

"There's a big meeting this evening to discuss the tunnel lights. Everyone will be going," Crispin explained as he grabbed a root to swing on.

"Come on my dear," his mother scolded, "This is no time to play, we must hurry."

"Can I come along with you," Tiberius asked. "Maybe I can help in some way."

"Yes of course, everyone's welcome. We can use all the help we can get," Crispin's father stated as they exited the tunnel.

The sun was sitting low on the horizon and casting strange shadows on the ground. The four companions found a nice soft tulip leaf to sit on and waited anxiously for the meeting to begin.

Gradually, out of the dusk, creatures of all sizes and shapes appeared and gathered around a large open grassy area.

Seven mushroom stools were carried in by the stag beetles and placed in a row near the central firepit. A group of ants built a fire and placed several brightly lit torches in several places too ward off the creeping darkness. The crowd which had been so gay and vivacious the night before was now quiet and solemn. Soon a low murmur went up from the crowd as seven slow moving insects made their way from under a wild blackberry bush. Tiberius recognized one as Mr. Icherio, the old Japanese beetle storyteller from the festival. The other six included two gnarled legged grasshoppers wearing blue striped vests, one shiny potato bug with grey bristly face whiskers; a chubby junebug attired in a red checkered waistcoat, and two dirty looking dung beetles.

"These are the village council members." Bertrand began explaining as he leaned toward Tiberius. "They are the oldest and wisest creatures from the tunnels. Perhaps, together they have found an answer to our dilemma."

Three brightly clad harlequin beetles rushed over and assisted Mr. Icherio and the two grasshoppers onto the stools. The spectators became silent once more and one of the grasshoppers stood up and in a raspy voice began to speak. "Good evening my dear friends. We have a serious situation which affects all the tunnel creatures in our forest. I'm sure you all know by now that our lights are failing us. The council discussed this for many nights and we have come to the conclusion that there is only one solution. We must find and bring back a new supply of crystals."

This bit of news caused quite a stir among the spectators who at once began to talk excitedly to one another. "Please, please everyone be quiet. We have a lot of things to discuss," the grasshopper pleaded.

The junebug raised himself off a log and waddled forward holding a scroll in the air and began to speak. "We have a map piece which shows a route to the Teepee Mountains, but that's all. The Fern Queen has the whole document which shows the way to the cave where the crystals can be found."

A large brown ant crawled out from under a pale yellow toadstool and addressed the crowd. "But the mountains are so far away," he began, "it would take forever to travel that far: and what about the stories of the nightmarish Gorboos who live in the cave.

Even if somebody finds the right cave they might be eaten or thrown in the river to drown."

"Those are just stories to entertain around the campfire," another ant began to argue. "We don't even know these creatures exist."

Mr. Icherio waved his arms in the air to stop the ants before they caused the crowd to become hysterical. "If these Gorboos do exist, they will have to be faced; but first someone will have to find the Fern Queen and get the rest of the map."

"I've heard of her," a centipede poked his head from under a rock and piped up. "She lives in the fern forest on the edge of the Teepee Mountains."

"Exactly," the elderly grasshopper stated. "And we must seek her out. Hopefully she will exchange the map for a very fine gift." He paused a moment; chuckled then added, "We all know how ladybugs hate to part with their treasures."

"That's right," a damselfly wearing a primrose hat exclaimed; "and she is after all, a queen."

"Well, that's good enough for me," one of the ants turned and said to the others.

"Okay," the grasshopper announced, "Now that we've settled the problem of where to go, we must think about how to travel such a great distance as fast as possible. Does anyone have an idea?"

For several minutes the crowd mumbled and scratched their heads, but no one offered any suggestions. Tiberius, who had been sitting in the shadows suddenly had a thought which hit him like a bolt of lightning. "I have an idea," he yelled out.

Everyone sat up and turned to peer into the darkness to see where the voice had come from. "Who was that? Come forward so we can see you," the old grasshopper ordered.

As Tiberius moved forward, he kept his wings folded tightly so no one would be knocked over. Some of the young creatures gasped in amazement at his large soft wings.

"Well now," the grasshopper began. "Where did you come from? You're a long way from home aren't you. We don't see very many of your kind around here."

"I was invited to enjoy your festival last night by my new friend Crispin the lightning bug and I might add it was a fabulous evening. I also had the pleasure of visiting one of the tunnels and seeing the mysterious lights. I was very upset to hear they may be loosing their power, so I decided to stay for the meeting."

"Yes that's all very well, but you did say that you had an idea," the grasshopper said in an impatient tone.

"Yes," Tiberius started. "It occurred to me that since you need to travel very fast I may be able to help. My wings are very large and I can travel long distances without getting tired. I can probably fly faster and higher than anyone else here. There's an old song which says we can reach the moon if we want to but I'm sure it's not true."

"But, you're not one of the tunnel creatures. Why would you want to help us," the junebug jumped off the log and asked.

"Because I'm a creature like all of you," he explained. "I just happen to be larger and live in a different place. I wouldn't want any of my new friends to suffer: so anything I can do to help, even if it endangers my life; I will do."

A cheer burst forth from the audience and Crispin, who could hardly contain himself, rushed forward and climbed on Tiberius' back. "And I shall go with him," the small lightning bug announced. "We can't let him go alone."

The council members looked at each other in amazement. They whispered to each other for several minutes and then the grasshopper came forward to speak.

"This is a great sacrifice, indeed. You will meet many dangers along the way and we're a little concerned. It's an awfully long journey for a young lightning bug who is not experienced in the dangers of the outside world."

"And that's exactly what I think too," Crispin's mother shouted in a panicky voice as she pushed forward with Bertrand in tow. "He's much too young to leave home and who knows what kind of devilish mischief they might get into. He could even be killed. Oh my. Oh my!"

Bertrand could tell his wife was on the verge of tears so he placed a wing around her for comfort. "Now, now, calm down," he coaxed in a soothing voice. "It might be good for the young fella' to get out and stretch his wings. When I was about his age I went on a fabulous adventure with my uncle Filby. We flew all the way across the great Shinatook Forest and let me tell you it got pretty scary down in the Milkweed Bogs. There must have been close to a thousand hungry frogs trying their best to catch us for their supper. Yes sir, I think Crispin would do just fine, especially with Tiberius' huge wings to protect him if the going gets rough."

"Well I sure hope your right," Katrina replied in a concerned voice. "I'll still worry my head off every minute that he's gone."

"But that's what mothers do best," Crispin chimed in as he gave his parents a huge hug.

"Well good. I'm glad that's settled. When can we leave," Tiberius questioned.

"First we must do some planning. Routes must be marked, strategies planned," the old grasshopper replied. "And we must not waste a single minute. Let's all meet in the council chambers after we have all had something to eat. All this excitement has made me terribly hungry."

Later, Crispin and Tiberius lounged lazily on a soft pine bough munching some pollen cakes left over from the night before while waiting to be summoned into the council chambers. They barely had time to finish the last bite when the junebug in the red checkered vest suddenly appeared from among the gnarled base of a pin oak tree and rang a small rusty bell. "Well, that's the signal for us to come in," Crispin piped up. "We better scurry on in before they all fall asleep. It happens quite frequently. I guess it's because they're all so old."

"Now don't be too harsh on them, one day you will be old too," Tiberius scolded.

As the two cohorts leapt from the tree and headed over, the old guide motioned impatiently, "Hurry up, the council members are getting tired and now that they have filled their bellies it is getting close to their bed time."

Tiberius smiled to himself when he saw Crispin roll his eyes upward and smirk to himself. As they entered, Tiberius noticed the tunnel was almost like the one he had spent the night in but a bit larger. Scattered here and there, hanging from tree roots were strange but interesting carvings of faces surrounded by vines and flowers.

"What are those," Tiberius whispered to Crispin.

"They are past council members. Some of the wisest men of the forest - long dead but never forgotten," he replied reverently.

As before in Crispin's tunnel, Tiberius had to sit outside with only his face peering through the door. What he saw was utterly amazing and his eyes grew huge as saucers trying to take in the spectacle. Illuminated by a soft golden glow were nine willow chairs with high backs and downy seats. They were arranged around a large wooden table, decorated with strange carvings of triangular shapes interwoven with vines.

On the walls were large maps made from leathery leaves which had been artistically woven together. On them were drawings of rivers, trees, rocks, pathways, and other strange symbols that Tiberius didn't recognize. On one map there was a face of a horrible hairy creature with glowing eyes and weird knobby shaped teeth forming a grin. He wondered if this was a portrait of the dreaded Gorboos that he heard so much about.

Crispin followed the old junebug guide into the room, took a seat close to the door, and soon the other council members entered through another passageway. To Crispin and Tiberius' chagrin, an invisible cloud of extremely unpleasant aromas followed the dung beetles to the table. Each member picked a particular chair and sat. A short time later, the old hobbling Japanese beetle appeared from the darkness and took his place at the head of the table. Crispin who had chosen the chair closest to the door leaned toward Tiberius and whispered, "Mr. Icherio is the head council member because he is the oldest."

The old beetle lit a small clay pipe, blew a few puffs of bluish smoke toward the ceiling then cleared his throat to speak. "Well my young friends, you have taken upon yourselves a great burden. You will need to find in yourselves great strength and bravery to carry it out and return safely. We would gladly go ourselves but as you can see, there isn't much of that left in our old bodies." A few council members chuckled out loud and nodded their heads in agreement. The others just rapped on the table with small nut shells.

"Also, our sentries are busy protecting the community from outside threats. Especially those pesky earthworms, whose relentless burrowing endangers our tunnels. Why, just the other day I was munching on a dogwood twig when much to my surprise I looked up and saw a pair of beady eyes staring down at me. Thank goodness the sentries ran it off. I might have been buried alive."

The old beetle paused as he took another puff on his pipe and leaned forward, his eyes narrowing. "So you see my young gallant friends we are most grateful for your unselfish sacrifice."

Crispin felt a shudder run up his back on hearing the word sacrifice, but was determined to hide his apprehension. He was, of course, supposed to be brave, but now he was feeling a little bit scared, and wondering what he had gotten himself into.

Suddenly one of the dung beetles spoke spraying a few unidentifiable smelly brown crumbs onto the table. "By golly! What brave lads they are!"

"Now, down to the business at hand," one of the grasshoppers with a high squeaky voice began as he removed a map with one jagged edge from the wall and placed it on the table. "Unfortunately we only possess one piece of the map," he pointed to the torn side and continued. "As you can see it was damaged and the other part was lost." Crispin slowly raised a front leg and the grasshopper looked up from the document. "My, my: questions so soon?" He commented.

"Well: just one at the moment," Crispin replied shyly.

The grasshopper twitched a leg up to his forehead and leaned closer. "Go right ahead Crispin. We're all ears."

Crispin started to speak when Mr. Icherio interrupted. "You'll have to speak up young fella'. This old timer's ears are not what they used to be."

"Yes sir," Crispin said in a louder voice then went on. "I was wondering how you got that piece of map, and how the other one was lost?"

"A very legitimate question indeed;" the grasshopper stated then gestured to Mr. Icherio, "and one which he could answer best."

Mr. Icherio nodded, removed his pipe and began speaking as a cloud of grey smoke momentarily obscured his gold shiny head. "I was just a lad when word came from the fern forest that the inhabitants of Lady Bug Town were in trouble. It had been an unusually warm winter and their stored food had begun to spoil. The Fern Queen sent a plea far and wide, asking creatures of great intelligence to help find a solution before starvation set in."

"Well, as it happened, Professor Picklepot; a fig beetle of much renown for his lifelong pursuit of knowledge, heard of their predicament and decided to help: and help he did!"

"He took off straightaway, and on arrival he was greeted by a group of gracious but somewhat thin ladybeetles who led him to the Fern Queen's chamber. Along the way he was mesmerized by the mysteriously glowing lights which lit their pathways. Of course; in no time he had solved their food storage problem so the queen and all of Lady Bug Town were extremely grateful. They rewarded him with a sack of the crystals, a map to their location and a warning about the dreaded cave guardians."

"On his way home he crossed paths with a particularly nasty tiger beetle. The two fought viciously and the professor narrowly escaped with his life and the crystals. Unfortunately, the map was torn during the fight and part was lost forever. Gravely injured, he made it as far as Dragonfly Landing, and after the village healers nursed him back to health he repaid their generosity by sharing the crystals and a copy of the map fragment."

Mr. Icherio knocked the ashes from his pipe into an ornately carved bowl and finished his tale. "And that my young friend is about all this old geezer knows about that. I hope that answered your question."

"Oh yes sir, it sure did," Crispin exclaimed. "I can't believe he actually survived the tiger beetle. That hardly ever happens."

Mr. Icherio nodded emphatically; then pointed at the map with the pipe stem. "Someone get a lantern on that so Crispin and Tiberius can get a better look at it." The junebug passed an acorn lantern to the grasshopper and he positioned it to one side of the map.

As the document brightened Crispin and Tiberius got their first good look at the map. The pair glanced in horror at it and then at each other: it was the map with the sketch of the fearsome hairy creature on it. "What is that?" Crispin stammered as he pointed to the apparition on the map.

"That unfortunately is a Gorboo or what someone imagines them to look like," the junebug sitting next to Crispin answered.

Crispin's eyes became so huge Tiberius was afraid they would pop right out of his head. "Relax my young friend," Tiberius spoke reassuringly from the doorway. "Don't let your imagination run too wild; things are never as bad as you may think."

"Okay," Crispin replied with a nervous smile.

The old grasshopper cleared his throat to draw everyone's attention back to the map. Pointing a gnarled leg at the document, he traced a line through its middle. "As you can see, you'll leave here from our forest and travel west along the Roaring Springs River until you get to the Milkweed Swamp. The river changes course to due south on the far edge of the swamp: but you must continue west to cross the Centipede River." He indicated a blue squiggly line and went on. "After that, hold your course, until you come to the Teepee Mountain range. He tapped a line of sharp peaked markings. The mountain nearest the fern forest will be the one with a flat top."

"After that we're not certain where the Fern Queen lives so you will have to ask someone who knows everything and everybody in the area. Oh yes, one more thing; try to stay away from the gypsy moths. We've heard if they catch you, you could be sold to the hoppers."

"Excuse me," Crispin said raising his front leg. "Did you say the Milkweed Swamp? That's where my father almost got eaten up by a hungry hoard of frogs!"

"Young man, you can't expect a swamp not to have lots of frogs in it now can you," the grasshopper answered impatiently.

"Yes, sir," Crispin replied sheepishly.

"Just be sure you are rested enough to fly over it as high and as fast as you can, then you'll be all right."

The potato bug who had spent most of the meeting munching on a bowl of fried potato skins finally stopped and commented, "At least we'll be sending the two fastest flyers we know. You will be on your own, since we don't have enough information on the maps." He continued in a sleepy voice, "You must keep your wits about you at all times and never let your guard down, especially since you will be going into unknown territory." A round of table thumping and nodding of heads went through the group.

"Last but not least is the gift for the Fern Queen," Mr. Icherio began. "It must be something very special, and the council decided on one of the villages' treasures. You must guard it with your life until it's safely delivered to her. It's a great sacrifice to make, but it's no use to us if our whole way of life is destroyed."

Crispin and Tiberius watched curiously as the old beetle pulled a small ornate box from his vest pocket and laid it on the table. He opened it and took out a pepperbush seed pod tied across the middle with a string. He very gently untied it and pulled apart the two halves. Inside, nestled in a white downy bed was the most beautiful blue gemstone they had ever seen. It was shaped like a heart and was the color of a summer sky. Crispin and Tiberius gasped in awe as they gazed upon its almost mystical beauty. The light that was reflected off the stone made it appear to have a rippling waterfall on the inside.

"This," the old beetle explained reverently: "is the Heart of the Sky. Legend says that one day a piece of the sky fell to earth and landed in the Lake of Tranquility at the foot of Obsidian Mountain. At the moment of impact, this very precious jewel was formed from the union of sky and water."

"And this is that jewel," Crispin asked breathlessly.

"Oh, yes indeed," the junebug chimed in, "and that is precisely why you must guard it with your life. It can never be replaced, and you might run into some unsavory characters who might want to relieve you of it."

"Time is of the utmost," Mr. Icherio announced rapping his pipe on the table, "You must prepare to leave at once."

After leaving the council chambers, the two friends made their way through the darkness to Crispin's home where his mother prepared a sumptuous feast, sniffing and dabbing her eyes with a velvety leaf during the whole meal. After their stomachs felt like they might burst, Bertrand disappeared, but returned with a small leathery box held together with grape vine ropes.

"Come here, Crispin, I have something for you," he said as he gently untied the vines and lifted off the lid. Inside was a well worn bag with braided straps on it. "This was my pack when I went on my adventure and I think you should have it for yours." He reached inside the box, pulled out the pack and retrieved a scroll of soft bark which was lying underneath. "I also thought you two might need this." Tiberius squeezed his head further through the door to get a better look at the mysterious object.

"My uncle Filby and I sketched this map on our adventure," his father explained unrolling the document. "It has some of the same general directions as the council members map, but we added a few details which showed what we encountered on the way. We didn't make it to the Teepee Mountains, but between our map and the council's, you should have a fairly good route to follow."

"Oh thank you father," Crispin exclaimed as he accepted the map, slipped on the pack and proudly marched around the room.

"Yes, thanks so much," Tiberius added. "We'll need all the help we can get."

Katrina had also prepared a bag for Tiberius which was sewn from very thick leathery leaves. The inside had been filled with pollen cakes and small acorn shells filled with water and nectar.

"Oh yes, I almost forgot," Crispin's mother beamed as she rushed out of the room and returned with a package neatly wrapped in fiery red leaves. "We were saving this for your birthday, but we thought now was a better time."

Crispin took the package and curiously turned it over and untied the green vine binding it. Inside was a tiny vest made from willow bark which had been beaten into a soft downy fabric.

"Look inside," Crispin's mother said excitedly.

He unfolded the vest, and opened it. Two hidden pockets had been sewn inside. "You can use the pockets for safekeeping the map and the stone," his father instructed.

"Thanks, this is the greatest gift ever," Crispin gushed. He slipped on the vest and his mother, laced it up for him still fighting back tears.

Chapter 3
The Milkweed Swamp

The next morning after a belly busting breakfast of poppy seed flapjacks and jasmine juice, Crispin and Tiberius gathered up their food packs and headed down to the tunnel entrance. Crispin's parents came outside to see the two off. "Oh, I can't believe we're letting you do this, you are just too young," Crispin's mother moaned as she dabbed here eyes with the hem of her apron.

"Now, now," his father said soothingly as he put his arm around his wife's shoulders, "all young ones must eventually leave the tunnel. It's just nature's way."

"But not this way, I always thought he would just move over to the next meadow," she said with a sobbing voice. After the two travelers food packs were securely fixed to their bodies, Crispin's parents gave them a final hug and watched as they turned and left.

"Well my young companion," Tiberius stated, "The time has finally arrived. Are you sure about this? You must have no doubts and your heart must be fully committed to our task."

"You bet..... I can hardly wait," Crispin chirped as he jumped up in the air and tried to click his legs together but fell down clumsily instead.

"Off to a great start," Tiberius teased. Crispin stood up and dusted himself off; straightened his pack, and the two friends marched out of the village and headed down the trail to the landing strip.

CRISPIN AND TIBERIUS couldn't believe the crowds of cheering spectators lining the trail and the clearing alongside the runway. They were dangling from trees and hopping up and down among the tall grasses as they chanted farewells to the pair. The two companions stopped at the end of the runway where a group of giggling and overly excited young female fireflies were standing on the sidelines throwing flowers.

"Come on," Tiberius chuckled. "We better leave before we get mobbed."

Crispin climbed onto Tiberius back, and snuggled down behind the food pack. Tiberius walked a short distance down the runway and unfolded his shimmery wings. He gave a few powerful flaps and lifted off into the air. Crispin looked back, waved a last good bye to the cheering crowd; and watched as his home slowly faded into the forest.

TIBERIUS HAD BEEN flying west along the Roaring Springs River for most of the afternoon following the path of the sun as it slowly slipped toward the horizon. Neither of the two adventurers had ever traveled this direction before and the terrain passing below them was excitingly unfamiliar and filled with unusual exotic smells.

Occasionally, seeing something which sparked their curiosity Tiberius would descend and hover momentarily so the two could investigate. They had just passed a long row of hills connected together by smooth reddish brown knobs when Crispin spotted something strange moving along the ground. "Hey, look down there. What are those?"

Tiberius glanced down, dipped one wing and soared earthward. A massive group of black, square bodied beetles with large hook snouts on their heads moved together in a tight heard. They kicked up billowy clouds of dust as they scurried across the vast open grassy plane. "Great grasshopper legs," Tiberius exclaimed. "That must be a heard of migrating rhinoceros beetles. I've heard about them but this is the first time I've actually seen them."

Crispin and Tiberius followed the heard for a short time, taking in the spectacle and then resumed their course. They flew over a birch forest clothed with their stark snow white trunks and several fields of brightly colored wildflowers. The one which caught their attention was a field awash in bright sky blue blooms. The two were so mesmerized by the scene below they didn't notice a huge flock of low flying geese heading in their direction. By then it was too late because as all educated flying creatures knew, geese thought they owned the airways and wouldn't stop for anyone.

"Ahhhh! Oh no," Tiberius screamed, but it was too late. They were immediately engulfed by a flurry of flapping black and gray feathered wings. Tiberius, being an expert flyer took immediate evasive maneuvers and avoided a catastrophe by flying through a hole in the geese's' formation.

"Oh gaads," Crispin yelled as he unburied his head from the food pack. "Where did they come from?"

"I don't know," Tiberius answered back. "It's really unusual for geese to be flying so low this time of the year." The geese began honking loudly as they flew off into the distance. "Isn't that just like a bunch of silly geese to give us a honking warning after almost running us over," Tiberius added in an exasperated voice.

"Yeah," Crispin added. "Let's try to keep an eye open for those guys from now on."

Tiberius glanced over at the setting sun, decided it was time to land and find a safe place to rest and have a snack. "There's a nice green forest down below," he shouted. "Let's stop for a while, get something to eat, and take a look at the map."

"Okay," Crispin responded. "I'm, beginning to get a little cramped."

After landing, the two friends decided to stretch their legs by hiking along a trail skirting the woods. The sun had slipped below the horizon quite some time ago, but the two travelers marched on down the dusty trail their spirits and energy never flagging.

Tiberius, whose shiny wings were folded tightly, was keeping a vigilant watch for impending disasters, while Crispin trailed behind, so small he looked like a speck, his backpack snugly on his back. He was weaving back and forth jumping and skipping stopping occasionally to pick up a treasure or peer into the woods at some strange rustling noise. Eventually Tiberius noticed a change in the sounds from the woods, which up until now had been quiet and benevolent. The chirping of crickets and buzzing of evening bees and moths had been drowned out by another louder and more ominous sound. The solitary sporadic croak.....'garroom, garroom'.....'peep, peep' had been getting louder with each passing bend in the road until they were now encircled by a full blown frog chorus.

Tiberius stopped abruptly and threw a protective leg in front of Crispin. "I think we better stop for a while and get a bit of supper. We also need to take a look at the map so we won't get lost and end up in that miserable swamp. I think the geese may have knocked us off course a little."

"We can build a campfire," suggested Crispin, "it might keep away any unwelcome guests from joining us. I'm sure I heard somewhere that frogs were deathly afraid of fire."

The two partners scrounged around the edge of the forest for a few minutes and collected enough bark, twigs, and nutshells for a small fire. Crispin rubbed his front leg and antennae together vigorously. There was a sharp crackling sound followed instantaneously by an electric orange dagger piercing the inky sky. It sparked and caught the twigs on fire. "Haha! Abracadabra," Crispin shouted out proudly as the fire blazed up. "I bet you're really glad you brought me along now aren't you?"

"You're absolutely right," Tiberius replied as his eyebrows shot up in amazement. "I've never seen anybody do that before. That's quite a talent you have there young fella."

"Well, not everybody can do it," Crispin started to explain. "It's a talent which only a few of us fireflies can do. We call it fire cracklings."

"My goodness; what a funny word," Tiberius stated. "Why do they call it that?"

Crispin rubbed his leg and antenna together again and a crackling sound was produced. "That's why," Crispin stated. "It the strange sound we can make when it happens."

"Well, I wish that was a talent I had. It would come in handy on those long cold winter nights," he said with a wistful look on his face. Crispin was still basking in his achievement when the two pulled up soft sycamore leaves and plopped down around the now blazing fire.

The air was heavy with the sweet sour smell of rotting vegetation. Tiberius, being the older and more experienced of the two had a sinking feeling in the pit of his stomach. The familiar odor pierced his nostrils. It was the smell of a swamp. He said nothing to Crispin, not wanting to worry his young friend. He hoped they were still far enough away from the Milkweed Swamp that it would pose no danger.

They pulled out the council map and studied it while munching on Katrina's dandelion pollen cakes which had been specially made to give the pair extra energy. The small round flattened disc were bright yellow, and had a delicate sweet honey like taste. They had been wrapped in maple leaves and tied with a small string. The two travelers didn't realize they were so hungry and attacked the cakes with great gusto. Afterwards while sipping their nutshell canteen drinks they studied the map.

"I would guess that we have come this far," Tiberius said as he traced a line along the map with his leg. "I remember passing the knobby snake knoll and this is the morning glory meadow that we crossed right before dusk, but the geese knocked us off course a bit so that means we must be right about here on the edge of...," as his leg stopped moving they looked up at each other and stopped chewing.

"Oh no," Crispin sputtered as he choked on a few crumbs. "We're on the edge of the Milkweed Swamp."

"Yes," Tiberius replied, "and that must be why we're hearing all the frogs. It's a good thing we stopped when we did or we might be someone's supper by now. We'll be all right for now with the fire going. Those croakers won't come near it even if they are starving to death." Tiberius looked up from the map and noticed Crispin staring off into the darkness with a frozen look of panic on his face. "What's wrong? Haven't you heard a word I've said," Tiberius demanded.

"Look!" Crispin pointed a shaky leg toward the edge of the woods.

It took Tiberius' eyes a few seconds to adjust to the inky blackness beyond the camp site and then he saw what had paralyzed Crispin. The forest was alive with hundreds of glowing orbs moving up and down and side to side. It took only a split second for him to realize what they were. He swiveled his head around in a circle and surveyed the surrounding area. To his dismay, he realized they were encircled and trapped by hordes of hungry frogs.

"There must be thousands of them," Crispin whispered in a terrified voice. "They must have crept up on us. We'll be gobbled up for sure, fire or no fire!"

"You might be right," Tiberius whispered back. "We have to get out of here right now."

The fire was beginning to die down so the pair moved closer and began grabbing everything within reach to keep the fire going but in no time they realized soon there would be nothing left to burn. As the fire grew dimmer, the frogs became bolder and came closer. They let loose a frightening serenade of thrumarum, garoom-garoom, ribbit-gribber, and peep-peeps. The two frightened companions realized they must act now or be eaten.

Tiberius crouched down as low as his huge body would allow and whispered a command to Crispin, "Throw that food pack on me and let's get the bettlebazzokers out of this horrid bog. The hungry hordes of hoppers will have to find supper somewhere else tonight."

Crispin, who fortunately was still wearing his backpack; very slowly re-loaded the other food pack and jumped onto his escort's back. Tiberius unfolded his wings, and in a split second they were airborne. It happened so fast, all the disappointed frogs saw was a brilliant green flash.

Crispin looked over the edge of Tiberius' wing for one last glimpse and saw a wave of darkness pouring over the abandoned campsite. He shouted in triumph. "Ha Ha! Take that you slimy devils!"

Chapter 4
A Terrible Storm

*O*nce the two companions became airborne, Crispin relaxed, and the rhythmic beating of Tiberius wings lulled him into a peaceful sleep. His tiny head was snuggled into the soft downy fur between the moth's wings.

Tiberius beat his powerful wings back and forth forcing himself to rise higher and higher. The moon was full tonight and seemed to magically draw him towards it as though it had a lasso around his body.

He gazed at the huge silvery orb and wondered what it would be like to land on its surface. What strange and mysterious creatures might live there? Would there be others like him? Was it just a big frozen chunk of ice hanging in the night sky like a dangling icicle? He didn't think anyone would ever discover its secrets. It just seemed too far away. He knew that no matter how far he flew, it never seemed to come any closer.

As Tiberius was pondering the mysteries of the universe; a mountainous formation of clouds had been advancing towards the two travelers. Tiberius trembled at the sight of the black billowing curtains which had been drawn over the once luminous moonlit sky.

Before he could decide how to outmaneuver the storm it was too late. The winds began to blow, and huge wet drops bombarded them like falling rocks. Crispin awoke with an uneasy start, and immediately knew that they were in trouble. He threw a foreleg over his face to block the rain and cried out to Tiberius. "Geezebees! What a horrible time to have a storm. Are we going to have to make a forced landing?"

"I don't know," replied Tiberius. "It depends on how long we have to fly through this. I am already getting quite worn out fighting against the wind. We have to make it across the bog. If we can't we will have to spend the night in a tree. I've had enough of those frogs for one night: haven't you? Just put your head down, be still and hope for the best."

Tiberius had been confident he could fly through the thunderstorm until the sky began to light up with sharp fiery daggers. Suddenly the two companions were surrounded by writhing blue and orange electric snakes.

Tiberius' frail body was no match for the ferocious monster that held them in its clutches. He was tumbled around like a leaf in an autumn wind. Crispin held on tighter and tighter too terrified to move. He was certain they would plunge to the earth at any moment. Even more frightening was the knowledge that for him to try to fly with wet sodden wings would only end up in tragedy. There was nothing left to do but try to hang on with all his might.

It was almost at this same moment that Tiberius was thinking that things couldn't possibly get any worse when suddenly they did. A bolt of lightening hit so close that the pair was temporarily blinded and a numbing electric heat washed over their tiny bodies. Tiberius was left so weak he could hardly flap his wings and the two unfortunate creatures began tumbling in a downward spiral toward the trees below.

Tiberius fought it with all his strength but the energy had been sucked out of his body. Crispin let out a terrified wail and tried to hold on but went flying off Tiberius's back. With all his might he clawed and grabbed for anything that might stop his fall; but down and down he kept sliding. Just as every ounce of his strength was giving out, he managed to grab hold of Tiberius folded leg. Tiberius, unable to flap his wings and being bombarded by leaden raindrops plummeted downward as a canopy of spindly pines grew dangerously close.

On the ground below, a peacefully sleeping raccoon was awakened by a strange wailing sound echoing through the forest. It peered upward through an opening in the thicket and blinked sleepily at the strange object silhouetted by the haloed moon. It was a large winged creature drifting back and forth in the heavy wet evening air with a tiny kicking creature dangling beneath it.

"Creeping crawdads, Crispin, stop kicking your legs. It's only throwing me off balance more!" Tiberius yelled through the buffeting wind.

Crispin tried to obey his orders, but it was hard to relax when he was shaking all over from fear. "I'm scared to death of those trees coming up towards us," Crispin screeched, "it looks like a forest of sharp needles, well be skewered for sure!"

"Just hang on tight and leave the flying to me. I'm beginning to get some strength back in my right wing so I'm going to try to open it." He cautiously unfolded his wing; then shouted victoriously, "Yes, I can move it now."

"Yiipie-yea," Crispin yelled excitedly as he looked up and saw the large wing gliding above him. "We'll make it for sure now! Nobody's going to be skewered tonight!"

The two voyagers immediately began to slow their descent as Tiberius caught a favorable air current. With his one good wing working, he let out a sigh of relief but was still anxious as he glanced down at his tiny friend dangling precariously beneath. 'I still have to make a safe landing,' he mused to himself. 'If I miss the trees and land on the ground, we might end up a bed time snack for those boggy frogs.' He immediately shook off the terrifying thoughts and made up his mind that he would not let it happen.

"Great grasshopper legs," Crispin yelled and startled Tiberius from his inward thoughts. "Here come the treetops! Oh gaads, were here already." He shut his eyes tight and pulled his legs up to his chest.

"Okay," Tiberius ordered sternly, "whatever you do, don't let go of my leg."

Crispin hit first and felt the prickly needles rush past his body with amazing speed. They didn't feel as sharp however as he feared, but the constant poking felt like he was being scrubbed by a giant bottle brush. "Ahhh Ahh Ahh Ahh," he kept screaming over and over as he plummeted downward.

Tiberius had closed his eyes, folded his delicate wings, and followed Crispin in a seemingly never ending spiral towards the earth. He lunged outward with his undamaged front leg grasping frantically for anything which might break their frightening descent.

After what seemed like an eternity, Crispin came to a dead stop with his two back legs straddling a small branch which was still bouncing up and down, threatening to pitch him off. His backpack however, hung precariously by its straps some distance below. The food pack was nowhere in sight. He immediately checked his vest for the stone and finding it was still there let out a sigh of relief. He then glanced upward and saw Tiberius swaying back and forth grasping onto a limb with his front legs.

"Crispin, Crispin! Are you alive?" Tiberius yelled breathlessly.

"Yes, I think so," he replied in a halting voice, gingerly rubbing his antennas. "Hmm. Let me see, legs, wings, yes all my parts are accounted for, just a few scratches. How about you? Are you all in one piece?"

"I think I will be all right too," Tiberius responded, "my left wing hurts something fierce. I think it was hit by the lightning."

By this time Crispin and Tiberius had managed to crawl onto a large and more stable branch. They stretched out and decided to take a much needed rest since they were both extraordinarily tired from their ordeal. Tiberius turned his head and spoke to Crispin, "I think we're very lucky to be alive, don't you?"

Crispin shook his head in agreement, "If it weren't for you, I would certainly have plunged to my death. How can I ever repay you for saving my life."

"Well, you can start by being quiet, and letting me take a nap," Tiberius replied with a laugh.

Crispin lay on his back gazing upward at the fuzzy haloed moon, listening to the distant rumble of thunder, and thanking his lucky stars that they were safe and sound. The storm had finally blown itself out leaving a clear high amber moon suspended in a diamond speckled sky. Below on the soggy forest floor the curious raccoon stood on its hind legs swaying back and forth stretching upwards for a better look at the strange creatures which fell from the sky.

Suddenly Crispin and Tiberius were startled out of their exhausted sleep by a scratching and rustling sound coming from the base of their temporary and uncomfortable bed. "What's all that racket down there," Tiberius shouted grumpily.

"I'm not sure," Crispin replied as he rubbed the sleep from his eyes. "Kind of looks like a pesky raccoon to me."

"I'll try to see what he wants and get rid of him, if I can; so we can go back to sleep," Tiberius stated.

Before Tiberius could say anything a loud gruff voice rose up through the branches. "Hey up there whoever you are, what's the idea? You guys crashing around making all kind of noise, waking me up just when I finally got to sleep. It's hard enough falling to sleep with all those swamp frogs and crickets!"

"Ribbet-ribbet, croak-croak skrac-skrac all night. It's enough to drive a raccoon nuts. Look at these dark circles around my eyes. I had just fallen asleep, when all this crashing in the trees woke me up. Well, what do you guys have to say for yourselves? I've a mind to bring the hoppers over here to eat you up."

"Oh please Mr. Raccoon I'm sorry, but it couldn't be helped. We were almost killed tonight," Crispin piped up.

"Yes, please just let us explain everything to you," Tiberius added.

"Well, sure why not, I'm a reasonable guy. It might be nice to talk to someone who isn't slimy for a change and a good story just might put me back to sleep."

"While you're at it don't call me Mr. Raccoon, makes me feel kinda like I ought to be wearin' a fancy hat or something. Just call me Rosco, that's my name after all. Sorry we got off to a bad start but I get cranky when I haven't had enough sleep."

Tiberius and Crispin looked at each other and shrugged their shoulders. "Sounds like a friendly enough fella, don't you think," Crispin asked.

"Okay," replied Tiberius. "But we still need to be cautious: I never really trusted those shifty raccoons. Always messing around where they don't belong and causing problems. Let's move down a little further and check him out." They crawled down to the lowest branch of the pine tree and peered down on Roscoe: his short pointy nose twitching back and forth sniffing the air.

"Don't worry I'm not going to eat you guys. Don't like insects much. Me: I'm into fish and just about anything slimy. What's your story? Don't see a lot of your kind traveling around together especially on a stormy night like this. You guys lost or something?"

"We're not sure," Crispin piped up. "My name is Crispin and this is my friend, Tiberius."

Roscoe let out a explosive belly laugh and fell down on his back kicking his legs up in the air. "Tiberius! That's the funniest name I ever heard. Where did you ever get such a stuffy name as that?"

Tiberius pulled his shoulders back and tucked his chin in indignantly while glaring sternly down at the rollicking raccoon.

"I'll have you know, in my part of the world; Tiberius is a very noble and dignified name. I would thank you not to make fun of it."

"Just our luck to get stranded in a tree guarded by an idiotic, insomniac raccoon," Tiberius whispered to Crispin.

"Yeah, I thought raccoons liked to stay up all night. This is a really strange forest we've landed in," Crispin whispered back.

"Hey you guys, where's your sense of humor?" Roscoe said as he picked himself up off the ground and brushed the damp pine needles off his fur.

"We're running a little short of that just now," Tiberius replied sharply. "We were almost the main dish for a bunch of revolting reptiles, caught in a horrendous rainstorm, skewered by thousands of sharp pine needles; and now my wing's been damaged by lightening. So excuse me if we don't seem too chipper right now. Oh yes - on top of it all we need to find somebody called the Fern Queen and have no idea of where to look."

"Okay, Okay, I get the message," Roscoe replied. "Man! And I thought my life was bad," Roscoe mumbled to himself. "Sounds like you two need some help maybe. I know these great guys who can take care of you for the night. You can get some food and rest, maybe even a little help for that wing problem of yours. Say, you never did tell me what you two are doing in my neck of the woods."

"Oh well," Crispin interjected. "We're on sort of a quest to save our world from dying out. It's kind of a long story."

"Well you better save it then until we get to where we're going. You might as well tell it only once....after all the gypsy moths just love a good story around the campfire."

Crispin and Tiberius both gasped in fright. "Gypsy moths! They're scoundrels! They'll tie us up, steal everything we have and then sell us to the boggy hoppers for food!" The two friends grabbed each other, their eyes wide with terror.

Roscoe laughed, "Don't be ridiculous, I've known the gypsy moths all my life. They're really great guys once you get to know them. They've just gotten a bad reputation that's all."

"Buuuut it must be true," Crispin stammered. "I've heard terrible stories about what gypsy moths will do if they catch you."

"Forget all that hogwash," Roscoe scolded.

"And my parents warned me never to go close to the gypsy wagons," Crispin whimpered.

"Well your parents, and every one else who thinks that way are wrong. They're just like every one else, just a little bit different. So, what do you say? If you're ready to go, just grab onto my tail, climb up my back, and we'll go meet some gypsy moths. I'll have you there in a jiffy. Don't worry about running into the hoppers. This is my turf and they know better than to mess with old Roscoe."

THE MOIST HEAVY pine scented air rushed passed Crispin and Tiberius as their furry coach took them deeper into the darkening forest. Tiberius had been sleeping soundly for some time but Crispin was too apprehensive at meeting the gypsy moths to close his eyes. Roscoe being the sure footed creature he was carried the two hitchhikers with amazing speed towards their destination. Only once did they stop. When Roscoe; with his keen sense of nocturnal vision spotted something glinting on the forest floor.

"Hmm. Hey, what's this," Roscoe mumbled under his breath as he picked it up and rolled the shiny object between his paws. "Can't really tell much in the dark, but I'm sure it's some kind of treasure. I better hang onto this." He quickly tucked it inside a small pouch hanging around his neck.

Crispin chuckled to himself at this strange creature who collected pieces of junk. "Come on, let's get a move on," he ordered impatiently.

"Hey you little twerp!" Roscoe teased. "How about a detour through Hoppersville? I could probably swap you guys for a big shiny ball of tin foil."

"No, No," Crispin pleaded, "I'm sorry. Please feel free to stop whenever you want... I won't make a sound."

Crispin, true to his promise, remained still and quietly nestled into his furry ride. After some time had passed Crispin was suddenly startled by strange sounds coming from off in the distance. He could barely make it out at first but as they drew closer, he was almost certain that he heard music and singing. It was a fast paced lively tune with a hauntingly beautiful tempo. For some reason it made his heart race excitedly. He poked out from his hiding place and spotted a warm fuzzy golden glow melting into the blackness of the forest. "Hey Roscoe. It that the gypsy moth's camp?" Crispin asked nervously.

"Yep sure is. They're the singing'est, dancin'est bunch of guys you'll ever see," Roscoe replied. "It's the same thing every night. You'd think that eventually, they'd wear themselves out. I'm glad they don't live in my neck of the woods."

"I have to admit it though, I've never heard such great fiddle playin', an' man what a brew they can cook up! Makes me drool just thinkin' about it."

Crispin decided Tiberius was going to miss all the excitement so he nudged him gently on the antenna. "All right. My goodness, I must have dozed off," the moth said as his head snapped up with a start.

"Look," Crispin cried out excitedly, pointing his front leg in the direction of the campsite, "it's the gypsy moths! We're here, we're here."

"Yes. Yes, I can see it," Tiberius replied laughing at the exuberance of his young friend.

Roscoe halted momentarily, pushed aside a dew covered maple branch and the three companions entered into another world.

Chapter 5
The Gypsy Moth Camp

Roscoe stepped forward into the glow of the campfire and called out with a wave of his paw, "Hey! How you guys doin' tonight?"

The revelry came to an abrupt halt and one of the moths setting by the campfire carefully laid his fiddle down on a bumpy log and squinted suspiciously in their direction. A huge smile of recognition lit his face as he rushed over and flew up into the air settling on the end of Roscoe's nose. "Roscoe, my old friend; how you have been? It is long time since we see you at our home. Come, sit and warm by our fire. We sing and dance for you tonight."

"Thanks a lot Bela, old pal," Roscoe replied. "But first, I want you to meet some new acquaintances of mine. Okay you two. Come on out," he instructed. Crispin and Tiberius shyly crawled down Roscoe's tail and moved forward into the bright light of the campfire.

Crispin stared apprehensively at their unusual host who was illuminated by the flickering campfire. He had very dark thick hair surrounding a swarthy face, and wore a bright orange and yellow vest with gold buttons on it. A wide green sash encircled his waist and a gold pendant hung from around his neck embossed with a mysterious design. Crispin pulled backwards in fear when he saw the necklace. It reminded him of an eyeball with a sword plunging into it.

"Found these two characters crashing around in some trees down by my place. They're kind of beat up. This one," Roscoe turned and pointed at Crispin, "says they're on some kind of important mission and got roughed up in a storm. You can bet that they have quite a tale to tell. I know you guys love a great story so I decided to bring them to you."

Bela stepped closer and with a quizzical expression on his dark hairy face; inspected the two visitors. "Yes.....yes. They look very tired. Come, we have plenty to eat and drink. Sit by our fire. Stay and rest as long as you need." Crispin and Tiberius moved closer to the fire and sat on a smooth log bench.

"Latslov, my eldest son will bring food and brew." Bela continued. "Latslov.... Latslov come quickly, we have guests in need of refreshment," he called out loudly clapping his forelegs together.

A younger gypsy moth resembling Bela appeared promptly holding two hickory nut bowls and passed them to the three companions. "So nice to meet you," Latslov said bowing low at the waist. He was dressed similarly to his father with the exception of a bright red striped scarf tied around the top of his head, and a small gold hoop dangling from his curly dark hair.

Roscoe moved forward suddenly and touched the glinting adornment in his hair, "Lovely....lovely," he murmured. "I don't suppose you'd consider a trade for this would you?"

"No..No. Was present from grandmother," Latslov said as he gently pushed Roscoe's paw away.

"Okay, fine, be that way," Roscoe whined and returned sulkily to his seat by the fire.

Crispin and Tiberius sipped the brew savoring the sweet musky flavor. It seemed to warm them instantly down to their tired bones. Next a dish was placed into their laps by two older and smaller lady gypsy moths. Their faces were slightly sunken in and very wrinkled. One of them smiled flirtingly at Tiberius which made him flinch.

"The girls around here aren't much to look at," Crispin commented.

"Hush," Tiberius ordered, "you better be careful not to insult these folks. They've been nothing but nice to us so far."

The two famished travelers ate the small sweet crunchy balls they were served with gusto and soon their bowls were replaced with a second helping. While eating, Crispin and Tiberius studied the strange world which they were now part of. Encircling the huge campfire were ten or twelve rectangular wagons made from strips of bark and twigs. They were supported by four round; sturdy looking chestnut wheels and a harness like object projected from the wagons' front. Several of the wagons were lit from the inside and their colorful curtains cast an eerie glowing rainbow pattern on the ground. Some of the wagons were decorated with intricate paintings of flowers and vines while the rest were left plain. Crispin had seen wagons like these before, as they came jostling down the road which passed by Dragonfly Landing. They would camp out in the nearby woods for a short time and then move on. At night when it was late and very quiet the village could hear the faint strains of music being carried on the night breezes.

Suddenly Tiberius nudged Crispin. "Hey, look over there," he said pointing at one of the wagons. "That whole roof is covered with blue mushrooms."

"Jumping junebugs! Those mushrooms are the weirdest thing I have ever seen!" Crispin exclaimed.

"Hey, what's weird, and what are you two talking about," Roscoe chimed in as he trotted up and lay down besides Crispin.

"Those blue mushrooms on the roof of that wagon," Crispin replied wiping crumbs from his mouth.

"I think they make a healing medicine from them. You know, salves and potions; that sort of thing. I hear they can work magic on all sorts of ailments."

Crispin's eyes shot up in amazement. "Wow, I wonder if they could put some of that stuff on Tiberius' wing."

"Well, it won't hurt to ask," Roscoe suggested.

Crispin turned his attention back to the food and commented, "Now this is what I call hospitality."

"Yes indeed," Tiberius agreed, "I guess all those bad rumors about the gypsy moths are definitely false. When we get back home we'll have to tell everyone what great folks they are."

Crispin nodded his head in agreement and added, "You're absolutely right." He said smacking his mouth and wiping it with a foreleg.

The three chums moved closer to the crackling campfire and stared groggily into the mesmerizing flames. The gypsy moths who had been busy doing odd chores around the campsite suddenly converged by the campfire and sat down on twig chairs and log benches. After setting down their cups of brew they pulled out an assortment of odd looking musical instruments and began to play.

A wizened moth wearing a poppy red patched vest pulled a fiddle up under his silvery fur framed chin and with a flick of his forearm the bow began to dance wildly across the strings. It was a fast hypnotic tune which was soon joined by the mellow lilting notes spilling from a reed pipe. The piper was a comical looking moth with twig-like legs wearing a very bizarre yellow hat with a green feather stuck in one side. His body swayed rhythmically back and forth as he waved his reed pipe through the smoky ember filled night air. To the left of the piper a musician in a brown waistcoat with white ruffles sat behind a square wooden stringed instrument called a cymballa which was perched on a three leg table. He was striking the strings with two long thin mallets with small round nutshell knobs on their ends. The soft "bing bong" tinkley sounds it made wove in and out of the beautiful tapestry of notes. Eventually more and more fiddlers joined in along with the jingling and clanging of a tambourine being thumped and beaten wildly by a twirling dancer clad in a vividly colored skirt.

Then, as suddenly as the music had started, it stopped. Bela, with his fiddle tucked under his arm; made his way from the shadows into the flickering firelight, stepped up onto a square wooden platform and announced, "Bela will play tune for special guests while Latslov sings amusing campfire song and dances for you also." He lifted his fiddle into the air and drew the bow slowly along the strings making them come to life as the sweet notes floated upward towards the halo rimmed moon.

Latslov who was standing statue like with a foreleg over his chest came to life with the first strains of the music. He thrust his arms skyward and began a wild jumping whirling and kicking performance which left the visitors awestruck. The faster Bela played his fiddle; the faster Latslov danced until they both reached a feverish pitch. Just when Crispin and Tiberius thought Bela's fiddle might explode into flames the music and dancing abruptly stopped.

Bela paused, adjusted his fiddle, and began to accompany Latslov in his song.

We love to dance, we love to sing
It's in our blood – that's the thing

We love the moon, we love the rain
It's in our blood – we don't complain

We love to eat, we love our brew
It's in our blood – it's what we do

We love our fiddles, we love our tunes
Been this way for many moons

We love the road so we're told
The song is done, the night is old

Towards the end of the song, several gypsy moths who were eating and drinking came forward and began dancing arm in arm. Crispin, who could contain his youthful exuberance no longer, jumped up and joined in the festivities. Soon he was dancing as though he had been a gypsy moth all his life. They sang and danced and sipped brew into the wee hours of the night and soon the flames in the campfire began to dim. He twirled, leapt, and jumped to the intoxicating melodies until finally exhausted, he fell dizzily onto a pile of soft lambs' ear leaves.

Tiberius, whose wing was still sore, remained sitting on the sidelines, content to watch the whirlwind of colors pass by. The whole spectacle of singing and dancing along with the never ending brew soon began to make his head spin. The colors spun faster and faster. The music grew louder and louder, and his body began to feel numb and sleepy. Suddenly, the whole troop of gypsy moths stopped and rushed to Tiberius who had passed out and was laying face down on the grass.

Bela and Latslov gently turned him over, and brushed the grass off his face. "He needs rest now," Bela instructed. "Lay him on those dandelion pillows by Maleva's wagon. She can attend to him."

"Be careful, he has an injured wing," Roscoe interjected.

"Yes," Crispin said in a concerned voice. "I'm afraid he's hurt more seriously than he lets on. Is there anything you could do to help him get better: maybe some of your blue mushroom medicine? We need to continue our journey as soon as possible."

"You must be patient," Bela instructed, "Your friend is of no help to you until he is fully recovered. Let us attend to him first and then you will tell me of your travels and the great howling storm that blew you into our camp. Perhaps our people can find some way to help."

Bela clapped his hands and with an authoritative voice called out in a strange language. A rose dotted drape covering an oval door at the rear of a nearby wagon parted and a bright light escaped piercing the darkness. A small silhouette appeared on the threshold; then descended the steps onto the spongy dew sodden ground. Everyone watched in silence as the small graceful moth made her way over to the injured visitor.

"This is niece - Maleva. She is wise in healing ways." Bela said to Crispin, then quickly clapped his forelegs. A group of moths rushed forward and gently carried Tiberius into Maleva's wagon with Roscoe, and a very concerned Crispin in tow.

"Quickly, make soft bed, and I will go to get salve," Maleva instructed in a sweet sultry voice. She turned quickly and left with the sound of tinkling bells following her.

Something soothing and ticklish on his wing woke Tiberius with a start. He looked up and saw a circle of strange faces staring down at him. A wave of panic came over him, but then he came to his senses, and remembered that he was among friends.

"You will be fine," Bela spoke softly. "Maleva is attending to your wounds. Just rest my friend and sleep."

Tiberius relaxed, and focused his eyes on the exotic and beautiful face hanging over him. "Yes, Bela is right," the angelic vision said. "The salve is very potent and has worked many miracles. Your wound is very painful...yes?"

"Yessss," Tiberius stammered, as he took in the vision before his eyes. Maleva resembled the other gypsy moths but her hair and eyes were lighter and softer as was her delicate face and body. She had a beautiful full mouth and large upturned eyes. Her clothes were still colorful but were softer and had a gossamer appearance. A small gold ringed object was braided into her shiny chestnut colored hair. Tiberius had a strange feeling inside his chest, and it was hard to breathe. 'Maybe I should pinch myself to see if I am awake,' he thought.

"Here, drink this," Maleva ordered as she gently lifted his head off the pillow. "It will help you sleep."

But Tiberius didn't want to sleep now, he was afraid of waking up, and finding that this beautiful creature was only a dream. But the more he fought the harder it became to stay awake. Before long, a heavy cloud of drowsiness invaded his thoughts and he fell into a deep sleep.

Crispin; reassured that Tiberius was resting comfortably, returned to the campfire and sat at the rough hewn table where Bela and Latslov were devouring something brown and slimy. It looked disgusting to Crispin, and he hoped they wouldn't offer to share the dish.

After a minute or two Bela put his bowl down, burped loudly, and patted his ample belly. "AHHHH! Nothing like a hot bowl of fungus stew before hearing a good story."

"Now," he began, leaning over conspiratorially and beaming with anticipation at Crispin. "Tell amazing story which brings two strangers on Roscoe's back to gypsy moths."

Crispin took a deep breath and began to tell of Dragonfly Landing and the rapidly dimming crystals. He then told about their narrow escape from the hoppers in the Milkweed Swamp, and their flight through the monstrous storm which left them lost and clinging precariously to life.

"Incredible....incredible," he repeated, "You are very brave one to come all this way. Tell me more. Where you will go from here?" Bela questioned.

Crispin threw his foreleg into the air hopelessly. "That's the problem. We don't know where we're supposed to go. Between the geese and the storm, we're off course and a bit lost. We need to find the Centipede River and cross it. After that we need to find the map keeper."

Bela lit a pipe engraved with the face of a wolf, and began blowing hazy smoke rings. As the rings rose melting into the misty night sky he nodded. "Yes, yes. I see problem. You perhaps know name of map guardian?"

"Well yes, we do know that much.... the Fern Queen," Crispin answered.

Bela pulled the pipe from his mouth, set up with a start and grinned. "Then it is fortunate, my young seeker that you have come to see gypsy moths. We have traveled much, to many different lands, and seen many strange things."

"Fern Queen is known to all my people. Queen dwells deep in the glen which grows at foot of white peaked mountains. There is much danger in the going. If friends' time is short, path must be through Woods of Forgetfulness. Would take many full moons to go around."

Crispin's eyes widened in wonderment. "The Woods of Forgetfulness? I've never heard of this place before. What is so bad in there?"

"You must travel very fast, and not linger: or eat anything in forest or you will forget everything," Bela explained.

"Everything?" Crispin replied.

"Yes," Bela nodded slowly. "Family, friends, even who you are and what you are doing there. You will remember nothing, and wander aimlessly for the rest of your life; but gypsy moths have something to help should you fall victim to evil woods."

Latslov pushed his empty bowl away, and spoke to his father in a strange language. Bela turned and motioned to a female moth nearby, and she hurried over. She was carrying a hummingbird nest basket and Crispin curiously peered inside. To his astonishment, instead of tiny eggs, it was filled with unusual roots and bunches of greenery. Bela addressed her in the same unfamiliar tongue and she scurried away. A few moments later she returned and placed a small glass phial on the table.

"What is it?" Crispin asked.

"Is potion to ward off sickness," Bela replied.

Crispin looked puzzled. "What's a potion Bela?"

"Is drink made from herbs gathered in the forest," Bela instructed.

"Sounds like it tastes bad," Crispin said puckering his face.

"Yes," Bela said, "but potion could save your life if overcome by forgetfulness. I do not envy you going into that cursed forest. If I were you I would not go in without the potion. That is what Bela, king of gypsy moths tells you!" He added thumping his pipe forcefully on the table.

Bela reached up and scratched one of his furry antennas and gave Crispin a purposeful wink, "Gypsy moths will help you on your quest." He jumped up on his stool and clapped his hands briskly three times. Bella's booming voice rose with great enthusiasm. "Two moons from now," he announced to the crowd. "Wagons leave to help new friends on journey. We take them to river bank where other friends will help them across. Now, sing and dance till the dawn shows her face on wagons."

TIBERIUS AWOKE THE next afternoon surrounded by a hazy fog. He stirred and decided to try his injured wing. Most of the pain was gone but it still felt stiff. He tried to sit up but a familiar voice scolded him. "Do not try to sit. Your head is still groggy...yes? It is from the medicine and brew we gave you last night. Soon it will clear up. I have a special nectar drink for you. For energy."

Maleva's enchanting face suddenly appeared through Tiberius' hazy vision. She supported Tiberius' head and shoulders and placed the drink to his lips. It was a cool tingly refreshing drink that reminded him of a beverage given to him once by his mother. It was almost like drinking sunshine. "Mmm, that's wonderful! What is it," Tiberius queried.

"Is very old gypsy moth recipe," Maleva explained. "Mostly, drink comes from wild pineapple mint with little secret ingredients."

Tiberius took a deep breath, "I feel stronger already and my vision is clearing. Can I try to sit up now?"

"Come, I help," Maleva said rearranging the dandelion pillows behind his back.

"Who are you?" Tiberius questioned.

"Am Maleva, niece of King Bela and healer for caravan."

"So nice to meet you," Tiberius responded. "And very fortunate for me," he added touching his injured wing.

"You have most beautiful wings," Maleva crooned, gently touching the unhurt wing. "You are lunar moth...no? Sometimes my people see your kind shimmering in the moonlight."

"Yes, I am," Tiberius began. "Do you know how we got our name?"

"No," she answered quizzically.

"A long time ago," Tiberius began, "in the beginning of our world when humans first saw us with our big pale green wings they thought we must have come from the moon. So we were named 'Lunar' which means moon in their language."

Maleva smiled and stifled a giggle with a forearm. "Humans very funny...yes?"

"I think they like to make up stories just as we do," Tiberius replied laughing. He cocked his head quizzically at Maleva. "Why are you awake so early? It's hours before dusk. I hope I didn't disturb your sleep."

"I do not sleep same as other gypsy moths. I am not pure gypsy moth blood: only half. Mother was monarch butterfly. She was lost and hurt like you. One day she fell in our camp and my father's people healed her. She was very beautiful, and my father loved her very much. Romantic, yes?"

"Where are your parents," Tiberius asked.

A shadow fell over Maleva's face and her eyes glistened with tears. "Was terrible flood. Mother was caught in tree, father tried to save her but no use. So now, I live with uncle Bela. Life here is okay but I am not like others. I wake in daytime, and do not like moving all time. I wish for home of my own someday in same place forever."

Tiberius felt an invisible hand close around his heart for this beautiful sad creature. "I wondered why you look different from other gypsy moths." As soon as Tiberius uttered these words, he knew Maleva might feel insulted so he quickly added, "I...uh..I uh, mean uh; what I mean is why you are more beautiful than other gypsy moths."

A fleeting smile played on her lips. "Oh, you just say that to make Maleva feel better."

"No, I really mean it," Tiberius said earnestly. "Last night I thought you were a dream. I was afraid that when I woke up you wouldn't be here."

Maleva's huge luminous eyes gazed tenderly at Tiberius and she spoke softly, "Well then, Maleva is happy too, that you woke up." The spell was broken by Crispin who knocked lightly on the wagon door. Maleva opened it and said, "All right to enter. Friend is much better."

Crispin hopped inside and sat next to Tiberius. "You look much better. We were really worried about you, but it looks like you've been in good hands," he said glancing over at Maleva.

"Yes, she's wonderful," Tiberius replied.

Just then, there was another knock at the door, and Crispin jumped up to open it. Roscoe's black shiny eyes stared through the tiny door. "How's the big guy doin'? I wanted to stop by and say 'Good-bye' to you two. I have to be getting back home before I get all my treasures looted by some squirrely chipmunk."

"We'll really miss you," Crispin said waving his leg. "Thanks for carrying us to the gypsy moths."

"Maybe we'll see you again," Tiberius added.

"Hey, you never know. You guys try to stay out of trouble now," Roscoe winked a dark, ringed eye and was gone.

"I'm going to miss Roscoe," Crispin said sadly.

"He is quite the character, isn't he," Tiberius added.

AS THE AFTERNOON melted into evening the gypsy moths began to stir around the campsite doing their chores. The male gypsy moths spread their brown and gray downy wings and flew off into the woods as the last rays of daylight licked at the horizon. They would be gone for several hours to collect delectable pollens and nectars for their evening meal. The pollen would be carried in pouches attached to their legs and the nectar would be scooped out of flowers and placed in tiny seed pod containers slung around their necks. The female gypsy moths accompanied by a few of the older children would search the woods for other treats to be loaded into twig pull carts. By the time they returned to the campsite the carts would be brimming with wild blackberries, mosses, pine nuts, tender young fiddle-heads and brown button mushrooms. The campfire was blazing fiercely when the food gatherers returned and the musicians were tuning their instruments in preparation of the night's entertainment.

Cooks wearing aprons over their boldly colored clothes rushed over excitedly to the carts of incoming food and whisked it away to the waiting bowls and cooking pots. Tonight the gypsy moth camp would feast on moss and fern fiddle-head salad, mushroom soup, and wild blueberry with pine nut pollen cakes. As always they would wash it all down with everyone's favorite drink – nectar brew.

Crispin lay back on a soft moss covered log watching in amazement at the well organized activities of the gypsy moths. As the night wore on everyone had a delicious meal and gathered around the campfire for singing and dancing. It was another festive night in the gypsy moth camp: just as it had been the night before, and would be for many, many nights to come.

Soon, Crispin was overcome with a string of very persuasive yawns so he decided to join Tiberius in Maleva's wagon for a much needed rest. He hopped up the stairs of the wagon quietly, pushed the flowered curtains aside, and crept inside.

Maleva was sleeping soundly on a plump feathery cushion at one end of the wagon, and Tiberius was snoring softly lying on a dandelion blanket at the other end. Crispin found himself a soft downy blanket, pulled it close to Tiberius and drifted off to sleep lulled by the sound of a solitary fiddle somewhere in the darkness.

CRISPIN AND TIBERIUS who had been sleeping soundly all day were jolted awake by the rattling and pitching of Maleva's wagon.

"How are you feeling today," Crispin asked yawning loudly and stretching his forearms upward.

Tiberius sat up slowly. "I'm much better thanks to that wonderful salve. It worked magic. My wing hardly hurts at all now. It is still a little stiff though, but I think we'll be flying again soon." Suddenly, the wagon pitched to one side.

"Let's go out and see what's going on," Tiberius said as he cautiously stood on his untried legs. "If I don't get up and start moving soon we'll never get back on the road."

Crispin held his friend's forearm as the two descended the wagon stairs. Outside in the gathering dusk there was a flurry of activity. Bela was scurrying back and forth instructing everyone to collect their possessions and get their wagons ready for the journey. Several other gypsy moths busied themselves hooking up objects that Crispin and Tiberius guessed to be harnesses to pull the wagons.

Tiberius reached up and scratched his antenna thoughtfully, glancing over at Crispin. "I wondered what they used to pull their wagons. They sure couldn't do it themselves, so whatever it is must be very strong."

"Well," Crispin piped up. "I have seen the wagons a time or two in the distance but they've always been too far away. I think I heard someone say that they used some kind of beetle."

"We can ask Bela – here he comes now," Tiberius announced.

Bela came striding out of the lengthening evening shadows and threw his arms out to the two friends. "Ah, there you are! Bela glad to see Tiberius up and about. You must be feeling much better. Maleva is good healer, yes?"

"She's marvelous," Tiberius proclaimed. "If we didn't have such an important journey ahead of us, I might be tempted to hurt my other wing just so Maleva could pamper me some more."

Bela's eyebrows shot up, and a mischievous grin crossed his face, "My large friend, you have been smitten by niece's charms, I think." Bela laid a forearm on Tiberius' shoulder and stated, "Maleva is different and sometime, a little lonely. I think, maybe she finds new friend."

"Yes," Tiberius stammered, feeling a bit embarrassed.

"Enough talk about women; caravan must leave soon. Moon is riding high on the horizon already," Bela said.

Crispin tugged gently on Bela's coat sleeve to get his attention. "Bela, we were wondering who pulls your wagons. I think it's a kind of beetle isn't it?" Crispin asked.

"Yes, Hercules beetles. You have seen our caravans then? From a distance perhaps?"

"A few times," Crispin responded, "but not close up. Someone told me once about the beetles."

Bela began to explain, "Hercules beetles are very strong, but also lazy. They wish to be fed instead of hunting for themselves. Our wagons are like feathers to them, so we give food and they pull us."

"Caravan must leave soon," Bela continued. "Crispin tells of your journey so we take you with us if you wish. I will tell you of our travel plans soon, but now Bela must go: there is much to do for leaving." At that, Bela turned and strode purposefully into the woods surrounding the campsite. Just then, a loud crashing noise in the woods made Crispin and Tiberius jump with fright. The foliage around the campsite suddenly parted and a dozen or more Hercules beetles entered the campsite herded in a tight group by two dozen experienced gypsy moth beetle wranglers.

Each beetle was flanked by four wranglers. The two by the front legs would guide their charges right or left by gently tapping the beetles' legs with a thin bamboo stick. The wranglers in the rear would control the beetles' forward or backward movements by tapping their back legs.

Some of the younger beetles found a delightful patch of mushrooms sprouting from a dead log and stubbornly decided they would stop and graze for a while. After a few minutes of stern coaxing by the gypsy moths they reluctantly decided to move on. The moonlight glimmered off the black metallic armored bodies as the wranglers maneuvered the beetles into position by the front of each wagon.

The wranglers scurried back and forth slipping halters and bridles over the beetles' heads. Next, a cinch was brought down, slipped under their bellies and tightened. The halters were made from shimmery red silkworm thread and decorated with bulbous copper bells. The halter and cinch were connected to a tongue made from long bamboo sticks which were attached to the front of the wagon. A square wooden driving seat with a red velvet cushion was positioned at the front of the wagon. Lastly, a set of shimmering gold reins spun from golden orb spider's web was attached to the bridle and halter.

While the wagons were being loaded and the beetles harnessed, the female moths busied themselves chopping and grinding special beetle food. They filled individual pine bark troughs with mosses, ferns, pine nuts and lichens. For an extra treat they threw in a few sprinkles of flaming orange parasol mushrooms which the Hercules beetles were especially fond of. A tiny amount of these rare mushrooms would give them extra energy for the long trip, but if too many were added, it could be a disaster. The beetles would get tipsy and go berserk while pulling the wagons.

The female moths carried the food troughs over and placed them under the beasts' heads. The beetles' short twig like antennas twitched excitedly as they began eating with great gusto accompanied by an odd and very loud symphony of sounds.

Crispin and Tiberius gasped in amazement at the largest beetles they had ever seen. Even stranger were the large hooked snouts atop their heads which were thrashing back and forth in their ferocious feeding frenzy. "They're not exactly quiet diners are they?" Tiberius exclaimed over the collection of chomp-chomp, snort-snort and click-click sounds being made by the beetles.

Latslov held his belly and laughed heartily, "Good appetite, yes!"

Crispin and Tiberius whose curiosity soon overcame their fear cautiously approached one of the lumbering giants being attended to by Latslov. "What are you feeding them?" Crispin asked quietly.

"Some of beetles' favorite mosses and fungus picked in woods," Latslov answered stroking the beetles head. "Come, you can touch. Beetles are nice, you have nothing to fear."

"I...I....I don't know," Crispin said keeping his forearms clasped tightly behind his back.

Tiberius, being a bit braver gingerly reached up and stroked the beetles head. "Ahhaha," he laughed. "They feel very strange. Silky smooth and hard at the same time." He began rubbing the creature more vigorously, and Crispin sensing there wasn't immediate danger tried to reach up and pet the beetle himself but couldn't quite reach.

Latslov seeing the disappointment on the young firefly's face bent over and lifted Crispin. "Young friend needs help, no?"

Crispin gently patted the massive head and a huge grin crossed his face. "Thank you Latslov. Wow! Wait till the friends back home hear about this," he announced proudly after being lowered back to the ground.

Bela, deciding that the preparations for the journey were going well, rejoined Crispin and Tiberius. He placed a forearm on Crispin and Tiberius' shoulders and led them to a shady spot under the drooping branches of an old gnarled willow tree.

"Come, sit. We rest for a while and talk. Bela is tired from preparations of journey." Bela reached up with a forearm and caught a trickle of sweat slipping towards his chin. "Ahh, being gypsy moth king is very hard job sometimes," he added with a slight chuckle. "You must be curious about journey, yes?" Bela questioned as the three sat on a smooth log.

"Yes we are," Crispin and Tiberius answered in unison.

Bela picked up a sharp stick and drew a line in the loose dirt beside him. "This is gypsy moth camp." he began, drawing a circle in the dirt. "Caravan will drive through forest most of night," he continued, drawing a straight line, "until river is near." He drew a row of wavy lines at one end representing water. "Big swamp is here to caravan's left." He placed an X to one side of the map. "But is far enough away so slimy creatures will not bother us. Gypsy moths must leave friends at river then travel north to join other caravans for wedding feast of Stefan...best beetle wrangler Bela knows!"

Tiberius and Crispin glanced at each other nervously at this bit of news. "Do not worry friends," Bela jumped in when he saw the concern in their eyes. "Gypsy moths have very good friend who take you across river in safety. Past river and mountain glen is where you find Fern Queen."

"But how will we find her," Crispin asked curiously.

"My friends, you not worry about that," Bela laughed. "Fern Queen and folks will find Crispin and Tiberius. Friends can ride in Maleva's wagon so she will have company for part of journey. We reach river banks before sun rises and must say our farewells."

Finally, after the food troughs were empty, everyone climbed into their wagons. The driver of the first wagon shook the reins attached to his beetle's harness and it moved forward out of the campsite. The other wagons followed one after another, until the abandoned campsite was far behind. The moon decided to hide its face from the travelers that night; and a heavy blanket of darkness wrapped itself around the caravan as they moved onward; a trail of soft glowing lamp-lit windows piercing the gloom of the forest.

Chapter 6
Terror Along the Road

As the night grew older a ghostly mist descended to the forest floor, snaked its way through the trees, and swirled around the gypsy moths caravan. Several hours had passed since the travelers had rolled out of the campsite. They were now jostling onward, deeper into the forest, accompanied only by the sharp sounds of snapping twigs under their wheels.

Frightened creatures which lay in their path went thrashing and skittering in every direction as the still night air was pierced by the strange rumbling tinkling sounds of the caravan. The wagon drivers could hardly make out the clawed horns of their charges in front of them which floated up through the heavy damp mist. No one was worried about getting lost however; because as everyone knew, Hercules beetles had an uncanny sense of direction, and were expert guides. There wasn't much left for the wagon drivers to do except grip the reins and keep a sharp eye out for any danger which might lie along the pathway.

Tonight, however, the soupy fog made their job that much harder. They sat hunched over with their hats pulled low and coat collars turned up to ward off the creeping damp mist.

Inside Maleva's wagon, Crispin and Tiberius sat on soft beds of pussy willow down; resting and talking to Maleva who had decided to stay awake and entertain her friends. She sang a few songs she had been taught while visiting butterfly relatives and then humored her two friends with stories about strange creatures the gypsy moths had encountered on their many journeys. Tiberius sat hypnotized, hanging on to her every word; dreading the time they would have to say good bye at the river's edge. The flickering amber glow flooding out from a small hanging lantern cast her silhouette softly on the wagon wall. Tiberius though to himself that even her shadow had an unearthly beauty to it.

Crispin sat nearby chewing on a sugar maple root studying his father's map. "Hey look at this," Crispin piped up, breaking the spell Tiberius was under. "Here on the map. This must be the Centipede River we're heading for."

Tiberius leaned over and gazed intently at the map. "Yes, yes, I see. I think you're right, and these sharp pointed markings must be the Teepee Mountain range. The fern glen must be in this area between the far river bank and the mountains." He added tapping the map with a foreleg.

Crispin tilted the map sideways and pointed to several strange symbols inscribed just beyond the river. Next to them written in very tiny red letters were the words 'Be wary travelers'. "Yikes," Crispin exclaimed. "What do you think these markings mean?"

"Let me see," Tiberius said as he took the map and held it up close to the light.
"Hmmm, I can't tell for certain but it looks like a drawing of some kind of plants."

"There's no way for us to be cautious of something if we don't know what it is," Crispin replied. "Do you think it could be the Woods of Forgetfulness that Bela told us about?"

"Well, we'll just have to keep our guard up and be ready for anything," Tiberius said, handing the map back to his friend. Crispin glanced briefly at the map again and announced cheerily, "It doesn't look far to the mountain range does it?"

Maleva's antennas twitched, as she chuckled softly and said, "Crispin, maps can be very deceiving. Even small spot on map can be very far away. I hope you are right however; trip is swift and you return safely." The wagon suddenly pitched to one side and slowly rolled to a stop.

Crispin jumped up pushed the curtain to one side and peered out the front window. The wagon drivers scurried around attending to their beetles as tendrils of mist swirled around them.

Crispin glanced upward at the muddy clouds skimming across the moon and wondered how much time had passed since they left the campsite. "I wonder why we stopped," Crispin questioned as he continued staring out the window.

"Sometimes the beetles get hungry and restless so we stop to feed them. It also could be broken wagon or obstacles on the pathway. We should be going soon. Maleva gets nervous when wagons stop for long time in strange place with no campfire."

A shiver ran up Crispin's back but he shook it off. He turned the knob on the wagon door and cautiously stuck his head into the darkness. The heavy smell of wet pine and rotting forest bracken smacked him in the face. The strange unsettled night air drew him outside, but being cautious of things unknown, he decided to go no further than the wagon driver's seat. He had been sitting alone for a few minutes watching the activity below when the door behind him opened and he was joined by Tiberius and Maleva.

The three friends sat side by side on the wagon seat enjoying the pungent night air which hugged their bodies like a cloak.

Maleva clutched her shawl tightly around her shoulders and announced. "Drivers are feeding beetle guides. Yes, see they are getting out food sacks." The aroma of tangy fruits and earthy smelling mushrooms drifted on eddies of mist shrouded night air and washed over the caravan.

"That's a really strange smell," Crispin said. The firefly rubbed his nose and wrinkled his face into a funny expression.

"Is beetle food," Maleva explained. "We hope other unwelcome guests will not be drawn to smell also," she added.

"What do you mean? What kind of unwelcome guests," Tiberius questioned.

Maleva got a strange mischievous sparkle in her eyes, and began to explain. "Most are harmless, just a few bugs or beetles. Maybe a few ants alone or traveling in small groups. But sometimes bad ones come also."

"Tell us about them pleeeeessssee," Crispin begged.

"Yes, but not Maleva's fault if you have bad dreams tonight."

"Hey, I'm not scared of anything, I'm not a baby."

"I think we can both take it," Tiberius laughed.

Maleva adjusted her shawl and began in a hushed voice. "Gypsy moths have heard story of ambush bugs for long time but never seen them. Fat little yellowish bugs with green glowing eyes. Most time bugs are harmless, hiding in goldenrod or other yellow flowers. When moon is full, bad things happen to bugs." She paused for a few seconds and peered suspiciously into the woods.

"Go on, what happens during the full moon," Crispin prompted.

"Bugs are driven mad from rays of full moon. Some creatures see them dancing and gyrating all night, as if possessed. Also, where there is full moon and fog, bugs think they are in water so dance and try to swim at same time. In few hours, bugs are exhausted."

"This is bad part now," Maleva leaned closer eyes widening and whispered to her captivated audience. "Ambush bugs are so mad with hunger; they sniff out food for miles around. Bugs lay hiding under leaves, and cling to tree limbs. And then," she paused for a second while her two friends held their breath. "Swoosh!" Maleva threw her forelegs outward toward Crispin and Tiberius who jumped backwards, almost tumbling from their seat.

"Bugs attack ferociously with no warning, raining down from trees and slithering from under leaves. They come from every corner of forest: wave after wave of glowing eyes, and thousands of writhing legs. Bugs cover food, grasping and clawing insanely: sometimes even fighting each other until every last morsel has vanished."

A collective gasp went up from the two friends as Maleva ended the frightening tale. Tiberius glanced nervously at the ghostly illuminated night surrounding the caravan. "I hate to bring this to anyone's attention, but isn't it a full moon, and welllll..," he didn't need to finished the observation. The worried look in his companion's eyes told him they had been struck with the exact same thought.

Maleva giggled, breaking the tension holding the three in its clutches. "Probably just scary tale for little ones; at festivals: no?"

"We hope so too," Crispin and Tiberius mumbled, not daring a glance into the tree shadowed mist.

"Look, there's Bela and Latslov," Crispin exclaimed waving at them through the fog.

They watched as Bela placed a bowl of food under one of the beetles and walked over to greet the three companions. "Ah! How are new friends and beautiful niece tonight? Is beautiful weather, no?" Bela announced cheerfully waving his arms in the billowing mist.

"We couldn't resist coming out to breathe fine night air uncle," Maleva chuckled. Tiberius and Crispin joined in nodding and laughing in agreement.

"Bela, I was just wondering how much further we have until we arrive at the river," Crispin blurted out excitedly.

"Oh, is not much further," Bela began, "Caravan will reach river bank before dawn. You are curious about meeting our friend from river, no?" Crispin nodded his head vigorously.

Bela laughed mischievously and shook a foreleg at Crispin. "Bela will make it mystery, keep you busy for rest of trip. Here is clue, gypsy moth friend is very large, with long tail, and is very good swimmer."

"But where will...." Suddenly Crispin's question was interrupted by loud panicky shouts slicing through the mugginess.

"Stay," Bela ordered sternly as he ran towards the shouting, fighting his way through the dense fog, straining to see the blurry shapes darting around the beetles.

"Ambush bugs after beetles' food!" Latslov yelled as he threw Bela a stick.

The fat yellow bugs had rushed in by the dozens; creeping and scurrying from under every leaf and twig in sight as they advanced towards the food. The gypsy moths could see they were worked up into a frenzy. The invaders clawed and jumped on top of each other until they were a surging writhing mound covering the bowls.

The moths madly rushed back and forth along the perimeter of the caravan swatting and whacking at the piles of marauders. Several groups of bugs retreated dejectedly into the woods and the moths were feeling some hope at driving the rest off, when suddenly, the foliage above them began to rustle ominously. They stopped fighting momentarily and ventured a glance upwards. To their horror, hundreds of the ambushers, their glowing green eyes piercing the fog, began dropping from the canopies above.

The Hercules beetles tried their best to protect the food by thrusting the invaders aside with their great horns and tossing them into the trees. The bugs however, were insanely stubborn fighters, and kept coming back for more. Now with the sky raining bugs, the beetles were thoroughly spooked, and began bucking and biting at their harnesses.

The wranglers rushed over in an effort to keep their charges from hurting themselves. They knew that if the beetles ran off, the caravan would be stuck in the forest. It might take days for them to round up the escapees.

Bela and Latslov looked around frantically and knew they were loosing the battle. For every bug they sent flying into the woods, there seemed to be dozens more taking their place.

Soon, every scrap of food in the bowls had vanished and the ambushers had discovered the food bags lying alongside the wagons. They were chewing and clawing at the bags working themselves into a frenzy at the aroma inside.

Back at Maleva's wagon, the three companions looked on horrified at the scene taking place on the ground below. "Should not have told that horrible story. Now look what happens," Maleva cried out covering her eyes with the ends of her shawl.

Tiberius placed a foreleg around her shoulder. "It's not your fault Maleva, it's just a strange coincidence," he glanced over at Crispin.

"I feel so helpless," Tiberius blurted out, "there's got to be something I can do."

"You forget injured wing," Maleva replied. "Is still healing."

"Yes, but you helped us when we were in trouble," Crispin added.

"That's right, and I can't sit by and watch my friends in trouble. I'm going to help the others," Tiberius said as he jumped to the ground. "You stay here with Maleva until I find out if we can do anything."

"Well okay, but hurry back," Crispin replied impatiently.

Tiberius rushed over, dodging the ambush bugs which had been knocked into the air, their narrow green eyes glowing like embers in the dense night fog.

"Why has friend come out? Wing could be re-injured," Bela yelled seeing Tiberius as he continued swatting at the ravaging bugs.

"Can I help," Tiberius shouted back.

"Must keep fighting bugs off: keep away from food wagons!" Bela yelled breathlessly.

Tiberius couldn't think of anything else to do, so he picked up a stick and began swatting at the bugs with his good arm. The ground around him had been transformed into a vibrating churning mass of frenzied ambush bugs with only one thing on their mind. FIND FOOD!

Tiberius glanced at Bela and Latslov who were dirty, sweating profusely, and wearing a very worried look on their faces. "What are our chances," Tiberius shouted.

"Loosing battle, there are too many," Bela responded wiping a bead of sweat off his chin.

"Must do something father," Latslov screamed above the screeching of bugs and panicked yells from the fighters. "Fire scares many bugs off," he added.

"No time to make fire; will be too late!" Bela shouted back in frustration.

"Can try, no?" Latslov yelled back.

Bela turned and yelled to a group of nearby moths, "Boris, Nikoli, bring torches!"

Tiberius' eyes went wide and he let out a gasp as he overheard what Latslov said. "Of course," he yelled throwing the stick down. "I'll be right back. I think Crispin can get us out of this mess," he blurted running toward Maleva's wagon. Bela and Latslov looked at each other quizzically and went back to fighting the bugs.

Crispin was practically jumping out of his skin from waiting when he saw Tiberius rushing towards them, yelling his name. "Crispin, Crispin. I can't help, but you can. The bugs are taking over - its very serious! They need fire very fast, and lots of it. Can you do that fire crackling thing or is it too wet?"

"I don't know, but I can try. Let's go and see," Crispin replied excitedly.

"Jump on my back," Tiberius ordered. "They might think you are an ambush bug, and accidentally smack you."

Tiberius and Crispin rushed over fighting their way through the sea of yellow bugs and found Bela and Latslov still fighting a courageous but loosing battle.

"Bela," Tiberius shouted to get his attention. "Crispin can start fires, watch!"

Crispin stood on Tiberius back, rubbed his leg and antenna together briskly and a piercing crackling sound followed by a brilliant orange spark shot up illuminating the darkness surrounding the caravan. The gypsy moths stopped fighting and gasped in amazement at the young firefly's demonstration.

"Hurry everyone, get torches and bring to Crispin," Bela ordered with renewed hope in his voice.

Soon all the moths were gathered all around Crispin, lighting their torches from the sparks flying off his body. The moth warriors spread out encircling the caravan jabbing and waving their fiery swords at the mass of invaders. At the sight of the flames the bugs reared onto their back legs, screeched in terror and darted back into the woods. The gypsy moths patrolled the area slowly sweeping the torches under and around the wagons looking for hiding marauders.

"Must check food wagons now," Bela stated. Tiberius and Crispin followed Bela and Latslov who cautiously approached the food wagon. "Stand back," he ordered.

Crispin and Tiberius nervously moved backwards. Bela crept up and in one swift movement thrust his torch inside. He jumped back as a hissing and screeching group of very annoyed bugs shot past him and disappeared beyond the nearby trees. "May you all be eaten by flock of starving bats tonight," the king yelled as he shook a fist at the trees.

Hearing the commotion, the other gypsy moths rushed over and gathered around Bela. Several of the wranglers jumped inside the wagon to take stock of the damage done to the food bags. A moment later a wrangler appeared in the doorway and reported, "Most food still safe. Can still feed beetles before we go on."

The area around the caravan was left in shambles, but they had beaten off the enemy and won the war. The moths collapsed on the ground in exhaustion still holding onto the precious torches in case the marauders decided to come back.

Bela threw an arm around Tiberius and Crispin. "You have saved caravan from ruin. From now, you are one of us: Wherever you go what ever you need, gypsy moth brothers will be there for you."

The moths let out an exuberant 'Hurrah'; lifted Crispin and Tiberius on their backs, and paraded the two heroes up and down the caravan; torches blazing triumphantly.

A few persistent ambush bugs stayed hidden under the bracken at the edge of the woods watching the revelry hoping the fires would magically go out. After a little while seeing the fires still blazing strong the last remnants of the marauders crept away dejectedly and disappeared into the swirling mist.

The food saved from the attackers was distributed among the beetles who were lolling about calmly as if nothing had happened. The moths however, were nervously milling around the campsite, jumping and twitching at every snap and snuffling sound around them. Tiberius and Crispin helped feed the beetles and stow the torches; then returned to the wagon where Maleva welcomed the two heroes with a grateful hug.

Crispin was explaining to Maleva in great detail and with just a little exaggeration, his talent of fire starting; when Tiberius noticed a commotion on the far side of the caravan. It was a rather large group of very excited female moths rushing over, their kaleidoscope of skirts flapping and tinkling in their wake. "Get in the wagon quick. We're about to be mobbed," Tiberius ordered.

It was too late. Before they had time to take evasive measures the heroes were surrounded by the cackling and cooing admirers. Tiberius and Crispin recognized the two older moths leading the pack as the servers from several nights before. Maleva moved forward and gently touched the shoulder of the older of the two females who had a halo of silvery hair peaking out from under a gold paisley scarf. "This is Natasha and sister, Maria. They are like mothers to us." The others gathered around nodding their heads in agreement.

"We speak for everyone," Maria said gesturing to the others as she began her speech. "Gypsy moths are very grateful to our new friends. From now on, we sing and tell stories of Crispin and Tiberius who save us from horrible crazy bugs. Also, here is gift for you." The sisters pulled shiny gold coin necklaces from their skirt pockets and placed them around the hero's necks. Natasha gestured skyward and proclaimed, "May your journeys always be safe and moon smile down upon you always."

As she finished the other females tried to surge forward, but were halted by Maria who clapped sharply and announced "They are tired and need rest. Come, caravan will leave soon. To the wagons my lovelies."

Tiberius and Crispin watched with relief as their exuberant admirers waved a tinkling good-bye and returned reluctantly to their wagons. "Yuck, I'm glad they all didn't try to kiss us," Crispin blurted out after the moths were out of earshot.

"Yes, I suppose we got off easy considering how excited they were," Tiberius replied.

Maleva lifted a coin on Crispin's necklace and caressed it, "Is rare for gypsy moths to give such important gift."

Tiberius bent over with a sweeping bow and said, "We will wear them proudly milady."

Fortunately for the moths who were exhausted from their misadventure with the ambush bugs, the rest of the journey that night was quiet and uneventful. Crispin and Tiberius tried to settle into a peaceful sleep for the remainder of the journey but their dreams were invaded by visions of hideous clawed beasts with vicious burning eye sockets. They jerked and twitched in an uneasy sleep slashing out with useless weapons drowning in a sea of thrashing legs and gnarling slathering jaws.

THE SWAYING MOTION and droning of wagon wheels beneath them slowed, and came to an abrupt halt, rescuing the two sleepers from their nightmares. The caravan had reached the shadowy twisting banks of the Centipede River shortly before dawn. They parked under a grove of stately old willow trees whose graceful arching branches reached down and caressed the silvery moon-kissed water below.

They sat up, rubbed the haze from their eyes, and noticed Maleva standing by the side window, peering outward. The first amber rays of morning streamed in and bathed her face in a soft gauzy halo.

"Come, look my friends. We finally arrive. River is beauti-ful...no?" Maleva announced.

Crispin and Tiberius rushed over and pushed their faces against the window. "Yippee," Crispin shouted bouncing up and down in excitement. "We're here, we're here! The river's huge. I wonder who's going to take us across."

"Never fear my young friend, Bela has a plan. I only wish my wing was completely healed so we could fly right over it," Tiberius replied touching his wing tenderly. "It should be healed soon, I can't hold up our trip any longer."

Maleva picked up her shawl and headed for the front door, "Come, we find Bela and talk about river crossing."

The three companions fluttered off the wagon and wove their way through the flurry of activity in the caravan. The Hercules beetles had been unhitched from the wagons, and were stomping their way towards the forest. The wranglers flanked the group tapping and waving their sticks through the dew fringed grass. Crispin, Tiberius and Maleva found Bela and Latslov at the river's edge perched on a pile of smooth gray stones. They were gazing out over the river's surface as the pale morning light broke loose from its dark prison of clouds. Bela and Latslov heard a scuffling sound coming from behind and turned.

"Good morning," Maleva said.

"Did friends have good rest," Bela questioned, giving his niece a hug.

"I had a few nightmares," Crispin piped up.

"Bela and others did too," he added laughing. "Bugs still gone when everyone wakes. Is all that matters, no?"

A young gypsy moth strode up to Bela, and placed a fiddle into his hands. "Thank you, Pavl. Run along now, play with others. Soon it will be time to sleep."

"Are you going to play for us," Crispin asked.

"Will play, but not for gypsy moths. Song will be signal to call river friend, so be patient and watch."

Tiberius and Crispin traded puzzled looks, and picked their way among the hills of time tumbled stones until they found a flat comfortable one and sat down. Maleva joined them a short time later but did not sit. "Little ones need bed time stories so Maleva must leave and go help others. Will see you in short time for saying good bye."

"Of course," Tiberius and Crispin replied in unison.

After Maleva disappeared into the woods, Crispin and Tiberius turned their attention back to the activities on the river bank. They watched with great anticipation as Bela tucked the fiddle under his fuzzy chin and readied the bow. He began playing an exceptionally loud, recognizable gypsy moth tune. The torrent of wild dancing notes skimmed their way down river and was heard for a great distance.

All the creatures in their watery homes and on the willow dappled banks stopped their morning rituals to listen in silence as the beautiful strange notes sailed past. Latslov stood next to his father, shading his eyes from the bright shafts of breaking dawn scanning the wide sparkling river.

"I'm so excited, my wings are vibrating," Crispin exclaimed.

Tiberius patted his young companion's shoulders. "I have to admit, this is quite intriguing. I can't imagine who or what is going to show up. One thing is for certain if Bela trusts this creature, I think we can too."

Just then Latslov yelled, "He comes," as he pointed towards the opposite bank.

Bela laid the fiddle and bow gently on a nearby stone, waved his arms in a broad sweeping motion, and called, "Ahoy old friend!"

Crispin and Tiberius, who were overcome with curiosity, left their stony perch and moved closer to the waters' edge. They watched as a pair of glistening bumps bobbed along the rivers surface leaving a long rippling gash in its wake. As the creature swam nearer, Crispin and Tiberius watched with fascination as the bumps transformed into a pair of narrow, reptilian eyes.

"It's an alligator," Crispin gasped.

"Settle down," Tiberius chuckled. "I know about 'gators. They're no danger to our kind. We're too small for them to waste time eating. Anyway, he must be a friendly fellow or the gypsy moths wouldn't have brought us here."

The alligator was now at the rivers edge and had pulled his massive dark green knobby body half way out of the water. The sharp claws on his crock'd front legs were sunk into the silty, gray oozing mud.

Tiberius cocked his head sideways and with a perplexed look inspected the newcomer. "I've seen quite a few alligators in my time, but there's something strange about this one. Let's move closer, so I can get a better view."

The two friends scurried up an overhanging branch giving them a bird's eye view of the massive creature. "Well, I'll be a four eyed bedbug," Tiberius exclaimed pointing downward. "I've never seen anything like this before."

Crispin studied the great bulky form lounging in the soft mud and gasped as his gaze fell upon the creature's head. He quickly glanced back at Tiberius and exclaimed, "Jumping junebugs. That alligator is wearing a pair of spectacles!"

A quirky smile slowly crossed Tiberius face as he laughed, "a 'gator who wears spectacles; and a gold rimmed pair at that. Must be an interesting fellow, don't you think?"

"I do indeed," Crispin agreed.

The two excited friends bounced off the branch and landed with a plop next to Bela and Latslov, who were chatting merrily with the bespectacled giant. "Ah, good," Bela announced. "Here are friends, Crispin and Tiberius we told you about."

Bela placed a foreleg on Tiberius's shoulder and said, "This is Tiberius. He is with injured wing."

Latslov patted Crispin on the head, "and friend Crispin who saved caravan from bug attack by starting fire, like magic."

Bela gestured grandly towards the reptile and announced loudly, "Bela pleased to introduce old friend, Mr. Gaylord Gator."

Tiberius bowed and replied. "It's very nice to make your acquaintance."

"And me too Mr. Gator," Crispin added ruffling his wings.

The alligator lifted one crook'd leg and said, "I'm pleased as a pig in a bucket of slop to meet you." He moved his large pointed snout back and forth to get a better look at Crispin and Tiberius. "Hmm, a giant moth and lightening bug traveling together on an important mission. Can't say I've heard tell of such a thing before."

"Bela and Latslov told me about y'alls perdikerment and I'm happy to oblige. Mr. Gator's at your service. Why shucks, you two little bitty guys couldn't weigh much more than a feather. I won't even notice y'all up there on my back."

Bela and Latslov smiled broadly at Crispin and Tiberius. "Gaylord was born in south where big swamps are," Bela said.

"How did you end up here," Crispin questioned.

"Well, I'll tell you," Mr. Gator began. "When me and my brother Jerry were babies there was this great gigantic flood, and quicker than a rattlesnake's tail the whole swamp was carried away, and us with it. When it finally stopped we landed in this big old beautiful river and never wanted to go back."

"And how did you meet the gypsy moths?" Tiberius questioned.

"Well now that tale's about as long as the mighty Mississippi. I'll spin that yarn later. We best get a move on if y'all want to get crossed over before that sun up there starts scorching our backs."

"Yes; and gypsy moths must say good bye to friends," Bela added. "Time to sleep soon. Caravan leaves tonight for north woods. Gaylord will wait, yes?"

"Why of course. I wouldn't dream of abandoning these two in their hour of need," Gaylord replied.

Crispin and Tiberius returned to the caravan where they were immediately surrounded. There was much back slapping from the wranglers and wagon drivers and fervent hugs from Natasha, Maria, and the other fluttering females.

Tiberius gazed over the throng of gray and black bodies in hopes of seeing Maleva's gold spotted wings. He found her standing alone by her wagon holding the food packs. "Time has come for leaving, no?" Maleva said sadly.

"Yes it has," Tiberius replied.

"Here are packs with fresh food for long journey."

He gently touched her shoulder and said, "Thank you for taking such good care of me. My wing is almost completely healed. Fortune smiled down on us the night Roscoe brought us to the gypsy moths."

"Maleva sorry friends had bad time in terrible storm, but if it were not so...." her voice hesitated, and she glanced down shyly at the ground.

"Yes, I know what you mean," Tiberius said. "We might have never met your people and......." his voice trailed off as the unspoken message passed between them.

They embraced tenderly for a few moments and then Tiberius reluctantly reached down and grabbed the packs. He turned and walked back towards the waiting well wishers with a painful heaviness in his chest. Crispin excited to finally continue their adventure rushed up to meet him. He took his backpack from Tiberius and waved a cheerful good bye to Maleva.

Bela and Latslov, accompanied them back to the river, and their waiting reptilian ferry. Bela un-slung a skinned bag on a string from his shoulder and pulled a pithy stopper from its mouth. Four tiny nutshell halves appeared from Latslov's pocket and were distributed among the group. They were filled with a sparkling amber liquid.

Bela and Latslov raised their drinks towards their friends and recited "May moon of gypsy moths smile down upon friends always and road you travel be smooth." "SALUTE!" they all chanted clinking their cups together and quickly downed the sweet nectar.

Crispin and Tiberius stood on the rocky bank watching with a tinge of sadness as the father and son wound their way back towards the caravan, and disappeared.

Mr. Gaylord Gator, true to his word was sprawled sunbathing in the same exact spot they had left him. Crispin and Tiberius crept cautiously toward the lumbering giant. His eyes were shut tight and they couldn't tell if he was sleeping or just doing what comes naturally to alligators. Tiberius decided it was probably a bad idea to startle the snoozing beast so they kept a safe distance and called out. "Mr. Gaylord, we're back. It's Crispin and Tiberius. Are you sleeping?" The alligator didn't move a muscle. In fact, he didn't even twitch. "Our voices are too tiny. We could stand here and shout all day!"

"He'll never hear us," Crispin moaned.

"I have an idea," Tiberius said. "I'll be right back." He scoured the area inspecting the rocky shore and returned several minutes later holding a long thin stick. "Come with me," he said. They moved forward slowly, stopping a safe distance from the pointy snout. Tiberius held out the stick and gently tapped the edge of Gaylord's mouth. He twitched, but continued snoozing peacefully.

"What now," Crispin asked.

"I'll try again," Tiberius replied. He tightened his grip on the stick, thrust forward and accidentally jabbed the reptile in a nostril!

Gaylord's eyes jerked open, let out a loud hiss, and his gigantic tail slapped the water sending a geyser into the air. Tiberius and Crispin scrambled for safety under an overhanging rock. "What in tarnation was that," Gaylord yelled.

Tiberius cautiously peered out from their hiding place and shouted back. "We're awfully sorry to disturb you sir but we tried calling out. Our voices weren't loud enough to wake you. We were afraid to startle a creature of your...." Tiberius hesitated to find the right word. "A creature of your....magnificence!"

"So you decided to punch me in the nose instead?" Crispin and Tiberius exchanged nervous glance, but relaxed when they heard a low growling laugh. "Ha ha, he he he. You two critters sure are smart. Poking an alligator in the nose to wake him up. Yep, it took a few brain cells to figure that one out, ha ha ha; ho ho ho! Now come on down here so we can get a move on. Daylight's burnin'."

The two friends retrieved their hastily abandoned packs and trotted nearer until they were standing under the alligator's gold rimmed eyes. "Good, there you are. See, I didn't gobble you up did I? Just because someone is bigger than you doesn't necessarily mean they are a monster; okay? Y'all got that?"

"Yes sir, Mr. Gator," they replied

"And let's get another thing straight right now. Stop calling me MR GATOR. Makes me feel like I'm ready for the boot factory. Just call me Gaylord."

"Now, set them packs down for a few minutes. There's a few things need talking about before we leave." Crispin and Tiberius dropped their packs to the ground and listened attentively.

"First, once you're settin' on my head, don't be movin' around too much. It makes my head itch something fierce. Second, there's a sand bar half way across the river. We might stop there for a while. I hear there's gonna' be some water bug races going on later, and we don't want to get tangled up in that mess. Third, don't worry about those stupid ducks. They won't come near me, yellow bellied cowards. They think I'm gonna' bite their heads off. If they had a lick of sense, they'd know 'gators in our neck of the woods only eat turtles and fish. All them feathers are sort of hard to get down."

Crispin and Tiberius were holding their breath trying not to laugh. They really didn't want to make fun of Gaylord when they knew quite well he was deadly serious, so they just nodded.

"So, If you guys are ready let's get goin'. Climb up my snout, find a comfortable spot, and make yourself at home. Oh yes; I almost forgot, number four. Don't mess with the spectacles."

Crispin and Tiberius crawled up and picked their way among the knobby green peaks until they were firmly seated. "Wow, this should be fun. I can't believe that we're actually going to ride on an alligator," Crispin gushed.

"Well, let's just relax and enjoy the trip. Look, we have a great view of the river from here," Tiberius replied.

Their water taxi suddenly and with a long powerful thrust backwards floated away from the water's edge. Crispin and Tiberius were jostled around at first, but once Gaylord turned around, and swam into deeper water they hardly felt anything at all.

Chapter 7
The Races

*I*t was quite out of the ordinary to see a moth and lightning bug floating down the river on an alligator barge. This interesting bit of news flew through the Centipede River inhabitants faster than a lightning bolt. Crispin, Tiberius, and Gaylord slid silently through the early morning haze followed by a hundred pairs of curious eyes.

Tiberius was gazing over the glassy pea green surface when suddenly the water below began to ripple and churn. "Don't look now, but I think we're going to have company," he announced.

"You're right," Crispin said pointing. "Look over there at those floating sticks and clumps of plants. They seem to be following us. What do you think they are?"

"We'll soon find out," Tiberius answered. "Here they come. I hope they're friendly."

"Me too," Crispin agreed.

The sticks arrived first bumping and bobbing in a churning mass. Crispin and Tiberius looked over Gaylord's huge body and inspected the flotilla of curious clinging creatures. The beetles were gray mottled, with huge front claws and twitching red antennas. They were hanging onto their stick rafts by one of their large claws, and waving with the other. "Ahoy, you up there, ahoy! Greetings from us long toed beetles."

Crispin and Tiberius waved and called back to the rafters. "Greetings to you too: from a luna moth and a lightning bug."

The beetles paddled around peering curiously and shouted, "We don't see many of your kind around here. Well, maybe some lightning bugs: but never ones wearing vests. Are you here for the water races?"

"No, we're on an urgent journey," Tiberius answered back.

"Oh. We were wondering if you wanted to join us on our rafts, and float around for a while?"

"It looks like fun, but we're having a grand time right here," Crispin replied. "By the way, I was wondering exactly where are your long toes?"

The beetles kicked their long legs up in the air and displayed an extremely fat oar-like appendage which sprouted from the side of each leg. "It comes in mighty handy for pushing our rafts along," one of the long toes said.

"Sure you don't want to come down for a closer look," one of the rafters shouted.

"Sorry, maybe another time," Tiberius replied.

"Good luck then, we must be moving along," the beetles yelled kicking off with their powerful toed oars.

The long toes were still waving good bye when another cheering and waving group of shiny green bugs floated by. They were sprawled on a clump of water hyacinths spouting water out of their mouth into the air. Crispin and Tiberius looked at each other and laughed. "Do you think that's how they say hello," Crispin asked.

"Maybe," Tiberius chuckled: "and look at these characters coming our way."

A group of fat orange spotted bugs came alongside hopping up and down on the waters surface, announcing their arrival in deep croaking voices. "Ahoy there travelers. Watch out for the water races, they're about to begin."

Tiberius and Crispin looked at the funny bugs and answered. "Thanks, we'll be stopping on the sand bar until the races are over."

"Wise decision, yes," One of the bugs croaked back. The other bugs shook their heads in agreement. "Yes, all the toad bugs agree, it's a wise decision indeed."

"We'll see you guys at the races then," the lead toad bug replied as they hopped off waving and yelling a croaky farewell.

Crispin and Tiberius were still having a great laugh over the comical toad bugs when the sky overhead suddenly darkened. They barely had time to duck when a squadron of dragonflies buzzed their heads inspecting the unusual ferry passengers. Green and blue darners tipped their wings gracefully, while violet damselflies turned somersaults around Gaylord's head. A few shy amber winged skimmers even showed up. They hovered overhead, their fragile golden wings buzzing a welcoming tune.

Crispin and Tiberius had been so distracted by the dragonfly squadron they hadn't noticed Gaylord's approach to the sand bar. He found a good landing spot and slid through the marsh plants fringing the island until the three travelers were on high dry ground. Crispin and Tiberius were amazed at the throng of spectators which encircled the sand bar awaiting the festivities. The toad bugs had arrived hopping and croaking excitedly; waving reedy grass sticks festooned with vibrant orange marigold petals. A group of yellow winged marsh flies sitting on a piece of driftwood were being entertained by several young bog beetles darting back and forth in a game of tag. Blue velvet shore bugs clung to a patch of fuzzy brown cattails munching happily on long strings of mossy river plants. Now and then one of the dark blue striped bugs would hop off his perch and disappear for a short time and return with a fresh batch of mossy snacks clutched between his front legs. The waiting bugs would cheer "Crickety clack, crickity clack. Horray! He's back!" and clap their long twiggy front legs as he passed out their treats. This went on for some time until the shore bugs, obviously stuffed, hung lethargically from their plush towers.

Damselflies, and dragonflies darted and dive bombed the perimeter of the sandbar entertaining the spectators with their aeronautical maneuvers. A squadron of green darner dragonflies approached, flying in a tight V formation. At the last second, they peeled off into barreling somersaults. Everyone except for the engorged shore bugs was on their feet cheering wildly as the darners buzzed overhead. The long toes floated up and anchored their bobbing rafts with reed grass ropes to a jungle of sturdy bulrushes. The beetles pulled their big toed legs from the water and stretched out on their rafts to bask in the golden morning rays.

"Well, this is a good place to park for a while," Gaylord announced. "You fella's can get down if you want or you can watch the races from up top."

"I think we'll have a better view from up here," Tiberius replied.

"Probably a good idea," Gaylord said. "There's no tellin' what critters are lurking around here. I'd hate to be responsible for gittin' y'all eatin' up."

Crispin and Tiberius had just gotten comfortable when suddenly a gray swirling cloud descended from above and surrounded Gaylord.

He shook his head vigorously and swatted at the dense droning mass with his legs. "Those darn punkies," he shouted. "Who invited you to the party? Y'all git on out of here and go bother someone else!"

"Yeeee," Crispin shouted flailing his legs at the unwelcome guests.

"Watch out," Tiberius ordered. "These guys are mean, and they have a nasty bite. Just be still, and keep your eyes shut and they'll soon leave."

Crispin tried to obey, but his curiosity got the upper hand, and he peeked out through squinted eyes at the punkies. The tiny flies had ugly squashed faces with a pair of extremely sharp teeth protruding from their mouths. Tufts of hair in a rainbow of pink, orange and blue jutted up like turkey feathers from the tops of their heads. Crispin, having seen too much for his own good quickly shut his eyes.

"You guys are getting on my last nerve," Tiberius shouted.

The punkies responded with a string of high pitched; 'Nyah nyah na na na', followed by a chorus of snickers.

Gaylord, at his wits end, sent a loud hiss into the air, and the troublesome punkie cloud suddenly scattered, swirling down the river.

"Good riddance," Gaylord shouted. "Those pests wouldn't be so bad if they didn't travel in packs. Are y'all okay up there?"

"We're fine, just a bit rattled," Tiberius answered.

"I hope they don't come back," Crispin whined.

"They won't," Gaylord said. "The punkies have had their fun with us for the day."

The crowd began cheering and whistling as two green lacy winged ripple bugs wearing red caps crawled up a tall stick tower at the center of the sand bar. They reached the very tip top of the spindly looking tower and stood at the rail waving their caps and bowing to the crowd. After a few minutes of revelry, the ripple bugs sat down on a bench and the spectators fell silent.

"Those must be the announcers for the races," Tiberius said to Crispin. "Those ripple bugs are notorious for being loud mouths. If the wind is right, you can hear them for a great distance along the river."

One of the announcers came back to the rail and called out in an extremely loud bellowing voice, "Welcome everyone to the 12th

annual Centipede River championship swimming races and what a grand day it is. We have entries representing every community along our fair river. They have come from as far away as Hob Nob Bend and Crab Cove to our very own town of Trout Hollow. We have six finalists in today's race. They are the winners of the elimination races held earlier this week along with the current Centipede River swimming champion back to defend his title; and here he comes now."

A raft decorated with blue and pale yellow water lilly swags floated up to the sandbar and a glistening ebony water boatman bug with huge oar like front claws stepped off and swaggered up a roped off path to the announcers tower.

"Ladies and gentlemen," the ripple bug began. "Please give farewell applause to our current champ, 'Neptune's Glory' as he relinquishes his crown. This water boatman bug broke last year's speed record and remarkably; did it swimming on his back!"

The magnificent bug climbed the tower; removed a small green leafy wreath from his head, and passed it to the announcer. He bowed proudly to the crowd as they roared with excitement and tossed flowers as he descended the tower and returned down the pathway.

"And now here comes the other contestants for this race-of-races," the announcer called excitedly.

A fleet of five other rafts each draped with colorful flowers stopped in front of the sandbar. Each one held an entourage of several bugs or beetles moving about in a flurry of activity. They were wearing brightly colored arm bands which matched the flower banners on their rafts.

"Ladies and gentlemen," the announcers began, "may we introduce this year's contestants. In raft number one we have the water treaders and their challenger 'Minnow War'." A cheer went up from the spectators as one of the lanky greenish water treaders waved an arm and twitched his long flowing antennas in the air.

"In raft number two, please welcome the water measurers with their champion, 'Sea Admiral'." The crowd again cheered wildly as an extremely long stick looking bug waved back.

"Also joining us in raft number three are the water striders with the graceful 'Lightning Sue'." A spider like bug with graceful long legs threw a kiss to the exuberant crowd.

"And here's our fourth challenger, the creeping water bugs, with their hopeful; 'River Biscuit'!" A small, but strong looking brown bug with webbed front legs jumped up and bowed. The spectators went wild.

"It seems we have a favorite with the audience today," the ripple bug shouted over the roaring crowd. "On raft number five, we have the water scorpions, with their challenger, 'Sailor's Son'." A grayish beetle with scorpion like front legs waved and kicked his legs up to the amusement of the crowd.

"And returning to defend their title on raft number six, we have the water boatmen, with the pride of the Centipede River, 'Neptune's Glory'." The beetle thrust his powerful oar like legs up into the air and fanned open a set of metallic wings.

"There you have it folks," the announcer called out: "Our six spectacular competitors. Now, let's get these races started."

The other ripple bug announcer pulled out a thin reed whistle and blew a series of trill like notes. The challengers dove off their rafts with an energetic plunge and swam to a row of orange flagged poles jutting out of the water.

"Will the contestants please take their place at the starting poles." The announcer called out. Each swimmer scurried over and grabbed onto a bobbing pole with their legs. At the sound of the whistle each contestant will circle the island once," the announcers instructed. "The one returning to the orange flag first will be this year's new champion. Anyone caught jumping the starting line or observed participating in foul play will be disqualified from competing for two years. Swimmers, take your marks."

The contestants let go of the poles and poised their bodies for take off. At the first pole, the water strider floated on the surface, tapping out messages with her long spider like legs. The ripples spread out and found their way to the other striders skating along the sand bar's shores. They responded by tapping a return message of good luck to their champion. At the next pole, the water treader stood on the water's surface, his spindly legs twitching impatiently. Next to them the water scorpion, and water measurer spread their twiggy bodies over the water like floating leaves. At the next pole, the water boatmen floated on his back stretching and splashing his extremely powerful oared legs.

Lastly, by the outside pole, the creeping water bug lay submerged with only his head and powerful webbed front legs protruding into the air.

The announcer lifted the reed whistle to his mouth and one long shrill note tumbled through the air. The swimmers thrust their powerful bodies forward leaving jets and sprays of water in their wake.

"And they're off," the announcer shouted. "Taking the lead is 'Minnow War', 'Sailor's Son' second, 'Neptune's Glory' third, 'Sea Admiral' fourth, 'River Biscuit' fifth and 'Lightning Sue' trailing."

"Splashing into the first turn it's 'Minnow War', 'Sailor's Son' in second, 'Neptune's Glory' moving up fast, 'River Biscuit'; 'Sea Admiral' and 'Lightning Sue' trailing neck and neck."

"'Lightning Sue's' in trouble. She's caught in a clump of Pickrel weeds." The water strider stopped and began tearing frantically at the web like foliage wrapped around her delicate legs. She finally chewed her way free and plowed forward to catch up with the others.

"Now in the back stretch it's 'Neptune's Glory' backstroking his way into first, 'Minnow War's fading, 'Sailor's Son' at third, 'River Biscuit' fourth 'Sea Admiral' fifth, and 'Lightning Sue' fighting her way back into the rear."

"Passing the three quarter pole it's 'Neptune's Glory', 'Sailor's Son' in close second, and 'River Biscuit' coming up on the outside neck and neck with 'Minnow War'. Oh, no! River biscuit and Minnow War have their legs tangled." The two bugs bobbed and flailed for a few seconds then parted. "They're back on course," the announcer shouted.

"Coming into the home stretch its 'Neptune's Glory', 'River Biscuit' passing 'Sailor's Son' is now second, 'Minnow War' is fading and is neck and neck with 'Sea Admiral' with 'Lightning Sue' still trailing."

"Here comes 'River Biscuit' pouring on the steam! He's neck and neck with 'Neptune's Glory' heading for the finish pole. He passed 'Neptune's Glory'!

'River Biscuit' wins by a length with 'Neptune's Glory' in second, 'Sailor's Son' third, "Minnow War" fourth, followed by 'Lightning Sue' and 'Sea Admiral'."

Crispin and Tiberius were on their feet shouting, cheering and jumping in the air along with the crowd. "What a great race," Crispin yelled out breathlessly. "Those guys can sure swim."

"It was one of the most exciting races I've ever seen: even better than the three legged grasshopper races!" Tiberius added.

"Three legged," Crispin said amazed. "That must be hilarious!"

"I'll take you to see the races next spring," Tiberius yelled over the screaming fans.

"That'l be fun," Crispin shouted back. "Hey look, the swimmers are coming back."

The contestants pulled themselves back to their rafts and flopped exhausted on piles of soft leaves. 'River Biscuit' however, jumped and threw his legs up in the air triumphantly as he made his way down the roped path to the announcer's tower. The jubilant crowd threw flowers and home made garlands at their new hero. He stopped at the base of the tower and stood on a tan flat topped mushroom.

The two racing announcers and an entourage of three important looking orange spotted toad bugs wearing black top hats and gold waistcoats encircled the podium.

"Joining us today to crown our new champion are representatives from our city council." The announcer shouted. The three spotted bugs tipped their hats, and waved ceremoniously to the crowd.

"Presenting the winner's wreath to 'River Biscuit', will be Mr. Theodore Toadbug." The council member removed his top hat and tried his best to execute a low gracious bow. He was however, quite fat, and his vest was already straining at its buttons. All Theodore Toadbug could manage was a swaying sweeping gesture with his arms as he waddled over to 'River Biscuit'.

"A thousand congratulations to you our new champion. We're all extremely proud of a job well done." He stated in a croaking voice. River Biscuit leaned over and Theodore Toadbug placed the green leafy wreath around his stumpy brown antennas.

"Ladies and gentlemen," the announcer began, "we present to you this year's Centipede River swimming champion and holder of the new record - 4.1 minutes, 'River Biscuit'!" The crowd went wild again as the newly crowned victor took a long well deserved bow.

The announcer raised an arm in the air to silence the crowd. "This year's winner will be the honored guest at all Centipede River functions and will ride in a place of honor in the lead raft at the annual Autumn Moon Festival parade. He will also be given the privilege of having the right of way anywhere along the Centipede River. Now, let's give a hardy round of applause for our other finalists in this year's competition." The five other competitors trotted down the roped path and one by one stepped up to the podium and shook River Biscuit's leg.

The spectators threw more flowers and shouted, "Hurrah, well done".

"We would like to thank everyone for coming to this years swimming championship and supporting our community," the ripple bugs announced. "For your farewell entertainment the mesmerizing whirligig beetle water troop will perform several dances for you. Enjoy the entertainment and have a safe trip home."

The rafts floated away from the sand bar and a group of shimmery green and black beetles gathered along the shore's edge. They formed a tight circle and started an elaborate gyrating water dance. They kicked and pirouetted in a synchronized display which left the onlookers clapping and yelling for more. The whirligig beetles responded with an encore ballet depicting a blooming water hyacinth. After the applause had died away, they leapt out of the water, bowed and swam off with a flash of metallic legs. The spectators gathered their belongings up and began to leave the sand bar.

"Well, I reckon it's safe for us to leave too," Gaylord announced. "How did y'all like the races? Pretty excitin' don't you think?"

"They were great," Crispin and Tiberius sang out. "We decided to cross on the right day, that's for sure."

"Okay, let's push off," Gaylord said, "Hold on." Gaylord slid back through the reedy marsh edges and plopped down into the river with a thundering splat.

Chapter 8
Gaylord's Story

A few stragglers crossing the river on their way home slowed Gaylord's progress, but soon their gator taxi deposited them on the far bank.

"Wow, that didn't take long at all," Crispin chirped.

"Will you be here later....when we're on our way back?" Tiberius queried.

"You bet," Gaylord replied. "I'm always hanging around these parts. Let's set for a spell, and have some lunch. I'm starved. I'm going to catch me a fish or two."

"Ick, fish," Crispin sputtered. "But I could go for some of those tasty gypsy moth cakes they packed for us. I have a rumbly tummy."

"Me too," Tiberius said. "And maybe, while we're eating, Gaylord will tell us a story about how he got those funny spectacles."

"Oh yes, I almost forgot. Please do tell us the story Mr. Gaylord," Crispin said.

"All right. Get comfortable under that sumac leaf, and eat while I go snag some fishies. I'll spin that yarn when I come back."

Gaylord headed off downstream while Crispin and Tiberius sat under the shady leaf and divided two of the little fluffy cakes. "Hey, let's get the map out and check our course," Crispin suggested. He unlaced his vest, pulled the folded map from its secret pocket, and spread it on the ground.

Tiberius finished the cake he was munching happily on, and turned his attention to the map. "Well, let's see...here is the Centipede River we just crossed," he said pointing to a wavy blue line. "Now, all we have to do is travel west through..." He hesitated a moment with a quizzical look. "I guess these green triangular symbols represent a forest."

Crispin jumped and gasped, "Oh no, I forgot to tell you! Bela told me when you were sick that we should try to avoid the Woods of Forgetfulness. I hope they're not in this forest."

"Did he say why," Tiberius asked.

"I can't remember all of it," Crispin replied scratching an antenna. "Just something about getting through it as fast as we can and not eating anything in the woods."

"Or what?" Tiberius queried.

"We'll forget who we are or where we're going," Crispin replied. "But don't worry, Bela gave us a potion to cure it if we're stricken."

"All right, I'm glad you remembered. We'll have to be fast and keep our wits about us," Tiberius added. "After the woods," he went on, "we should come to the Teepee Mountains. The fern glen grows along the foothills."

"Well, we're getting closer," Crispin added cheerfully as he refolded the map and tucked it away.

A few minutes later Gaylord returned and stretched out on the spongy grass. "Mmm mmm! Had me a couple of fat juicy piggy perch. Those little guys practically jumped down my throat." He grinned and licked his lips with a slurp. "Okay, I promised somebody a story: didn't I. Where do I start," he mused.

"At the beginning," Crispin giggled.

"All right then," Gaylord began. "Me and my brother Jerry were hatched out from two identical eggs. Yep, that's right, like two peas in a pod. At first that is. But later on when we got a little older something very strange started happening. Every time I tried to catch a turtle or fish, I would snap at it and miss. Funny thing was, Jerry would catch the little rascals every time. Before long he was catching all the food or I would have starved to death. He was getting pretty tired of it too. We were almost grown up and well, you can imagine how that made me feel."

"The other gators made fun of me too! Called me names like 'Jerry's baby', and 'Slow Joe'. Well, one night I was laying on the bank feeling real sorry for myself when along came this really dirty mangy stray dog. Poor thing looked like he'd been chewed up and spit out. He was so bad, I forgot about my problems and went over to see if I could help. Turned out his name was Chester, a terrier mix from the city a few miles away. Got himself lost in the woods and was half starved. I helped him catch a turtle to gnaw on and we struck up a conversation. I told him I knew what it was like to starve, and explained about my problem. Well, low and behold, this dog's got some city smarts and starts tellin' me he knows what's wrong with me. Turns out I've got this condition called nearsightedness. That means my eyes aren't exactly workin' right. Things around me always looked fuzzy and out of focus. Chester told me about this animal doctor back in town who could probably help; so we found Jerry, and told him the good news. We decided to help Chester find his way back home in exchange for takin' us to the animal doctor."

"Here's where it gets really weird. We finally got to town, but before Chester could get us to the doctor me and Jerry got chased around by two men with ropes on long sticks, and captured. We fought like the dickens; but they drug us into this huge truck and took us to a place called 'Gator World' where they put us in a pen with some other; not too friendly 'gators."

"We tried every trick we knew to get out, but nothing worked. The fence was too high to climb over and the dirt around the edge was too hard to dig through. So day after day, we swam around in this little fenced lake while all these funny humans came and stared and screamed at us."

"As you can imagine, we were really depressed. Twice a day this man in a uniform would throw meat over the fence to us. All the other 'gators would rush over and hog all the food. I just set in the corner and waited for a few tidbits Jerry managed to get. Well, I guess the man in uniform got worried about me and one day two other guys came with the rope on a stick, and took me to the animal doctor. They put me on a big shiny table and poked and prodded me all over. The doctor laughed and told the other men, 'The only thing this gator needs is a pair of glasses. He's not eatin' because he can't see his food.'"

"'We can fix that,'" one of the uniformed men said. He left and came back with a big brown box. Next thing you know, they're puttin' these strange glass and metal things on my head. They put me down on the floor, and lay a chicken leg in one corner. After having a bunch of these objects taken on and off my head, I finally see the chicken leg clear as day; run over and gobble it up. I'm taken and locked back up, but I'm too excited to care at the moment because everything is so beautiful, the sky, clouds, leaves on trees, even Jerry and the other grumpy old gators look mighty fine."

"Me and Jerry ware so happy, we danced around, and the other gators stared at us like we had lost our marbles. I could take care of myself now and Jerry could start a life of his own. There was only one problem. We were still prisoners of 'Gator World'."

"Our big break came one night when they installed this big bright night light by the gate of our fence. As you know, gypsy moths love lights, and this one attracted a huge flock. We started talking to the moths, and told them about our perdikerment. The gypsy moths said they might be able to help and would return the next night. True to their word, they came fluttering back along with a raccoon who I think was named ....mmm...Roger or something like that. I forget his name."

"Was his name Roscoe," Tiberius interjected.

"Sounds right to me," Gaylord answered.

"He is a friend of ours. He took us to the gypsy moths when we were in trouble," Crispin added.

"Well, he was good with locks, but a mite skittish around the gators," Gaylord continued. "Didn't take any time. The critter climbed up the fence, and managed to pick the lock. We were out of there in a flash. Some of the other 'gators refused to go: idiots! Said they had been there too long, and were afraid to be in the wild."

"Me and Jerry made a beeline for the woods and didn't stop until we made it safely back to the river. The other 'gators called me four eyes for a while, but I didn't care; these glasses opened up a whole new world for me."

"Where's Jerry now," Crispin asked.

"Oh, he lives down the river a piece. He has a family to feed now, but I see him off and on."

"That explains why you're friends with the gypsy moths," Tiberius said.

"Yep, I owe them big time," Gaylord said. "Anytime they need help, I'm there lickety split. Especially Bela. He's the one that brought Roscoe that night."

"Wow, what a great story," Crispin gushed. "I'm glad everything worked out all right, and your eyes are better."

"Me too," Gaylord said with a toothy grin as he proudly adjusted his gold spectacles.

"Well, the day's wearing on," Tiberius stated. "And we have to be moving along. It's been a grand trip, we can't thank you enough. Perhaps someday, we can repay the favor."

"It was my pleasure. Y'all have a safe journey," Gaylord replied lifting a stumpy front leg in farewell.

Crispin and Tiberius gave Gaylord a heart felt pat on the end of his snout, slung their food packs over their shoulders and marched into the reed grass jungle.

Chapter 9
Crispin's Narrow Escape

The grasses edging the river eventually changed and Crispin and Tiberius found themselves hiking through a tall meadow guarded by ancient hickory trees. Their gnarled bark reminded Crispin of stretched out preying mantis faces. Some of them seemed to smile back with a friendly grin while others had a frightening sinister countenance.

"Do you have any idea where we're going," Crispin asked.

"We need to be traveling west, so I'm following the afternoon sun. Let's hope he's right and we don't get too lost. This grass is so tall it's hard to see over," Tiberius stated. The two companions trekked on for some time until suddenly Tiberius stopped dead in his tracks, and dropped his food pack.

"Is something wrong," Crispin said in a concerned voice.

"Nothing. That's just it," Tiberius replied. "I don't think anything's wrong with my wing anymore. It feels fine, so I'm wondering why we're still walking." Tiberius slowly stretched his giant soft wings and cautiously flapped them up and down several times.

"How does it feel," Crispin queried.

"It feels wonderfully normal. I'm going to circle a few times just to be sure before I try to carry you," Tiberius replied.

"Okay, let's go together, I could use a good stretch myself," Crispin said.

One good strong flap was all it took for Tiberius to clear the tops of the meadow grass. Soon, he and Crispin were fluttering about merrily side by side in huge swooping circles amongst the tops of the hickory trees.

"Whee...Whee," Crispin shouted ecstatically. "It's great to be able to fly. I'm so glad I'm a lightning bug! Hey! How does your wing feel?"

"It feels one hundred per cent. I won't have any problem with you on my back. Come on let's go get the food packs and do some serious air travel for a change."

Crispin and Tiberius landed and retrieved their packs which by this time were noticeably lighter. "We're getting low on food," Crispin said concerned.

"Don't worry we'll find food along the way. Remember, I'm used to feeding myself," Tiberius replied.

"Well, I can take care of myself too," Crispin said, puffing out his tiny chest.

Tiberius raised a knowing eyebrow and replied, "Oh, of course my young friend, I have no doubt in my mind about that."

"I can fly alongside for a while and keep up too. You don't have to carry me the whole way," Crispin added.

Tiberius chuckled softly, and teasingly bowed. "Whatever you say young squire; but I must remind you if we stand here talking all day we'll never get any place, so is it all right to leave?"

Crispin, playing along laughed and said, "Yes, you have my permission to take off."

Still chuckling; the two friends swooped upwards, skimmed the treetops, and headed into the freedom of the sky. Crispin, true to his word flew alongside Tiberius, but before long became exhausted. Tiberius noticed his small companion lagging behind, and slowed. "Hey, you've done a great job," he shouted. "Jump on now, I'll fly for both of us for a while." Tiberius slowed into a glide as Crispin buzzed overhead, and landed gracefully onto his back. They followed the sun as it made its decent toward the horizon watching as it was consumed by the ravenous evening shadows.

"I'M SORT OF hungry," Crispin called out.

"So am I, let's land," Tiberius shouted as he began floating earthwards. On their way down, the fragrance of a honeysuckle vine danced in the evening warmth and pulled the hungry travelers towards it.

"Mmmm, that smells divine," Tiberius exclaimed. "I haven't had honeysuckle nectar in a very long time; it's one of my favorites. There's usually a lot of pollen hanging around inside the blossoms too. We'll dine like royalty tonight."

"Yipee!" Crispin yelled in expectation as the two friends landed with a bounce on the vine. They chomped, sipped, and sucked on the pale yellow blossoms until their bellies were happily swollen.

"Ohh, Ohh," Tiberius groaned. "I can't fly any more tonight. I couldn't even take off."

"Let's spend the night here. I'm really tired," Crispin moaned.

"Well, we've got a reason to be tired. It's been a very long exciting day. This seems to be a safe place. Let's find a cozy spot, and get some rest," Tiberius said.

"I saw a tree over there with a hole in it. We would be really snuggly inside," Crispin suggested.

Tiberius followed Crispin to a hawthorne tree, and the tired travelers crawled into a comfortable dry hole, and fell into a deep sleep. The next morning Tiberius woke with a start. A shaft of sunlight beamed into the darkened hole and caressed his face. He yawned, sat up and peered at his surroundings. He was alone. Crispin was gone.

"Now where can that whippersnapper be, he must be some-where close by," Tiberius mumbled sleepily as he glanced down and noticed the tiny vest.

Tiberius crawled from the hole, and flew towards the honey-suckle vine. "Crispin..... Crispin, are you over here eating again," he shouted.

There was no answer. Tiberius flew around the area for a few minutes and returned to the tree. He hoped Crispin was back, but as he peered into the empty hole, a wave of panic washed over him. Crispin wouldn't have left his vest if he wasn't planning to come back. Something must have happened to him. He flittered to the honeysuckle and back to the tree frantically calling his friend's name over and over.

Despondent, Tiberius slumped against the base of the tree. Then he heard it. A tiny frightened voice, not much more than a whisper, was coming from a shallow ditch nearby.

"Ahhh! Ahhhh! Somebody help; please help. Can anyone hear me? I'm stuck inside something!"

Tiberius jumped up and hurried toward the panicked cries. He stepped into a strange, eerie landscape, and a wave of wet cool air immediately chilled his body. The ground looked solid, but the moss below his feet squished and moved with every step. Everywhere he looked, there were odd, low growing green trumpet shaped plants with cobra like hoods covering the ground.

A foul odor of stagnating vegetation and something much worse he didn't want to know about hung in the air like an invisible phantom. A sick knot formed in the pit of his stomach and his legs started shaking. He had been in a place like this before. He was in a pitcher plant bog surrounded by a forest of carnivorous plants. Tiberius squeezed his eyes shut, but a frightening memory locked away in the dark corners of his mind clawed its way loose.

He gone on a nectar hunt with his father one warm summer day when they stumbled upon a pitcher plant bog, much like this one. His father warned him to stay close by, but he saw some very strange looking plants growing in a nearby ravine. Plants this exotic must have really great nectar he thought to himself. It won't hurt to have a quick look. He fluttered into the ravine and glided low over the odd hooded plants. Suddenly, he heard a pathetic cry for help, and followed it to one of the trumpet shaped plants. Tiberius remembered peering inside at an unfortunate bumblebee who was frantically treading water in the base of the monstrous plant.

"Don't worry, I'll get you out," Tiberius called down to the struggling creature.

As he drew closer however, his leg slipped off the lip of the pitcher plant and he began sliding downward through the tubular neck. He tried to climb back up, but the harder he tried, the farther down he slid. It was gooey and nasty on the inside and Tiberius was heading straight for the watery trap below.

Before long he would join the struggling frantic bumblebee. He glanced down at the frightening spectacle below. The bee had become exhausted from fighting and was floating dejectedly in a pool of dismembered dissolving bodies. Tiberius screamed as a fly head bobbed up to the surface next to the bee. Fortunately, after what seemed like an eternity, his father heard his screams and before long Tiberius saw the familiar welcoming face gazing down over the plant's lip.

"Don't worry, I'll get you out," his father yelled as a vine came plummeting into the foul tunnel. Tiberius grabbed it, and glanced down at the bee who was thrashing about again.

"Come on, you can get out too," Tiberius called.

"I'm too tired to reach up and grab the rope," the bee answered in a weak trembly voice.

"Okay, I'm coming down to help you," Tiberius answered.

Fighting back disgust and fear, he slid down to the rope's end, plunged into the revolting pool, and tied it around the bee's middle. Tiberius yelled for his father to haul them up.

The two victims held on as the vine was pulled up and out over the lip. Tiberius and the bee dropped to the ground exhausted and covered with sticky ooze. The very happy but exhausted bee thanked the moths, and hobbled off. The terrifying experience had haunted Tiberius' nightmares ever since.

Crispin's panicked cries for help brought Tiberius back to reality and he shook off the gripping fear.

"I'm coming," Tiberius yelled. He plowed forward into the carnivorous jungle and fluttered from one menacing trumpet to another peering into the pools of death. He glanced into one, and jumped back in blinding horror as he caught sight of a partially digested luna moth wing. His heart jumped in his throat and another wave of paralysis spasmed through his body.

'I have to keep going,' he braced himself. 'I have to save Crispin.' Just then he heard Crispin scream again, and it was much nearer.

"Keep yelling, I will follow your voice. Sing a song, you won't be as scared," Tiberius yelled out.

Tiberius followed the muffled shaky notes as Crispin began singing a silly song about possums swinging in a sweet gum tree.

"Tiberius, I see your wing. Here I am," Crispin shouted frantically.

Tiberius looked inside a nearby plant and to his relief, saw his frightened friend struggling in the putrid slime coating the plant's throat.

"You'll be okay now," Tiberius reassured him, "I know how to get you out, just hold on."

Tiberius glanced around and spied a sturdy vine snaking its way over the ground. He tugged at it and a length broke away. Crispin clawed wildly at the slippery tunnel and stared expectantly at the shaft of sunlight above his head.

"Grab the rope," Tiberius ordered.

"Okay, I've got it," Crispin responded, as he gripped the lifeline. Tiberius pulled the rope with his front legs and soon, much to his relief, he saw his friend's head pop up over the pitcher plant's hood.

Crispin, covered with the foul slime, fell to the ground, kicking and crying hysterically. Tiberius still shaken and out of breath tried to console Crispin by patting him on the back, but it wasn't doing much good. His tormented young friend kept flailing his arms and legs, screaming incoherently at his invisible enemy.

Tiberius, frustrated by his inability to help suddenly had an incredibly wild idea. He jumped up, grabbed a stick, and began whacking a nearby pitcher plant while yelling at the top of his lungs. "You...rotten...stinky...disgusting plants. You mean, foul smelling, bog slime!" Whack, whack, whack, whack. "Scum sucking bug eaters!" Tiberius yelled and pummeled the pitcher plant until it collapsed in on itself. His sudden mad outburst pulled Crispin back to reality and the firefly lay staring curiously at Tiberius' continued rantings. "You slimy, piece of fly spit....."

Crispin, even though his legs were still a bit wobbly, stood; grabbed a stick, and joined Tiberius. "You smelly bog dwelling bags of slime!" Crispin shouted. Whack, whack, whack. "Green devils! Fly boogers! I hope the slugs gobble you up."

After Tiberius and Crispin knocked over several of the carnivorous plants, they fell exhausted onto their backs laughing hysterically. After a few minutes their side splitting laughter dissolved into an occasional chuckle.

"Well, that should teach those pesky plants a lesson," Tiberius said breathlessly.

"I certainly hope so. That was the scariest thing that ever happened to me," Crispin gasped.

"I know exactly how you feel. The same thing happened to me when I was your age," Tiberius replied.

"Really? How did you survive," Crispin asked.

"My dad pulled me out. He used a vine rope, just like I used to rescue you," Tiberius said.

"You must have been petrified to come in here and search for me," Crispin stated.

"I was. I almost didn't make it, but the thought of you inside that dreadful plant kept me going," Tiberius replied.

"I've learned my lesson. I'll never going near those bug suckers again," Crispin declared.

"Good. Now, tell me, how did you end up falling into that monster," Tiberius coaxed.

"I woke a little before dawn, and my tummy felt empty," Crispin began. "The thought of that yummy honeysuckle pollen was making my mouth water, so I flew around looking for it. I smelled something sweet, and went to check it out. That's when I landed on the strange plant, and slipped inside. I tried to crawl back up but these hairs were pushing me back down. I yelled and yelled for so long," Crispin cradled his head in his legs. "I was so scared. It was so nasty and slimy inside." Crispin lifted his head, glanced wide eyed at Tiberius, and stammered, "There...there were horrible things floating in a pool at the base of the plant!"

"Yes, I know," Tiberius said sympathetically. "I lived over it, and so will you. When bad thing happen we have to pick ourselves up, and go on."

"Now, if you feel ready, we'll get your vest and our packs and find some water. You'll feel much better after washing off that filth."

"I just want to get as far away from this wretched place as I can," Crispin moaned.

They followed a small trickling stream which ended its journey sliding over a shelf of algae covered stones into a deep sapphire pool. Crispin, having learned his lesson glanced around suspiciously and then made a mad dash for the clear refreshing water. He splashed and paddled around while Tiberius sat with his wings spread wide sunbathing on a toasty rock. Sometime later Crispin emerged dripping wet but squeaky clean and much happier.

"Wow, I feel so much better," Crispin announced.

"Is your skin sore from the plant's juices," Tiberius asked.

"Just a little, it's not bad," Crispin replied rubbing his legs.

"Good. As soon as you're dry, put on your vest, and we'll visit that honeysuckle vine before we leave. And this time; we'll go the right direction," Tiberius chuckled.

Chapter 10
Into the Woods

"I sure hate to leave this honeysuckle vine. The nectar is practically dripping off the petals," Crispin said wiping the sweet juice off his face.

"Maybe we'll find some more along the way. They're all blooming like crazy right now," Tiberius replied with a wide grin. "Let's get going. We lost most of the morning getting acquainted with carnivorous plants; didn't we," he added with a wink.

"I'm really, really, reeeaallyy sorry," Crispin said throwing his front legs into the air.

"Well, If nothing else, you learned a valuable lesson – the same one I learned when I was your age," Tiberius said.

"Don't worry – from now on, I won't be poking around in things that could be dangerous," Crispin responded sheepishly.

"Good. And don't be running off. It worries me when I don't know where you are – okay?" Tiberius instructed.

Crispin shook Tiberius' leg. "All right, you've got a deal."

"Hop on, and lets get going," Tiberius said.

Tiberius found a nice comfortable cruising altitude and held his course until a thick bank of low dense clouds rolled in. A few times Tiberius could see nothing but a wall of solid white in front of his eyes. He dipped his wings one way and then another trying to find a patch of clear sky. 'I hope I don't loose my bearings and fly us into the ground,' he thought. Then suddenly, the clouds parted and a welcoming ray of sunshine beamed through. He glided through the cloud break and was rewarded with wide open blue sky.

Crispin leaned over and shouted to Tiberius, "I hope you're not lost."

"No, we're fine, see the sun is behind us. That means we're going west."

The sky remained calm and blue for quite some time, but shortly after the sun had reached its zenith, another bank of clouds floated above the horizon. The massive stacked cotton boles were heavily grayed at the base and poised for a midday rainstorm. Crispin leaned forward and pointed in its direction. "That's a nasty looking thunderhead coming up," he yelled.

"They're still a long way off. I don't think we'll get caught in it," Tiberius called back

True to his word, the two friends watched from afar as the gray clouds turned oppressively darker. Lightning bolts skittered through the thunderheads leaden base, and a chorus of rumbles answered back. No longer able to contain its watery burden, the thunderhead dropped a gray curtain of rain earthward.

By the time Tiberius and Crispin approached the rainstorm it had softened to a gentle sprinkle and shafts of sunlight were peeking through. Suddenly, Tiberius felt Crispin almost leap off his back shouting excitedly. "Tiberius! Look! It's magnificent!"

Tiberius gazed upward at the most beautiful and perfect rainbow he had ever seen. The bow went from horizon to horizon and the vivid iridescent bands of color loomed directly in front of them. "Wow, this is great! Let's fly right through it and see what it's like," Crispin shouted excitedly.

"All right, here we go, but it's not as easy as you think to catch a rainbow," Tiberius chuckled.

Crispin was practically vibrating with expectation as they drew nearer. He was imagining cascades of shimmering colors washing over his body. As they flew toward the rainbow Crispin noticed something unusual and a little disappointing. The colors seemed to be fading away and it was hard to tell where the rainbow actually was. "Hey! Where is the rainbow going? Oh no, it's dissolving," Crispin cried.

"It's still here," Tiberius replied. "That's the funny thing about rainbows. The closer you get, the further away they seem. We're probably flying into it right now."

Crispin looked around sadly. He didn't see any colors at all. There was something strange however that struck him. A sweet fragrance hung in the air. "Tiberius! Do you smell that," Crispin yelled.

"Yes, it smells like spicy spring violets."

"Do you think we could be inside the purple stripe in the rainbow?" Crispin questioned.

"I've never heard of rainbows having smells," Tiberius replied.

"Maybe this is a special rainbow," Crispin wondered.

"You might be right. There are a lot of strange and fascinating things in this world no one knows about. Maybe we stumbled into a one in a million rainbow."

The two mesmerized friends flew on and soon the sweet odor began to fade. "Oh no, it's going away! Wait, what is that," Crispin said sniffing the air. "Great grashopper legs. Now I'm smelling wild blueberries. "We must be in the blue stripe. Wow! Nobody's ever going to believe this. Whee! Whee," Crispin shouted throwing his arms up into the air.

Crispin and Tiberius left the delicious aroma of blueberries behind and suddenly found themselves surrounded by a pungent pine forest odor as they glided through the green stripe. Next the two excited travelers passed through the sweet fragrance of jasmine blooms in the yellow stripe followed by a tangy orange blossom aroma which tickled their noses. Lastly they flew through the red stripe which smelled like juicy ripe wild strawberries which made them drool with hunger. Finally the two travelers emerged from the astonishing rainbow ecstatic and speechless. They flew in silence too stunned to speak for some time following the sun's journey westward.

Crispin, exhausted from his ordeal in the bog, quickly fell asleep, and Tiberius pushed onward hoping to find the Woods of Forgetfullness before sunset.

To his dismay however, there were only spotty clumps of trees below which became increasingly sparse and eventually disappeared. The terrain changed into a flat desolate plane with no signs of vegetation except an occasional scraggly juniper or tall prickly forked cactus. Tiberius stared mesmerized at the strange rock formations which cropped up out of the gravely earth. Huge gold and rusty red boulders were balanced precariously upon each other in a gravity defying display. He spotted a gigantic ridge of rough hewn pink stone which reminded him of a gigantic turtle's back and another mysterious formation carved into a huge open arch. The waning afternoon sun painted the landscape with a pallet of soft hues. Tiberius gazed at the blue, lavender, pink, and gold streaks splashed over the rocky plane and decided this was the most beautiful and exotic place he had ever seen.

He was also wondering how much further the unusual terrain would continue when suddenly a huge canyon loomed below him. He peered into the deep gaping wound tearing through the earth and saw a tiny glistening ribbon of water at the bottom of the abyss snaking its way towards some unknown destination. Tiberius flew alongside the canyon until it opened up and flattened into a blue twisty stream which hooked sharply to the north. After the river vanished, Tiberius was relieved to see the familiar clumpy groves of trees reappear. The sun was brushing the horizon when finally the trees became so dense Tiberius was certain he had finally arrived at the Woods of Forgetfulness.

Crispin was dreaming about frogs jumping out of hissing snake headed plants and chasing him through a mossy quagmire when suddenly he was jostled awake. He sat up, brushed the sleep from his eyes and looked around. Tiberius had landed on the branch of a pine tree at the edge of a forest.

"Where are we," Crispin asked. "Are these the Woods of Forgetfulness?"

"They should be," Tiberius answered. "I've been flying in the right direction all afternoon. My wings are quite tired. They must still be a little weak from my injury."

Crispin jumped off Tiberius back and grabbed onto a cluster of pine needles. "Let's find a comfortable place for you sit and rest for a while," he suggested.

"That sounds great but first, let's get something to eat. I'm famished. My antenna caught a whiff of an apple orchard as I was flying past that ridge," Tiberius said pointing over Crispin's back.

"I don't feel like anything sweet tonight, but I might have some nice apple leaves," Crispin said patting his belly.

The two friends flew over to the apple orchard and Tiberius sucked the delicate nectar while Crispin munched on the tangy crunchy leaves. Afterwards, they returned to the woods edge and found an abandoned raggedy but soft oriole nest to snuggle into for the night.

Early the next morning, they awoke to the annoying split-splat of huge messy raindrops on their faces. "Ugg," Tiberius groaned glancing up at the angry sky. "Let's find some shelter before this gets worse." They crawled out of their cozy bed and made their way down to the forest floor.

"Over there," Crispin pointed urgently.

Crispin and Tiberius hurried over and ducked under a large umbrella shaped white mushroom and it began to pour viciously; cascading in sheets off the cap's curved edge. The pair huddled against the spongy stalk surrounded by a circular waterfall and stayed perfectly dry.

Finally, the rain slowed to a gentle pit-pat, then stopped altogether. Crispin and Tiberius stepped out from under their shelter just as the first morning rays of sunshine escaped from the rapidly dissipating storm clouds.

"I hope the rain moves on down the road," Tiberius said.

"Me too," Crispin replied. "If that had kept up for much longer we would be looking for a pecan shell to use as a boat."

"I think the rain is over for a while so let's go see if we're in the Woods of Forgetfulness. We're in no danger if we don't eat anything in the woods," Tiberius stated.

"Okay, I'm ready," Crispin said excitedly, swinging on a vine. "I'm really curious about this mysterious place," he added.

The two companions entered the woods and noticed nothing unusual at first. A short distance later they spotted something white staked at the edge of an elderberry bush. They rushed over and Tiberius brushed away a branch revealing a white paper birch sign posted on a crooked stick. Written on the sign in dark purple berry juice was a warning.

"DO NOT EAT ANYTHING IN THE FOREST"

Below the message it was signed: CRAB E. ROCK.

"I guess we've found the Woods of Forgetfulness." Crispin said. "I wonder who Crab E. Rock is."

"I don't know, but is sounds like he runs this place," Tiberius replied. "Come on, we don't have to worry about the warning since we brought our own food," he added.

As they hiked deeper into the woods Tiberius began to notice something puzzling. He stopped and surveyed the area scratching his feathery antennas quizzically.

"What's wrong," Crispin asked.

"There's something quite out of sorts in this forest. Haven't you noticed it too?" Tiberius asked.

A worried look crossed Crispin's face, "No, but I hope it's not too bad," he replied.

"Look around and listen," Tiberius ordered.

Crispin stood perfectly still and glanced all around the woods. Suddenly, his eyes widened as it hit him. "I don't hear any sound but the wind. There are no animal or insect sounds. It's perfectly quiet."

"That's right," Tiberius began. "Not only that – look at all the trees and plants. The berry bushes are so loaded down with fruit they're practically breaking. There's rotten fruit and old nuts covering the ground, and that patch of toad lilies we just passed was overloaded with pollen."

"This is really bizarre," Crispin stated.

"Not really," Tiberius said. "When you think about it logically; if you can't eat anything in the forest then you wouldn't have anyone wanting to live here. They would starve to death. Therefore; nothing ever gets eaten – so it just sits here and rots."

"Well, it gives me the creeps," Crispin said. "It's not natural."

"I'm not so sure we should go any deeper into these woods," Tiberius said. "They give me the willie-worms too. Maybe we should get out now while we can and fly over them."

"Well, if you think so, then let's get out of here," Crispin replied.

He mounted Tiberius' back and they fluttered upwards. Tiberius was almost clear of the tree canopy when a sudden and unexplainable force bore down on his wings making it impossible to fly higher. He flew to another opening in the trees and tried it again with no luck at escaping. Frantically, he darted from one area of the woods to another, but each time the oppressive invisible weight sent him back down into the woods. Finally he gave up and landed.

Crispin; frightened out of his wits gasped as he jumped off Tiberius back. "What's going on? Why can't we leave?"

"I wish I knew," Tiberius replied. "It's some sort of invisible force. Did Bela mention anything to you about this," he questioned.

"No. Maybe he didn't know about it," Crispin replied starting to pace nervously.

"Well, we can either go back the way we came or keep going," Tiberius suggested. "This place is creepy but we should be fine as long as we eat our own food."

"If we go back, we'll lose more time, so I vote to go on," Crispin stated.

"Okay," Tiberius agreed. "Let's get going."

They marched silently through woods which earlier had seemed to them only strangely benign. The shadows cast by the trees and bushes now took on a sinister countenance made even more frightening by the unnerving absence of living sounds.

The dense pine and nut trees they had been traveling through for what seemed like an eternity began to thin and were gradually replaced by strange twisted corky trees. Crispin grabbed one of the fuzzy dark green triangular shaped leaves and sniffed it.

"Yuck, these stink. They smell like earthworm breath! What kind of trees are these?" Crispin asked.

"I've never seen trees like these before," Tiberius replied.

Just then Crispin jumped in the air and pointed at something ahead. "Hey – there's another sign," he shouted. They hurried over and Tiberius read it out loud.

"Enjoy the flowers and remember: DON'T EAT ANYTHING IN THE FOREST! Signed: Crab E. Rock."

Crispin and Tiberius glanced at each other with puzzled looks on their faces. "I haven't seen very many flowers, have you?" Crispin said.

"Just those toad lilies we passed a while back and a few wild strawberry blooms. Most flowers don't bloom well in a shady forest," Tiberius replied.

"Yes, but this is not your ordinary forest, is it," Crispin suggested.

"You have a point," Tiberius responded. "And we'll never find out just standing here will we," he added.

The two companions passed the warning sign and resumed their journey through the unchanging landscape. They hiked in silence for some time until finally Crispin spoke up. "I'm still looking for those flowers."

"Maybe we're here in the wrong season," Tiberius said looking over at his small friend who had a forlorn expression on his face and was kicking a stick irritably. "Are you getting tired," Tiberius asked. "If you are, you can ride on my back for a while."

"No, I'm fine. I wonder how much further these woods go on," Crispin replied.

"I wish I could answer that," Tiberius said. "Maybe we can stop soon and check the map. It might tell us how far we've traveled."

"Oh yeah, I forgot about the map! I bet we can find out exactly where we are," Crispin said his voice cheering.

Tiberius smiled to himself as he noticed Crispin hopping a few steps. A while later they halted when the thick twisted forest abruptly ended and opened into a large sun bathed meadow of brightly colored flowers.

"Hurry," Crispin shouted. "We found the flowers!"

"We most definitely have found them," Tiberius announced his antenna twitching from the overpowering scent of nectar wafting through the air. They plunged forward into the welcoming meadow skipping and fluttering merrily at the chance to leave the monotonous forest behind.

Tiberius quickly scanned the perimeter of the meadow, hoping to see an end to the forest. To his dismay, he noticed it was bordered by more of the same terrain. He then glanced up at the unobstructed sky and wondered if the invisible obstacle was here as well. 'There's only one way to find out,' he told himself as he called out. "Crispin, let's see if we can fly out of here. There aren't any trees around. Maybe there is a hole in the Woods of Forgetfulness."

"Wow, you might be right," Crispin said.

"Come on. Jump up and let's try it," Tiberius ordered.

Crispin arranged himself behind the food packs and Tiberius soared skyward. They were feeling hopeful when suddenly the same oppressive weight began to bear down on Tiberius' wings and he had to descend.

Back on the ground, Crispin dismounted, pulled the food packs off Tiberius back and let them slide to the ground. He plopped down, and planted his chin in his hands dejectedly. "I thought for sure we'd get out this time," Crispin groaned.

"Well, it was worth a try," Tiberius said throwing up his front legs. "Come on. As long as we're here we might as well enjoy this beautiful field of flowers and all this wide open space. I don't know about you but I could use a little wing exercise. We can fly up a storm here and not have to worry about thick branches getting in our way," he added.

"All right, I guess I could use the exercise too," Crispin piped up.

Tiberius fluttered off the rock he was standing on and Crispin followed buzzing upward in a swooping motion. "Hey, let's have a race," Crispin yelled over to Tiberius.

"Okay," Tiberius called back hoping to cheer up his small friend.

"When I yell GO," Crispin began. "We'll race over to those bright orange flowers in the distance."

"I'm ready," Tiberius replied gliding along side Crispin.

"Ready! Set! GO!" Crispin shouted as the two friends shot off as fast as they could; making a bee-line for the orange flowers.

Tiberius, realizing he had an advantage over Crispin because of his huge wings, slowed; and soon, Crispin passed him reaching the orange flowers first. "Wow, you must be the fastest bug around," Tiberius gushed.

"It's like I told you! I'm really light because my tail is hollow," Crispin remarked.

"Oh yes! I had forgotten," Tiberius stated. "Anybody would be crazy to challenge you! You're the champ today," he added feigning disappointment.

"Don't be sad, I bet you win the race next time," Crispin said cheerfully

"I don't know. You're awfully good," Tiberius said, shaking his head.

"Well, there aren't many of my friends at Dragonfly Landing that can beat me," he said wistfully.

Tiberius noticed a shadow cross his friend's face and realized he was thinking about home and feeling a little home sick. Just then, an interesting idea came to mind and he wondered if it might cheer Crispin up. "I have a great idea," Tiberius announced.

"What is it," Crispin piped up.

"I've noticed some of these flowers are really quite bizarre, haven't you?" He began.

Crispin glanced around, his curiosity aroused. "No, they look normal to me. Why? What did you see?"

"Come with me and I'll show you," Tiberius ordered with a silent smile. He fluttered off with Crispin in tow and landed in a patch of yellow and red spotted ruffled flowers.

"What are they," Crispin asked.

"They're clown orchids," Tiberius explained. "If you listen really close you can hear them laughing."

"No, I don't believe it. You pulling my legs," Crispin replied frowning.

"Put your ear really close and listen," Tiberius ordered.

Crispin climbed up the orchid stalk and laid his head close to the exotic flower's petals. Unnoticed, Tiberius very quietly crept underneath an orchid leaf and cupped his front legs around his mouth. In a tiny disguised voice he let out a chorous of 'Hee Hee Hee', 'Ho Ho Ho', and 'Ha ha ha'. Crispin: startled, jumped back and fell to the ground just as Tiberius reappeared.

"Leaping ladybugs! I heard it! I really did," Crispin exclaimed. "The clown orchid was laughing. This is fun. Are there more flowers like this around here?"

"Lots more. In fact, I think I see some over there," Tiberius gestured. "Come on let's go. See those spiky bright blue flowers growing low to the ground. They're bugle weed – and they trumpet."

"No they don't, I don't believe you," Crispin said stubbornly.

"Go lay in the patch and listen," Tiberius instructed.

Crispin did as he was told and plopped down on the thick mat of dark green leaves. Tiberius hid in the foliage of a nearby honey bush and made a trumpeting sound several times.

Crispin jumped up and yelled, "I heard the bugles, I heard the bugles. You were right again. Quick let's find another one."

"Okay, follow me," Tiberius said.

They flew to a patch of silvery gray fuzzy leaves and Crispin nestled down inside. "You listen and this time tell me what they are," Tiberius suggested

He listened intently and heard a string of 'baa, baa, baa', and yelled excitedly, "This must be lambs ears. It's got to be. I heard bleating."

"You're a smart little whippersnapper," Tiberius proclaimed.

"What are those over there," Crispin sang out pointing towards a group of yellow – daisy like flowers.

"Hurry over and find out," Tiberius called out laughing.

Crispin grasped a clump of the lacy foliage and listened quietly. Tiberius in the meantime had crept under the edge of the plant.

Presently Crispin heard a sound of 'Achooo! Achoo! Achoo! Achoo!' He buzzed off the bloom, landed and found Tiberius standing nearby. "I'm, not sure what this flower is, but it sneezes," he said scratching his head in thought.

"It's sneezeweed my dear boy," Tiberius answered.

"Of course I've heard of sneezeweed, but I never knew it actually sneezed," Crispin responded throwing his arm into the air.

The two friends jumped and fluttered about for some time playing their game which took them to a viciously growling tiger orchid; a cluster of cat mint that meowed, and a lavender patch of dog-toothed violets which; Crispin swore, barked like a real dog.

Crispin was somersaulting through the air gleefully after the game and Tiberius was sure his little ruse had cheered his friend. He also noticed the sun angled low towards the horizon and knew it was time to head back into the woods. Crispin had been so cheered by the afternoon of fun he didn't even complain when Tiberius suggested they move on.

They flew to the edge of the flower meadow and fluttered through the sparse trees until the forest became so thick they had to resume walking. They hadn't covered much ground when dusk crept upon the forest like a stealthy predator.

"It's getting too dark to see where we're going. We need to camp for the night," Tiberius said halting his steps.

"You're right. It's so dark, I can hardly see," Crispin responded.

"Let's fly up into one of these tree canopies. Maybe we can catch some moonlight to read the map by," Tiberius suggested.

Just as the two friends were about to ascend to a soft leafed tulip tree, Crispin cried out, "What on earth is that!"

"Where are you looking? I can hardly see you," Tiberius exclaimed.

"Over there," he pointed. "See that eerie green light glowing low down on the ground?"

"Oh, ooh yes! I see it," Tiberius exclaimed. "It's really bright. Let's go see what it is. Stay close by so we don't get separated."

The travelers picked their way through the curtain of darkness and crept cautiously towards the strange beacon of light. The glow grew brighter until they were standing right in front of the mysterious object. Growing up against a huge decayed stump was a gigantic cluster of phosphorescent mushrooms. The two stunned companions moved closer; their mouths hanging open in disbelief.

"There must be at least a hundred of them," Tiberius gasped. He glanced over at Crispin who was bathed in the bizarre green glow.

"My dad told me once about glowing mushrooms, but I thought it was a fairy tale," Crispin said his eyes huge as saucers. "I've seen some really weird things, like fairy rings, turkey feathers and gigantic puff balls, but these are definitely beyond strange."

Tiberius paused and rubbed his face in thought. "They're simply unearthly, and very bright. In fact, I think we should be able to read the map in this light. They seem harmless enough, so let's make our camp here," he added.

"I still can't believe this," Crispin exclaimed shaking his head and dropping his food pack by one of the luminous pimply topped mushrooms.

Tiberius found a patch of velvety moss growing under several mushrooms. "Crispin, I found us a nice comfortable bed for the night," he called out.

Crispin scurried over and fell down with a relieved sigh. "Ahh, this feels great," he said. "This must be what lying on a cloud feels like." Tiberius chuckled at Crispin's enthusiasm and settled in next to him.

"You look really weird," Crispin said inspecting Tiberius' green haloed body.

"You're pretty strange looking too. Your face reminds me of a little green apple," Tiberius laughed.

"Oh great, now you reminded me of how hungry I am," Crispin moaned. "I'm glad we brought our food."

"Let's see how much of the gypsy moth's food is left," Tiberius said opening the sack. "Well there are several of the small wild berry cakes left and a bundle of dried milkweed," he reported.

"I vote for the berry cakes," Crispin spoke up.

Tiberius passed two of the small cakes to him and helped himself to the other two. They were so starved the cakes disappeared in no time. Crispin, still chewing reached into his vest, pulled out the yellowed map, and handed it to Tiberius. He gently unfolded the fragile creased document and held it up to the bizarre light.

Tiberius pointed to an area covered with small green triangles. "We now know these are the Woods of Forgetfulness. How far we've come will be a little harder to calculate," he said. This wasn't news Crispin wanted to hear and his face soured. He peered over Tiberius' shoulder and scanned the map more intently. "Wait just a minute," he practically screamed. "Look at this section of the forest!"

Tiberius eyebrows shot up as he saw what Crispin had found. About half way through the green triangles was a blank space with a tiny sun symbol in it. "That has to be the open meadow of flowers we crossed earlier," Tiberius said emphatically.

"Whoopee," Crispin sang out, "We're not lost after all! We should be out of the woods by tomorrow afternoon," he added.

Tiberius was busy turning the map around in his hands when suddenly something caught his attention. He held it closer to the light and chuckled. "My goodness, guess what I found." Crispin moved in for a closer look. "Remember when we were looking at the map in Maleva's wagon," Tiberius began.

"Sure I do," Crispin piped up.

"Read these three small red words," Tiberius said tapping on the map.

"Travelers be wary," Crispin recited.

"Look at the symbol next to it. What does it look like," Tiberius questioned.

"It looks like a tiny pitcher plant," Crispin groaned. "Then this must be.....Jumping junebugs," he glanced at Tiberius.

"This is the location of the carnivorous bog we stumbled into," Tiberius interjected.

"And I was stupid enough to walk right smack into it," Crispin said shaking his head.

"Don't be too hard on yourself," Tiberius replied sympathetically.

"If I had studied the map closer, we might have avoided the area altogether. Well, we survived, that's all that matters," Crispin said stifling a yawn.

"Come on, it's late. Let's get some shut eye so we can get an early start in the morning," Tiberius said returning the yawn.

They lay down on the soft mossy bed and shut their eyes. Several minutes later Tiberius noticed his young friend tossing and turning. "What's wrong? Can't you sleep," he asked.

"These mushrooms are glowing so bright I can see them though my eyelids," Crispin complained.

"Wait a second, I'll be right back," Tiberius said shuffling over to a nearby bush. He returned and handed two thick holly leaves to Crispin.

"Here we go, put these over your eyes. They will block out the light," Tiberius said.

Crispin laid the leaves over his eyes and exhaled a sigh of relief. "That's much better. Now every thing is dark. I'll be asleep in a wink. Hey Tiberius, thanks for the leaves," he added.

"You're welcome," Tiberius responded.

"Oh yes: thanks for playing that really fun game with me in the flower field today. For a second you almost had me believing there really were clown orchids that laughed."

Tiberius sat up with a start and glared at Crispin. He was snuggled comfortable in his green velvety bed with a huge satisfied grin on his face.

"Why you little stink-bug! You knew all along it was me making those sounds and you didn't say a word," Tiberius scolded.

"Yep, sure did," Crispin said. "I wasn't born yesterday you know. Anyway, you were having so much fun I didn't want to spoil it for you."

"I was trying to cheer you up," Tiberius said.

"I know, and it worked," Crispin replied.

Tiberius lay back down and said with a smile on his face. "You better get to sleep before those mushrooms start singing."

Chapter 11
Help from the Watch

Two shiny black death-watch beetles sat on a pine cone that was lying on the cluttered, untouched floor of the Woods of Forgetfulness. If there had been any other creatures close by they would have heard an odd click, squeak, click-click sounds coming from their direction. They also could have seen that the two beetles were obviously having an important discussion.

"Now listen to me Vinney, since this is your first day on the watch I'm going to cut you some slack. Crab E. Rock hired you 'cause you're Sal the Slug's friend but that don't mean much to me. You either do the job right or you're outta here," he said jerking a foreleg up in the air.

"Sure, sure Sergeant Mudd. I know whatcha' mean! You can count on me. I got no place else t' hide – uh; I mean no place to go: and I need the dough," Vinney replied twisting an antenna nervously.

"Now listen up," Sergeant Mudd instructed in a gravely voice. "It's our job to patrol the woods searching for poor unfortunate victims who are in trouble."

"What kind of trouble boss," Vinney said.

"Mostly it's creatures that strayed in here and either didn't see the 'Don't Eat Anything In The Woods Sign', or couldn't read it."

"Oh yeah, Mr. Rock gave me the scoop on that already – about loosing their memories. What a tough break," Vinney said.

"We find them and then we escort them to the watch house where Mr. Rock takes care of the technicalities. Then we go back on patrol. Have you got all that now?" Sergeant Mudd added as he stuffed a rolled up nicotina leaf into his mouth.

He thrust a leaf at Vinney. "It's good for the itchy kudzu. You might run into it on night patrol. I caught a bad case of it last week chasing a freaked-out fungus bug. They can't read you know. Come in here and stuff themselves silly on all the fungus. Then they can't remember anything and go berserk. We get a lot of them in here. Sometimes I just want to club them over the head," he added rearranging the clump in his mouth.

Vinney's eyes narrowed and he grinned maliciously, "Hey, you want me to whack a few of these guys for you. I'm good at whacking."

"Are you some kind of idiot? Didn't you hear what I've been saying," Sergeant Mudd growled, his eyes bulging. "We're here to take them to Mr. Rock in one piece."

"Okay. Don't loose your marbles. I got it, boss," Vinney spat out.

"And stop calling me boss. We're professionals here," Sergeant Mudd said scratching his backside. "Argggh *@#$%, this kudzu itch is killing me! Come on, follow me. I've got our equipment stashed over there in a log hole."

Vinney crept along behind Sergeant Mudd; chuckling to himself at the strange way his partner's rump swayed back and forth as he scurried along. Sergeant Mudd reached into the log and pulled out a bundled up collection of watch accessories and weapons. "All right tough guy. Here's your helmet," Sergeant Mudd began. He unfolded a half moon shaped hat made from leathery possum haw leaves and stuck it on Vinney's head. "You'll need this when some half-crazed, out of their mind suspect starts chucking things at you."

"I look stupid," Vinney complained tugging at the helmet.

"Wear it you knucklehead. You'll be glad you have it on later - believe me," Sergeant Mudd glowered as he picked up a utility belt woven from quack grass. "This goes around your shoulders," Sergeant Mudd demonstrated how to hook the belt up. "And this club hangs in the belt loop," Sergeant Mudd hung a smooth rounded poplar stick from Vinney's belt.

Vinney gazed expectantly at the stick. "I'm good at whacking."

"Yes. So you've told me," Sergeant Mudd said exasperated. He handed a thin hemp rope to his charge. "Tuck this around your belt. Sometimes we have to tie someone up until they calm down."

"Hey, I think I'm going to like this job," Vinney exclaimed, "Whacking and tying poor unfortunate creatures up. Sounds like it's right up my alley." His beady eyes squinted with enthusiasm.

"Whatever," Sergeant Mudd said shaking his head. "Let's get going. We need to survey sector 7 first. There's a lot of trouble with renegade squirrels in there; they can't resist all those acorns.

You take the south trail, and I'll go north. We'll circle around and meet back here at 1300 hours. Whoever finds suspects, signal with six clicks - and don't do anything until I get there. No whacking or tying up. If you do, I'll whack you - hard head – you got that?" Sergeant Mudd growled spitting a stream of pea green nicotina juice onto the ground. Vinney jumped back, saluted and headed towards the south trail.

"What a numbskull. Why do they give me all the flakes," Sergeant Mudd mumbled under his breath as he headed north.

A short time later, Sergeant Mudd was poking his stick under a quince bush searching for a renegade fungus beetle when he heard a succession of six clicks. "I'll come back and catch you later," he mumbled as he holstered his club and waddled off towards the signal.

He found Vinney hiding in a bracken fern at the edge of a clearing. Inside was a gigantic decaying hollow tree stump surrounded by an enormous grove of pale yellow bumpy topped mushrooms.

The watch beetles however weren't concerned with the mushrooms. They were studying the two creatures pacing back and forth with a 'Nobody's Home' glassy look to their eyes.

"I've been scoping these two guys out for a while. There's definitely something fishy going on," Vinney reported.

"Good job Vin," Sergeant Mudd said slapping him on the back. "They've definitely lost their memory. We don't get many of their kind around here. I think the big one is some kind of moth and the little one is a lightning bug. These weird glowing mushrooms pop up every now and then after a rain. The moths are really attracted to them for some reason."

"There's a couple of sacks over there on the ground," Vinney pointed out. "I say we try to get a look inside. There might be some valuable loot we should confiscate."

"We don't steal in the watch," Sergeant Mudd said through clenched teeth.

"Whadda-ya mean," Vinney responded. "I didn't say nothing about stealing."

"We're taking them AND their packs to Mr. Rock! If a watch beetle ain't got integrity, he needs to turn in his club and take a hike."

"Okay...okay. Don't bust a gut. Geez, your eyes look like they're gonna' pop out. You're scaring me." Vinney whined backing up in self defense.

Sergeant Mudd straightened his helmet and tried to regain his lost composure. "Now follow me, and be quiet. You never know what reaction these wack-o's are gonna' have."

Crispin and Tiberius had awakened that very morning feeling refreshed but with absolutely no memory. They stared at each other for the longest time until Tiberius broke the silence.

"This is really bizarre, but I don't know who I am, or who you are, or where I am. It's driving me crazy. Do you know who you are?"

"No, I don't. It feels like someone stole part of my brain while I was asleep. I'm scared," Crispin whimpered.

They paced in circles for a while longer and then Tiberius noticed the food sacks. "Are these yours," he asked.

"What makes you think I can remember that," Crispin said.

"Oh, right. I forgot that too," Tiberius replied. "There are two of them, so they must be ours and since we woke up on the same place it's a safe deduction that we're traveling together. But to where and from where," Tiberius said scratching his head in deep thought.

Just then the two victims heard a succession of click-click's coming from the forest. "Did you hear that," Tiberius frowned.

"Yes," Crispin nodded.

A short time later, Crispin and Tiberius heard a deep gravely voice call out from the edge of the clearing. "Hello you two. My name is Sergeant Mudd, and we're here to help you. Don't be afraid. You've lost your memory because you ate something in the forest. You don't remember it but you have to take my word for it. Me and my partner Vinney are going to come out now. Is that all right?"

Tiberius and Crispin glanced at each other and shrugged their shoulders. "It's okay. Come on over," Tiberius answered.

The two watch guards slowly crept into the clearing and stood a safe distance away.

"We're going to take you two out of the forest to see our supervisor, Mr. Crab E. Rock for a nice visit. He'll try to sort out what happened to you. You might have to stay for a while until you get your memories back."

Sergeant Mudd hadn't noticed Vinney slink away and circle around behind him; but he had a sneaking suspicion he was up to no good. His fears were confirmed when he noticed a long stick appear from behind a dead stump and hook through one of the pack straps in an attempt to drag it away.

"Excuse me gentlemen; if you will have a seat, I'll be right back. I have to go check on my partner," Sergeant Mudd grumbled.

Keeping an eye on the confused pair, he scurried over in Vinney's direction. "You little no good...." Sergeant Mudd stopped dead in his tracks when he saw Vinney jump on top of another bug, and wrestle him to the ground. In the flash of an eye, his trainee whipped out his rope and began tying his prisoner.

"Hey, what's going on," Sergeant Mudd yelled.

Vinney jumped up leaving the bound bug thrashing on the forest floor. "I saw this guy lurking around in the bushes and figured something fishy was going on," Vinney explained. "When I saw him try to snatch the loot...I mean the packs; the only thing I could think of, since I'm not supposed to whack anybody, was to subdue the suspect with my rope."

Sergeant Mudd sidled up to the struggling prisoner for a closer look. The green and yellow striped bug lay on his back kicking his legs and hissing through a gag of brown moss.

"Well, I'll be a two legged centipede," the sergeant shouted excitedly. "You just captured Frenchy Lee Fernrucker, the ring-leader of the assassin bugs."

"I did?" Vinney spat leaning closer to re-inspect his capture.

"Frenchy and his gang are a bunch of low lives. If you pay them enough they'll jump anybody and rough them up. They hate the watch beetles and try to knock us around every chance they get. Oh, did I mention that they're thieves? I guess that's obvious, isn't it. Frenchy must have the authorities hot on his tail or he wouldn't be hiding in these woods. I'm surprised you saw the rascal. They're experts at camouflage."

"What should I do with him sir," Vinney asked.

"Check his ropes," the sergeant ordered, "be sure they're tight, but loose enough so he can walk. I'll go collect those other two and we'll head in to the station."

"Yes sir," Vinney said with a crisp salute.

When he returned, Crispin and Tiberius were sitting on a log still shaking their heads as if to clear the fog imprisoning their minds. Sergeant Mudd picked up the food packs and announced, "Okay, up and at 'em you two. We'll carry the packs since they're evidence. Mr. Rock will ascertain if they are yours or not. We're also escorting a very special guest, one slimy character named Frenchy Fernrucker. My partner nailed him just as he was about to abscond with our evidence. Now I don't want any funny stuff out of you two. Okay? No wandering or flying off and if anybody feels like screaming, try to warn us first. Have you got that?"

Crispin and Tiberius both shook their heads.

Vinney joined the others with his uncooperative captive in tow. Frenchy stood glaring menacingly at Sergeant Mudd, while twisting back and forth fighting his ropes. "Stop trying to escape," he growled. "Vinney's an expert at knot tying, right Vin?"

"That's affirmative sarge," Vinney replied.

Frenchy tried to scream a nasty word at the sergeant through his mossy gag, but all that managed to escape was 'hagga-hagga, hiss-hiss'.

"Oh, poor thing, cat's got his tongue," Sergeant Mudd teased. "Come on. Let's get this piece of fungus back to the watch house," he ordered.

The party of five started their march with Sergeant Mudd and Frenchy in the lead, Crispin and Tiberius in the middle, with Vinney bringing up the rear. They trekked onward for some time with no mishaps, except for once when Frenchy feigned tripping. He fell and rolled away from the group in an unsuccessful attempt to escape. In a flurry of excitement he was recaptured, and they resumed their march.

As the noon sun began to beat down upon their backs they came to the edge of the woods and left it behind. They started passing huge redwood trees which soared miles above their heads and clusters of silver edged lacy ferns which hugged the forest floor.

Soon Sergeant Mudd halted in front of a rectangular gray stone building covered with patchy pale green lichen. A series of black and white signs were posted above a round wooden door with a well used polished chestnut doorknob. Sergeant Mudd and Vinny halted momentarily. This gave Tiberius and Crispin a chance to read the sign above the door. It read.

Department of Lost Insects and Other Small Creatures

Sergeant at Arms Crab E. Rock
Hours of operation: Sunrise to Sunset
Every day except Major Holidays
Knock before entering.
Please wipe your paws, claws, feet, toes, legs etc.

Sergeant Mudd knocked and they heard a muffled crackly voice coming from the other side of the door. "Enter and don't let any flies in."

The door cracked open and a cricket in a gray vest with a stiff white collar peered out and spoke. "Oh, Sergeant Mudd, it's you. Come on in. Found some strays, I see."

They wiped their feet on a bristly hedgehog snoozing by the entrance, and filed into the building. The cricket led them through a short hallway which opened up into a large room. Inside, there was a peculiar round window in the ceiling illuminating a rough hewn wooden desk holding a gourd pitcher, and a small hollowed out rock. Behind the desk was a large chair with a strangely curved back, and in front were two small backless benches.

"Vinney, you guard the victims until Mr. Rock comes with the paperwork. I'll put this piece of worm slime in the lockup where he belongs," Sergeant Mudd growled, giving Frenchy a push into another hallway.

Crispin and Tiberius sat on one of the benches and surveyed the rocky walls of the room. There were tortoise shells of various colors and patterns hanging on almost every surface. Another black and white sign was displayed on the wall behind the desk.

Please have as seat and be patient.
No cussing, No spitting, No web spinning

Vinney took a seat on the other bench and began practicing a quick draw with his watch club. He would stop now and then and execute swift jabs and slashes at some imaginary foe. He looked up and noticed Crispin and Tiberius staring at him. "Hey, a watch beetle's got to be prepared. You never know, we might have to whack some more of those assassin bug-thugs."

"Oh yeah. Right," Tiberius replied trying to sound interested.

Crispin was becoming impatient and fidgeted on the uncomfortable bench. He was about to express his frustration when suddenly a large square door behind the desk opened.

The cricket who had answered the door earlier scurried in and announced "Hear ye! Hear ye! All rise for the Honorable Sergeant at Arms, Mr. Crab E. Rock."

Crispin and Tiberius stood and watched expectantly as Mr. Rock made his entrance. He was indeed a crab. A rock crab to be exact and a very large one at that. His armored body and claws were a grayish blue hue and his beady eyes were black as onyx. What was most amazing and somewhat strange about the Sergeant at Arms was the turtle shell strapped onto his back by a pair of blue and gold striped suspenders. A bronze star shaped badge inscribed with unrecognizable symbols and writing hung from one of the suspenders. An untidy cigar, obviously rolled in haste, smoldered between his tightly clamped, inward curving mandibles. A cloud of greenish acrid smoke hovered around his head like a swamp gas helmet. "Sit down. Sit down everybody. Don't know why we have all this fanfare just a waste of time if you ask me," Mr. Rock grumbled with a wave of his claw.

Sergeant Mudd returned and rushed over just as everyone was being re-seated. The cricket clerk produced a stack of papers and laid them on the desk. Mr. Rock placed his sodden ended cigar on the carved rock ash tray and began shuffling through the paperwork as he mumbled to himself. "All right, what have we got this time. Hmmm.... moth...lightning bug...found in woods... backpacks...no memories."

He glanced up at Crispin and Tiberius. "Yep, that's you two all right." He laid the paperwork down and reintroduced the cigar to his mouth. He chomped on it and sent several puffs upward as he scrutinized the pair. "Sergeant Mudd," he belted out.

"Yes sir," Sergeant Mudd snapped back.

"Are you in possession of the backpacks," Mr. Rock asked, rattling one of the papers.

"Yes sir. They're in the holding room."

"Let's see them," he ordered.

"Vinney. Grab the packs." Sergeant Mudd instructed.

Vinney disappeared from the room, and returned a few seconds later. He laid the food packs on Mr. Rock's desk. "All right, let's see what kind of paraphernalia they have," Mr. Rock said dumping the contents on his desk. "Mmm.....two nut shells. A lot of crumbs and two gold necklaces...well this is really, really helpful. Isn't it," he mumbled rolling the cigar around in his mouth. He lifted one of the necklaces with his claw and inspected the linked gold coins.

"I was hoping to find something to tell us who you are. Maybe we could help you get back to where you belong. We can't let you loose with no memory: that's asking for trouble, and our job is to keep that from happening." Crispin and Tiberius shook their heads in agreement.

"Believe it or not, this happens all the time," Mr. Rock continued. "We let the unidentified victims hang out here until their memories return. Of course you can't just lie around twiddling your legs. We'll have you help out with various chores around the watch house. Don't worry, they won't be too difficult and we won't turn you into slaves. You'll help the others collect food and firewood and do some light cleaning. Maybe polishing these," he gestured to the wall of shells.

"How long will it take for our memories to return," Tiberius asked.

Mr. Rock blew a succession of smoke rings and watched them float toward the round window. "Can't say for sure...depends on the critter. I can say that in my experience, I've never seen it take longer than one complete moon cycle. Of course, in that instance, the victim was a potato weevil. They haven't got much of a memory to begin with," he began to chuckle. "What could they possibly have to remember, maybe where the potato patch is? Ah ha ha ha, ho ho he he, oh my, ah haha," Mr. Rock's body was shaking with spasms of bellowing laughter. This caused a large chunk of ashes to drop off the end of his cigar and in a flash; a black hole began to eat its way through the paperwork. Mr. Rock quickly scooted his chair back and splashed water from the gourd pitcher onto the smoldering documents.

"Great goose eggs," the crab exclaimed. "Got to stop smoking these dog rockets. I'm going to burn this place down one of these days." He snuffed the cigar out in the ash tray as the cricket appeared and began soaking up the water with a spongy wart mushroom. What no one had noticed during the cigar fiasco was that one of the packs had slid off the desk and onto the floor. Mr. Rock leaned down and grabbed one strap with his claw. As he picked it up a small object fell out with a thump. It was long and slender, wrapped in wilted leaves and tied with string.

"What have we here," Mr. Rock announced holding up the mysterious package. He placed it on the desk, untied the string, and cautiously unrolled the wrapping. Inside was a thin round brown corked vial affixed with an aged parchment label. Written on it in tiny black print was a message: '**If you can't remember, drink this**.'

"All right you two," Mr. Rock motioned to Crispin and Tiberius. "See if you can identify this."

They started to rise from the bench. "Wait, never mind," the crab motioned. "Sit back down. I don't know what I was thinking," he continued. "You can't tell me anything about this bottle if you have no memory of it."

He held the vial up into the shaft of light streaming down from the ceiling window and the thick amber liquid inside sparkled with flecks of gold. He sat the bottle back onto his desk and scratched his head in contemplation. "Okay. Here's what I think." He finally said. "You can either hang around here waiting for some undetermined time for your minds to clear, or you take a chance and drink this stuff. I'm almost positive these packs belong to you, so take a while and discuss the matter while I take a short break."

"Hear Ye, Hear Ye, there will be a short recess," Mr. Cricket sang out. "All rise for the departure of the Honorable..."

"Could we please dispense with the protocol for now," Mr. Rock interrupted with a snap.

"Yes sir," Mr. Cricket saluted smartly and hurried off.

"That cricket is going to drive me loopy some day with all this 'Hear Ye'- mumbo-jumbo; as if I don't have enough to put up with," he mumbled under his breath as he turned to leave.

Crispin and Tiberius watched the Sergeant at Arms exit the room. His scurrying gait made an annoying tap-tap scratch-scratch sound as his claws drug along the stone floor. Vinney and Sergeant Mudd stood huddled in the corner whispering and clicking to one another as if they were the ones having to make the decision.

Crispin and Tiberius jumped off the uncomfortable bench and approached the desk to inspect the mysterious vial of liquid. "Wow. Am I glad to get off that bench," Crispin groaned rubbing his behind.

"Me too," Tiberius said. "I hope we don't have to be here much longer. I still can't remember anything but I have this weird feeling I can't explain; like we're supposed to be doing something really important instead of hanging around here." Tiberius picked up the vial and rolled it between his front legs hoping it would spark his memory – but it didn't. He let out an exasperated sigh, "I have no clue where this came from, but I have this strange gut feeling we better drink it." He turned to Crispin who was shaking his head in agreement.

"I'm going to drink it too. I have that same funny feeling."

"Okay, it's settled then," Tiberius said relieved at their decision. "When Mr. Rock comes back, we'll drink it."

They didn't have to wait long for Mr. Rock to return and when he did they remained standing, hoping they wouldn't be sent back to the dreaded bench. The Sergeant at Arms took his seat and gave Mr. Cricket a warning glance.

"Fine, if that's the way you want it," the cricket said throwing his arms up in defeat and retreating into the corner.

"Have you guys reached a decision yet," Mr. Rock asked.

"Yes sir," Tiberius spoke up, "We've decided to drink the potion."

"Carry on then," Mr. Rock said as he leaned forward expectantly. He held out two small bone cups and filled them with water from the gourd. "Just in case it tastes bad," he said.

Tiberius popped the cork stopper off the vial's lip, and cautiously sniffed the viscous liquid inside. "Well, it doesn't stink. That's good I guess. I'm going to drink half, and leave the other half for you."

He brought the potion up to his mouth, hesitated for a moment and quickly sipped a small amount; then looked at the vial, and took another tiny drink. "Okay, here's your half," he said passing it to Crispin. "It really doesn't taste bad, just kind of earthy, like mushrooms."

Crispin drank the rest of the potion in one gulp, "Yuck! It's icky," he said reaching for the cup of water.

Vinney, Sergeant Mudd and Mr. Cricket stood close by, their eyes glued to Crispin and Tiberius; waiting for something miraculous to happen. "How do you feel," Mr. Rock asked.

"My head feels kind of hot," Tiberius replied.

"So does mine," Crispin added.

"Any memories coming back yet," Mr. Rock asked.

"Not yet," Tiberius said.

Crispin shook his head back and forth, "Nothing here either."

"It might take a little while for it to take effect. Why don't you have a seat and give it a chance," the crab suggested.

He noticed a pained expression cross Crispin's face and laughed. Or maybe you would rather stand. Those benches ought to be in a torture chamber. That is, if we had one. Nope, don't do torture here, although that Frenchy Fernrucker character deserves some."

"Why don't you make him sit on one of your benches," Crispin quipped.

"Holy smoke, why didn't I think of that," Mr. Rock said with a raucous laugh. Tiberius liked Mr. Crab E. Rock. He decided to ask about the shells on the wall. "Oh, those," he replied scuttling over to the ornamental shells. "Well now, there's a story behind those if you care to hear it."

"Yes please," Crispin prompted.

"I'd be interested to hear it too," Tiberius added.

Mr. Rock laid a claw on one of the shells which looked old and very worn. "This was my first shell. But I have to go back a way before I get to this one."

He got a far away look in his eyes, and began his story. "I haven't always lived here, or had this job. I was born along a rocky seashore a long way from here. I loved it there. I would swim in the cool salty water all day; and play hide and seek among the rocks with my friends. At night we would hunt for shrimp and cockles. Life was good. Then one day I decided to swim way out past the shoreline just to see what was out there. Eventually my legs grew tired from swimming and I decided to head back to the shore. That's when it happened." Mr. Rock's voice grew thin and trailed off.

"What happened," Crispin spoke up.

"I heard a loud thumping, swooshing sound and then everything went black. My friends found me later washed up on the rocks. My back shell had been cut very badly from something moving through the water. The pain was very bad and the salt water only made it sting worse. I lay on the burning hot rocks day after day, too weak to move. After a while my friends stopped coming to check on me because they couldn't stand to see me in such pain, and not be able to help."

"That's when I decided it would be better if I wandered off to die. I drug myself away from my home and waited, but I didn't die. I kept going until I came to a cool river. The water didn't sting my cuts, so I stayed for a while, and began to recover. Then one day, I caught my reflection in the glassy surface of the water and was horrified at my scarred body. I became very depressed, and found a rotted log to hide in. I stopped eating and soon was barely able to move."

"One day it started to rain, and a squirrel came into my log for shelter. Her name was Sally Chestnut and she had the most beautiful reddish brown fur I had ever seen. I told her so, and she said I was the most interesting creature she had ever seen. She especially liked the decorative stripes on my back. I was flabbergasted, and told her they were scars, and I hated them. Sally was very understanding and brought me food and water until I began to get my strength back. We became friends and one day, she showed up dragging a beautiful yellow spotted shell. Together, we worked on different ways to attach it onto my back, and finally came up with these." Mr. Rock stopped momentarily and snapped one of his suspenders. "I thought it looked magnificent; and so did Sally: although she never did really understand why I hated the stripes on my back. I decided life was worth living after all, and we wandered around exploring the neighborhood. One crisp autumn day while Sally was out gathering nuts for the winter I heard a frantic commotion off in the distance. I headed over and found the watch house in the throes of an assassin bug attack. Wanting to help, I ran towards the bugs with my claws flying. They must have thought a monster was after them. They took one look at me, screeched, and scattered in a thousand directions."

"By the time Sally found me I was surrounded by a throng of very grateful watch beetles, and more strange creatures than I could shake a stick at. They had been terrorized by the assassin bugs for some time and saw no hopes of winning the onslaught: that is until I showed up."

"They pleaded with me to stay and as a bribe, started bringing me every unoccupied tortoise shell they could find." He gestured to the wall. "So I decided to stay. It was a nice place and the critters were friendly and made me feel special. The best part was that I felt needed and could help others. Eventually I wanted something else to do, so I was unanimously voted as the Sergeant at Arms of lost insects and small creatures."

"I bet you miss your old friends at the seashore," Crispin began. "I miss my parents and family back at Dragonfly Landing."

For a split second, Crispin didn't realize what he had said. When he did, his whole face lit up, and he gasped. "Oh! Oh! I think my memory is coming back. Yes it is. I can remember who I am, and where I live!" He turned to Tiberius triumphantly and said, "You're my friend Tiberius, and we're on an important mission to save my village."

Tiberius grinned, patted Crispin on the back and said, "Yes, I know. My memory started to come back while Mr. Rock was telling his story, but I didn't want to interrupt."

"Great Grasshopper legs," Crispin shouted. "How much time have we lost?"

"Almost a whole day - near as I can tell." Tiberius replied. "It could have been much worse if the gypsy moths hadn't given us that potion."

"So that's where it came from," Mr. Rock's shiny eyes widened with interest. "It would really come in handy in this place. It certainly would make my job easier if I could get my hands on the formula. We might have to send out a search party and make friends with these gypsy moths."

"You would like them," Crispin said. "They were very nice to us and took care of Tiberius when lightning injured his wing."

"I don't suppose you know where we can locate them," he asked.

"Not really," Tiberius said. "They travel around a lot, but they're easiest to find at night. If you see a huge campfire, and hear music that makes your legs start to jump you probably found the gypsy moth camp."

Sergeant Mudd cleared his throat and interrupted, "Mr. Rock sir. We'll be on our way if it's all right. We need to get back on patrol."

"Yes. Yes of course. And you," he pointed to Vinney. "Great job on capturing that Fernrucker fugitive. He's slipped through our traps more than a few times. There might be a commendation patch in your future!" Mr. Rock winked at Vinney.

A huge grin split Vinney's face and Sergeant Mudd clapped him on the back. The two watch beetles saluted, turned, and marched away. Before leaving the room, Sergeant Mudd turned and called out, "Hey you two guys, take care and remember don't ever eat anything in the woods again."

"We'll try to remember that," Tiberius chortled.

Mr. Cricked rushed ahead of the watch beetles and opened the door for them.

"Oh yes," Mr. Rock inquired. "That reminds me, I forgot to ask just what it was you ate in the forest."

"We didn't eat anything in the forest," Crispin answered.

"That's right, we brought our own food," Tiberius added.

"But the sign told you not to eat ANYTHING in the forest," Mr. Rock explained.

"But we didn't...Ohhhhh!" Tiberius said as he suddenly understood and turned to Crispin. "We did eat something in the forest. We ate our own food. We thought the sign was warning us not to eat anything growing or lying around in the woods." Crispin rolled his eyes as it finally sunk in.

"I guess we need to work on the wording of that sign," Mr. Rock said. "It's a little misleading." He yelled for Mr. Cricket, and the small clerk scurried in. "Take a memorandum," he ordered. Mr. Cricket pulled a small pad and tiny writing stick out of his vest pocket.

"To all sign makers," he dictated. "From this day forward, all warning signs in the Woods of Forgetfulness will read as follows: 'Don't eat anything in the forest. This included food brought in on your person'. Signed Crab E. Rock."

"Very well, I'll see to it immediately," Mr. Cricket said.

"As for you two," he turned his attention back to Crispin and Tiberius, "we can't send you off starving. I'll have the kitchen whip you up a meal."

Tiberius coughed nervously and replied. "We don't mean to be rude sir, but would it be all right if we took our food with us? We need to get going as soon as possible."

"Certainly, certainly, I'll have someone see to it right away. "Mr. Cricket," he yelled. He waited but the clerk didn't come.

"Now where is that...Oh yes. I sent him to the sign makers. I'll go myself and have someone make you a sack lunch."

Mr. Rock hurried off and returned shortly with two round pouches wrapped in corn husk. "This trail mix should keep you going for a while. It's light but filling. We always keep a barrel of it handy for our watch beetles to snack on." Crispin and Tiberius tucked it away in their packs.

A green and red shield bug wearing a seed pod helmet and tin foil armor on his stocky leaf shaped back entered the room and saluted Mr. Rock. "This is Corporal Dirt," the crab said. "He will be your escort. Don't worry. There's no danger it's just procedure. He will take you to Twin Falls overlook so you can be on your way."

The shield bug Corporal stepped forward. "Follow me gentlemen." Crispin and Tiberius followed Corporal Dirt with Mr. Rock tapping and scratching behind. The cricket suddenly appeared from the shadows and opened the door. Tiberius and Crispin turned to bid Mr. Rock farewell.

"Thanks for all the help," Tiberius said.

"And the story, and the food," Crispin added.

"That's what the watch house is here for. You guys have a safe journey," Mr. Rock said.

They exited into the bright mid-day sun and followed Corporal Dirt down a narrow winding gravel path. At the end, where the stately trees began, they turned and waved to Mr. Rock who was conversing with the hedgehog. He waved back and watched as they stepped into the woods.

Crispin and Tiberius were glad to be back in a forest that teemed with life. Corporal Dirt was a lively chatty sort of fellow, and had not stopped talking since they left the watch house. After telling them practically his whole life history he plunged into a story about escorting a group of rowdy grasshoppers through the Woods of Forgetfulness. "I mean to tell you, that was a tough assignment," Corporal Dirt went on. "Those hoppers wouldn't listen to a thing I had to say. It was all I could do to keep them from munching on something or other along the way, and I couldn't get them to walk along normal like. It was walk....jump....buzz; jump.....buzz.....walk, all the way through the woods, it really drove me to the edge. Don't you know I was glad to finish that escort duty."

There was an unexpected lull in Corporal Dirt's monologue as he hesitated at the base of a wild ginger leaf. "Now, be careful," he warned, "I don't want you two falling into the canyon."

Crispin and Tiberius moved forward slowly following their escort until they stood at the end of the redwood forest and gazed down into Twin Falls canyon. It was not the deepest canyon Crispin and Tiberius had ever seen but it definitely was the most beautiful. Lush green vegetation covered the floor and walls of the canyon and a rainbow'd waterfall spilled from the canyon's mouth. A spike of rock divided the flood and sent a curtain of shimmering ribbons into a boiling, frothy, azure cauldron below.

Chapter 12
The Stink Bug Boys

Crispin and Tiberius were much relieved to finally be on their journey once more with their memories intact. Their escort had returned to the watch house some time ago after making sure his charges were headed in the right direction. The woods they were now flying over were mostly a thick tangle of sweet briar, horse chestnut and wild persimmon bushes. Occasionally they would see a solitary spindly pine tree standing sentinel over the vegetation at its feet.

They flew over a sparkling stream winding its way through the woods and decided it looked like a perfect place to rest and eat their sack lunches. Tiberius found a toasty smooth rock to sunbathe on while Crispin stretched out in the shade from the rock's overhang.

They unwrapped the corn husk pouches and found a tasty mixture of nuts, berries, seeds, and something puffy and yellow which they didn't recognize. Crispin rolled over, craned his neck toward the rock's edge and shouted. "Hey, what are these funny puffy things?"

"I don't know, but they taste okay." Tiberius answered then added; "You know what they say 'Beggars can't be choosers'."

While eating, they watched a family of beavers swim by and disappear under a jammed mound of sticks and dead logs clinging to the stream bank. Sometime later a heron circled the stream twice and then gracefully swooped down to pluck his meal from the water. He rested momentarily on a rock jutting out from the stream, and gulped down a small twitching fish. Crispin flew up to Tiberius and hid beneath his wing. "Will he come eat us," he asked concerned.

"Not unless we sprout fins and start living in the water," Tiberius chuckled.

"Oh," Crispin said relieved. "He only eats fish. Okay, in that case, I like the bird."

Eventually the heron unfolded his soft gray wings, flapped twice, and soared into a nearby sweet gum tree.

The two friends reluctantly left the refreshing stream and continued their journey. The bushy woods soon merged into a rocky landscape with a thick green carpet of growth creeping amongst boulders so white and sparkling they looked like icy jewels.

They flew through a dense bank of low hanging misty clouds for a short time and when they emerged the majestic Teepee Mountains loomed before them like glistening white temples. The range of triangular peaks rose so high that their pointy heads disappeared in a veil of billowy clouds and lush velvety tendrils crept around their feet like fuzzy emerald slippers. "I can see now how they got their name," Tiberius stated. "They really do look like teepees."

Suddenly Crispin shouted. "Look over there at the mountain to our left. It's the only one without a peak."

"Yes! That's the flat topped one shown on the map," Tiberius called back excitedly. "I'll head straight for it."

As the travelers moved closer they began to see clumps of deep green lacy foliage and realized the velvety tendrils crawling up the mountain sides were ferns. Some were stiff and straight, and so dark green they almost looked black. Others were bright green the color of a newborn katydid with soft intricate lacy fronds. There were also some so strange with unusual colors and patterns they reminded Crispin of bird feathers. "Well, I think we can safely assume we're in the beginning of the fern forest," Tiberius stated.

"I absolutely agree," Crispin replied. "They're beautiful, and look so soft. Could we sleep here tonight? They would make such nice soft beds," he added.

"I don't see why not," Tiberius said glancing upward. "The sun is getting low and I think we're both a little tired. We can get a good night's rest and start fresh tomorrow searching for the Fern Queen."

"Bela told me we wouldn't have to look for her because they would find us. What do you suppose that's all about?" Crispin questioned.

"I don't know," Tiberius replied. "But we can't sit around and twiddle our legs. We need to keep moving."

As night fell a soft cool mist descended on the fern forest. Crispin and Tiberius snuggled under a velvety fern frond, and were lulled to sleep by the serenading of crickets.

TIBERIUS AWOKE AT the crack of dawn and looked over at his friend's tiny form curled up under a nearby fern. He couldn't help chuckling silently at the way Crispin's gentle snoring caused the frond above his head to float up and down. The morning doves hauntingly peaceful coo's echoed from a distant tree welcoming a new day. Early rising bees were already at their tasks of buzz diving and nuzzling their heads into patches of glistening dew covered clover. Their foraging reminded Tiberius they would need something to eat before continuing their journey. He stretched his delicate legs and sauntered over to inspect the packs for remaining food. Peering inside he decided there wasn't enough trail mix left for two and not wanting to compete with the nearby bees, he began searching the area for other food. After scrounging for some time with only a few worm hole riddled nut shells to show for his effort; something white creeping along the ground caught his eye. He rushed over, and to his delight was rewarded with thick vigorous mounds of bindweed clothed in pale pink funnel shaped blooms. This was nectar that no self respecting moth with a refined palate could pass up but not wanting to leave Crispin alone for too long he postponed his feast and returned. He was however, already awake rubbing his eyes and wearing a confused look.

"Oh, there you are," Crispin said groggily. "For a while I couldn't remember where I was. I was afraid we were back in the Woods of Forgetfulness."

Tiberius hurried over and plopped down sporting a huge grin. "I was out scouting for extra food and stumbled upon a magnificent stand of bindweed in full bloom. Have you ever tried it," he asked.

Crispin shook his head. "No, I don't think so," he answered scrunching up his face. "It must be wonderful though. You're practically drooling," he laughed.

"Ah, you're right my boy. One of nature's finest accomplishments if I may say so. We need to go right now, before we have to fight off an invasion of hungry honey bees for it."

On returning, they found the bindweed had not been disturbed by the local bees and the two friends dived right in. Soon their stomachs stopped growling and the extremely sweet juice gave them so much energy they decided to save the remaining trail mix for a snack later.

Crispin wiped a dribble of the heavenly nectar from his mouth and looked up just in time to see a colony of excited honeybees heading straight for the coveted bindweed patch. "Great beetle bazookers," Crispin cried out. "Here they come."

"Time to fly," Tiberius exclaimed.

Crispin grabbed the packs, jumped on Tiberius' back and they fled. They glanced down and laughed as the ravenous hoard touched down and plunged their heads into the empty funnels.

"Where are we headed," Crispin yelled over the noise of wind skimming past Tiberius wings.

"Not far. I just wanted to get us away from those bees before they realized we had emptied the bindweed blooms." Tiberius explained. "The little nippers can be a bit short tempered when they're upset," he continued. "We'll have to land soon. If the Fern Queen and her subjects are supposed to find us, I don't think it will be up here," he added.

"I think I see a trail over there," Crispin called out pointing towards the foothill of the flat topped landmark. Tiberius followed the pathway with his eyes and noticed it wove alongside the mountains' base for quite a distance. He speculated to himself that this might be a good spot to land, so he dipped one wing and glided in for a landing. "I think we should hike along this trail until either they find us or we find them," he explained as Crispin dismounted.

"Sounds like a good plan to me," he responded as they began strolling along.

The path was obviously well traveled as evidenced by the smooth worn down stones embedded beneath their feet. The lush growth of ferns, creeping jenny and mosses surrounding them was also noticeably absent from the trail except for a few tenacious tufts of scratchy bristle moss which had taken up residence in the fissured stones. They were flanked on their right by the sheer glittering cliffs of the Teepee Mountains and the rocky fern covered foothills on the other. The air was cool and a heavy mist dripped off the ferns and collected in the shallow depressions of the time etched rocks. A sweet pungent earthy smell enveloped the two travelers as they marched on. Occasionally, boggy recesses belched up a sulfurous mixture of stagnant water and decomposing vegetation and the travelers held their breath as they passed.

As the morning wore on the two companions kept up a steady pace of hiking, hoping to cover most of the trail by late afternoon unless by some chance the Fern Queen's folk found them sooner. Several times hearing rustling or buzzing close by, they stopped and waited, hoping someone would come out to greet them.

"I hope we're in the right place," Crispin said.

"I'm sure we are," Tiberius replied. "This seems to be the only trail along here. We really haven't been walking that long, it just seems like it," he added.

"Let's stop and get a drink, I'm thirsty," Crispin said.

They found a rock holding a puddle of fresh rainwater and sipped it until they were refreshed and ready to move on. Just as Crispin lifted his head from the puddle he caught a glimpse of something moving about in the ferns behind him. He quickly turned around but it had disappeared. "Did you see that," he asked Tiberius.

"No, but I thought I heard something," he replied.

Back on the trail, Crispin and Tiberius heard a crunch-crunch, thwack-thwack sound behind them. Once again, they saw nothing, and kept walking.

After the fourth time they were almost sure something was following them.

"Let's sit on that log and wait a while," Tiberius suggested. "When we start walking again and hear the same commotion, we'll know for sure we are being followed."

The pair hopped up and perched on the log trying to act as if they were just taking a rest. They chatted nonchalantly back and forth and watched the nearby ferns for signs of movement.

"There, did you see that. I saw something in that bird nest fern to our left," Crispin whispered.

"Yes. Something bright green was moving along the ground," he whispered back.

"What should we do," Crispin asked.

"Let's just sit here for a while, and see if it leaves," Tiberius replied.

They watched as the green mass stopped directly across from them and completely disappeared into the vegetation. "Are they still there," Crispin asked in a hushed voice.

"Yes, they're camouflaged," Tiberius whispered back.

"Maybe they're afraid of us," Crispin said.

"You could be right, but that wouldn't explain why they're following us. This is a real conundrum," Tiberius pointed out.

A puzzled look crossed Crispin's face. "What's a com-nim-crum-drum?" He asked.

Tiberius tried not to laugh at Crispin's mispronunciation. "A conundrum is a puzzle which needs to be solved," he whispered.

"Oh, well, have you any idea of how to solve this con-nun-doo-rum." Crispin asked.

"I think so," Tiberius began. "They must be watching us for a reason. It's almost as if they're spying on us and usually spies are trying to collect information so if we give them some, maybe they will leave. Of course, there's another possibility," he continued. "What if they're the ones who are supposed to find us?"

Crispin's eyes widened at the idea. "You're right, it could be them, but someone has to make the first move."

Tiberius shut his eyes and scratched his head in contemplation for a few moments. Finally his eyes shot open and Crispin knew he had come up with a bright idea.

"You've got something haven't you," Crispin whispered excitedly.

"Well, it might work," Tiberius began to explain. "Let's talk in a normal tone of voice to each other about trying to find the Fern Queen."

"Ah, I see," Crispin said. "That will give them the information they might be after."

"Yes, that's using the old noggin," he replied tapping Crispin on the head.

Tiberius started the loud conversation "Well Crispin, where do you think we are?"

"I'm not sure, but we must be in the fern forest. Look at all these ferns," Crispin threw out his front legs with a flourish.

"Well then," Tiberius said. "If this is the fern forest, where is the Fern Queen? We really need to find her soon; she is the only one who can give us the information we need."

There was a slight rustle in the foliage at the mention of the Fern Queen. Crispin and Tiberius glanced hopefully at each other, and resumed their conversation.

"If only we could find someone who could tell us which why to go," Crispin moaned with a loud sigh.

"Well, we won't find her sitting on this log all day, so we better get moving," Tiberius replied.

They jumped off the log, adjusted their packs, and started walking at a deliberately slow pace. The pair had taken only a few steps when a gravely voice behind them called out, "Howdy."

Crispin and Tiberius stopped dead in their tracks and slowly turned around. A lime green bug with a shield shaped body and short legs stood in the middle of the pathway. The bug moved a bit closer and Crispin and Tiberius noticed he was wearing a triangular piece of red cloth around his neck.

"Me and my boys happened to overhear your conversation back there on the log." The bug gestured into the foliage as several groups of the green bugs trotted out. Eventually ten bugs, all wearing the same red neckerchiefs stood behind the lead bug.

"As I was saying," he continued, "When we heard y'all were looking for the Fern Queen, we reckoned you boys might need some help finding her."

"Yes, that would be great," Tiberius exclaimed.

"Me and the boys will be right glad to help you, and we're heading back that way directly."

"My name's Jessie, I'm the trail boss," he said extending a leg.

"Pleased to meet you. I'm Tiberius and this is my friend Crispin."

"Boys. Come round and meet the strangers," Jessie called back to the group.

They surged forward and surrounded Crispin and Tiberius. "Howdy. My name's Tex," said one of the bugs shaking their legs. One by one, the other "boys" introduced themselves. There was Wes, Frank, Dusty, Wishbone, Rowdy, Wyatt, Billie, Roy, and Hank.

Crispin and Tiberius were bombarded with questions about who they were, where they were from, and what they were doing in their neck of the woods. They answered all the questions and eventually the boys settled down.

"All right boys, let's get moving. Got to report back before sundown," Jessie ordered.

Crispin and Tiberius followed the group as they wove their way through the foliage flanking the trail. Every once in a while, the group would pause and inspect some of the ferns. "They seem to be looking for something," Crispin whispered to Tiberius.

"I'm sure we'll eventually find out what it is," he replied.

Later they stopped again, and Jessie called out, "Roy, you and Wishbone scout out those bracken ferns down in Gobbler's Glen. We've had a run of bad luck up there lately. The rest of us will mosey on over and check out the sword ferns at Snooty Hollow." Roy and Wishbone immediately scurried into the brush and the rest of the group continued on.

"This is really strange behavior; I wish I knew what was going on." Tiberius said.

"Why don't we just ask," Crispin suggested.

"Maybe they don't want us to know," Tiberius pointed out.

"Well, I'm going to ask anyway," Crispin replied.

"All right. I can't stand the suspense any longer, I'm coming too," Tiberius said. They quickened their pace, and came alongside the trail boss.

"Howdy you two. Need something," Jessie inquired.

"Wellll....," Crispin began. "We don't mean to pry, but could you explain exactly what you boys are doing?"

"Just working," Jessie replied coyly.

"Yes, but what is it that you do," Crispin asked.

The trail boss laughed and replied in his gravely voice. "We work for the Fern Queen. Our job is to scout the fern forest for aphid attacks which could kill the ferns. We also keep a look out for ants on foliage."

"Why ants," Crispin asked.

"Because aphids excrete honeydew, a sweet juice which ants go loco over. They follow the aphids around, and lap up the juice. Sometimes they even milk them."

"Really," Crispin's eyes widened. "How can they do that?"

"The ants rub the aphids backs," he explained. "I guess the little guys really like it too, because it makes them excrete more honeydew."

"Wow," Crispin exclaimed.

"So you do all this to protect the ferns," Tiberius commented.

"Good gravy no," Jessie exclaimed. "That's only part of it. When we find a heard of aphids, we report back to the Fern Queen."

"What does the Fern Queen do with them," Crispin asked.

He was about to answer when suddenly Wyatt rushed up and began frantically signaling with his front legs.

"Get down, and be quiet," Jessie whispered to Crispin and Tiberius. "Rowdy spotted a tiger beetle heading straight for us."

The group crouched down low hiding in the foliage and watched as the ferocious beetle stalked towards them. The tiger beetle was shiny and dark green with six white spots circling its oval body. Its powerful sharp pincher claws on its head clenched back and forth menacingly, ready to devour unsuspecting victims.

As the predator came closer, Jessie caught the boys attention and signaled something to them. They pulled their red neckerchiefs up over their faces, leaving only their eyes uncovered. Suddenly the air surrounding them began to stink horribly. Crispin glanced over at Tiberius and wrinkled up his face in disgust. Tiberius eyes were bulged out as if he was holding his breath, and both of their eyes began to water. The tiger beetle stopped abruptly; covered his face with one leg, and scurried in the opposite direction as fast as it could.

"Okay boys, we're in the clear," Jessie announced as soon as the tiger beetle was well away. "Good work. That varmint took off faster than a ten legged cockroach."

"And he stunk too," Crispin said.

"Well, something around here sure did," Tiberius added.

Jessie and the boys started laughing so hard, they had to hold their sides.

"Well if it wasn't the beetle making that stink, what did? I know it wasn't me," Crispin said.

"They thought it was the beetle." Rowdy managed to say between spasms of laughter. Billy rushed forward and placed a leg on Crispin's back and stated, "I reckon they don't call us the 'Stink-Bug Boys' for nothin'."

The rest of the boys all shouted, "Yahoo! Time to move on out."

Trotting along in two's with Crispin and Tiberius sandwiched in between, the stink bugs returned to their strange weaving walk.

"What does 'yahoo!' mean," Crispin asked Tiberius.

"I can't say I've ever heard that word before," Tiberius answered.

Crispin scratched an antenna in thought, and started laughing. "It must be one of those shout-out-loud-excitedly words," he snickered.

Tiberius grinned broadly and replied. "And who ever said lightning bugs weren't smart."

It wasn't long before Roy and Wishbone came charging out of the brush. The group halted while Jessie and the two scouts carried on a very animated conversation. After a flurry of waving and pointing into the distance, Roy and Wishbone rejoined the group, and they continued on. It was late afternoon before the group reached their destination.

They crossed a small babbling brook, edged in orange tinged autumn ferns and then followed a termite riddled fence on the verge of collapse. The fence ended in a rusty gate hanging askew from a broken hinge and the group marched under it into a field of soft plumy goldenrod. The first thing that caught Crispin and Tiberius attention was all the ladybugs crawling and dangling from the yellow weeds.

The next thing they saw was an old tumbled down stone structure with an ancient weather etched door partially attached to it by one rusty hinge. As they drew nearer Crispin and Tiberius could see that several of the stones formed what was left of a set of stairs leading into a large rectangular hole set into the ground. The entrance was flanked by two giant graceful pink and silver banded painted ferns. Dark green lustrous ivy and flaming orange trumpet vines twined their way around the sad clinging door. Hundreds of ladybugs crept gingerly around the entrance and steps. Every now and then one of the bright red and black spotted bugs would fly gracefully over their heads.

"Geeze bees, there are ladybugs everywhere," Crispin pointed out.

"That's because ladybugs like cool dark places," Tiberius replied. Crispin and Tiberius followed Jessie and his boys up the steps and down into the mysterious dark hole.

They entered the gloom and walked down a gently sloping dusty path, covered with thousands of tiny ladybug footprints. Shafts of sunlight filtered down through cracks above their heads, illuminating the group as they passed under. White gnarly roots from the ivy's above dangled and clung to the dirt ceiling and pale brown spotted mushrooms sprang from the walls at crazy angles.

As they continued further in, the shafts of light weakened and an earthy musty smell floated up to meet them.

The dirt walls and ceiling were alive with clusters of ladybugs milling about or snoozing peacefully. As the group passed, some of the bugs swiveled their heads, smiled, and called out, "Welcome back boys!"

The boys waved back. So did Crispin and Tiberius. Even though they weren't 'the boys', they still wanted to be courteous.

The stink bug boys were now passing single file through a narrow rock walled passage way, and Tiberius had to hold his wings tight against his body to fit through the entrance. As soon as Tiberius and Crispin entered the tunnel, they both gasped in surprise at what they saw. Nestled into tiny crevices in the walls were the same crystals used at Dragonfly Landing!

"Look," Crispin whispered excitedly. "They're using the crystals too!"

"This is most unexpected." Tiberius mused. "I hadn't expected to find the Fern Queen using them."

"This is great," Crispin gushed. "Since they use them too, they most certainly know the way to the cave." He paused, and his eyes bulged wide as an idea struck him.

"Great grasshopper legs! If they have a lot, maybe they will give us enough so we don't have to go face those scary Gorboos!"

"Don't get your hopes up," Tiberius cautioned. "They might not have enough to give us or they could be having the same problem as Dragonfly Landing."

"You mean these could be wearing out too," Crispin replied.

"Don't worry, it will all work out somehow," Tiberius said reassuringly.

The group made its way through the tunnel and Crispin and Tiberius felt it growing cooler the further they went. Tiny rivulets of condensed moisture had trickled down the walls and they had to wade through the shallow, cool pools in several places. The passageway eventually widened and Tiberius was now able to relax his wings. They rounded a corner and entered a large cavernous chamber. Lined against one wall were spider web covered rows of gigantic rectangular bottles crowned with rusty circular lids. Inside, floating in liquid were strange shaped blobs resembling fruits and vegetables. Some were filled with smooth red or pale orange orbs while others held smaller yellow seed like granules or long thin green stalks. Four strange symbols were embossed on the glass bottles' surface. They continued on and saw other large, mysterious objects lying in a disorganized pile next to a rotted board. These were round rusty metal containers with yellowed, tattered paper coverings, depicting faded images of fruits and vegetables. The group made another sharp turn and suddenly stopped in front of a round shiny tin door embossed with a circle of ferns enclosing the letters - FQ.

"FQ: do you think that stands for Fern Queen," Crispin asked.

"We'll soon find out," Tiberius replied.

Jessie leaned forward and spoke to a crack in the rock wall next to the door. "Howdy, it's Jessie and the boys to see the Fern Queen."

The small round bald head of a sow bug poked out of the crack. His bulging eyes narrowed as he surveyed the group and their unusual companions. "State your business," said the sow bug in a nasally voice.

"Quit bein' so dad burn uppity, Winthrope. You know we're here to give our daily report. So stop beating around the bush and open that door," Jessie ordered.

The sow bug snorted, "I know what you're here for...but what about those two. Where did you pick them up? We can't just let anybody in."

Jessie's face darkened and he replied impatiently, "Winthrope, if you don't open that door right now we'll let you have it. You'll have to hold your breath till you pass out." The boys turned around and waggled their back ends threateningly at Winthrope.

"No! Not the stink spray – please! I'll let you in right now. I'm just trying to do my job," Winthrope whined. He jerked his head back, and disappeared into the crevice.

A few seconds later there was a series of clicks and the door swung opened, and the group entered. The door banged behind them followed by another click after which the sow bug rolled up into a ball and disappeared under a rock.

Chapter 13
Ladybug Town

"Come on in boys," a soft whispery voice called out from the other side of the room.

Crispin and Tiberius followed the group as they crossed to a pink stone fireplace with a chair along side which had been carved from a pecan shell. Dancing flames in the hearth and three glowing wooden lanterns on the mantle bathed the room in soft cozy light.

In the chair sat a ladybug with long dark eyelashes, a tiny pouty mouth, and shimmering black spotted - red wings. She batted her long lashes and addressed them softly, "My, my. We have visitors. Where on earth did you find them?"

"Found them down on the trail, ma'am. They seemed sort of lost, and were asking for you," Jessie answered.

Her eyes widened. "For me?"

"Yes ma'am. Some sort of quest they need your help with."

She rubbed her feet together briskly and a twinkle came to her eyes. "Oh, I do so love a good mystery."

"It's a map we're really after. We were told you have the one we need," Tiberius explained.

"Come closer so I can get a good look at you two," she prompted.

The pair moved closer to the Fern Queen and she reached out and gently touched Tiberius' wing. "AAAh. A luna moth I haven't seen one of your kind for some time. Can you open your wings so I can see them?" Tiberius surveyed the room and deciding there was ample room slowly unfolded his wings. "They're magnificent," the Fern Queen gushed fluttering her long lashes at Tiberius. "And do you have an equally marvelous name?"

"My name is Tiberius," he answered, slowly refolding his wings.

"A very honorable name," the ladybug nodded, then turned to Crispin. "And you young fella'; what's your name?"

"Crispin ma'am. It's an honor to meet you, your highness," he said bowing.

She threw back her head and let out a string of bubbly giggles. "Please just call me Queenie. I'm really not a queen. It's more of an honorary title."

"Honorary," Tiberius said puzzled.

"Yes, let me explain," she began. "Ladybugs have anywhere between two and twenty-eight spots on their back, and I happen to have the most spots a ladybug can have," she stood and turned. "Count them. I have 28 spots. I am also one of the oldest in my family. I'm 2 and half years old. Since I have so many spots and I've been around for so long, the other ladybugs think I'm special. The main reason however, is that I'm in charge of the cake factory and whoever is in charge has always been called the Fern Queen. Don't ask me why. It has something to do with some strange tradition."

"Cake factory! We didn't see that on the way in. What kind of cakes do you make," Crispin asked trying to ignore the grumbling in his belly.

"Aphid cakes of course," the Fern Queen replied. "We store them for winter; otherwise, we would starve."

"I'm not especially fond of aphids, but we would like to see your factory," Crispin said.

"I'd like to see it too, ma'am." Tiberius added.

"Ma'am!" Queenie snickered, "You've been hanging out with the boys too long. I like these two, Jessie." She announced waving grandly; then continued. "Let's get the daily aphid report over with so I can find this mysterious map they need. Winthrope, it's time for the reports," she called out.

The pudgy sow bug rolled from under the rock, uncurled and skittered over to the fireplace. He picked up a small bound tablet made of smooth sycamore leaves and a sharp pointed sooty stick. He scribbled something on one of the pages, glanced up, and nodded at the Fern Queen.

Jessie and the boys moved closer. "Well now ma'am; me and the boys found a pretty good heard of aphids on the bracken fern down in Snooty Hollow. Roy and Wishbone spotted some rustlers up in Gobblers Glen and we also saw a might good size heard grazing on the sword ferns in the south meadow this morning. I reckon' by now, the ants will have found them too."

The Fern Queen was now all business, and stated in a stern voice. "Very well, let's send some of the girls out right away to start control maneuvers. Let's hope we get to those aphids before the rustlers steal too many. Our production line in the factory has slowed because of those pesky ants runnin' off with all our aphids. Sorry about the delay," she added glancing apologetically at Crispin and Tiberius.

Queenie crawled down from her chair, crossed the room, and removed a cone shaped object hanging on the wall. "Okay, I'm going to make the aphid announcement to the girls," she said. "The sooner they get out there the better. Winthrope!" she called out. "Bring the notes so I don't send them to the wrong place. My memory's not as good as it used to be." The bug grabbed his notes, and scurried behind the Fern Queen as she followed the stink bug boys towards the door.

"Come on you two," she waved at Crispin and Tiberius. "This won't take too long. I'll give you a tour of our factory afterwards. It's quite interesting and we're very proud of our facilities, if I may say so."

IT WAS A long and eclectic group which marched single file back through the tunnel. Heading towards the entrance were a ladybug carrying a strange cone shaped object, a sow bug clutching a notebook, eleven tired and dusty stink bugs, a luna moth with tightly folded wings, and bringing up the rear, a young lightning bug skipping along merrily. They stopped at the front steps, and squinted at the burning red sun setting lazily on the horizon.

Jessie approached the Fern Queen and cleared his voice to get her attention. "Ma'am; me and the boys are going to mosey on over to the bunkhouse for some grub and a little shut eye. It's been a long day. We'll be going out at sunrise as usual."

"Yes, of course," Queenie responded. "As always, you and your boys have done us a great service. Come by the factory soon and pick up your plant juice and cakes. Go get some rest now, you look very tired."

"Yes'm, we are. Hope you and your gal's have a great round-up tonight," Jessie responded as he looked over at Crispin and Tiberius. "It's been mighty nice meetin' you fellas'. Let us know if you ever need a good trail boss again."

"Thanks for all your help. You've saved us a lot of time," Tiberius replied.

"Yeah, and you guys are fun too," Crispin added.

The stink bug boys trotted down the steps, turned for a final wave and shouted "Happy Trails" as they moseyed off into the sunset.

"What amazing characters those stink bug boys, wouldn't you agree," the Fern Queen said turning towards Crispin and Tiberius.

"Yes ma'am," they both sang out.

"Now what did I tell you about that ma'am thing," she scolded wagging a front leg.

"Oh yes; Queenie," Tiberius corrected himself.

"I promise not to call you ma'am again," Crispin said sheepishly.

"Good. Now that we have that straightened out, I better give the girls their marching orders."

Crispin and Tiberius waited at the entrance while the Fern Queen and Winthrope moved down and stood on the lowest step. The cone shaped object Queenie was carrying turned out to be a megaphone made out of rolled up paper birch bark. She brought it to her mouth and began speaking. Her quiet, whispery voice, now came out loud and powerful, traveling past the front steps to the fields beyond. The ladybugs near and far suddenly stopped their activities at the sound of her voice. "Gather around girls. I have the nightly aphid reports from the Stink Bug Boys." A loud cheer went up from the gathering ladybugs. "Here are the locations of the aphid sightings." She paused and glanced over at Winthrope. "Can I have the notes please," she whispered.

He rushed over and handed her the notebook. She cleared her voice and began speaking again. "There's a rather large infestation over in Gobblers Glenn on the bracken ferns; and another one over in Snooty Hollow on the sword ferns. Also, some of you might want to check out the south meadow."

"Oh yes. Rustlers were sighted in Gobbler's Glen, so be on your toes. We need to get there soon, and let them know we're not going to be pushed around." Another cheer rose up from the audience. "Don't forget girls: after you've had supper, fill your backpacks as full as you can; and drop them off at the factory. Good luck ladies, and happy hunting!" The ladybugs cheered again, then rose from the fields in a massive humming red cloud.

A moment later, the excited swarm split into several groups and disappeared into the forest and glens beyond.

The Fern Queen and Winthrope returned to the entrance and traveled back down the tunnel with Crispin and Tiberius in tow. After passing the room full of strange containers, the tunnel became very cold and Crispin and Tiberius started shaking. To their relief, when they entered the Fern Queen's chambers, the warm cozy fire was still ablaze in the fireplace. "Winthrope. Bring our two guests some pillows to sit on," Queenie ordered.

"Yes Queenie. I'll only be a minute," he answered.

The sow bug scurried out of the room and quickly returned dragging two plump, white, round pillows. He placed them across from Queenie's chair and the two visitors made themselves comfortable.

Queenie clapped her hands and two ladybugs in pink spotted aprons came in carrying acorn bowls. "I thought you might be hungry, so I had the cook's prepare you a meal," she said.

Crispin glanced at Tiberius nervously as the bowl was placed into his hands. He immediately relaxed as he inspected the bowl's contents. Instead of the expected aphids, he found to his delight it was filled with rolled up leaves and a few spongy cakes. They quickly downed the tart savory leaves and sweet honey cakes; then washed them down with a cup of water which Winthrope served from a rectangular wooden tray embossed with the FQ seal.

Crispin smacked his lips and looked at Queenie. "Aren't you hungry too," he asked.

"Goodness no, I ate a long time ago: before you arrived. I wanted to be sure you were fed before taking you to see our factory," she replied.

"Do we have enough time to discuss the map and still see the cake production?" Tiberius asked, hoping he wasn't being too impertinent.

"Yes of course, the factory will be operating most of the night, but some of the machines may shut down earlier; so let's do the tour first. Oh yes," she added wiggling her lower legs, "the document room is beyond the factory, so why not save ourselves some steps. These old legs aren't what they used to be."

"Now, why don't you start at the beginning, and tell me about your journey," Queenie prompted.

"Everything," Crispin asked.

"Yes of course, and don't leave anything out," she replied.

"This could take a while," Tiberius chuckled.

Queenie nestle back into her pillowed chair as the visitors began the tale of their adventures. By the time they had finished, the roaring fire had withered down into a pile of softly glowing orange embers.

"That's the most amazing tale I've ever heard," the Fern Queen said. "I'm glad Tiberius pulled you out of that horrible bog plant. And that rainbow! My, my: I never dreamed there could be such a thing. I'm glad those gypsy moths don't eat aphids," she added. "As much as they travel there might not be any left for us. So, you two have come all this way to find the crystals your village needs."

"Yes, that's right," Tiberius nodded.

Queenie pursed her lips and replied. "I'm sure you've noticed by now the crystals are very important to us as well."

"Yes, we were very excited to see them on our way in," Tiberius said.

"Unfortunately," she went on, "we have also noticed a slight dimming of our crystals. Some day in the near future we will have to replace ours as well, but since we have the map, is shouldn't be too much of a problem."

Crispin was perplexed at Queenie's seemingly nonchalant attitude about replacing her people's crystals. With a puzzled look, he asked, "But aren't you worried about encountering the Gorboos?"

Queenie's eyes widened as a mixture of amazement and confusion registered on her face. "Gorboos? I've never heard of them. What are they?"

Tiberius leaned forward and began to explain. "We don't know much about them either but the council of elders at Dragonfly Landing said that they are the guardians of the cave and if we want the crystals we'll have to get past them somehow."

Crispin twisted an antenna nervously; then added. "And if they catch you, you will be eaten or drowned in the cold cave river."

Queenie sat up sharply in her chair. "Oh dear me! It's been a long time since the ladybugs around this part of the forest have needed to collect crystals, and since I'm the oldest, I would certainly know something about these Gorboos, but I've never heard of them. Perhaps a past Fern Queen knew of these creatures, but the knowledge has since been lost." She relaxed into her chair and went on. "I wish I could offer you a few words of advice, but unfortunately, the most I can offer is our hospitality, and a copy of our map. I wish I could be more help."

"Thank you, Queenie. The map will be invaluable I'm sure," Tiberius said.

"Wonderful then, let's go get that map for you: shall we," Queenie said rising stiffly from her chair.

She called out to Winthrope who was once again snoozing under his rock. "Winthrope. Wake up." The sow bug twitched, but didn't waken. "Oh well, I don't need him; he's probably exhausted anyway. I'll let him sleep for a while," she muttered to herself as they exited the room.

The threesome started down a passageway going in the opposite direction from the entrance. It was much the same as the one they had traveled through earlier with the stink bug boys; except this one had doors lining both sides. They resembled the door to the Fern Queen's chambers, being round and tin with letters embossed into them. They approached one bearing the letters W-P.

By this time Crispin's curiosity had gotten the better of him, and he spoke up. "Excuse me Queenie, do you mind if I ask you what's behind the other doors?"

"No, of course not," she began. "Some are living quarters for the older lady beetles; the one we just passed with the big S on it belongs to Scarlett. She's in charge of quality control at the factory." She paused in front of the WP door. "This is our wing polishing room. Come, have a peek," she said opening the door.

Crispin and Tiberius squeezed together and peered into the room. They saw a dozen or more ladybug beetles of various colors and sizes stretched out on wooden benches with their wings flared outwards. Other lady beetles in blue and white polka dotted aprons hovered over them rubbing their wings briskly with soft lambs ear leaves. A lady must always try to look her best," Queenie commented.

She closed the door and the group continued down the passageway. A short time later they stopped in front of another door marked AR. "This is the aroma room," she explained. "Inside, our chemists produce a body spray we wear when we go outside. We think it smells divine but a lot of our enemies think it stinks to high heaven so they won't even come near us!"

"It's sort of a defense mechanism then," Tiberius interjected.

"Exactly; let's see what's going on inside," Queenie said opening the door.

Inside were six very serious looking ladybug beetles in purple polka dotted aprons scurrying around carrying bowls and flasks. In the background several bubbling, steaming pots sat inside a glowing hearth. A sharp sweet acrid smell wafted out the door and stung Crispin and Tiberius' noses. Tiberius quickly pulled his head back.

"Ick!" Crispin moaned covering his nose.

One of the chemists close to the door peered over the top of her spectacles and came over to greet the inquisitive group. "Oh, Queenie: how are you? Can I help you," she inquired.

"No thank you Poppy, I was just showing our guests around. Carry on: and in case I haven't told you lately, you're all doing a great job."

"Thank you, thank you. We're happy to do what we can to help out the other girls," she replied smiling and straightening her apron. "Have you taken our guests to see our cake factory yet?" She added.

"No ma'am we're on our way there now," Crispin piped up.

Poppy giggled and patted Crispin's head. "Now there's something I haven't been called in a long time. How did you two happen to end up here anyway?"

"We came to see the Fern Queen for a map we need," Tiberius answered.

"Oh! A map. I see. You'll find that in the documents vault," Poppy offered.

"Yes, I'm taking them there after the factory tour," Queenie informed her.

"Right then," Poppy replied. "I better get back to work. Can't fall behind you know. Have a nice visit you two," she waved as Queenie closed the door.

Chapter 14
The Factory

The threesome continued on following a gentle downhill passageway for a short distance. Crispin and Tiberius soon caught a whiff of an unusual sweet, spicy aroma lingering in the air.

"Something smells delicious," Crispin exclaimed.

"We're getting close to the cake factory," Queenie said.

They halted at a highly polished knotty pine square door. The letters CF encircled with a fern wreath had been burned into it. Crispin and Tiberius didn't have to ask what the initial meant this time. They knew they stood for cake factory. Queenie pulled on its smooth hazelnut door knob and they filled through.

Crispin and Tiberius eyes' widened in amazement as they scanned the entry room. It was lit with a dozen or more crystals nestled inside a great hanging chandelier skillfully crafted from a collection of unusual translucent seed pods.

Hanging on the wall was a collection of paper birch signs painstakingly drawn with colorful messages. Queenie paused long enough for Crispin and Tiberius to read most of them. The largest sign was decorated in green and gold with the FQ fern encircled logo which read 'Home of the Renowned Aphid Cakes – Best in the Forest'.

A smaller sign to one side of the exit door with bright red letters stated 'All Employees Must Wash Legs Thoroughly Before Returning to Factory Floor'. Next to the message was a happy, grinning ladybug beetle clasping her sparkling legs together.

On the opposite side of the door hung a sign stating in purple letters 'No unauthorized personnel permitted beyond this point'. Along the other walls were groupings of signs showing various degrees of aging as evidenced by the faded colors on several. One triangular shaped sign depicted a very pale ladybug eating a round cake. It read 'FQ Cakes - When Only the Best Will Do'. Alongside of it was a round red and blue sign which simply stated 'Fern Queen Cakes - A Satisfying Winter Treat'.

The group approached the exit door, and when she opened it there was an annoying squeaking sound. "Better get that door oiled," Queenie muttered to herself as they entered the next room.

"Okay, here we are in the wardrobe room," their guide announced. Hanging on twig hooks were rows of lime green polka dotted aprons and shelves stocked with white mushroom looking hats. "Everyone entering the factory floor must wear a hat." Queenie stated grabbing several off the shelves. She put one on her head and handed the others to Crispin and Tiberius.

"Here's a size extra large for you Tiberius, and I think you will take a medium Crispin." Tiberius slipped on the strange hat and then helped Crispin who was struggling with the unaccustomed head wear.

"There, you look adorable," Tiberius teased.

"Thanks a lot Mr. Mushroom head," Crispin quipped back.

"Come on you two comedians," Queenie laughed. "There's a lot to see."

They left the wardrobe room and walked through a narrow passageway. Even before the group reached the factory floor they could hear strange noises echoing through the passageway. As they drew closer, the vague sounds resolved into a cadence of whistles, hissing, clanging, a 'thawump thawump' sound, and a symphony of other noises which blended into a continuous loud hum. The passageway stopped abruptly and opened into a large room brightly illuminated from shafts of light streaming down through an old four pane windowed ceiling. Queenie paused and let Crispin and Tiberius take in the view.

The factory floor was long and rectangular, with hundreds of polka dotted apron'd and mushroom hatted ladybug beetles manning strange machinery and devices. Cogs, belts, ropes, pulleys and paddles squeaked, wheezed, clicked, clacked and whistled in an industrious rhythm. Gauzy clouds of hissing steam and belches of colored smoke bathed the room in a sweet smelling, floating haze.

"First we'll stop at the power station so you can see how we generate energy to run our machines," Queenie explained. She led them to a door at one end of the factory floor with a sign featuring a lady beetle thrusting a very muscular arm upwards. Underneath were the words '*Lady Bug Power*'.

Inside, dozens of ladybugs wearing green polka doted bands across their foreheads, and unusual lace up shoes, were working feverishly at their stations. Some of the strangest contraptions Crispin and Tiberius had ever seen were whirling, spinning, pulling, bouncing, springing and rocking.

"This is incredibly unbelievable," Tiberius commented. "I've never seen anything like this before."

"It's out of this world," Crispin added.

Queenie chuckled and said, "No. I don't imagine you have. We pride ourselves on having the most modern and up to date factory. Would you like to take a closer look?" The visitors nodded excitedly.

The first place they stopped consisted of six round cages on spindles all in a row. Each one held an energetic ladybug who was running, causing the cage to spin. They moved to the next station where the ladies jumped up and down on bouncy round platforms, engaging a set of springs which lay coiled beneath the strange device. They waved cheerfully to the visitors as they bounced up and down.

The next industrious group pushed a huge wooden spoked drum in circles causing a round shaft to turn engaging a rubbery black belt.

The last station they visited consisted of four chairs, each having a thin spoked wheel and a set of pedals. Ladybugs with bulging legs sat pedaling at lightning speed, sending sparks flying into clear boxes filled with bubbling water.

Suddenly a whistle blew and more workers dressed in the same attire rushed in and stood next to each station. The workers driving the generators very quickly stopped and their replacements deftly took over. The change over was timed so perfectly the generator mechanisms hardly missed a beat, and continued churning out power.

"Amazing," Tiberius commented. "How often do they have shift change?"

"Quite often," Queenie began. "We have six groups of power ladies. They're all very strong, but we don't want to over work any of them. And let me tell you these gals can really eat," she added with a chuckle.

"Well, they're in the right place to get food," Crispin said.

"We're all very proud of our power ladies," Queenie stated. "We would have a pretty rough time running the factory without them. Of course, all the workers in the factory are important. I guess you could say it's a team effort; so, what do you say we go meet some of the others?" She added leading her charges back through the door.

They followed her to the far end of the factory floor where ladybugs scurried about; carrying rough woven sacks, filled with leaves. They took turns emptying the leaves into a large steaming kettle.

One of the workers with a very plump cheerful face sat her sack down and approached the group. "Hello Queenie. What have we here - visitors?" She asked.

"Yes. I'd like you to meet Crispin and Tiberius," she said touching a foreleg on their shoulders.

"Nice to meet you both," she said executing a crisp curtsey.

"This is Cherry. She's in charge of the juice extractor department," Queenie said.

Crispin and Tiberius nodded their heads politely. "Would you like to explain what's done in your department?" Queenie asked.

"I would be glad to," she replied, gesturing toward the sack carriers. "We start the juice extraction process by collecting these sacks of leaves with aphids on them which are brought to us by the ladies out on aphid patrol." She moved the group over to a large white enameled vat full of water being agitated by three fin shaped blades attached to a cylinder. Crispin and Tiberius peered in at the mat of green leaves being sloshed back and forth. The machine clicked twice and the agitator stopped.

"Next the water will drain out filtering the tiny aphids," Cherry pointed to a clear hose attached to the vat's underside. "They will be collected and pumped through the hose to the next station for further processing," she went on. "The leaves stay here where they are boiled." Cherry maneuvered the group to a large bubbling kettle where several workers prodded the stewing leaves with long wooden spoons.

"After they boil for the required time, we transfer them to a barrel press where the juice is squeezed out. It's this way," Cherry said as she led the group to it.

They stopped in front of a large metal banded barrel like gizmo with a small set of stairs leading to its brim. Several ladybugs carrying oil cans scurried up the stairs and oiled a belt driven wheel perched on top of the juice press. They ran back down the stairs and another group of workers carrying baskets of boiled leaves went up and dumped their cargo into the press. After the workers descended the stairs, someone yelled out "All clear!" A worker nearby, rushed over and threw a lever on the barrel's side and the wheel began a slow squeaking rotation.

"Keep an eye on the spigot," Cherry indicated, pointing to a brass tube protruding from the machine's base. A green liquid came trickling out and was deposited into a bucket below the spigot. "We store the plant juice until the stink bug boys come to collect it," Cherry added.

Queenie stepped up and patted Cherry on the shoulder. "Thank you," she said. "You've been a great guide. Keep up the good work."

"Yes, thank you. This is all so amazing," Tiberius commented.

"All right you two; let's move on to the batter assembly station," Queenie said gesturing in its direction.

They followed along side a clear hose with a pale green clumpy solution flowing through it until they came to a round sign with a button stating in red letters 'Batter Assembly Station: Ring for Assistance'. Queenie pushed the button, and a loud buzzing announced their arrival.

Almost immediately a large strong looking ladybug with an up turned nose and an abundance of wing spots appeared and greeted them in a loud raspy voice. "Hello. Hello, Queenie. How are you today? I see you have brought us some guests."

"Yes. This is Crispin and Tiberius," Queenie replied.

"Pleased to meet you boys, I'm Rosy. I'm the boss here at the batter assembly station," she said extending a foreleg.

"Perhaps you could show our visitors what you do here Rosy," Queenie said.

"Be glad to. Come right this way," Rosy replied as she moved the group past the sign and led them to the base of a chestnut shell mixing vat. Seven flat top petrified mushroom footstools encircled the vat's base and Rosy had Crispin and Tiberius step up to look inside.

Peering over the side, they saw four thin rod shaped wooden blades affixed to the bottom of the bowl, and the clear tube they had passed earlier went up and over its rim.

While elevated on the footstools, they got a good view of the surrounding work area. On nearby shelves were baskets and bottles holding various colored powders and strange looking seeds with wooden spoons and scoops hanging neatly on pegs above them.

"Okay. Here's where the batter assembly process starts," Rosy began as she patted the mixing vat's base. "The clean filtered aphids will be pumped through the hose and deposited into the mixing vat where they will be combined with other ingredients." Rosy gestured to the baskets and bottles behind them. "Unfortunately, some of them are secret, so I can't tell you what they are," she explained with a teasing wink. "But it's pretty obvious by the smell in here that one of them is honey."

"We're not mixing right now because my ladies are on a break, but if you can come back...well, by golly!" She exclaimed, "Here they come now. I guess break time ended early today."

Crispin and Tiberius stepped off the footstools and Rosy guided them safely away from the machine as the returning workers began opening the bottles and measuring out the powders and seedy looking substances into the baskets. They carried their baskets back to the mixing vat, climbed up onto the footstools, and poured the ingredients in. After repeating the tasks several times, one of the ladybugs called out, "Rosie, we're ready for the next batch."

Rosie scurried over and pushed a lever at the vat's base. There was a low humming sound and the green aphid solution shot out of the tube into the mixer. The machine clicked twice, and the solution stopped. Almost immediately the blades began to whirl, followed by a sharp liquidy 'slap-slap' sound.

Queenie appeared with two wooden boxes for Crispin and Tiberius to stand on, so they could get a better view. Now they could see the lumpy greenish yellow mixture being mashed and slung against the bowl's sides, transforming it into a smooth satiny batter. There was another series of clicks, and suddenly the machine stopped.

"The batter is now ready to be transferred to the next station," Rosie informed them. She led the group onward, stopping next to a thin white pipe connecting the mixing vat to a long thin wooden table. Ladybug workers wearing clean white mitts stood lined up on both sides of the table, poised for action.

"The dough will now pass through the extruder pipe and be deposited for further processing," Rosie explained. "I'll turn this next part of the tour over to Ruby who's in charge of the cutting and stamping department," she added.

Queenie shot her a warm smile and said. "We appreciate you taking the time to show us around your station. You're all doing a wonderful job."

"Thank you," Rosy said. "I hope you enjoy the rest of the tour. They'll be extruding the dough shortly. You won't want to miss that," she added as she headed back to her station with a wave.

"Wonderful," Queenie said. "Let's go find Ruby, shall we? Oh, there she is now. You can't miss Ruby. She has an unusually dark red body. That's how she got her name you know," Queenie added.

Crispin and Tiberius hurried after Queenie as she headed towards a cluster of ladybugs standing next to the white extruder pipe. "Ruby, how are you," Queenie said.

"I'm great," Ruby replied. "But my extruder machine seems to be malfunctioning."

"Well now, perhaps I can help. What seems to be the problem," Queenie asked.

"There doesn't seem to be any power," Ruby replied.

Just then, the factory became very quiet and there were several shouts of 'NO POWER!' "I'll go see what's wrong," Queenie said as she scurried off towards the power station.

While she was gone, Tiberius whispered to Crispin, "I didn't expect this to take so long. I hope we're almost at the end of the tour. We need to get the map soon."

Queenie quickly re-appeared, and announced loudly "You all should have power now, everything's been taken care of." A collective shout of 'Hooray' rippled through the factory floor. She then rejoined the group at the extruder pipe.

"Well, what happened," Ruby questioned.

As Queenie began to explain, Tiberius glanced over at Crispin and rolled his eyes impatiently. "It seems a wolf spider sneaked in through a wall crack and scared all the power ladies out of their wits and right off their machines. It was pandemonium for a while."

"I can imagine. Eeek! A wolf spider! I'd run too," Ruby said cringing. "They ran him off, right," she added nervously.

"Oh yes, he's long gone," Queenie said. "Marigold threw a bottle of our body repellent perfume at him, and after he got a good whiff they heard him yell, 'Oh my...Phew, I'm outa here!'"

"Good riddance too," a group of nearby workers chanted all nodding their heads.

"Now that the spider problem is solved, let's see if we have power," Ruby stated.

She turned a knob and the extruder pipe began to hum and vibrate. It wasn't long before a thin rope of dough began to snake its way out of the extruder and crawl along the cutting table. "Here's where our job really starts," Ruby announced.

Crispin and Tiberius watched fascinated as the first group of workers grabbed the serpentine length of dough and sliced it into discs. The small smooth dough circles were then shuffled down the table to the next group who lined them up and mashed a small wooden block stamp into their surface. After stamping, the workers farther down the line took the dough discs and placed them in tight flat rows on round stone pans. The tour group moved and was now standing next to a huge stone fireplace at the table's end.

"Here's the next step in the process," Ruby began. "The cakes will bake over a low temperature fire until they are golden brown and delightfully crunchy. It looks like there's a batch ready to go in now," she announced.

Workers outfitted with thick padded gray mitts placed the cake covered pans onto long handled wooden paddles. They slowly approached the fireplace mouth and shoved the paddles into it. With one quick thrust they slid their paddles back out leaving the pans sitting on a platform suspended above a mound of crackling logs.

"This is where my job ends," Ruby said. "The wrapping and boxing department takes over from here. You've been a great group, and we hope to see you back again soon," Ruby said. "I must be getting back to my workers."

"Well," Queenie stated. "We're getting towards the end of the process. Let's go see the finished product."

The group made their way around the opposite side of the fireplace and watched as workers with similar paddles removed the cake pans from the hearth. Queenie spotted someone; waved, and a bright orange ladybug wearing a fuchsia pink flower necklace rushed over. "Hello Sunny," Queenie greeted her. "Would you mind showing my friends Crispin and Tiberius the wrapping and boxing department?"

"Hi, fellas. I would love to show you around," Sunny replied with a bubbly giggle. "Just follow me."

As the group continued on, Queenie leaned in towards Sunny and began talking. "Where did you get that stunning necklace," she asked.

Sunny giggled again and explained, "Wyatt gave it to me when the boys came to get their rations." Crispin and Tiberius both rolled their eyes and shook their heads when Queenie wasn't looking.

"Oh yes, Wyatt." Queenie said. "He's the really quiet one isn't he?"

"Yes, that's him," Sunny replied sheepishly. "I think he's kind of cute though."

"But that smell they make some times...Phew," Queenie said waving a foreleg in the air.

"Well we all have our little problems, don't we," Sunny said with an understanding smile.

They finally stopped in front of a large round rotating table full of jostling cakes. After several rotations, the cakes were funneled into a narrow chute. They slid downward and came to rest on a table where gloved workers sifted through them.

"Our lovely ladies will first inspect the cakes for imperfections," Sunny explained. "The rejects are eaten right away. The energy ladies get quite a lot of them, but we usually have enough so everyone in the factory gets a treat now and then. The ones that pass inspection are then sent to the wrappers." They moved on down the table, and paused to watch.

A wrapper took a large soft sycamore leaf from a pile and wrapped the cake by rolling and tucking the leaf edges inside. She then passed it around to a coworker who tied it snugly with a fuzzy rough vine and she finished it with a tiny loop bow.

"Here's the final step in the cake's processing," Sunny announced as they moved past the wrappers.

They watched as the last group of workers arranged the cakes in orderly rows inside paper birch boxes bearing the inscription 'Fern Queen Cakes – Factory Fresh'.

"Well, there you have it the entire process from start to finish. What do you think of our little factory," Queenie asked.

"It's simply incredible. What an operation. I can see why you're proud of it," Tiberius replied.

"I love this place," Crispin exclaimed. "It's fantabulious."

"I'm glad you liked it," Queenie added. "I think Sunny has something for you. A little souvenir," she added.

Sunny strolled up carrying two of the cake boxes. "We didn't want you to leave without a sample of our wares she said handing the boxes to them."

"Thank you very much," Tiberius responded.

"Yeess, thank you," Crispin added a little warily.

"Oh don't worry you two," Queenie chuckled. "These are the same cakes the stink bug boys eat. They don't like aphids much either. They're just plain honey cakes."

Crispin's eyes lighted up, "Oh yummy, I love honey. I bet these are the best cakes ever."

"Of course they are," she said, then turned to Sunny. "Thank you for all your help. I hope you saved some honey cakes for Wyatt," she said with a playful wink.

"Oh Queenie, hush. You don't want to start rumors," Sunny said as she waved 'Good bye' and turned to leave.

"Where do the cakes go after they're boxed," Tiberius asked.

"They go downstairs into cold storage where they stay until we need them when food is scarce," Queenie explained.

"And they stay fresh," Crispin wanted to know.

"Yes," she replied. "Somehow, the sycamore leaves preserve them. I would take you down there, but I'm afraid the cold would make you sick. Why don't I take you to the documents vault, and we can look for that map you're after?"

"That's sounds great," Tiberius said, relieved that she hadn't forgotten about it.

Chapter 15
Queenie's Map

Crispin and Tiberius, with their scrumptious souvenirs tucked under their wings, followed Queenie through a nearby door and down a short tunnel until they came to a door inscribed with the letters DV.

"Well, here we are – documents vault." Queenie announced as she manipulated a complicated puzzle like door latch. After a few clicks and a rasping noise she pulled on the door knob, and it opened.

Crispin glanced over at Tiberius who had a look on his face which could only be translated as; 'Finally – it's about time'. They crossed the threshold, and a musty un-aired odor met them. Crispin and Tiberius surveyed the room, which was lit by a small crystal filled walnut lantern perched on a sideboard with two smooth rock stools on each side. Stacks of dust covered paper birch boxes marked with indecipherable letter groupings stood against the gray slate walls.

Queenie crept from one stack to another occasionally peering into a box to inspect its contents. "Now, I know it's here somewhere. It's been a long time since we had any use for that map," Queenie said scratching her head as if it would help her remember. "Please, just give me a few minutes. I'll eventually find it. I know you must be growing impatient - you've traveled such a great distance," she kept talking, but it became muffled as she disappeared behind a skyscraper of musty boxes.

Crispin and Tiberius resigned to waiting sat on the rock stools. Suddenly, Crispin bolted upright and patted his vest. Tiberius, startled, turned and looked at Crispin. The two friends' eyes widened as they were struck with the same thought.

"The stone," Tiberius whispered excitedly. "Have you still got it?"

"Yes, it's still in my hidden pocket," Crispin replied in a low, relieved voice.

"I forgot all about it," Tiberius confessed.

"So did I," Crispin added. "What should we do? The Fern Queen is giving us a copy of the map without asking for anything in return."

"Yes," Tiberius began. "And we were supposed to use the stone in exchange for information about the Gorboos which we didn't get."

Crispin fondled the tiny box in his vest and then said thoughtfully, "We could keep the stone and return home with it and the crystals. Not only would the village have new crystals, but they would have their treasure back too."

There was a momentary silence and then Tiberius whispered back, "Hmm, yes, we could do that but our mission was to give it to the Fern Queen and she is giving us a copy of their map. I think we should fulfill our promise to the council elders and at least offer it to her."

Crispin contemplated this momentarily and finally replied, "You're right of course. I wouldn't feel right otherwise. I'm just glad we remembered before it was too late."

"Good, I was hoping you would say that," Tiberius said, sounding relieved. "We'll give her the stone after she finds the map."

The quiet discussion ended when a muffled 'TA DA' escaped from among the files. Queenie reappeared somewhat dusty and disheveled carrying a framed object and a scroll in her front legs. "Well, here it is. The long awaited map and a copy for you. They had been misfiled just as I feared. The original map had been stuffed into a box of other forgotten documents." She blew on it and a gray cloud of dust dissipated into the stale air. "I'm afraid it's seen better days." She examined the framed map reverently, tracing a front leg over its surface, and went on. "This is really quite irresponsible, shoving an important document like this into a dark corner. The survival of our community might one day depend on this map. From now on I'm going to make sure it's properly cared for."

She glanced back at Crispin and Tiberius with an expectant smile. "Let's go back to my quarters so we can examine the map more closely."

"That sounds like a good idea," Tiberius responded.

"And I'm going to sample these yummy smelling honey cakes while we're at it." Crispin piped up sniffing his gift box.

When they returned to Queenie's chambers, nothing had changed except for the fire in the hearth which had been rekindled. Winthrope was still snoozing under his rock and their food bowls with a few left over morsels were right where they had left them. Queenie gestured towards the pillows. "Have a seat. I'll be back faster than a bee's wing. Oh, and get your map out while I'm gone." She added disappearing into an adjoining room.

The two friends plopped onto their billowy pillows, glad for a rest after their hike through the cake factory. Crispin reached into his vest and retrieved the councils' map and the seed pod box.

"We better give her the stone as soon as she comes back, and I think you should present it since it's from your village," Tiberius suggested.

"Yes. I can't stand the suspense any longer," Crispin replied.

Tiberius gave him a quizzical look. "What? You mean, giving her the stone?"

Crispin laughed and rattled his cake box. "No, I mean trying these. The aroma is driving me crazy."

Tiberius groaned and rolled his eyes. "Okay wise guy, open the box, and let's try one." Crispin untied the cake package; removed one of the goodies, and inspected it carefully. The cake was golden brown, and soft, with the FQ fern encircled logo stamped into its surface. He took a bite and offered one to Tiberius who quickly gobbled it down, smacking his lips.

"Wow, these are delicious," Crispin gushed. "And so fresh: the honey tastes like it just came from the hive."

Tiberius was enjoying his second cake when Queenie returned carrying a similar white pillow. "Good, I see you're enjoying our wares." She dropped her pillow beside her guests, folded her delicate black legs under her body and sat down.

"Yes, and they are marvelous," Tiberius said.

"They're the best I've ever tasted," Crispin mumbled through a mouthful of crumbs.

A proud smile crossed Queenie's face. "Of course. We only make the best here at our cake factory. All right," she continued. "Let's get down to this map reading business, shall we. I'm sure you two are anxious to get a look at my map." She laid the rolled up document between them.

Tiberius cleared his throat loudly then spoke. "Before we start, there is something we would like to give you." Crispin held out the box, and set it gently in front of her. "This is a gift from my village for all the help you've given us."

Queenie hesitated, took the box, untied it, and pulled the two halves apart. A gasp escaped her lips as the blue stone glittered back.

"It is one of the most precious treasures of Dragonfly Landing. They call it; 'The Heart of the Sky'," Crispin explained

After hearing the story of how the stone got its name, she removed it gingerly from its cradle, and held it up to the lantern light, admiring it from every angle. After what seemed like an eternal silence, she let out a sigh, returned the stone to its nest, and handed it back to Crispin. "I'm very flattered, but I couldn't possibly accept such a grand gift, especially one as important as this one." She hesitated thoughtfully. "You did say it was a valuable treasure to your village."

Crispin and Tiberius glanced nervously at each other, not quite knowing how to respond. The council elders had painted quite a different picture of the Fern Queen: one in which she wasn't quite as gracious. There was an awkward moment of silence, and finally Tiberius spoke. "But our mission was to find you, and exchange this stone for the map, and other information you might have."

Queenie shifted nervously on her pillow. "Yes, I understand your position, but let me explain something. I'm an ordinary ladybug with an ordinary life." She gestured around the room, and shrugged modestly. "Do you see any crowns, or jewel encrusted scepters. I would have to hire a guard to protect it, and I don't mean you know who." She pointed to the snoozing sow bug in the corner. "No, I won't take it," she added softly. "You should take it back where it belongs."

"But, but what about our mission," Crispin stammered.

"I'm so sorry," Queenie smiled wistfully; "But look on the bright side. You've only partly failed. I did give you the map. Unfortunately, as you already know, I can't help with the other information."

Tiberius rubbed a foreleg across his face in defeat and smiled sheepishly. "Then there's nothing we can say to change your mind?"

"Nothing." She hesitated a moment and added. "There is one thing you can do for me." The two friends nodded and sat up attentively as she continued. "The whole ladybug community will be grateful if you could send back any relevant information you collect about the cave and these mysterious Gorboo creatures. I'm sure it will come in handy sooner or later when we need to replace our lights."

"Of course," Tiberius replied, "We'll move heaven and earth to get the information back to you."

Crispin returned the seed pod case to his hidden pocket, and said with a beaming face, "My village will always be in your debt."

"Good, now back to the business at hand," she announced. "May I see your map?"

"Of course," Crispin replied handing the document to her.

Queenie reached to one side of her pillow and retrieved the copy of her map and put on a pair of silver rimmed spectacles which made her eyes look huge and owlish. "I don't want to handle the original map too much," she continued. "It's very fragile and I can feel its frame loosening, but you two can examine it while I'm studying the others." She placed it in front of her guests and they leaned into the lantern light for a better view. They were excited to finally get a look at the document they had risked life and limb for.

It was slightly smaller than theirs and its crinkled amber blotched surface made it look much older. The map's center was adorned with a faded maroon colored compass rose consisting of two double pointed crossed arrows indicating North, South, East, and West.

The script flanking the map's features was strange and indecipherable, but several of the symbols stood unmistakably for mountains, trees, and bodies of water. A pale blue line sliced diagonally from one corner of the document to the other obviously symbolizing a river. It made only one sharp curve in its course, jostling to one side of the compass rose. At the top of the map and slightly to one side of the river sat a row of gray peaked drawings standing like sentinels, guarding a line of green filigreed drawings at their feet.

"I bet these are the Teepee Mountains with the Fern Forest below," Crispin pointed out.

Tiberius shook his head in agreement. "I'm sure you guessed that one right," he traced the blue line. "And this is obviously a river, but some of the other drawings..." he hesitated, shaking his head. "It's hard to say. I really wouldn't want to guess."

Queenie; after shuffling and studying the maps intensely peered over the top of her spectacles. "I hadn't realized how far you two have traveled. You have had quite the journey: and it's not over, is it?"

She sighed wistfully and laid the maps down side by side. "It would be fun to go on an exciting adventure, but I'm a little too old for that now."

"It hasn't all been fun," Crispin declared. "Some of it like almost getting digested by a pitcher plant; was downright horrible."

Tiberius nodded. "And there were several other incidents we could have done without as well, but," he quickly added, "I wouldn't have missed meeting the gypsy moths for all the nectar in the world." Crispin smiled, thinking to himself that Tiberius was probably remembering the time he spent with Maleva.

Queenie stretched and repositioned her legs on her pillow. "Well, I think you should both be very proud of what you've accomplished."

"Thank you," they chorused.

She laid a leg on the maps and went on. "After studying both maps, I've determined how they match up. It really wasn't hard. The symbols for the Teepee Mountains are similar on both." She indicated the area of peaked symbols. "Of course some of the markings on your map are a bit unusual and I'm sure you've found the same true with our map..." The pair nodded empathically. "Which isn't surprising since they were made by different cartographers."

Crispin and Tiberius shot each other a puzzled look. "A cart... what," Tiberius asked.

She laughed, a little bit embarrassed, and explained, "A cartographer is just a big word for someone who makes maps."

"AAAh," they exclaimed, mumbling the new word under their breath. "I guess you're never too old to learn another word," Tiberius stated.

Queenie readjusted her spectacles and turned her attention back to the maps. "Okay, we are here," she pointed at the peaked symbols which converged on the borders of each map. "And this is where you want to end up." She traced her leg across her map and stopped at a drawing at the far edge.

Crispin and Tiberius leaned in for a closer look. It was a black, half moon shaped drawing with slender dagger shaped objects hanging underneath it.

"This is the Devil's Gullet Cave," Queenie announced. "Since I assume you'll be flying most of the time -" She hesitated and glanced up at Crispin and Tiberius who nodded. "Let me show you the best route to take and the landmarks you will see from the air." She pointed to the blue line at the top of her map, "This is the Triton River, and if you follow it south," she slid her leg along its length. "It will take you directly to the cave. In fact, it will take you into the cave since it flows through it."

Crispin touched the strange script alongside the river. "Does this say Triton River?"

"Yes," Queenie answered. "It's written in Coccinelliese, the ancient language of the ladybug beetles. It's obvious we don't use it any more." She picked up Crispin's box of cakes, pointing to the writing on it.

She smiled and continued her instructions. "After you leave the fern forest, the first obvious landmark you will see is Stag Mountain." She moved her front leg to the left of the river and stopped on a large brown double peaked drawing surrounded by tiny green squiggles.

"You can't miss it," Queenie instructed. "Stag mountain stands alone surrounded by the great kudzu forest. It's very large and has two sharp peaks which resemble a pair of horns."

She traced the river and continued, "Now; as you move southwards, look to the west and you should see Hoot 'n Hollow." She stopped at a strange symbol which resembled a branched tree.

"That's a funny name," Crispin commented. "It sounds like owls live there."

"They do," Queenie replied. "Lots of them. It's also home to the famously unusual topsy-turvy mushrooms." She tapped a spot on the branch symbol. The two friends had to squint to see the tiny orange balls dangling below one of the limbs.

"Very curious," Tiberius observed. "Why do they call them topsy-turvy."

"I've heard they grow upside down," Queenie explained.

Crispin sat up with a start. "What! Upside down! I'd sure like to see that."

Queenie threw her head back and laughed at Crispin's youthful exuberance. "Well, if you decide to stop for a look, be sure to do it during the day, when the owls are asleep. It probably gets pretty wild at night with all that hooting and hollering going on."

She laughed again louder at her own joke and Crispin and Tiberius couldn't help but join in. They finally settled down, and Queenie went on with her directions. "Where were we now? Oh yes, after passing Hoot 'n Hollow, you'll pass by the Last Stop Sinkhole on the east side of the Triton." She pointed to a black spiraling circle and went on. "It will look like a deep dark hole from the air."

"What exactly is a sinkhole," Crispin asked.

"It's a spot in the earth where the roof of a cave has collapsed. They can be very deep and dangerous."

"Why is it called the Last Stop Sinkhole?" Crispin wondered out loud.

"Think about it," Tiberius said with a wink.

Suddenly Crispin's eyes widened. "Ooooh!" He exclaimed, "We'll be sure to admire that landmark from the sky."

"Probably a wise thing to do," Queenie recommended. She moved on down the map. "Next; you will see off to the west, Dancing Fish Lake." She indicated a large circular blue feature with fish symbols inside.

"Those must be very talented fish," Crispin pointed out.

Queenie smiled and replied, "I've heard the lake is filled with great schools of golden perch which jump out of the water and scoot around on their tails. It must be an incredible thing to see."

Crispin squirmed excitedly on his pillow. "I hope we can catch one of their performances as we fly over."

"Maybe you'll get lucky," Queenie suggested winking at Crispin. "Just be sure to keep your altitude up. You don't want to be the main course."

"Okay," Queenie went on. "Here is the last landmark before the cave," she said tracing along the Triton River. She stopped at a pale green rectangular area with several brown squiggly lines inside. "This is Annelid Valley."

Tiberius scratched an antenna and furrowed his brow. "I think I've heard that word before." He muttered it several times. "Oh yes, isn't that another name for earthworms?"

"Yes," Queenie chuckled. "It is. The valley is just crawling with the slimy fellows and the underground is riddled with tunnels. That's another place that's crazy at night. I wouldn't recommend stopping in there either, if you need a good night's sleep. The dirt really flies when they're excavating. Now," she continued, "from there it's only a stone's throw from the cave entrance." She moved her leg over to the arched symbol.

"What are those sharp pointy objects?" Crispin asked. "They look scary, sort of like fangs."

"Oh, those," Queenie began to explain. "They're supposed to represent cave formations. Stalactites or stalagmites I would imagine."

"I've never been in a cave before," Crispin said.

"Neither have I," Tiberius added.

"I was in one when I was younger," she began. "I flew in there to get out of a hail storm. It was pitch black and filled with bizarre formations that looked like stone icicles. Some of them were so beautiful they took my breath away." Suddenly Crispin and Tiberius looked uneasy and shifted nervously on their pillows. "Is something wrong," Queenie asked.

"It's the pitch black part which has us worried," Tiberius began. "We don't have lanterns with us."

"Don't concern yourself about that," she reassured them, "we will be happy to donate a couple of ours."

"We'd be ever so grateful," Tiberius replied.

She pointed back to the black spiraled disk and continued. "The Last Stop sinkhole could be a part of the cave. There might be a huge connecting cave system in this area. Heaven knows we certainly have enough limestone for it."

Tiberius eyes widened. "Were those sparkling white rock we passed on our way here limestone?"

"Yes," she answered. "They fell during a landslide on the Teepee Mountain range."

Crispin stifled a yawn, but its effects were contagious and soon a string of yawns overtook the group.

"It's getting late," Queenie announced, "and I've shown you just about everything I can about the map."

"I can't believe how much you know about the world outside your town," Tiberius stated.

"Well," Queenie explained. "I flew with my parents to many places in my younger days and by the time you get to be my age you've learned a lot just by talking to others. In fact you're never too old to learn new things. Why just think of all the new things I've learned since meeting you two. There are gypsy moths, scented rainbows, the Woods of Forgetfulness, and...." she lay a foreleg on the map, "most importantly, I've learned more about the world outside my home."

She removed her spectacles and smiled at Crispin. "You should never miss an opportunity to learn new things. It's what makes life interesting."

"Yes ma'am," Crispin replied his eyelids fluttering sleepily.

"Now," she continued, folding the maps. "Tuck these away safely in that cute little vest of yours and I'll show you where you can sleep for tonight."

Crispin placed the maps into his hidden pocket, and they followed Queenie back into the tunnel.

"We have a nice comfortable room prepared for you," Queenie announced as they walked. "It's not far, in fact, we're here all ready."

They halted in front of a door marked SR. Crispin and Tiberius were curious about what it stood for but right now all they cared about was a nice soft place to sleep.

Then Queenie said. "Oh, In case you're wondering; SR stands for spare room."

"Ooooh." They both exclaimed trying to act interested.

She opened the round door and they entered into a room which looked similar to Queenie's but smaller. There was a warm cozy fire blazing in the hearth with two glowing lanterns on its mantle. The room was also furnished with two nutshell chairs against a square bark table and a collection of assorted size pillows in one corner. On the walls were several faded paintings which reminded Crispin and Tiberius of the advertisement signs in the cake factory. Most of them were flowers, but one was a portrait of a young ladybug resembling Queenie.

Crispin crossed the room to the portrait. "Is this you Queenie," he asked.

"Hruumph," she snorted. "I'd forgotten that old picture of me was in here."

She came over and inspected it. "Yep, that's me in my younger days. I don't know what possessed them to hang it in here. They probably didn't know what else to do with it." She laughed, "I hope you can sleep with that thing staring down at you."

"I think you were quite lovely," Tiberius commented: then added, "of course, you still are."

Queenie glanced at Crispin and chuckled, "You could learn a few things about flattery from this guy."

She headed towards the door and added, "If you need anything, just ask Winthrope for it. He'll be awake most of the night on door duty."

After Queenie left, they sorted through the mountain of pillows, selected two cuddly green ones and placed them close to the fireplace. Tiberius pulled the lantern covers down dimming the crystals, and soon the two exhausted travelers were sound asleep.

Chapter 16
A Disturbing Night

A sharp rapping noise startled them from their sleep and they realized it was morning. Then they heard a tiny muffled voice outside the door. "Hello. Good morning, I'm the maid. Are you awake in there?"

Tiberius was still rubbing the sleep from his eyes when he answered the door. "Oh hello," he said staring at a ladybug in a yellow dotted apron carrying a tray.

She flashed a warm smile and announced, "I'm Sunflower; the maid. I have your breakfast if you're ready for it."

Tiberius looked over at Crispin, "Are you hungry yet?"

"I'm starving," he answered.

Sunflower bustled into the room and placed the tray on the table. It held a large bowl and two cups. "I hope you like buckwheat pods," she said cheerfully. "They just came out of the oven too. They're maaaaarvelous, and very nutritious."

The two friends sat and sniffed the bowl of glistening pods which had a sweet earthy aroma. Tiberius popped one in his mouth and chewed it. Then Crispin did the same. "Yum! These are excellent," Tiberius exclaimed.

"I really like them too," Crispin added.

A satisfied smile crossed Sunflower's face. "Is this your first time to eat buckwheat pods," she asked. They both nodded. "Well, enjoy them, and then when you're ready, Queenie would like to see you before you leave."

Tiberius gulped and replied, "Thank you for breakfast Sunflower."

"My pleasure," she said hustling out the door.

They quickly made the large bowl of pods disappear, and washed it down with cups of cool sparkling spring water. Tiberius pushed away from the table. "Well; we better find Queenie and say good bye."

"Yes, it's a very interesting place with yummy food but we need to be on our way," Crispin added.

They collected their belongings and started down the tunnel towards Queenie's chambers. The passageway was crowded compared to the night before with ladybugs in their multi-hued dotted aprons scurrying to their various work places.

Sunny and a group of other factory workers stopped when they saw Crispin and Tiberius. "Good Morning," Sunny greeted them. "Good luck on your journey. It was all the talk last night. It went through Lady Bug Town like a wildfire. Everyone thinks you're just peachy!" She glanced over at Crispin. "And you're adorable in that sweet little vest!" She reached out and tweaked him on the cheek. Crispin grimaced and squirmed causing the other factory workers to giggle.

"We're on our way to find Queenie to say good-bye," Tiberius announced in hopes of rescuing Crispin from his ardent admirers.

"You're in luck then," Sunny sang out, "She's already at the factory and we're heading that way ourselves. Let's go together."

Tiberius could tell by the pleading look on Crispin's face that he wanted to run the other direction but he saw no way out if they wanted to see Queenie any time soon.

"Wonderful idea," Tiberius said, and then glanced apologetically at Crispin. He mercifully placed himself between Sunny and Crispin as the group continued down the passage way. As luck would have it, they hadn't gone far when Queenie was spotted standing by the aroma room door. She waved, and motioned for them to come over.

"Ah, I was just looking for you. I didn't want you to come all the way to the factory to find me. I hope your breakfast was enjoyable."

"Yes, thank you, it was great," Tiberius answered.

"We had buckwheat pods, and they were yummy," Crispin chimed in.

Queenie giggled and patted his shoulder. "Well, I'm so glad you liked them. I guess you're anxious to be on your way then."

"Yes. We need to leave soon," Tiberius replied.

"Then let me walk you to the entrance," she offered.

Much to Crispin's relief, they bid farewell to Sunny and the other ladies and headed back towards the entrance at a leisurely stroll. When the threesome arrived, the sun was streaming through the ivy framed entrance, and the unaccustomed brightness made them wince as they crept down the stone steps. They paused on the last one to say good-bye.

Tiberius turned to Queenie and smiled warmly. "We can't thank you enough for the help, and your hospitality was..." He hesitated and cleared his throat. "Well, we didn't expect such a warm welcome. We did drop in unannounced."

"Nonsense," Queenie snorted. "It doesn't matter at all. You'll always be welcomed at Lady Bug Town, and I've really enjoyed your company. It's been a nice diversion from my daily routine. Now, you two better be on your way." She gave Tiberius a hug, and Crispin, a peck on the cheek. "When you get back to Dragonfly Landing, be sure to spread the word about Fern Queen Cakes. We ship you know."

"Wouldn't they be stale by the time they got there," Crispin asked.

"Oh no," she explained. "We use the snail express."

Crispin and Tiberius shot each other a puzzled look.

"What?" She replied incredulously, "You've never heard of it? I thought everyone knew about the twelve legged double shelled mountain snail. They're only the fastest and most rugged snail on earth!"

"They have two shells?" Tiberius asked rubbing his jaw.

"Yes," Queenie responded. "And the dip between their two shells is perfect for strapping cargo into." She laughed and added, "I'll send something your way one day, so don't be surprised when the snail express shows up on your doorstep."

"That would be fantabulous," said Crispin gleefully.

"Well, we really must be going now," Tiberius stated as he picked up his food pack.

Crispin scrambled onto his ride and secured the packs as Queenie watched in fascination. "This is certainly a first for me. A lightning bug hitching a ride on a luna moth, and I thought I had seen it all." She threw her head back and giggled. "Boy was I wrong!"

By this time, the two visitors had drawn a large crowd of curious spectators, and a murmur of excitement rose from the crowd of well-wishers as Tiberius spread his shimmery wings for take off.

"Have a safe journey," Queenie shouted.

Tiberius caught a gentle updraft, and rode it skyward. They waved a final farewell to their new friends and watched as Lady Bug Town dissolved into a soft green haze.

Once they had gained altitude, Tiberius banked gently southward, in search of the Triton River. Off in the distance, the majestic Teepee Mountains slowly miniaturized into a string of sparkling points. Below, lay a huge expanse of dense forest with groves of pines: some having been completely overtaken by kudzu vines. Crispin peered over a wing for a better view, straining against the buffeting winds. To him, the strange vine covered apparitions resembled a creepy gathering of green draped ghosts, rising from the earth. Soon afterwards the twin peaks of Stag Mountain loomed into view, jutting above the green sea of kudzu. "Look, it's the first landmark on Queenie's map!" Crispin yelled excitedly.

"Great, then we're on the right course." Tiberius answered.

Leaving the suffocated forest and Stag Mountain behind, they flew over a desolate rocky plane populated with small grayish shrubby sage bushes and juniper trees with bizarre, contorted branches.

Gradually the scenery below turned green and fertile once more, and Tiberius noticed a group of unusual trees directly below. For some reason, they seemed to jump out of the landscape, begging to be noticed. He couldn't quite figure it out, but somehow they seemed strangely familiar. Then, it hit him. They resembled the branched symbols on Queenie's map. "This must be Hoot 'n Hollow," he called out to get Crispin's attention.

"What? Where?" He shouted back. "All I see are endless trees."

Tiberius, jubilant, having found the landmark, dropped a wing and glided towards the ground.

Crispin, aware of the altitude change, leaned over, "Are we landing," he yelled over the rushing wind.

"I'm going in for a closer look."

"What about the owls," Crispin responded with concern in his voice.

"They're asleep right now," Tiberius reassured him.

He continued downward in a spiraling pattern, circling the tree tops and then entered the woods fluttering back and forth zigzagging between the dense branches. The trees were short and stout with tiered rows of stubby branches jutting horizontally from the trunks. Their tiny acorn shaped, orange hued leaves were arranged in tight, whorled bunches on the branch tips and cast deep shadows onto the ground below. The thick girthed trunks were cloaked in a mottled white and dark gray pattern, which from a distance, made the trees look almost reptilian. Every tree they flew by had at least one perfectly owl-sized hole in it; and some of the larger diameter trees even had several openings in a row. Luckily, as they suspected, there wasn't an owl in sight, but their presence was made known by a strange wheezy snoring noise coming from several of the apartments.

"I think it's safe to assume they're all sound asleep," Tiberius commented.

"That's good," Crispin said. "I'm hungry. Let's look for those topsy-turvy mushrooms. They sound so weird."

"All right," Tiberius chuckled; landing on a branch a safe distance from any owl hole. "Let's eat," he continued, "but not the mushrooms. You should never, ever eat any mushrooms in the wild. They could poison you."

Crispin looked puzzled. "Even if they look like the ones my mother cooks?"

"Yes, even those," Tiberius warned. "There are poisonous ones which look just like the edible kinds and only an expert on mushrooms can tell the difference."

"Okay, but we can still look at them, right," he questioned.

Tiberius chuckled at his young friend's exuberance. "Of course we can. That's the main reason I landed here. I knew you wanted to see them and I'm curious myself. I'm starved though," he went on. "Lunch first: then mushroom hunting. Okay?"

"That's fine with me," Crispin said flapping his arms. "I'm sure they're not going to grow wings and fly away."

After gobbling down several of their gifted honey cakes, Crispin and Tiberius set off in search of the mushrooms. They fluttered amongst the trees for quite some time and had almost given up when suddenly Crispin shouted, "I think I see them! Over in that tree to our left."

Tiberius dipped a wing and with Crispin's guidance glided to the indicated tree.

"There. There," he shouted, "Yes, just a bit lower. We found them, we found them!"

Tiberius gently landed on the mushroom covered branch and Crispin bounced off excitedly. They stared, their mouths hanging agape with disbelief. The fungi were indeed growing upside down and in a perfectly straight line. Their milky white stalks were attached to the underside of the limb, and their vivid red parasol shaped caps were dangling in mid air. Peering down they had a perfect view of the tan gilled underside of the caps.

"Wow, these are so weird," Crispin exclaimed. "I wonder what makes them grow topsy-turvy?"

Tiberius puzzled the matter for several moments. "I haven't got a clue," he answered, "but nature usually does things for a reason. I bet the owls could tell us."

"Oh no," Crispin blurted out. "I don't want to hang around for the answer and end up someone's meal. I've seen them and that's enough for me."

"I agree," Tiberius said. "Mount up and let's get back in the air."

They exited the woods and flew on hoping the Triton River wasn't too far away. Fortunately for the two travelers, they spotted the wide muddy green body of water shortly after leaving Hoot 'n Hollow. They both felt a wave of excitement when it came into view knowing the prize they had come so far to retrieve was finally in reach. In the pit of their stomachs however, they also felt a stab of apprehension at the knowledge of what might be waiting for them in the cave's mysterious depths.

Tiberius followed the rivers course southward until the sun began to dip below his right wing, and began searching the landscape for a safe looking place for the night.

Crispin who had the better eyes of the pair tapped Tiberius on the head. "Hey, look over to your left. What's that?"

Tiberius banked gently for a better view. "What do you see?"

"There's something big and dark in the ground," Crispin answered.

The spot in question was only a short distance away and soon the travelers were approaching its edge. Suddenly, the earth opened up beneath them in a chasm so dark and unfathomable they could only gasp in wonder. Tiberius hovered over the gaping mouth trying to estimate its depth but a short distance down the rocky throat it disappeared into oblivion. He landed on a rock perched on the pit's rim. Crispin dismounted and the friends leaned over, staring transfixed into its inky blackness.

Tiberius finally broke the silence. "If I'm not mistaken, we're looking into the Last Stop Sinkhole."

"Of course," Crispin said. "It's just as Queenie described." He picked up a pebble and tossed it inside. It vanished silently into the pit's gut. "It must be incredibly deep." He commented. Crispin tossed another pebble in and listened for it to hit. "I wouldn't want to find out, would you?"

"No, I wouldn't," Tiberius replied.

They sat on the edge for a time imagining what might lie at the bottom, if indeed there was one until Tiberius noticed the ocher sun touching the horizon. He yawned noisily.

"Let's find some place to spend the night," he suggested and pointed to a nearby fir tree. "That looks comfy, don't you think? If we stay here on these rocks, some slithery night lizard might get us."

"Eeek," Crispin jumped up, "Let's go."

They found a soft thick bough, settled into it, and watched the sun melt into a deep purple horizon. Sometime during the night Crispin and Tiberius were awakened by a loud crackling and rumbling. Panicked they grabbed on tightly as the branches underneath them began to sway and pitch violently. Fortunately, the commotion didn't last long and soon the night was once again quiet and still.

"What was that," Crispin gasped.

Tiberius was sitting up, apparently having been shaken to alertness. "I don't know, but it seems to be over. Whatever happened was close by, but I think we're safe up here for now. Try to go back to sleep."

Tiberius decided to stay on guard for a while, but eventually deciding there would not be a recurrence allowed himself to drift back to sleep.

The following morning, Crispin and Tiberius were horrified at what lay below their tree. The sinkhole's opening was now twice as big and had apparently experienced a cave in during the night. There were fresh fracture lines in the rocky walls surrounding the pit's throat, but what frightened them the most lay directly at their feet. The fir tree they had been sleeping in was now precariously clinging to the hole's edge! Most of its exposed gnarly roots were dangling over the abyss.

"Great grasshopper legs," Crispin cried out. "What happened?"

"I don't know," Tiberius exclaimed breathlessly, "but let's get out of this tree. It's only hanging on by a few roots."

They flew down to the newly exposed rock edge, and gaped downward in stunned silence. Finally Tiberius spoke, "Remember Queenie telling us this sink hole could be part of a huge cave system?" Crispin nodded.

"I think she was right." He hesitated a moment thinking. "And last night, more of the cave's roof collapsed."

Crispin's eyes flew opened. "Holy bog beetles. We could have ended up at the bottom of that hole."

"Yes," Tiberius replied. "We were lucky that tree hung on. I don't know about you, but that's not the way I want to go spelunking."

"What's a spee-lunking?"

"Just a word for exploring caves," Tiberius answered.

"Oh, in that case, I don't want to go spelunking either."

Tiberius grinned. "Good, we'll do our spelunking the normal way then."

Their narrow escape from an untimely plunge into the dark recess of the pit's nether regions left Crispin and Tiberius with a cold emptiness in the pit of their stomachs. They decided to remedy their discomfort, by eating a comforting breakfast.

Tiberius with his acute sense of smell located a nearby patch of toadflax in full bloom, and bursting with nectar. He sipped from the dainty pink snapdragon like flowers while Crispin munched on a piece of tender green mottled lichen from a log which had fallen in the night. They topped off their meal by splitting one of the honey cakes.

"Are you ready to go," Tiberius asked, knocking some crumbs off his leg. Crispin; whose mouth was still full, answered by jumping up and grabbing his pack. Tiberius cocked an eyebrow. "I'll take that as a yes."

Back in the air they hovered momentarily for a bug's eye view of the newly expanded sink hole, and then resumed their journey southward. They had been flying for quite some time as evidenced by the traveling sun, over vast stands of deciduous forest punctuated occasionally by stark outcroppings of gigantic grayish blue boulders. The monotony of the landscape was suddenly broken when a tributary sprouted from the Triton and snaked eastward through the forest. Crispin was scanning the stream's path as it disappeared into the surrounding forest, when something unusual caught his eye. Not far from the tributary's mouth lay a stick and vine structure spanning the water's girth, connecting the opposite banks. Crispin had seen bridges before, but what really peaked his interest was the movement on it. He tapped Tiberius' wing to get his attention. "Hey, take a look down there. It's a bridge, and there's something crossing it. Can we go down for a closer look?"

Tiberius responded by dipping a wing and circling over the bridge. They landed on one of the bridges' end post, and watched as a caravan of camel crickets with bundled sticks on their backs filed across.

One of the crickets took notice of the strangers, hesitated; gave them a polite nod and called out in a creaky voice. "Hey, how you doing."

"Just great," Crispin sang out.

Tiberius looking puzzled asked, "I thought crickets only came out at night."

"You're a smart guy," the cricket answered, "but we're behind schedule on a big delivery...buildin' a big tree house up north." He wiped his brow. "Man, this heat's killing me. Gotta get goin'. See you guys around." He adjusted his bundle, and marched on.

"Now, that's a hard working bunch of crickets," Tiberius commented.

"Yeah, everyone knows how much crickets hate daylight," Crispin added.

The last cricket stepped off the bridge just as Tiberius fluttered skyward. Soon afterwards, Dancing Fish Lake came into view. The crescent shaped body of sparkling blue water looked so inviting they decided to have lunch on its banks. They stretched out on a nice soft patch of Irish moss under a willow tree which draped gracefully over the water's edge.

Tiberius broke out the honey cakes, and passed one to Crispin. "I'm sure glad the Fern Queen gave us a lot of cakes."

"So am I," Tiberius replied. "It saves us time, and we don't have to worry about starving."

A worried look crossed Crispin's face. "What are we going to eat on the way home?"

"Don't waste time worrying about things that haven't happened yet," Tiberius said somewhat sharply. "Besides: we've been able to find lots of food so far, haven't we?"

"You're right," Crispin said peevishly then added more cheerfully. "At least it's not winter. This time of year, there's food everywhere."

"That's right," Tiberius agreed. "You know I wouldn't let you starve. Here, have another cake."

They finished lunch, and decided to kick back for a well earned rest. The gentle lapping of water on the rocky bank and monotonous buzzing and droning of the lake shore's winged inhabitants finally took its toll on the weary travelers. Before long they were snoozing peacefully unaware of the lengthening afternoon shadows. Sometime later Crispin and Tiberius bolted upright, startled from their sleep by a loud thrashing churning sound.

Crispin rubbed the sleep from his eyes. "Am I dreaming?"

Tiberius blinked rapidly and chuckled, "If you are, we're having the same dream."

Directly in front of them were at least a hundred golden fish gleaming in the sunlight. They were balanced on the water's surface, propelling themselves along with their tails. Suddenly the performers began twisting, swaying, and flopping in unison. Crispin couldn't help but jump up and down, clapping. "It looks like some kind of mad dance," he yelled.

Tiberius mouth hung open in disbelief. "I thought it was all just a wild story, but," he shook his head in wonder. "I never would have believed it if I hadn't seen it with my own eyes." The bizarre dance lasted only a short time and then it abruptly ended as the fish slipped back under the still churning surface.

Crispin turned to Tiberius, his eyes huge as saucers. "Great beetle bazookers!" He threw his arms up in the air. "What a show, and what a stroke of luck. If we hadn't fallen asleep, we might have given up, and left before the show started."

Tiberius was still gazing over the water's surface shaking his head with a huge grin on his face. He turned to Crispin. "I never knew fish could be so entertaining. This is certainly one to write home about."

Crispin, still worked up, cut in, "Woopdie do, what a day. Let's get going and see what other adventures we can get into."

"All right, but settle down, you might fall off my back."

Crispin jumped on and Tiberius soared upwards still chuckling and muttering to himself. 'Gotta stop giving the kid so many honey cakes. He's going to wear me out.'

Dancing Fish Lake was quite large and Crispin and Tiberius flew along its shimmering shoreline southward for the better part of the afternoon. Eventually, the lake disappeared behind them and Tiberius knew; if he remembered the map correctly, that Annelid Valley lay directly south of the lake so he was confident they would pass over it before nightfall. The only thing that bothered him was how they would recognize it.

'What should we be looking for,' Tiberius thought to himself. 'It's just a valley with a bunch of worms living in the ground. What possible features could they make that could be seen from the air.'

The land they were passing over at present didn't look at all like a valley. It was a reappearance of the parched rocky plateau they had flown over the day before. Crispin leaned over and yelled out, "This sure does look familiar."

"Yes," Tiberius called back. "But don't worry; we're going the right way."

He had barely finished his statement when a cluster of small hills came into view. They looked as bleak and parched as the plateau, but as Tiberius flew over, a noticeable change was apparent. The opposite side of the hills was clothed in a velvety green cloak of vegetation.

Tiberius scanned the valley floor for evidence they were indeed passing over a land inhabited by thousands of worms. At first all he saw was smooth lush terrain, but soon he spotted a small brown ripple rising from the sea of green. This was followed by several longer ridge lines which snaked their way along the valley floor. The pair flew on, and it wasn't long before the whole valley was covered in tiny mountain ranges of brown furrows.

"Those must be worm trails," Tiberius called out.

"Wow," Crispin shouted back. "And none of them run into each other. I wonder how they can tell where to dig."

"It must be some kind of earthworm technology we don't know about," Tiberius answered. "Let's go down for a closer look."

They landed on a small rock jutting up from an immense field covered in a variety of thick and vigorous tufted grasses. Crispin climbed down to give Tiberius a rest and stretched out on the rock.

"Jimminy junebugs," he announced, "Everything is so green and healthy."

"It's the earthworms," Tiberius stated. "They help transport organic material into the soil, and it fertilizes the plants."

"Oohh," Crispin replied. Then he pointed at something in the distance. "What's that over there?"

"I can't tell from here," Tiberius answered. "Why don't we stretch our legs? We can check it out on the way."

Happy to be investigating the unknown again, Crispin hopped down energetically. After learning his lesson in the carnivorous bog, he stayed close to Tiberius as they strolled towards the mysterious object.

As they drew nearer, it became obvious it was a sign. A piece of bark was wedged between two limbs of a dead tree stump. On the bark were three lines of script crudely written in purple mulberry ink. Crispin and Tiberius didn't understand the strange letters in the first two lines, but the last one seemed familiar to Tiberius.

"Hmmm," he mumbled pointing to the third line. "I've seen this before, written on rocks at Blow Fly beach. I go there sometimes when the sea oats are blooming. Ah yes," he added triumphantly, "I've got it now."

"What does it say," Crispin asked impatiently.

"It says, 'Earthworm excavation in progress. Caution; soft ground'."

"OOOO," Crispin replied glancing below his legs nervously. "Do you think we're safe?"

"Of course. Now a snail or rhinoceros beetle might have to worry about cave-ins, but we're too light for that to happen."

Crispin glanced around. "I guess they're sleeping. There's not much dirt moving going on."

"You're right. I think we should be moving on," Tiberius suggested. "The cave shouldn't be much further. Let's see if we can reach it by dusk."

Crispin, somewhat disappointed at not seeing one single solitary worm; glumly mounted his ride. As Tiberius fluttered over the valley, Crispin watched in hopes of spotting the elusive creatures. Sadly, all he saw were more of the mounded dirt trails. Eventually, even those disappeared as they left Annelid valley, and its nocturnal inhabitants behind.

Chapter 17
A New Friend

nnelid valley was far behind and as the setting sun melted into an indigo evening, Tiberius knew the time had come to end their day's journey. He glanced earthward and noticed that the Triton River had narrowed into what now looked to be a very wide stream. It also seemed to be flowing slightly downhill. With the fading light, it became hard to follow its course, so he landed on an oak branch. The jarring awoke Crispin who; worn out from the day's excitement, had been napping since leaving Annelid valley.

"Where are we," he asked rubbing his eyes.

"I'm not sure, but I have this feeling we're getting close to the cave. The river has narrowed quite a bit."

"Maybe we can see it when the sun comes up," Crispin said expectantly.

"That's what I'm hoping," Tiberius replied. "It would be useless to try and locate the entrance in the dark, so we better try to get a good nights rest. We're going to need all our energy for what might lay ahead."

"After my nap, I don't feel very sleepy," Crispin announced. "Why don't I stand watch for a little while so you can get some sleep?" Crispin glanced around warily. "This place gives me the creeps for some reason."

"What do you mean," Tiberius prompted.

"It makes the hairs on my feelers stand up."

"Well, we're really close to the river. Maybe it's the muggy air," Tiberius suggested.

"I hope so, last time I had this feeling, a bat was poking around the entrance to our tunnel."

"Okay, you stay awake if it makes you feel better, I'm tired." Tiberius yawned, folded his wings, and was asleep as fast as an owl's wink.

Crispin lounged on his back listening to the serenading crickets and followed the silvery blue moon on its nightly journey. Sometime later, Crispin felt a recurrence of the prickly sensation on his feelers and bolted upright with alarm. He searched the moonlit sky, but saw nothing. Maybe I'm letting my imagination get the better of me he thought. He laughed nervously, but it caught in his throat as he noticed an eerie shadow crossing the moon. A feeling of dread rose in his throat as he realized the dark swarming mass wasn't a cloud. To make matters worse, it was coming straight towards them.

"Bats!" He screamed.

Tiberius didn't move. Crispin jumped over, and shook him violently. "Wake up! Bats! They're heading this way!" Tiberius jerked his head up and glanced upwards. The voracious throng of bug eaters was closing in, blotting out the luminous night sky.

"Hurry," Crispin whispered. "We have to hide or we'll be eaten!"

They saw no safe place in the tree's canopy, so in terror, they flew to the ground hoping to find a rocky crevice they could disappear into. They scurried back and forth, but all they saw were sparse bushes which offered no safety.

"They're almost here," Crispin shouted over the deafening rustle of the flying hoards.

Tiberius couldn't breathe, panic gripped his throat. In desperation, he grabbed Crispin's foreleg and headed back to the tree. Luckily he saw a dark spot on the trunk, and on closer inspection, found it was a hole. He pushed Crispin in and followed him. Fortunately, the rotten spot went deep, and they squeezed in tight as far away from its opening as they could. They had barely caught their breath when the bats descended on the tree.

Crispin and Tiberius couldn't see much out of the small opening, not that they wanted to, but the wild rustling of wings announced the marauder's presence. They heard a scratching sound outside, and a twitching pug nosed rodent face poked itself into the hole, and leered at the frightened pair. They gasped, and squeezed together trying to move further back into the hole. The hideous face disappeared momentarily, but was replaced by a black clawed leg. It grasped around in the space, searching for its prey, but fortunately, Crispin and Tiberius were out of its reach.

Crispin was trembling and Tiberius tried to calm him. "Don't worry he can't reach us," Tiberius' voice quivered slightly, betraying his own unease as he continued. "I've heard bats really aren't mean. I think they're just hungry and will move on before daybreak."

Crispin, his throat paralyzed by fear, tried to respond but could only manage was a raspy 'Oooo-kay'.

The bat, finally tiring of the hunt, withdrew his claw in defeat. His dog like face reappeared for one last frustrated glimpse of his intended victims: blinked several times, and flew away.

"Will they be here much longer?" Crispin whispered.

"There's no way to know," Tiberius answered. "We better stay hidden until sunrise. There will undoubtedly be a few stragglers lurking around."

"All right," Crispin said reluctantly. "It's kind of stuffy in here and awfully dark, but I wouldn't get a wink of sleep out there worrying about a lone bat picking me off."

"Oh no!" Tiberius said. "We left our packs hanging on the tree branch. We sure could have used those lanterns in here."

"Great grubs!" Crispin exclaimed. "I hope the bats leave them alone."

"Well then; let's try to make the most of an uncomfortable situation," Tiberius suggested, shifting his position.

Crispin wiggled to find a more comfortable spot and before long he drifted off into an unsettled sleep. Several times during the night he heard scratching and the disturbing tic-tic sound of wings, but in his hazy dream filled state, he wasn't sure if it was real.

Sometime before dawn, he dreamt a giant snarling, drooling bat was crushing him in its sharp talons. Just as it was ready to bite his head off, he woke and bolted upright, barely missing the ceiling and accidentally kicking Tiberius in the leg.

"Ouch. Take it easy," he mumbled. "I might need my legs later. What's the matter?"

"I'm sorry, I had a horrible nightmare. A really ugly bat was about to bite my head off!"

Tiberius massaged his leg gently and tried to stretch out in their cramped quarters. "Oh well. No harm done. I probably would have woken up kicking too."

"Hey, look at the light streaming in," Crispin pointed. "It's morning, and all the bats will be gone."

"Great," Tiberius said, "My wings can't take this cramped space any longer. Come on then," he continued. "Let's go find some food. There's nothing like a full belly and fresh air to help shake off a bad bat dream."

Warily, Crispin poked his head out and surveyed the area. He knew Tiberius was right about the bats early dawn retreat, but the dream still haunted him. Finally reassured his winged nemesis was only an apparition of his subconscious, he exited the hole with Tiberius close behind.

They fluttered to the sparkling dew covered forest floor, and stood for a moment stretching and basking in the warm sunshine. Tiberius found a flat rock nearby and perched on it with his wings stretched wide to catch the sun's energizing rays. Crispin was close by; doing a few push ups and leg stretches to work the knots out of his tight muscles.

Once they were warmed and limbered up, the night's ordeal seemed to fade and the two friends realized the last time they had eaten was at Dancing Fish Lake.

"Come on; let's go find something to eat." Tiberius suggested joining Crispin on the ground.

"What about the honey cakes," Crispin asked.

"Let's see what's available around here first. We might need to eat them once we're inside the cave."

"Oh, I hadn't thought about that. I was thinking with my stomach."

Tiberius patted Crispin's shoulder. "My stomach's talking to me too. Why don't you jump on my back? We can cover more area from the air."

"Good idea" Crispin said cheerily as he mounted up.

Tiberius flew to the edge of the oak forest where it skirted the Triton River. They decided to cross and try their luck on the opposite shore where the tall grasses and shrubs looked more promising. The hungry friends had circled the area along the shore several times when Crispin sang out. "Hey, down there. Those look like berry bushes."

Tiberius descended and much to their delight he touched down in the middle of a wild blueberry patch loaded with ripening fruit. Crispin hopped off, grabbed a branch, and began munching on the juicy sweet balls; while Tiberius sucked the juice with great relish. The berries were so ripe, their skins exploded when bitten, and before long, the two diners' faces and legs were dripping and stained blue. Crispin pointed at Tiberius and laughed so hard he almost fell off the branch. "You're all blue," he said, managing to catch his breath.

Tiberius squinted and replied teasingly, "You've no room to talk: you look like a blue darner."

Crispin glanced at his legs and gasped. "Is my face as blue as yours?"

"Bluer," Tiberius replied.

"Will it wash off?"

"There's only one way to find out," Tiberius answered. "Let's go back to the river bank, and give it a try."

The colorful friends landed in a still, shallow pool, and they scrubbed vigorously. Although the stain remained, they had managed to fade it to a lighter lavender hue.

"Well, that's about the best we can do," Tiberius said. "The rest will eventually wear off."

"It's okay," Crispin rubbed his belly. "Those blueberries were worth it."

"I agree," Tiberius replied. "Now, let's get flying. Today's the day we find the cave. It couldn't be far. Not with all the bats flying around last night."

Crispin buried his face in his hands. "Oh no: not more bats."

"Don't worry," Tiberius assured him. "If we keep our wits about us, we can avoid them."

"How will we do that," Crispin asked with a skeptical look.

"Well," Tiberius began tapping his forehead. "We have the lanterns. The light might keep them at bay, but I wouldn't count on that. It might just make us an easier target. Also," he went on, "We could search for another entrance that's beyond the bats roost."

"Ohhh," Crispin said, a light going off in his head. "In that case, what are we waiting for, let's go find the cave."

Tiberius, with his young passenger's head tucked low to lessen the drag, sped over the Triton in search of their destination. The river below danced with jewels scattered upon it by the newly born sun and the travelers' spirits soared with expectation.

About the time the sun reached its zenith, Tiberius noticed another change in the river. The water, which had been flowing very fast, became sluggish as if something was impeding its course. The something became obvious when suddenly; looming directly ahead lay the cave's entrance. At first glance it looked like nothing more than a large hill, but on closer inspection they saw a darkened arched fissure cut into the rock.

At the base of the cave entrance the muddy river slapped gently against yellow sulfur stained rocks which had been polished smooth as glass. They found a mossy ledge overhang to sit on and stared at the cavernous opening in awed silence.

Finally, Crispin spoke, "I'm afraid that if I blink, it will disappear."

"I know how you feel." Tiberius replied, "It's hard to believe we're actually here."

"It sure looks creepy," Crispin observed. "Like a giant rock monster gulping water."

Tiberius leaned in close and whispered, "It's only a cave. An imagination is a good thing," he went on; "but try to control it while we're in the cave. You'll be conjuring all kinds of nightmarish beasts from the shadows. Your fears can transform perfectly ordinary things into your worst nightmares." He paused to be sure Crispin was paying attention and added, "If you learn to master your fear, it will never become your master."

"I understand," Crispin replied soberly.

"Now," Tiberius continued, "Most importantly we have to stay together, no matter what."

"You don't have to worry about that," Crispin replied emphatically. "The last thing I want to do is get lost in there alone."

"Good," Tiberius stated with a firm nod, "and remember; together, we can face anything."

"I feel braver already," Crispin said confidently.

"Hold that thought," Tiberius said, "and If you start feeling scared, just repeat this to yourself....I'm brave, I'm very brave."

"Yes, yes!" Crispin shouted thrusting a foreleg upwards. "Bravery will be my motto!"

Tiberius, satisfied at the results that his pep talk had on Crispin; decided it was time to make their move. "Are you ready to go in then?"

"Yep, sure am," he replied straightening his vest.

They jumped off the overhang and fluttered down to a group of small stones lying in a quieter area of the cave's border. With straining eyes, they attempted to see what awaited them beyond the entrance. A short distance in, they saw the faint outline of mist shrouded boulders, which like great rows of teeth from some unimaginable beast, faded into the oblivion of its cold gullet. Adorning the entrance were gigantic lush ferns, thriving in the cool translucent mist and pendulous mosses framing the arched roof like emerald hair ornaments.

They were about to enter the cave when a gravely voice called out, "Ahoy there! Who be commin' into my cave?" They turned towards the sound, and saw a shiny black reptilian head poked out from a patch of moss.

"It's a salamander," Crispin gasped, "he might eat us!"

Tiberius glanced upwards. "You're right, we better keep our distance. Let's fly to that higher ledge for safety."

"Ahoy there," the voice shouted louder this time.

They watched anxiously as the salamander dropped from the moss and slithered across the rocks in their direction. They moved even higher. "Oh no. He's coming closer," Crispin whispered.

"I think we better get out of here, right now," Tiberius exclaimed.

They were poised, ready for a quick escape when the salamander looked up and grinned a huge, almost toothless smile.

"Look! He has no teeth." Crispin pointed.

"I see," Tiberius replied. "Maybe he's harmless." They flew a bit closer in curiosity, but remained at a safe distance.

"Well, blow me down mateys." The salamander shouted. "There be no reason for ye afearin' Captain Jack. No harm will be comin' to ye here. Me insect eatin' days are over. Captain Jack be fillin' his belly with mosses since me teeth got knocked out."

Crispin and Tiberius decided the old salamander, as crusty as he seemed, wasn't a threat, so they hopped down and crossed to the rock where he was perched. Captain Jack threw his head back, and belted out a laugh which echoed around the cave. "Har, har. What brings you two swabs into me port." He moved closer and stared with a squinted eye. "I've not seen the likes of you two in these parts, that's for certain ...and in such an intriguing shade of blue."

They glanced at their legs, having forgotten about the stains. "We had blueberries this morning," Crispin explained.

Tiberius cleared his throat to speak, "Oh...I'm Tiberius, and this is my friend, Crispin. It's a pleasure to make your acquaintance."

"Argh. You'll be callin' me Captain Jack; if you don't mind."

"Yesss," Tiberius stuttered a bit. "Right, Mr..., I mean, Captain Jack."

Crispin couldn't tear his eyes away from the salamander's shriveled mouth and accidentally blurted out. "What happened to your teeth?"

"Argh. Well me lad, I'll tell you what happened. A scalawag crawfish name of Davie Fang from upriver tried to steal me treasure. A right bloody fight it was too. He'll not be try'n that again for certain." His yellow spotted belly shook with a raucous laugh.

"After Captain Jack finished with the blackguard, he'll be changin' his name to 'One Eye Davie'." Crispin and Tiberius didn't quite know what to make of the colorful tale but chuckled politely anyway.

Captain Jack ran his tongue over his one remaining front tooth, and asked, "Now, tell old Jack what brings ye here?"

"We need to find some very special crystals to save Crispin's village. They're supposed to be in this cave," Tiberius answered.

"So, crystals be your prize," Captain Jack said, flicking his narrow pinkish tongue.

"And we have to get past the Gorboos too," Crispin added.

"I'll not be knowin' any Gorboos," Captain Jack exclaimed, "You'll not be talking about bats, will ye? Captain Jack sees them scurvy beasts every night."

"No," Tiberius answered, "We don't know what the Gorboos are, but we've been told the fierce creatures guard the crystals in the cave's depths."

"I'll not be goin' into the cave's belly," Captain Jack said. "Dark and cold as Davie Jones' locker in there, and no moss to fill me belly. You'll not be seeing a thing in that beasties throat. Black as midnight it'll be for sure."

"We have some lights," Crispin announced patting his backpack.

"Yes," Tiberius added, "We're hoping they will help us pass the bats safely."

"Captain Jack hides from the scalawags at night too. I'm not wantin' me bones to be stripped clean."

"Can't we just fly in when the bats are asleep," Tiberius asked.

"Argh. There's always a few of the beasties keepin' an eye on them what's sleepin'. You'd be picked off for certain."

"But won't they get you too?" Crispin blurted out.

"Don't ye be fearin' for Captain Jack lad. Those scalawags be no match for the likes of this old sea dog."

Captain Jack scratched his head in thought for several moments. "I'll make ye a bargain then. Ye swabs bring a crystal back for me treasure trove and I'll steer ye past the scurvy beasties in me ship."

Crispin and Tiberius glanced at each other in amazement. "You have a ship," Crispin blurted out.

"Aye. To be certain, and a right sturdy ship she is too."

"But will we fit into it." Tiberius asked gesturing to his large wings.

Captain Jack moved closer and inspected the wings. "Aye, you'll be fittin' for sure." He glanced at Crispin, "and you too matey."

"Oh. In that case, riding in your ship would be a wonderful idea," Tiberius added enthusiastically, "it's a bargain."

"Well, blow me down. Captain Jack's not had a crew in a right long time. Look sharp now and follow Captain Jack to me ship. She's moored in them there ferns."

Captain Jack slithered into the water and swam towards a clump of bushy ferns with Tiberius and Crispin fluttering behind, just above the surface. The salamander disappeared into the lush foliage while they waited expectantly on a nearby stone.

"What kind of ship could a salamander possibly have," Crispin asked.

"I have no idea," Tiberius answered. "I don't really care as long as it's safe and gets us past the bats."

They heard a rustling sound and the ferns' fronds began to bend and quiver. Captain Jack's head poked out followed by his front legs which were pulling on a rope. Then the most amazing contraption Crispin and Tiberius had ever laid eyes on emerged from the fronds and floated into the open.

"Wow! Would you look at that?" Tiberius exclaimed.

"Jumping junebugs," Crispin added. "Let's go check this ship out."

"Ha har. This be the good ship: *Chameleon!*" Captain Jack roared as Crispin and Tiberius landed on the bottle.

The Chameleon was made from a brilliant collection of river debris which the Captain had craftily assembled into what appeared to be a very seaworthy vessel.

The main body of the ship consisted of a clear rectangular glass bottle with a short neck which flared into a large round opening. It lay lengthwise and was kept afloat by a barge made from old wine corks and vividly colored, battered fishing bobs.

The floating objects were strung together with mismatched pieces of wire and fishing line. At both ends of the vessel the barge extended into a V shaped deck with a woven net covering. Thin wooden strips encircled the bottle in several places anchoring it to the barge. Crispin and Tiberius; unaccustomed to the bottle's slick surface, tiptoed carefully from one end of the craft to the other inspecting the floating marvel. The most unusual feature which left them scratching their heads in puzzlement was a group of blocky symbols raised from the glass surface. The inscriptions surrounded a circle enclosing the head of a cow.

"Drop anchor," Captain Jack suddenly shouted. Crispin and Tiberius startled: turned just in time to see a rope with a rock tied to its end being thrown overboard. They crossed to where Captain Jack stood, and peered transfixed over the bottle's edge.

"Well now me hearties," Captain Jack beamed with pride. "Do ye like me ship? A right beauty she is, and never left Captain Jack stranded."

"Yes, it's magnificent," Crispin gushed.

"I've never seen anything quite like it." Tiberius admitted shaking his head. "It must have taken you quite some time to build it."

"That's for certain, but a fierce storm be me good fortune." Crispin and Tiberius listened wide eyed as he went on. "Captain Jack'll be findin' lots of treasure washed up on shore." He slapped his tail on the bottle and continued. "Found me bottle trapped in a tree root."

"Where did you find the wood," Crispin queried.

Captain Jack pointed up river. "Beaver's dam. Critters ran off after the storm, so helped meself. Lashed some good strong sticks to the bobbins, and round me bottle. Stand by mates, Captain Jack will show ye his pilot's chair." He gestured and they followed, trying to keep up with the agile toed reptile. He slithered onto the deck while Crispin and Tiberius sat aloft watching intently through the green fibrous netting.

Captain Jack grabbed a sturdy looking clear plastic rod hanging from the netting. "This be for pushing off rocks and such," he said jabbing the air, "and this be my paddle." He plunged his tail into the river, swishing it back and forth.

The vessel moved forward a bit and Crispin and Tiberius grabbed onto the netting to steady themselves. All they could manage was to shake their heads in astonishment at the remarkable vessel, and its creator.

Captain Jack gestured at them to join him on the steering platform. It was a little crowded, but all three managed to fit. "Now, if ye swabs be sailin' with Captain Jack, I'll be needin' to teach ye some seafarin'."

Crispin's face broke into a huge grin. "Oh boy, I've never ridden in a ship before."

"Neither have I," Tiberius added. "This should be very interesting."

"Listen up mateys," Captain Jack began. "This be the stern," he instructed tapping the platform, "and this be the bow," he pointed to the opposite end of the ship." Crispin and Tiberius repeated the instructions pointing to the indicated locations.

"And now," the captain continued. "This be port side," he said pointing to the left of the platform, "and this be starboard," he turned and gestured to the right side.

Crispin and Tiberius went through the drill once again and the Captain beamed at his able students. "Ye be shipmates for certain." Crispin and Tiberius shook each other's legs in congratulation.

Captain Jack picked up a cork with a rope attached to one end, "and this be the hatch." He demonstrated by crawling into the bottle, and pulling the cork behind him. Once inside, he gave a firm tug on the rope and with several high pitched squeaks, the stopper sealed him in. He then pushed from the inside, and it popped out onto the deck.

"'Tis easy for certain: but keeps her seaworthy."

Crispin looked skeptical. "What if it gets knocked out?"

"You'll not be needin' to worry matey, Captain Jack will give it a swift kick back in."

"Oh, all right," Crispin replied, "seems safe enough."

"Will we be leaving soon," Tiberius asked, secretly hoping they would get past the bats before dusk.

"Aye, that we will. Captain Jack will be wantin' to carry ye well past them scurvy beasties."

"Tiberius says they're really not mean," Crispin piped up. "Just hungry and looking for food."

"Har har, well spoke lad. You might have a point, but Captain Jack'll keep his distance if ye don't mind."

"And so will we," Tiberius added.

"There be no time like the present," Captain Jack belted loudly, "all hands on deck, and weigh the anchor." Crispin and Tiberius looked around puzzled. "And where would an anchor be?" Tiberius asked.

"Captain Jack's forgettin' you be landlubbers." He gestured for them to follow and slithered towards the ships bow where he grabbed a rope trailing into the water. "Anchors be them what holds the ship fast."

"Of course," Tiberius exclaimed. "Otherwise, you'd be floating out of control."

Crispin studied the water's surface expectantly. Captain Jack began hauling up the rope, and soon a square rock broke the surface. He wound the rock weighted rope into a neat coil, and slid it onto a sturdy wire hook. "Now, she be ready to sail," Captain Jack announced with a grand gesture. "If ye shipmates climb aboard we'll be pushing off: and a grand journey it will be for sure!"

Chapter 18
The Chameleon's Journey

Crispin and Tiberius entered the bottle and looked around. Inside, at the forward end lay what appeared to be a pile of junk. It was an assortment of small multi-colored glass pieces, rocks, wooden sticks, metal of various sizes and shapes; and a curious clear glass ball with red, blue, and yellow swirls inside.

"What do you suppose all this stuff is for," Crispin puzzled.

"He probably needs weight at this end to help steer the ship," Tiberius guessed.

Next to the strange junk collection sat a small clam shell filled with bits of dried moss and a woven straw mat. "I hope that dried moss isn't for us," Crispin groaned. "I can eat fresh moss, but if it's too old it gives me a belly ache."

"It looks like it has been here for a while," Tiberius observed.

"House cleaning probably isn't the Captain's favorite thing to do," Crispin chortled.

"Shush," Tiberius whispered. "Here he comes."

Captain Jack stuck his head through the bottle opening. "Have ye found a comfortable spot?"

Crispin saw his chance, and asked, "What's this pile of stuff back here?"

"That be me ballast. Helps the ship settle a bit. Keeps her nose up so we won't be takin' on water."

"Oh, of course," Crispin said glancing at Tiberius who had a smug look on his face.

"And what about that pretty glass ball?" he went on.

Captain Jack winked, "A right beauty that one. Found it on the river bank. Captain Jack be havin' lots of treasures stashed aways in the cave. If you've a fancy to see it, Captain Jack'll be steerin' the ship close by."

"Yes, yes, I want to see all of your treasures," Crispin sang out.

"We can stay in the bottle; can't we," Tiberius asked still thinking of avoiding any bat encounters.

"Aye, for certain. Ye can spy me treasure through the port side. Keep an ear open for me signal."

"All right then, we'd like to see it....for certain!" Tiberius quipped.

Captain Jack returned topside and the two friends moved to the far end of the bottle and sat on the mat. Because of the ballast, it rode lower here and the water line came even with their heads. Suddenly, they were submerged into a bottomless alien world of jade green. Luminous arrows of sunlight pierced the river's surface and shot downwards in a constantly changing dance of colors.

"It's beautiful," Crispin gasped. "Who would have thought a lightning bug could ever go under water?"

"Or a luna moth," Tiberius added, almost in a whisper.

"I'm going to lie down so I can see better," Crispin said pressing his face against the glass bottom.

"What a great idea," Tiberius replied stretching out along side his shipmate.

The world which greeted them was unlike anything they could have imagined. Water creatures of all sizes and shapes; some finned and others with a bizarre insect like appearance swam, scuttled, or floated by in a fascinating aquatic parade.

Suddenly, Crispin's head shot up. "Ugh, there's a huge bass coming our way. One of these guys almost ate me once."

The fish spotting the two insects through the glass; circled underneath several times and then came closer to investigate. It pressed a gigantic, magnified eye up to the glass and ogled the strange object and its inhabitants.

The bottle swayed gently as a swell formed from the unwelcome guest. The bass seemed confused as to why his delectable meal was in plain sight, but beyond his grasp.

"Hey, you're wasting your time Mr. Bass," Crispin shouted even though he knew the fish couldn't hear him.

"I hope he gives up before he damages the ship," Tiberius said somewhat sharply. "Let's alert Captain Jack. I'm sure he deals with this sort of thing all the time." he suggested, moving towards the hatch.

"No, wait," Crispin protested, "I have an idea. Let's see if it works first."

"All right, be my guest," Tiberius said throwing his forelegs up.

The fish swam off, but they could see it circling underneath faster and faster; then the finned nemesis suddenly shot upwards, towards the bottle.

Crispin picked up one of the sticks from the junk pile and readied it. Tiberius sat back down, and waited for the impact. At the last moment, the bass slowed and came to a dead stop. It stared momentarily; once again pressing its eye up against the glass.

"Okay Mr. Bass: take this!" Crispin shouted, and with a quick succession of taps, he brought the stick down on the glass directly above the fishes eyeball. It jerked and swam off covering the ships bottom in a turbulence of frothy bubbles. Crispin threw the stick down and laughed smugly at his triumph over the troublemaker.

"Well done, well done," Tiberius sang out giving him a congratulatory thump on the shoulder. "You didn't damage the bottle did you," Tiberius asked, scrutinizing the ship's bottom.

"No," Crispin said matter-of-factly, "I was careful. Then he spat out, "I'd rather be back in that nasty pitcher plant than face Captain Jack after cracking his ship."

Tiberius peered intently into the watery depths. "Well, it seemed to do the trick. There's no sigh of the slimy beast at all."

The Captain thrust his head in once more and announced, "Time to close the hatch." His face disappeared and was replaced by the cork stopper.

Crispin and Tiberius hurried over, grabbed the rope and pulled it taut. The cork slid into the neck accompanied by the high pitched squeak. They returned to the scratchy straw mats and watched their pilot prepare for launch.

With steering pole in hand, he pushed off the rocks, and began paddling with his strong tail. The ship rocked and bobbed and soon, they were being carried along with the gentle current toward the misty boulder lined entrance. Crispin and Tiberius; knowing they would loose the light soon, readied their lanterns and resumed their vigilant examination of the mysterious realm beneath them.

"Look at those cute little fish," Crispin pointed out gleefully.

They watched amused, as a school of minnows and several spidery rock shrimp escorted them into the cave. As the ship passed underneath the arched entrance, a garden of gossamer grasses and sword like plants swayed and brushed against the ship's bottom.

Strange bugs and other aquatic inhabitants disturbed by the passing ships wake abandoned the safety of their watery forest and disappeared into the murky distance.

Tiberius touched Crispin's shoulder. "I think we're slowing. We might be coming up on Captain Jack's treasure. Watch closely, you don't want to miss it."

"I sure don't want that to happen," Crispin said. "Wow, a real live treasure. I wonder what he has."

"Well," Tiberius replied pointing to the ballast behind him. "If it's anything like this, I wouldn't get too excited."

The ship slowed to a crawl, and there was a sharp rap on the bottle. Crispin and Tiberius glanced up to see Captain Jack pointing to one side of the cave. They jumped up excitedly, crossed to the port side, and pressed their faces against the bottle's glass side. Captain Jack steered them out of the current, and the bottle floated into a channel between two glistening rocks with a recessed ledge beyond. Sitting on the ledge were two large mountains of every imaginable kind of debris. They saw hills of colored glass pieces, piles of tarnished metallic buttons, more corks and bobbins, balls of twine and wire, old rusty bottle caps and several more of the beautiful glass globes. Sitting alone to one side were strange shaped metal objects; round and very thin with a coppery appearance. Embossed on them were funny faces surrounded by strange script.

"Great beetle bazookers!" Crispin exclaimed. "You were right, a lot more of the same things." He threw his arms up to his head. "It must have taken Captain Jack an eternity to find all this stuff."

"He probably has a lot of free time," Tiberius grinned. "What else could a moss munching salamander have to do?"

Captain Jack's long, thin, almost toothless face beamed with pride as he gazed into the bottle and gestured toward his magnificent treasure trove. Crispin and Tiberius feigned astonishment, then smiled broadly and gestured excitedly at what they really considered more piles of junk. They returned to their seats and gazed up at Captain Jack through the glass.

He was maneuvering them slowly and cautiously into the river's center, thrusting his pole when necessary as the few remaining boulders passed dangerously close. After successfully navigating the obstacles he took shelter under the netted canopy. Swishing his tail rhythmically, he propelled the ship forward on the now smooth open river.

A twilight darkness overtook the voyagers and their lanterns began to give off a dim glow, becoming brighter as the ship left the waning sunlight far behind.

Waves of golden light spilled from the glass vessel illuminating the arched ceiling and dark grey, white spattered walls of the cave. "What's that white drippy stuff all over the walls," Crispin pointed out.

"It's guano," Tiberius replied.

"Guano? What's that?"

"Bat droppings," Tiberius answered pinching his nose.

"Oh, you mean bat poop," Crispin laughed.

"You got it kid," Tiberius winked. Suddenly, a dark shadow passing overhead caught their attention.

"Wh...wh...whaat was that?" Crispin asked nervously.

Tiberius scanned the roof and replied in a hushed tone. "We're moving under the roosting bat colony. Look." he pointed upwards.

Crispin dared a look through the glass, and was amazed at what he saw. The cave ceiling was covered with a dangling mass of dark brown slumbering forms clinging effortlessly to their rocky perch. The creatures' heads and tightly folded wings hung suspended in mid air transforming the smooth rock into a seemingly never ending carpet of furry bumps. Several awake and alert bats protecting the colony flitted back and forth.

"Jumping junebugs," Crispin gasped. "There are so many of them."

"Yes," Tiberius whispered. "I'm glad we're inside this bottle, and not out there."

Suddenly Crispin thought of Captain Jack. "I hope he's all right out there all alone."

Deciding to check up on their crusty navigator, they moved aft, and spotted him crouched under the protective netting, keeping a sharp eye on the acrobatic sleepers.

"Well, he looks safe enough," Tiberius observed.

Crispin rapped on the glass. Captain Jack turned and grinned confidently at his two passengers.

Reassured he was okay, they returned to their seats and watched the spectacle above, until the colony began to thin. Eventually, as the fading twilight deepened, only a few stragglers could be seen.

Shortly afterwards, they felt the vessel slow, turn slightly, and bounce several times. A few moments later, they heard the squeaking of the hatch being popped out, and then Captain Jack's illuminated face appeared and he motioned for them to come out.

"All ashore lads," he sang out. "Don't be afearin'. Narry a winged beastie in sight."

He pulled his head out: then Crispin and Tiberius; lanterns and packs in hand; followed him onto the deck. They were glad to be out of the bottle which had become increasingly stuffy, and took a deep breath.

"It smells weird out here," Crispin commented wrinkling his nose. He took another lung full and added, "It's damp and musty too."

"And chilly," Tiberius said rubbing his forelegs briskly.

"You'll not need worry about it growing colder," Captain Jack began to explain, "Went a right long way in once and it never changed."

"That's good," Crispin spoke up, "If I get too cold, my joints freeze up."

"And my wings start to ache," Tiberius added.

"Are you sure you didn't see the Gorboos when you went exploring," Crispin inquired.

"If Gorboos be small blind cave fish, then - aye. There be a small lake a short ways in full of the wretched creatures."

"No, I don't think those are Gorboos," said Tiberius shaking his head.

"Maybe you didn't go that far in." Crispin suggested.

A shadow crossed the captain's face. "I'll not be wantin' to find out then. If good fortune be your lot, I'll be spyin ye again in my lagoon." He slapped Tiberius cheerfully on the back and Crispin on the shoulder. "Well now mateys, ye been right good company, but best be getting back before the beasties start to fly." Crispin and Tiberius stepped off the pilot's deck onto a nearby rock.

"Can you see to get back without a lantern," Tiberius questioned him.

"Aye, Captain Jack be havin' good dark vision, and you'll be needin' both lanterns to find yer way through the cold beast's belly."

The crusty but now endearing seafarer backed his ship away from the rocks, executed a sharp turning maneuver, and slipped into the darkness. They stood for a few moments listening quietly as the swish-swish sound of Captain Jack's tail faded away. The two friends, alone once more exchanged a look which relayed their unspoken anxiety. They picked up the lanterns, and Tiberius whispered, "Remember, stay as close as you can."

Crispin executed a crisp salute and quipped, "Aye, aye sir."

Tiberius amused, winked and they began winding their way between the boulders lying along the river bank. Eventually, after walking for some time, a wider, easier pathway led them away from the river. The rocks here were different, and unlike anything they had ever seen above ground. Scattered in various places were huge dome shaped formations which seemed to melt into the cave floor. From a distance they resembled translucent, amber colored columns of beeswax. As they drew nearer however, instead of being honeycomb, the formations were smooth as glass.

"These are strange," Crispin said. "They're so shiny, I expected them to be wet, but they're not. This is certainly a conundrum," he stated glancing at Tiberius; proud that he had remembered the long word.

Tiberius returned a broad smile. "Yes, it certainly seems so, but it's just our lights reflecting off their smooth surface."

"Hey," Crispin pointed. "Look at that funny little knob sitting on top of the dome. It looks like one of my mother's poppy seed biscuits."

Tiberius cocked his head, examined the formation and then replied. "I think it looks like a mushroom cap."

"No," Crispin challenged. "It's flat top makes it look more like a biscuit."

Tiberius studied his friend, and noticed he was practically drooling at the sight. "You aren't hungry by any chance are you?"

Crispin tore his eyes away and laughed. "I must be; that stone biscuit is looking pretty good right now."

"Let's go just a little further," Tiberius coaxed. "Then we can sit down then and have a honey cake."

"Okay," Crispin replied cheerfully, "Maybe we can find that lake with the blind fish that Captain Jack was telling us about."

They passed more of the tall columnar domes, but occasionally there would be short squatty ones with small still pools of water sitting in a hollow on their tops. A single 'plip-plop' would sometimes echo through the large chamber; but when they held up their lanterns to investigate, all they saw was the army of domed sentinels guarding the silence.

"I hope it doesn't start raining," Crispin said in a hushed voice.

"I'm not an expert on caves," Tiberius began, "but I don't think it rains inside them. The water dripping is probably seeping through small cracks from above."

Suddenly a loud ringing clash echoed through the cave. Crispin and Tiberius scared out of their wits; jumped into the air. They swung their lanterns in a wide arc scanning the dark recesses but didn't see anything sinister.

"Wa...wha...what was that?" Crispin finally managed to say.

"It was probably just a falling rock. Things can't always stay in one place, you know," Tiberius said trying to sound calm.

"I hope you're right," Crispin replied peering into the inky void, more spooked than reassured. Tiberius laid a foreleg on his frightened friend's back, and suggested they move on.

No more crashing sounds were heard, but the effect it had on Crispin's fertile imagination was immediately apparent. Several times, Tiberius noticed Crispin jump as shadows cast by their lanterns darted among the formations in an eerie game of hide and seek. Then he heard Crispin chanting under his breath: 'I'm brave... I'm brave'. Later it escalated to 'I'm very brave....I'm very brave' and eventually to 'I'm very, very brave.'

'He's beginning to get on my nerves,' Tiberius thought to himself, 'but I was the one who suggested he say it. What can I do?' Suddenly, he came up with a solution, and stopped dead in his tracks. Crispin glanced at him with a questioning look.

"You know how sounds echo really well in parts of a cave," Tiberius began.

"Sure," Crispin replied.

"Well, whispering can be magnified too, and we wouldn't want to alert the Gorboos if they're close by would we?"

Crispin shook his head.

"Good. Then why don't you try to think 'I'm brave'. It will be safer."

Crispin nodded and they continued on, eventually leaving the domed chamber and entering a narrow passage with pale grey limestone walls. Tiberius' strategy must have worked because he didn't hear another peep from Crispin until they stepped into another chamber. As their lights fell upon the room, they froze; too awestruck to move. What they saw was unlike the previous chamber's hulking dome statues. This room was decorated with thin ivory colored icicle shaped formations clinging to the ceiling and sprouting from the floor. In several places the two met and formed columns. They moved inside slowly in reverence of this masterpiece of nature, holding their lanterns high to illuminate as much of the room as possible.

"Look," Crispin exclaimed pointing upwards at the spiky formations. "Aren't those the stalactites that Queenie told us about?"

Tiberius stopped and surveyed the rocky icicles. "I believe you're right, but if I remember correctly, there was another name for them."

Crispin scratched his head deep in thought for several moments then pointed to the ground. "I remember, the ones on the floor are stalagmites." He glanced around the room then added. "I feel like I'm in the throat of a gigantic fanged sea monster."

Tiberius chuckled and wagged a foreleg at Crispin, "Oh my. That imagination is on the loose again."

Crispin puffed out his chest. "That doesn't mean I'm scared though."

"Of course not," Tiberius replied with a wink.

The fascinated travelers wound cautiously through the spiky jungle and it became denser the further in they went. Crispin let out a loud sigh. "If these formations get any thicker, we won't be able to get through."

Tiberius stopped, and held up his lantern. "Maybe we can see an easier path."

Their lights penetrated the surrounding darkness as they strained to see into the distant shadows. At one spot it illuminated a set of dark pools connected with a narrow channel, rimmed in a snow white crusty deposit. The water's surface, not having the reflection of a sky resembled a sheet of onyx glass floating on the cave's floor.

"This must be the lake Captain Jack told us about." Crispin whispered as they drew nearer.

"Don't get too close," Tiberius said laying a protective foreleg on Crispin's shoulder. "The shelf surrounding the pool could be very thin, and if there are fish in it, they might be able to jump."

"But Captain Jack said they were blind," Crispin protested. "If they can't see us we wouldn't be in any danger."

"Not necessarily," Tiberius corrected. "Creatures which hunt in the dark have special abilities to help them find food. Their other senses can be extremely well developed."

"Like the bats," Crispin asked.

"Yes." Tiberius went on. "But bats aren't blind. The sounds they make echo off objects and help them navigate at night."

"Is that how you can find nectar from far away," Crispin asked.

Tiberius smiled and touched his feeler, "I can actually smell with these."

"Wow," Crispin replied, "Even though the fish can't see me, they might be able to smell or hear me?"

"Or feel the vibrations of our steps," Tiberius added.

"Okay, I'm convinced now, I'm staying away from the edge."

"Good," Tiberius nodded. "We can see just fine where we're at." He stomped the floor and added, "It seem safe enough. Let's have lunch here – or whatever meal it is. It's hard to keep track of the time when you can't see the sun."

They sat against a stalagmite and Crispin broke a honey cake in two. He handed a piece to Tiberius and they began eating ravenously. "What a strange world," Crispin exclaimed between bites. "No season, no sun to tell you if it's day or night." He looked around the chamber. "It's beautiful here but there's no sky or trees. I wouldn't like to live here."

Tiberius swallowed and replied, "Neither would I."

After eating, they chanced a closer look at the hour glass shaped lake and found the pool's edge to be very sturdy. With their lanterns held high, the opaque glassy surface dissolved, revealing crystal water with visibility so good, they could see straight to the bottom. "I can't tell how deep it is, can you," Tiberius asked.

"No, the water is so clear it is hard to tell."

Tiberius pointed to one side. "It seems fairly shallow here, but when you look at it from another angle, it seems deeper."

Crispin moved along the edge and stopped when something caught his attention. "Come look at this," he motioned.

Tiberius went over and saw several of the rocky icicle formations scattered about the pool's bottom. He glanced over their heads, and pointing to a group of small round scars on the cave ceiling. "The stalactites must have broken off and fallen in."

"What caused them to fall," Crispin asked.

"It probably happened sometime in the past when the earth shook," Tiberius informed him.

"Well, I sure hope it doesn't happen while we're down here. We might be skewered."

"I don't think you need to worry about that," Tiberius reassured him, "it doesn't happen very often."

"But what about the other night at the Last Stop," Crispin blurted out. "It shook really bad. Maybe that's when it happened."

"Mmmm," Tiberius replied with a raised eyebrow, "I hadn't thought about that. You could be right. In fact, I think it's a brilliant deduction."

A proud grin spread across Crispin's face. Suddenly, a small glint of silver flashed through the water; immediately followed by several others.

"Hey, I think I saw the fish," Crispin shouted.

"I saw them too," Tiberius said, waving a leg. "They went that direction."

"Can we throw some honey cake crumbs to them," Crispin inquired.

"Sure, just don't get too close. They might mistake you for a crumb."

Crispin retrieved some from the food pack, and tossed them in. The surface rippled, and the fish darted underneath the crumbs. "Here they come." He whispered.

All at once, the glassy surface was transformed into a boiling cauldron of glittering silver as the fishes lunged for the crumbs. Deciding that the fish were too small to be a danger, they moved closer and studied the ravenous creatures as they jostled one another for food. They resembled, in size and form, the common minnow, but that was where the similarity ended. These strange fish had hooded bumps instead of eyes, and their skin was almost transparent, revealing a shadowy skeleton beneath.

"Why don't they have eyes?" Crispin asked sadly.

"I guess they don't need them since they live in total darkness," Tiberius explained. "And they've never developed any coloration for the same reason."

Suddenly Crispin gasped, "Look, I think I can see that one's heart beating!"

Tiberius leaned in for a better view. "Jumping junebugs! You're right. That's the most bizarre thing I've ever seen."

"I wonder what they eat," Crispin questioned.

"There must be smaller creatures in the water we can't see, like algae," Tiberius guessed.

"That's got to be it," Crispin nodded, then asked, "but what do the algae eat?"

"That I can't tell you either," Tiberius said throwing up his legs. He laughed and it echoed around the lake room, then added in a whisper, "One thing I can tell you though, if we sit around trying to solve the mysteries of life, we'll never get back home. Let's think about it while we're walking."

Crispin wanted to feed the fish again, but Tiberius reminded him they might need every spare crumb for themselves. He agreed and they continued on choosing the easiest open trail through the lake room. Before leaving however, they turned for one last glimpse.

"It looks like a jewel encrusted forest," Crispin observed.

Tiberius nodded. "For once, I agree with your imagination."

THE LAKE ROOM was some distance behind now and the stalagmites and stalactites had eventually disappeared, leaving a smooth cave floor free from obstacles. They were making good time when suddenly, three tunnels lay before them.

"Great," Crispin blurted out. "How do we know which one to take."

"Well," Tiberius pondered. "The middle one looks bigger. Let's check it out first. If it's a dead end, we'll try the next one."

Crispin sighed, "This could take a while."

"I know," Tiberius said hearing the fatigue in Crispin's voice. "I'm getting tired too. We'll stop and rest soon, I promise."

They entered the tunnel and saw nothing unusual at first, but a short distance in, their lights fell upon something unbelievably amazing. The tunnel twinkled like a night sky full of purple stars.

They swept their lanterns upward and found massive clusters of amethyst crystals growing from the walls.

"They're beautiful," Crispin exclaimed, "What are they?"

"Some kind of crystals," Tiberius said, then quickly added "but not the ones we're after."

Crispin picked up a loose one from the floor and replied wistfully, "That's too bad. There's no one guarding these. Can I have a few to take home? My mother would love these. They would make a great birthday present."

"I guess it would be okay," Tiberius replied, "but only a few. We need to save room for the more important crystals."

Crispin chose a few of the smaller shards lying at his feet, and tucked them into his pack. Meanwhile, Tiberius was admiring a particularly large solitary lavender crystal suspended over his head and commented. "I didn't see any of these in Captain Jack's treasure; he obviously didn't make it in this far. There's no way he would have left these behind." He quickly bent over and picked up several from the floor. "I bet Captain Jack would like some of these as well."

"You're right," Crispin agreed. "We should also tell him where we found them so he can come get more."

Tiberius tucked a crystal into his pack, looked around the tunnel, and shook his head. "This place is amazing, but we have to keep moving."

Soon, after passing the crystal tunnel, the passageway dead ended at a wall which resembled a frozen waterfall. "Well, so much for this tunnel," Tiberius announced.

"Maybe we'll have better luck in the next one. At least this passageway wasn't very long and we found these great crystals." Crispin said rattling his pack.

"You're right," Tiberius replied, "there's so many fascinating things in this cave getting even a little bit lost isn't a waste of time." They retraced their steps, slowing for one last look at the amethyst crystals; and exited the tunnel.

"Okay, now which one do we take," Crispin asked.

Tiberius studied the two remaining entrances. "This one looks easier," he said pointing to their left, then went on as they headed in its direction. "The other one has a steep uphill slope. I don't know about you, but I sure don't feel like climbing."

Crispin kicked a pebble out of his way. "Neither do I."

This passageway looked much the same as the crystal tunnel, except for a small rivulet of water which sprang from a hidden recess in the ceiling. It trickled silently down one side of the entrance; then dripped from a ledge into a shallow eroded basin with a funny 'plip-plop' sound. They skirted the pool of water and entered slowly holding their lanterns out, cautiously scanning the unknown darkness. Tiberius stopped suddenly, and Crispin bumped into him.

"Shhh. Did you hear that?" Tiberius whispered.

"No, I didn't hear anything."

"Just be quiet and listen."

A moment later they both distinctly heard a chirp-chirp sound echoing through the tunnel. "It sounds like a cricket," Crispin said.

"That's what I thought too," Tiberius replied, then gestured further down the tunnel. "It seems to be coming from that direction."

"Can crickets live in caves," Crispin asked.

"Let's go see if we can find the cricket," Tiberius suggested. "It might have wondered in here and gotten lost."

Several moments later, they heard the chirp, chirp, chirp again and headed towards it. Finally the cricket song grew so loud they knew it had to be close by. Swinging their lanterns slowly, they searched every nook and cranny in sight. Suddenly, a flurry of white jumped into their light, startling them so badly that they fell backwards; their lanterns rolling along the tunnel in a chaotic light show.

Chapter 19
A Terrifying Encounter

Shakily, they retrieved their lanterns and inspected the cricket standing before them.

He seemed unfazed by the stray visitors and the unaccustomed brightness of their lanterns. At once, they saw why. Like the fish in the lake, the cricket was blind. Instead of normal eyes, his were white and cloudy. He also looked to be very old, with bristly antenna hair, and wings of grayish white. Crispin, wary of the strange cricket moved behind Tiberius and peered around his wing.

"Do not fear me," the cricket began in an infirm sing song voice. "You are travelers from a far away land and seek an important treasure."

Crispin and Tiberius glanced at each other, their eyes wide in amazement. "Yyees," Tiberius stammered, "but how do you know that?"

The old cricket lifted a leg and waved it slowly, "I am blind, but I can see many things in the darkness."

Crispin, feeling a bit braver, came closer, "You're right. We are looking for a treasure. We need to find the glowing crystals to save my village from disaster."

"Yes," Tiberius added, "Can you help us?"

The old cricket spoke again, louder and with great passion. "The treasure you seek is here, but the road will be filled with much danger." He pointed a shaking leg down the tunnel.

"Do you mean the Gorboos," Crispin spoke up.

"Yes, the crystal guardians dwell in the deepest recesses of the cave. Go if you must, but move in the darkness as they do, or you will not succeed." He paused and tilted his head upward, then added, "Do not despair when things are darkest. Help will come from above, and," he looked directly at Tiberius, "things are not always as they seem."

Tiberius was about to ask what the old cricket meant when, with an unexpected rustle of wings, the cricket disappeared into the darkness. They swung their lanterns upwards, illuminating the walls, but saw no movement.

"Thank you Mr. Cricket," Tiberius called out.

There was no response, only the echoes of his voice. A moment later, a series of chirps echoed through the tunnel.

"What a strange cricket," Crispin exclaimed.

"Strange indeed, but very helpful," Tiberius replied. "He told us which way to go."

"Good, now we won't have to waste time investigating the other tunnel," Crispin said cheerfully.

"We could rest here for a while," Tiberius suggested, "it seems safe."

"I'd rather not. Mr. Cricket's singing might keep me awake."

"Why should that bother you? You're used to hearing crickets singing."

"I know, but that particular cricket gives me the creeps for some reason. Didn't you think he was spooky?"

"No," Tiberius replied. "Mostly I felt sorry for him, being so old, and blind. But if he bothers you, we can go on down the tunnel."

"Good. Let's get going." Crispin said glancing behind his shoulder as they marched on.

"I HAVEN'T SEEN anything like those purple crystals in this tunnel," Crispin stated quietly after they had traveled for some time.

"Well," Tiberius whispered back, "it's like I said before. This place seems to have a surprise around every corner."

Just then, the tunnel took a sharp turn and the travelers felt as though they were headed back in the opposite direction. "Ha," Tiberius said "and here's one of those corners."

"Aren't we going in the same direction we just came in," Crispin asked sounding confused. "Maybe the tunnels are connected and we're traveling in a circle."

"No," Tiberius reassured him. "That tunnel was definitely a dead end. They couldn't be connected. Beside, it feels like we're going down hill."

Crispin slowed and stared at his feet. "I hadn't noticed before, but I think you're right."

They continued their decent for some time, occasionally feeling as though the tunnel was twisting into a spiral. They came upon a section of the pathway which was scattered with unusual shaped stones. Crispin stumbled on one and dropped his lantern.

"Are you okay," Tiberius asked inspecting his young friend.

"Yes, I'm okay. What are these things on the ground?" He bent over, picked one up, and rolled it curiously between his forelegs.

Tiberius studied the strange tubular object. "I don't think its ordinary rock." He glanced around the ground, and went on, "There seems to be quite a lot of them. They had to come from somewhere nearby."

He tilted his lantern upwards and the light came to rest on a fissure slicing through the tunnels' smooth brown and ivory marbled ceiling. Suspended along the crack was a line of tightly packed thin white tube structures. Most of the straw-like formations were hanging vertically but others were attached at crazy angles and bizarre spirals.

Crispin trying to contain his enthusiasm whispered loudly, "Great grasshopper legs. Look at all those strange tubie things. They're so weird! Can we sleep here?"

Tiberius gave Crispin a quizzical look. "Do you think that's a good idea?" He pointed to the broken formations lying on the ground.

"Oh, I guess not," Crispin replied with a disappointed look.

"We'll find a resting place soon," Tiberius said patting his friend on the back. He winked and went on, "I don't want to explain to everyone back at Dragonfly Landing how their brave little hero survived lightning storms, hungry frogs, carnivorous plants and bats only to be killed by a falling tubie thing." The two friends laughed quietly as they continued on in search of a safe resting place.

It wasn't long before they found a cozy niche along the tunnel's ceiling to slip into. After splitting one of their few remaining honey cakes, and taking a nice long refreshing drink from a nearby pool, they lowered the lids on their lanterns.

Suddenly Crispin whispered, "I've never seen it so dark. There's no moon or starlight. I can't see you, or even my own legs."

"Don't worry, I'm still here even if you can't see me," Tiberius reassured him. "We're experiencing total darkness. If you're scared, we can open one of the lanterns a bit, but we'll be safer if we leave them closed."

"I'll be all right," Crispin replied sleepily. "I won't know the difference with my eyes closed."

TIBERIUS AWOKE SOME time later startled by a strange noise in the distance. Because of the cavern's echoes, he couldn't get a fix on where it was coming from but deep in his gut, he knew it wasn't a falling formation but something alive. The noise eventually subsided and he fell back asleep grateful it hadn't wakened his skittish companion. The pair woke later feeling refreshed, but very confused.

"This is too weird for me," Crispin confessed. "I can't tell if it's day or night."

Tiberius adjusted the lantern light brighter. "There, now it's daytime, do you feel better."

"Yes, but I hope we don't have to spend a long time in here I'm..."

"Shh," Tiberius cut him off, and closed the lantern cover again.

"What's wrong," Crispin whispered.

"I heard this strange sound last night, and there it is again."

Lying extremely still, they listened with great apprehension to the ominous noise in the distance. They weren't certain what they were hearing, but it sounded like claws scratching on the rocky tunnel floors accompanied by the sound of something being dragged. Every now and then, a series of raspy clicks would echo through the cave. Soon, the sounds grew louder, and seemed to be coming their way.

Crispin shifted nervously and knocked a small pebble out which hit the floor with a loud 'ping'.

"Shh," Tiberius warned, "We have to be quiet."

"Don't worry," Crispin replied. "I feel like I can't even breathe."

The frightening sounds grew louder and suddenly, the pitch black tunnel took on an eerie pale blue glow. Crispin and Tiberius inched forward, just enough to see who or what was coming. "Don't stick your head out too far," Tiberius warned, "we don't want to be seen."

Crispin pulled his head back into the crevice. "I just want a good look."

Tiberius pointed downward, "Don't worry; we will get our chance when they pass below us."

The mysterious pale blue light grew brighter and they watched petrified as the mysterious creatures marched single file directly below them. The creatures were smaller than they had imagined, being only as long as Tiberius' wing span but their hideousness made up for their ordinary size. They had the long segmented body of a centipede flanked by numerous twitching legs, each ending in one sharp curved talon. At the torso's end being drug along the floor with a throoshing sound was a long spiked tail resembling a bee stinger. Occasionally the appendage would jerk upwards; then drop back to the ground with a dull thud.

The pale blue glow radiating from the creatures' bodies was so intense it bathed them and the surrounding area with an eerie luminescence. Their heads were held low to the ground as if sniffing out smells only they could detect.

Suddenly, one halted and looked upward. Crispin and Tiberius froze hoping they hadn't been heard or smelt. What they saw next was the most frightening face they had ever encountered. The creature had a triangular mantid like head but instead of the usual round bug eyes, its' were narrow and snake like in a sickly shade of greenish yellow. Two small holes lay underneath the eyes and below them a mouth only seen in one's nightmare. At the end of its narrow jaws lay a round puckered hole with strings of yellowish ooze dripping from the orifice. Another of the creatures stopped, gazed upward, and spoke to its companion.

What Crispin and Tiberius saw next chilled them to their bones. The shriveled crack in the creature's jaws opened into a wide circle revealing an inner ring of gnashing dagger like teeth. Several series of the clicking sounds they had heard earlier were exchanged between the two companions, and after one last look upwards, the pair continued along the tunnel.

Crispin and Tiberius silently let out their breath, but soon another one stopped below. Instead of looking upwards however, it glared at the tunnel wall for a moment then flicked a long strap like tongue at something on it. After the creature had moved on, the pair shrank back into the crevice wishing they had not gotten such a good look at their nemesis. They sat in silence for some time, afraid to speak. Finally, when the throoshing, scratching and clicking noises faded away and the only sound to be heard was the benign plip-plop of a nearby pool did they dare to whisper what they were both thinking, but afraid to say. "It's the Gorboos!"

"We must be close to their lair," Tiberius speculated after the pair left the protective niche and continued on in the direction the Gorboos were traveling.

"Yuck!" Crispin groaned. "I've stepped on something slimy." They stopped, inspected the tunnel floor and their lights reflected off a pile of yellow gelatinous muck. "Smells nasty too," he added.

"No doubt the Gorboos left this behind for us," Tiberius said disgusted. "We better watch where we step from now on," he added holding his lantern a bit lower as they continued onward.

"I was wondering," Crispin asked trying to keep his voice down. "Where do you think the Gorboos came from. We saw no signs of them before we entered this tunnel."

"They could have come from the tunnel we didn't take," Tiberius began, "and for all we know there might be a corridor connecting the two."

"I'm, sure you're right," Crispin remarked. "You're a genius. In fact, I think you're smarter than a two headed cranioptera beetle."

Tiberius chuckled. "Just using a little deductive reasoning, my dear Crispin."

The tunnel widened and twisted sharply in a U turn which sent the travelers on a laborious uphill hike. Soon, much to their relief, it leveled and they entered a large room filled with more of the beeswax colored domes.

"Please don't tell me we're back where we started," Crispin whispered frantically.

"No, no," Tiberius reassured him swinging his lantern upwards. "Look, there are stalactites in here. The other chamber didn't have any."

"Good," Crispin sighed, "I don't want to walk in circles for the rest of my life. Oh great! There are Gorboo glops in here too."

"Well, at least we're on the right track," Tiberius said then added, "Let's dim our lanterns. We don't know how close we are to their lair."

They moved on, their pace slower because of the dim lights, and began crossing an arched limestone bridge. It spanned a section of the chamber's floor which was bathed in a thin sheet of flowing water. In several places, swirling eddies had pooled and were being funneled into a thin fissure where they disappeared into unknown regions of the cave. As the pair neared the far side of the bridge, they became aware of a low rumbling sound in the distance which grew louder with each step they took. Until now the pair had remained silent in fear of being detected by the Gorboos, but now, Tiberius felt their voices were masked enough to speak safely. "It sounds like a waterfall," he said loudly.

"But where is it?" Crispin called back swinging his lantern around the darkened chamber.

Tiberius shook his head and gestured for them to continue. They reached the bridges foot and were faced with a sheer wall of limestone which seemed to have no entrance.

"There must be a way around it," Tiberius shouted placing an ear to the wall. "The roaring sound is definitely coming from the other side." They crept from one end to another inspecting the obstacle looking for an obvious way in.

Suddenly, Crispin cried out, "Hey! Here's one of those Gorboo glops."

Tiberius rushed over and carefully inspected the wall above the malodorous pile. He was running a foreleg along the smooth surface when he discovered a narrow glop filled crawl space. "They must have come this way," Tiberius observed. He stuck his head inside for a moment and came out with a pinched up face. "Oh, they came this way all right. The smell is enough to knock over a rhinoceros beetle."

"I guess there's no other way for us to go," Crispin moaned.

"Unfortunately: no. Just try not to breathe too deep; and you might want to stow your vest away." Tiberius suggested as they entered the crawl space.

"Oh, great grubs! Thanks for reminding me." Crispin exclaimed as he began unfastening the ties.

A moment later, the pair reluctantly entered the Gorboo tunnel with Tiberius in the lead. The crevice was so narrow the pair had to drag their packs with a hind leg while pushing the lanterns ahead for guidance. Gasping at the smelly muck they traversed the tight passageway hoping it would be a very short trip. "I wonder how much further we have to go?" Crispin asked after they had crawled some distance.

"Couldn't be much further now," Tiberius answered breathlessly. "I'm starting to feel a puff of fresh air."

"Thank goodness," Crispin replied. "This is almost as bad as being in that nasty pitcher plant."

Tiberius had been right and shortly the passageway mercifully began to widen and soon they entered a larger chamber. The exhausted pair was greeted with a thunderous but beautiful cascading ribbon of crystal water gushing over a ledge from far above. They washed the ooze from their bodies in a quieter pool fed from the waterfall and rested for a short spell wondering what to do next.

Tiberius leaned over and cupped his forelegs around his mouth. "Let's move away from the waterfall so we don't have to shout."

Crispin nodded, stood up, slipped back into his vest, and adjusted his pack. They chose a path leading away from the waterfall, but unfortunately a short time later the corridor ended. It was however, much quieter and seeing no Gorboo glops, they felt it safe enough to rest for a while and plan their strategy.

"We'll have to keep following the Gorboo glop and hope it eventually leads us to them." Tiberius scratched a leg and went on. "My skin still doesn't feel clean, and it's sticky."

"So is mine," Crispin added. "I don't see any glop left on us, but I'm itchy and..." he paused and sniffed his leg, "I smell really weird, like skunkweed."

Tiberius smelled his foreleg, and wrinkled up his nose. "You're right. Phew whee."

"I hope it wears off before we get home," Crispin moaned. "If we come dragging in to Dragonfly Landing purple and stinky we'll be living alone on the village outskirts."

Tiberius chuckled, and reassured him it would probably would be gone by then. "We could try another bath," Crispin suggested.

"Not for me," Tiberius said grimacing. "I almost froze to death from the first one. Go ahead if you want to, but I would rather be sticky and smelly than catch bug-pneumia."

"Oh yikes. I don't want to get sick either. My uncle Philby had bug-pneumia once and he almost died. He couldn't fly for the longest time."

Tiberius gestured towards the corridor opening. "Well, we better be off. There's no way to plan anything until we see what we're up against."

"I hope we find their lair soon," Crispin sighed. "The suspense is getting to me."

They retraced their steps to the waterfall and scoured the ground until they found the trail of glops. The putrid piles led them up a steep rocky trail where they traversed several tight switchbacks. Their encounters with the glops now increased and the wary travelers positioned their lantern lids so low they could hardly see.

Suddenly, Tiberius heard Crispin gasp, and turned to see what was wrong.

Crispin was holding his forelegs up in the air. Neither of them could believe their eyes. Their bodies were glowing in the exact same shade of blue as the Gorboos. Tiberius closed the lantern lid completely and their bodies glowed even brighter.

"Great grasshopper legs," Crispin whispered, "What's going on?"

"It must be the glop we got on us," Tiberius replied waving his antennas around.

"Why didn't it wash off?" Crispin wondered.

"I don't know, maybe it soaked into our pores."

"I hope it comes off soon. It will be hard to hide if we're glowing."

"Wait just a minute," Tiberius whispered excitedly. "Yes, it just might work."

"What might work," Crispin asked expectantly.

"Now, think about this. If we're glowing the same way as the Gorboos, they might think we're one of them!"

"But we look different." Crispin protested.

"Yes, I know," Tiberius gestured wildly, "but it could give us a chance to sneak up on them." He sniffed a leg and continued, "especially if we smell like them too."

"Let's hope they have bad eyesight, like all the other creatures in this place," Crispin added.

"Yes, keep your legs crossed my little friend."

They continued on, their body glow leading the way, staying silent and alert for any signs of the Gorboos. At one spot in the trail, they came to a junction. One branch continued through a hole lying between two boulders, and the other to a nearby ledge.

"Which way," Crispin asked.

Tiberius pointed to the ledge, "Let's see what's below."

They lay on their bellies and peered over the abrupt drop off. Far below, a sea of tiny blue glowing dots were milling about in the inky void.

"Holy horseflies," Crispin gasped. "If those are the Gorboos, it must be a long way down."

"Those are the Gorboos all right," Tiberius stated. "They're at the bottom of a canyon."

Crispin nudged Tiberius and pointed to one end of the canyon. Two lines of Gorboos moving in opposite directions snaked along a switch back trail etched into the sheer wall of the abyss.

Tiberius leaned in close and spoke softly to Crispin. "That trail must be their way in and out of the canyon."

"Do we have to go that way too," Crispin inquired.

"Only if the crystals are down there."

A skeptical look passed over Crispin's face. "What if the crystals aren't down there?"

Tiberius studied the creatures moving along the canyon trail and replied. "There is a chance the crystals could be somewhere other than the canyon." He scratched an antenna in deep thought and went on. "It's obvious the Gorboos are doing something in other areas of the cave, but what?"

"Maybe this isn't their lair," Crispin suggested.

"You have a point," Tiberius agreed. "I just assumed it was here because there seems to be so many of them."

Crispin leaned further over the ledge, twisting for a better view of the trail. "I wonder where that trail exits. We didn't see any Gorboos at the waterfall junction."

"Well," Tiberius suggested, "they could have been in the other passageway."

"But we didn't hear any Gorboo sounds," Crispin pointed out.

"As we found out, the passageways in this place are full of bizarre twists and turns. They could have gone on any number of trails."

Crispin thought about what Tiberius had said for a moment. "So the Gorboos could have been close by, and we just didn't hear them."

"Exactly," Tiberius said throwing a foreleg up.

They watched the activities on the canyon floor a bit longer and then Crispin's whisper broke the silence. "Have you figured out what we need to do?"

Tiberius nodded; then replied. "First we need to follow the Gorboos to see what they're doing in other parts of the cave. Hopefully our first endeavor will bring us to the crystals. I don't know about you, but I would like to avoid going down into the canyon."

"Me too," Crispin agreed.

"All right, we'll follow the Gorboo procession around and see if they lead us to the crystals. If that doesn't work..." Tiberius, not needing to finish his statement, pointed down into the abyss. Cautiously, they crept back to the waterfall junction, and squatted behind one of the large boulders.

"I don't see the Gorboos," Crispin said peering around the formation's edge.

"I'm positive they're down that tunnel somewhere," Tiberius stated emphatically. He stood and stretched his legs. "And we'll never find them sitting here. It's now or never. Come on. Let's investigate that tunnel."

Crispin followed Tiberius from behind the bolder's safety, and they entered the hole. Immediately they were assaulted by the now too familiar malodorous Gorboo piles. Tiberius leaned close to Crispin and whispered. "When we see the blue glow ahead, slow down, and try to stay as quiet as possible. If we're spotted, and they come after us, we'll have to fly. It's the only advantage we have over them."

After rounding numerous corners and negotiating a slippery incline they stopped, baffled at the abrupt disappearance of glops. "Do you think we'll ever catch up with them," Crispin asked wearily.

Tiberius, looking confused, scratched one of his feathery antennas. "I'm beginning to think we've taken a wrong turn. We've lost the glop trail." He glanced at Crispin who was rubbing a leg and realized how tired the small bug looked. To Crispin's relief, Tiberius suggested they find a safe place to rest and have a honey cake. They found a large drapery looking formation, and slipped behind it. Later, with a full belly, Crispin was overcome with sleep, and he nodded off. Tiberius stood watch hoping they wouldn't have to retrace their steps, and start over. Fighting to stay awake he did a series of wing flapping exercises and high kicks. Suddenly, something thick and wet fell from somewhere above and smacked him on the head. He looked up and noticed a crack in the rock with the yellowish glop drizzling from it.

"I need a better look at this," He mumbled as he reached for his lantern. He directed the beam of light upwards and discovered a wet slick trail of glop on the tunnel walls. He followed it with the beam until it disappeared into a vertical shaft directly above his head. Another glop fell, and landed on his face, barley missing his eyes. He groaned and wiped it away with a foreleg. Afraid of loosing the Gorboo troop he woke Crispin.

"Oh no! I didn't mean to fall asleep," Crispin groaned.

"It's okay." Tiberius whispered, "but you need to wake up now. I've found the Gorboo trail."

Crispin sat with a start. "You did! Where?"

"Come this way," Tiberius ordered as they left the safety of the rocky wall. He shone the light upward and explained. "The reason we lost them was because they went up this shaft." He swept the beam along the wall illuminating the ascending path of slime.

Crispin clasped his head between his forelegs and shook it sadly. "Oh no. We have to crawl through another smelly hole."

"I'm afraid so," Tiberius replied apologetically.

"Oh well," Crispin said solemnly accepting his fate and removing his vest, "If we have to; let's get it over with."

"That's the spirit," Tiberius said giving Crispin a supporting thump on the back.

The two explorers flew up to the opening, took a deep breath and entered the yellow ooze covered shaft. Fortunately, once inside, the shaft opened up enabling the pair to avoid the walls and its inevitable slime bath. Until now, they had not encountered any perceivable air movement in the cave, but now there was a rather stiff current flowing through the shaft. Even with the buffeting breeze, they flew quickly and in no time, the exit was in sight. Hanging on with their forelegs, they peered over the opening into the adjoining chamber which was illuminated in the very familiar shade of Gorboo blue.

Tiberius signaled for Crispin to be quiet, and they slowly stuck their heads out into the chamber for a better look. It was a large room with another lake and a sprinkling of stalactites and stalagmites. It reminded them of Captain Jack's lake, but instead of being dark and glassy; this one had a milky consistency and glowed a beautiful summer sky blue. Along its edge and on the nearby rocks grew a thick fringe of stringy green vegetation. A dozen or more Gorboos mingled about, splashing in the water and tearing off chunks of vegetation with their razor like teeth.

Wisps of steamy fog rising from the pool swirled around the creatures, shrouding them in a hazy blanket. Suddenly, a fight erupted between two Gorboos over a particular patch of the mossy growth. A few of their companions glanced over as the altercation began, but others went about their bathing and plant collecting with total indifference. After a vicious exchange of talon swiping, hissing, clicking, and teeth gnashing, the looser skulked to a far corner licking his wounds. Tiberius motioned for Crispin to follow him back down the shaft, and they returned to their hiding spot.

"Geez bees," Crispin exclaimed, "Do you think that's their lair?"

"It's probably not," Tiberius replied. "There weren't very many of them there. If I had to guess, I'd say the pool was a place for food gathering."

"The stringy plants," Crispin questioned.

"Yes," Tiberius began, "and they certainly seemed to be enjoying the water as well."

Crispin's eyes widened. "It's like the glowing mushrooms in the Woods of Forgetfullness?"

"Sort of, but not quite the same," Tiberius nodded, and went on to explain, "It's called phosphorescence. The pool is full of very tiny creatures which produce a chemical in their bodies that glows."

"Like a glow worm," Crispin guessed.

"Yes, that's possible," Tiberius answered, then paused scratching his chin.

Suddenly, his face lit up, and he continued. "Maybe the Groboos are glowing because they eat and bathe in the pool."

Crispin rolled his eyes in thought for a moment. "Well, they do glow the same color of blue." He inspected his legs, and went on. "I'm confused about one thing though. If we're glowing because we're covered in glop, why doesn't it glow on rocks and the trails?"

"You've got me stumped," Tiberius admitted. "Unless the creature's body heat activates it somehow."

"That pond did look rather warm," Crispin added.

"Jumping junebugs," Tiberius said slapping a leg, "We may have solved the mystery of the glowing Gorboos. Now, if we could only solve the mystery of the glowing crystals."

"I didn't see any crystals around the pool," Crispin stated.

"Neither did I," Tiberius said. "We probably should go back and investigate the area. There could be an adjoining chamber we couldn't see."

A puzzled look crossed Crispin's face. "How can we do that with all those nasty Gorboos lurking about?"

"We'll wait here till they are all gone, and then return up the shaft to investigate."

"What if more Gorboos come while we're searching," Crispin asked skeptically

Tiberius waved a foreleg in the air, "If that happens, we'll just try to blend in."

Only a short time had passed before they began to hear the telltale clicking and scraping of talons coming down the shaft.

Chapter 20
The Lair

"They're coming." Tiberius whispered urgently as he motioned for Crispin to move deeper into the recess. "We don't want them to see us glowing," he warned. "They will surely come to investigate."

The ominous sounds and their accompanying spine tingling glow announced the creatures approach. Petrified, the pair held their breath as the glow intensified and outlined the drapery wall in a brilliant halo, pulsing with each passing creature. Crispin and Tiberius silently counted each one until the tunnel was once again plunged into darkness.

"I counted at least twelve," Tiberius reported. "That's about the same number of Gorboos we saw at the pool. I don't think there will be any more, but let's stay put for a while just to be sure."

"Sounds like a great idea," Crispin replied. "I'm in no hurry to meet those guys."

"That goes double for me," Tiberius added with an emphatic nod.

A short time later, Tiberius stood, brushed the gravely dust off his legs, and announced. "It's time to investigate that pool room." Crispin hopped up, and they crept from behind the alcove. "The coast is clear," Tiberius reported with a wave of his leg.

Re-navigating the loathsome shaft opening, and buffeting winds they ascended into the now deserted phosphorescent chamber. The wary cohorts circled the pool and began investigating the area for unseen chambers. A billowy moisture laden fog rose from the sapphire pool, and hung on its surface like a ghostly shroud. The air surrounding it seemed to wrap them in a lulling warmth and Crispin felt strangely drawn towards it. He leaned over the moss covered rocky edge and plunged several legs into the hypnotic water.

Tiberius, with a look of concern on his face, rushed over and laid a gentle but restraining hand on Crispin's back. "I know it looks very inviting, but remember where we are. There could be another Gorboo troop heading this way."

"Oh, sorry," Crispin said sheepishly, jumping up and shaking the water from his legs. "I...I...I couldn't help myself," he stammered.

"I understand," Tiberius replied sympathetically "I had the same urge myself."

The pair continued their search around the pool's perimeter but to their dismay, found no crystal filled chambers.

"Well, this room is a dead end," Crispin moaned. "I guess that means we have to go back to the canyon floor and deal with those creepy bugs."

"Yes," Tiberius replied, "If the crystals are down there, it's the only way to find them."

"Okay, I'm ready," Crispin unexpectedly sang out kicking his legs and dancing a jig around Tiberius. He stopped momentarily and a huge grin spread across his face. "For some reason, my legs seem to be full of energy. I'm beginning to see why the Gorboos hang out around this pool."

Tiberius glanced at Crispin's legs and a puzzled look crossed his face. He took Crispin by a foreleg and led him into a darkened crevice lying between several tightly packed stalagmites.

"What's going on," Crispin blurted out impatiently.

"Ah ha!" He pointed to his friend's legs. "I knew I wasn't imagining it."

"Imagining what," Crispin said stamping his legs in panic.

"Take a look at your legs, and see for yourself."

Crispin glanced down and let out a gasp. "Jumpin' junebugs, they're glowing a lot brighter than before. It must have been the water in the pool. These are the same legs I was soaking."

"I knew there was something unusual in that pool," Tiberius said rubbing an antenna thoughtfully; then added. "And you said your legs felt rested?"

"They don't feel tired at all, not like before. The water made them fell tingly and warm."

"Hmm." Tiberius mumbled narrowing his eyes.

"What," Crispin asked expectantly.

"Shhh," Tiberius ordered. "I'm hatching a plan."

They returned pool side and Tiberius paced, forelegs crossed, and head down in deep thought. Suddenly he halted and jabbed a foreleg into the air. "I've got it," he declared.

Crispin jumped excitedly. "What, what have you got."

"Come with me," Tiberius ordered, heading towards the pool.

"I think we should both take a little dip," he began. "The way I see it we need to recharge our glow so we can blend in better once we reach the canyon. Also, if that water re-energized your legs, just think what it will do for the rest of our body. I know we're not swimmers, but we can use those floating clumps of moss as rafts."

"That's a marvelous plan," Crispin exclaimed slapping one side of his head in amazement. "But what if the Gorboos show up while we're bathing," he added nervously.

"Don't worry," Tiberius reassured him. "We'll take turns. You go ahead and climb in. I'll go stand watch at the shaft entrance."

Crispin slowly but eagerly slid into the pool causing the fog to roll back in wispy tendrils and gentle waves to lap over the rocky edge. It splashed onto Tiberius legs and he let out a sigh. "Oh my! That does feel warm and refreshing. I can hardly wait for my turn."

Later, Tiberius was keeping a sharp eye on the shaft when he heard Crispin cry out. He rushed over, and found Crispin treading water frantically. "Help, my moss raft broke up."

"Don't panic, there's another clump behind you. See if you can reach it."

Crispin was thrashing in a circle trying unsuccessfully to reach the patch of vegetation when suddenly he flipped onto his back and began laughing. He kicked his legs effortlessly and back stroked over to the pool's edge.

Tiberius stared down with his mouth agape. "What in the world. How are you doing that?"

"I'm floating," Crispin shouted merrily. "But I haven't a clue how I'm doing it. I got so tired of fighting the water I had to rest, so I relaxed and that's when I noticed something pushing me upward."

"Whoopie! This is great. I can swim. Look! Watch this. He flipped over on his belly and dog paddled around the pool's edge."

"Oh no" Tiberius cried out. "Now I'll never get you out."

Crispin swam another lap around the pool and finally came to rest alongside Tiberius; who was soaking his legs motioning for Crispin to get out.

"Oh, do I have to?"

"I'm sorry," Tiberius said extending a foreleg to Crispin, "but the longer we stay here the more danger we're putting ourselves in."

Reluctantly, Crispin crawled out and shook himself sending a shower of blue shimmering droplets into the air.

"Oh!" he blurted. I forgot to tell you. The water is salty and has a really weird smell."

"I hope you didn't drink too much," Tiberius scolded.

"Nope. I kept my mouth shut most of the time."

Tiberius leaned over and sniffed. "It does smell rather strange: kind of like rotten eggs." He stuck a foreleg in and tasted a droplet of water. "Yep, it's salty all right." He spat and went on. "This is a mineral pool. I've heard stories of great bodies of water which are so dense with salt they hold you up."

"I've seen butterflies sipping minerals from mud puddles before," Crispin chimed in. "My father says it gives them energy. This water is kind of like that isn't it?"

Tiberius chuckled. "Well, not exactly. We're not drinking it. Traveling in this cool air for so long has cramped our muscles, and the warm water is relaxing them....AND it's my turn in the pool; so hurry and stand watch for any unwelcome guests."

"Oh, all right," Crispin said reluctantly. "But believe me, once you're in that pool, you won't want to get out."

Tiberius warily stepped into the pool, wings opened wide for extra buoyancy and began floating effortlessly around the edge. After becoming accustomed to the watery realm, he rolled back and forth dipping one wing, then the other; letting the miraculous waters relax his tired body.

Meanwhile, Crispin stood at his post humming a funny little tune his mother had sang to him as a baby. He hadn't thought about the song for a long time, but now, for some strange reason, it came floating back into his memory comforting him in this dark and lonely place.

Tiberius, worried the Gorboos might return, cut his swim short and exited the pool flapping his wings vigorously to dry them. "I sure hate to go back up that nasty shaft after getting squeaky clean," Tiberius complained as he strolled over to Crispin.

"Yep! I was just thinking the same thing," Crispin said giving the shaft opening a distasteful glance.

"Okay, let's get it over with," Tiberius stated as they headed to the opening. The two friends, now with an energetic spring to their walk, retraced their steps, and in no time were gazing over the cliff's edge.

"It's really rather beautiful," Tiberius commented; then added, "From a distance of course."

Crispin threw Tiberius a puzzled look, "What do you mean."

"Oh come now," he replied. "I thought you were the one with the vivid imagination. Look at that canyon floor again, and tell me what you see."

Crispin leaned over the edge a bit further knitting his brow. "There's nothing but..." he hesitated, and then a smile played across his mouth. "...wait, of course, now I see it."

"What do you see," Tiberius prompted.

"It's a night sky filled with stars...except..." Crispin covered his mouth and chuckled. "The stars are all moving."

Tiberius winked. "Well, I'm glad you haven't lost your imagination. That would be a pity."

"Don't worry, I'll always have that," Crispin grinned.

Now that the friends were sure that this was the creatures' lair, they decided it was time for a closer look. Armed with only their wits, bravery, and somewhat questionable camouflage, they crept stealthily towards the two way Gorboo highway. They crouched patiently behind a boulder at the roadway entrance observing the blue bodies coming and going along the steep cliff wall.

After some time Crispin whispered painfully, "My legs are all numb and prickly. I'm afraid if I don't stretch, I won't be able to move at all."

"It shouldn't be long now," Tiberius answered. "It looks like the Gorboo troops are thinning."

"Look." He pointed down the roadway. "There's only a few going back into the canyon, and I haven't seen any of the creatures come up for a long time now. They might be settling down for a rest period."

"Maybe it's their night time," Crispin interjected. "Although I can't see how they would know."

"They wouldn't," Tiberius replied, then went on. "Creatures without a sun or moon probably have something inside their bodies telling them when to wake, and sleep."

Crispin raised an eyebrow and whispered. "Well, I hope whatever tells them to sleep does it soon, before I'm permanently crippled."

Tiberius urgently peered over the boulder's edge and then let out a relieved sigh. "The road seems to have cleared. I don't see any of the creatures at all now." He turned and glanced back at the cliff overhang, "In fact, there isn't a single Gorboo anywhere."

"Good. Can I stretch my legs now?"

"Of course you can," Tiberius replied.

He tried to stand, but stumbled and fell over. "I can't feel my legs," he groaned. "It's like trying to stand on wooden stumps."

Tiberius smiled reassuringly. "Don't worry, just stretch out and rub them."

Crispin massaged his legs slowly. "Ouch! Now it feels like I fell into a stinging nettle."

"That's the circulation coming back," Tiberius said. "Just give it a little time. You'll be all right."

True to his word, Crispin's legs were soon back to normal and feeling fit as a fiddle. With the highway now devoid of any glowing bodies other than their own, the pair started down. They stayed close to the boulder lined edge to avoid detection and the glop piles concentrated along the middle of the road.

Occasionally they would stop after negotiating another laborious switch back and chance a look over the edge. The Gorboo lair seemed to rush up to meet them and with each passing view their steps grew heavier with dread.

After a time, the roadway flattened, and a large rocky embankment rose along one side of the highway, completely blocking their view. Tiberius held out a foreleg halting Crispin.

"Not being able to see where we're going makes me very nervous," he said in a low voice. "It's impossible to tell how close we are. The last thing we need is to stumble un-warned into Gorboo central."

Crispin swallowed hard. "I could have done without that piece of news."

"Don't panic," Tiberius replied. "We'll just slow down and keep a sharp eye out. Stay close behind me and watch for my signals." Crispin nodded and managed a feeble half smile.

Moving at a snail's pace, it seemed to take an eternity to cover the last leg of the road. Gradually, the embankment tapered off but the highways angle still hid the lair. Just when the pair felt the tedious trek would never end, they came upon a huge arch spanning the highway. The stone edifice seemed to stand detached from any surrounding structures, and it's inside curve dripped with the same straw like tubes they had seen earlier.

Finally Crispin broke the silence. "I wonder if the Gorboos use this for a highway marker."

"We'll find out soon enough." Tiberius replied indicating they should move on.

They passed under the arch and peered cautiously to see what lay beyond. To the right was only blackness and to the left stood a giant boulder blocking their view. They decided to go left, and crept towards the huge obstacle following its curve and bracing themselves for whatever lay beyond.

Suddenly, Tiberius jumped back and grabbed Crispin's shoulder. The look on Tiberius' face said it all. They had found the lair. He gestured for Crispin to peek around the boulder. He was about to get his first close up look at the lair when Tiberius noticed Crispin's antenna conspicuously sticking beyond the boulder's edge. He grabbed his friend's vest and gave it a tug. Crispin turned and saw Tiberius holding his feathery feelers down close to his face. Crispin almost let out a laugh but then understood what Tiberius was trying to tell him. He nodded, pulled his own antennas down, and resumed inspecting the lair.

Sprawled below was a city with hundreds of writhing glowing bodies, jostling to and fro, some crawling and clawing over their companions to reach their destinations. Others swarmed up the lower canyon wall weaving their way in and out of narrow fissures and strange honeycomb like pockets. A line of Gorboos carrying the mossy clumps from the pool room on their backs crawled along a narrow raised ledge encircling the city and disappeared into a large oval shaped portal. The noise rising from below was a continuous irritating symphony of clicks, tail thumping and scraping of claws. As the initial shock wore off, Crispin and Tiberius noticed that not all the Gorboos glowed with the same intensity and also varied in size. Some were longer and thinner while others had a chunky appearance and moved along at slug's pace. A chorus of angry hisses erupted from among the crowd and several of the Gorboos jumped on one another forming a vicious intertwined ball of slashing claws and clubbing tails.

Tiberius motioned for Crispin to sit tight while he studied the Gorboos routines and habits. It would be almost impossible to infiltrate undetected and search for the crystals with so many of the Gorboos moving about. They needed a plan and possibly a back up plan. Holding his feelers back out of sight, he first searched the area for signs of the crystals. He saw nothing other than the illumination from the creatures' bodies. 'If the crystals are here, they're somewhere inside,' he thought.

The constantly moving Gorboo mass and occasional fights were too haphazard to be of any use, but the moss carriers along the ledge seemed to be more predictable: coming and going at regular intervals. There were too many crevices and smaller pockets to safely search, so Tiberius decided the larger oval shaped portal the moss carriers were entering would be the most promising place to begin their search. His plan would also have to contend with the food packs and Crispin's vest which left conspicuous dark holes in their glowing camouflage. Leaving them behind wasn't an option, so additional coverage would need to be located. 'Hmm,' Tiberius mused, 'what could we use?'

While trying to solve the dilemma his eyes rested on the moss carriers. One possible solution hit him like a bolt of lightning. "Of course," he almost yelled out. It was an ingenious strategy, but to carry it out they would have to wait for the Gorboos' activity to slow....if it ever did. Watching the frenzied dance below, he had his doubts.

While waiting, he focused on the moss carriers and their puzzling journey along the ledge. It began at the pile of moss where a helper pinched off a layer of vegetation with his lobster like front claws and placed it on the carriers back. It then returned to the ledge and slowly moved along the trail until it came to the portal and disappeared. Other Gorboos, their backs empty appeared from the opening and returned for another mossy cargo.

A tap on Tiberius wing broke his concentration. He glanced at Crispin who had a look on his face which clearly translated as 'Well?' Tiberius smiled back reassuringly and mouthed 'I have a plan'. Crispin nodded and returned a silent 'Okay'. He returned to his observation and a short time later noticed that the main road seemed to be less congested. Many of them had migrated to the cliff wall and were squirming their way into the crevices and honeycombed pockets. As the chambers filled with the glowing bugs a soft blue light radiated from the walls and melted into the surrounding darkness. Several groups of the larger, slower Gorboos didn't attempt to climb the cliff, but instead lay along its base. Tiberius studied them for some time and seeing no motion other than an occasional leg twitch concluded they were sleeping. A few Gorboos still stirred along the main road and several moss carriers continued transporting their cargo.

He realized that this might be the opportunity they had been waiting for even if they had to side step several sleeping Gorboos. He leaned close to Crispin's ear and in as quiet a whisper as possible, began to explain the strategy. "We'll disguise ourselves by laying the moss on our backs; move along the ledge, and enter the portal. If we find the crystals, we'll fill our packs and try to sneak back out."

He hesitated momentarily and went on. "If we're discovered, we'll try to fly away. If not, run as fast as you can: and since you're faster than me, well..." He swallowed hard... "Getting the crystals back is the important thing. One pack is still better than none."

Crispin frowned and shook his head emphatically.

"Okay, okay," he said laying a steadying leg on Crispin, "if we get separated, make for that chamber we discovered by the waterfall. Don't wait too long. Keep moving and head for the entrance. Hopefully, we'll meet up along the way." He sighed heavily and asked, "Are you ready?" Crispin nodded.

After tightening their packs, they moved cautiously from behind their hiding place. Holding their bodies low to the ground in Gorboo posture, the pair slowly crept along the cities' outskirts hoping to avoid its inhabitants until the last possible moment. The pair halted momentarily, and surveyed the movements of the remaining active Gorboos. To Crispin and Tiberius' advantage most had gravitated to one particular spot well away from the moss heap; so they began weaving their way between groups of sleepers, choosing the shortest route to their objective.

The Gorboos were even more sinister up close; their thickened tails ringed with overlapping scales and talons sharp as any hawks'. Some of the sleepers were making a nasal clicking, snuffling sound, while others remained motionless, heads thrown back, and mouths agape revealing their dagger rimmed orifice. Suddenly one of the creatures twitched violently and its strap like tongue flicked out slapping Crispin's leg. It was cold, rough and wet with slime.

Crispin threw a leg up to stifle a scream and they froze as the eel like appendage retracted with a disgusting slurp.

Drawing near to the moss station they ducked under a rocky projection; and seeing none of the carriers or their attendants, Tiberius motioned for Crispin to follow him. Positioning themselves on the side facing away from the busy Gorboos, they began slowly pulling at the vegetation. It came off in thin sheets, and they took turns maneuvering it onto each others back. Once covered they discovered that when properly balanced it was relatively easy to carry. With Tiberius in the lead; and one last glance to ensure the ledge was unoccupied, they left the relative safety of the hill and began their trek along the ledge.

It was narrow and hard to navigate but to their relief, not steep. They passed several alcoves set into the cliff which Tiberius noted were probably used for the carriers to safely pass one another. After covering half the distance and hearing no commotion or alarms from below; they began to breathe a little easier. The entrance was drawing nearer and the pair was feeling a small amount of triumph when a glowing form exited the opening and headed in their direction. Tiberius' heart jumped into his throat as he realized the creature would surely see them at close range and he quickly searched their surroundings for an escape. Relieved, he spotted an approaching alcove, and the pair ducked in. They moved as far back as possible and squatted close to the floor. There were a few tense moments when the Gorboo stopped and squinted its reptile-like eyes into the crevice. His curiosity must have been satisfied because soon, they heard the dragging and scratching sounds pass on by. The pair looked at each other and managed a shaky smile. So far their ruse was working.

They covered the remaining distance with no other encounters and finally drew up alongside the portal. Tiberius chanced a quick look inside and seeing only darkness, stepped in. There was nothing unusual about the space, being low roofed and wide with small clumps of vegetation scattered about. Using the discarded moss as a trail marker they followed it deeper into the recess. After rounding several tight corners they noticed a pale blue glow coming from an intersecting corridor accompanied by a foul oily smell.

Tiberius motioned for them to take the path leading towards the light source. They crept along, hugging the wall until they stood next to an opening, and peered in. A smooth shallow pit carved into the stone floor held a writhing mass of very young Gorboos in varying stages of development. The newborns had a soft almost transparent quality to their bodies and had no glow. The older infants' bodies had begun to harden and take on a weak blue glow. Half a dozen adults lounged nearby shredding and chewing the stringy vegetation. Occasionally they would spit juice into a stone bowl receptacle positioned nearby. Tiberius noticed that the Gorboos were not the best shots, and some of the liquid would miss, landing on the floor. In one spot, it trickled down a narrow crack and disappeared. The babies were sucking and smacking away at the mulched concoction while the older ones chewed and batted it about playfully. Tiberius thought they almost looked cute, but he reminded himself what they would grow into. He began scanning the nursery for signs of the crystals, but saw nothing. He turned to Crispin, shook his head, and mouthed 'NO CRYSTALS'.

They returned to the intersection and decided to investigate the original corridor which seemed to extend farther in. Along the way, they found a darkened chamber and poked their heads in for a closer look. Again, there were no glowing crystals, only another shallow depression littered with bits of petrified moss and groups of stony debris. Tiberius glanced up and saw an old scar line across the ceiling revealing a possible reason for the abandoned nursery.

Crispin held his arms up in a 'what-now?' gesture, and Tiberius indicated for them to continue along the corridor. Shortly after leaving the abandoned nursery, the path dropped off dangerously on one side, and the ground became damp and slippery. After almost losing their step several times, Tiberius decided it was becoming too dangerous to continue. Reluctantly they retraced their steps and were passing the nursery when a pack of tiny, running Gorboos came charging from the chamber! Tiberius was frantically looking for a convenient hiding spot when suddenly Crispin shoved him into a small crack between two triangular shaped boulders. Immediately, the ground fell from under their feet, and they began a terrifying plunge downward. They tried to spread their wings, but found them useless in the tight shaft. The drop was a short one but to the plummeting pair it seemed to take forever. They landed with a bone jarring thud on a pile of loose gravel. The stunned victims both had the wind knocked out of them but jumped up immediately ready to flee if necessary. A blinding glare greeted them and they threw forelegs up to shade their eyes.

Chapter 21
A Fortunate Accident

After traveling for so long in the darkness it took a while for their eyes to adjust, but when they did, what lay before them had to be the most welcoming sight they would ever see. The chamber they had accidentally fallen into was filled with the very crystals they had traveled so far to find. Crispin jumped up and threw his forelegs into the air dancing madly in a circle, wearing a grin so big Tiberius thought his face would split in two. Tiberius couldn't help but join the celebration. He hooked arms with Crispin, and whirled until they were both dizzy, breathless, and hot!

Tiberius suddenly broke loose and whispered, "Why is it so hot down here? I wonder where..." He was cut off when a loud hiss followed by a cloud of steam erupted from somewhere in the chamber.

"Where is that coming from?" Crispin exclaimed waving at a patch of the muggy fog.

"I can't see anything either," Tiberius replied.

The steam quickly dissipated and Crispin glanced around the room. "Have you noticed the crystals are not all glowing with the same brightness? In fact, look, some aren't glowing at all."

"I probably should check it out." Tiberius began. "It could be important. We wouldn't want to get crystals that are going dead. You start filling your pack with the brightest ones and I'll be back shortly to help."

Crispin ran to a particularly brilliant cluster and began shoving the tiny treasures into his pack while Tiberius crossed to the far side of the chamber and picked up one of the darkened crystals. He turned it over in his hand and it cracked into two halves.

"Hmm. Very curious." He mumbled. The pieces were very hot, and he dropped them just as a loud hissing belched under his feet. Startled, he fluttered away just in time to avoid being engulfed in the steam cloud. After it had subsided, he investigated the ground where the steam seemed to enter and found a series of small cone shaped vents. Still nervous from the steam eruption, he jerked his body sideways as something wet hit his wing. He looked up to see what was falling from above, and saw a tiny fissure with several amber colored droplets dangling from its edge. Another fell and he jumped aside. It landed on the floor, rolled once, picking up a layer of dark blue dust, and finally came to rest near one of the vents. He leaned in for a closer look at the mysterious droplet, and noticed a strangely familiar odor. It was the same oily smell they had encountered in the nursery. Then he remembered the spitting nursery workers, and the juice draining into a crack in the floor. Suddenly, another steam eruption belched forth shooting the forming crystals towards the far end of the chamber. Once the air cleared, he glanced around one more time and realized the farther the crystals had been blown from the steam vents the more brilliant they glowed. "Of course," Tiberius muttered excitedly, "that must be how the crystals are formed!"

He wanted to rush over and explain his theory to Crispin, but knew it would have to wait so he began filling his own pack. Crispin had already tied his filled bag, and was stuffing the almost weightless crystals anywhere he could find a spot. He tucked several into his hidden vest pocket and a few others into the 'Heart of the Sky' box.

Satisfied that he had collected as many crystals as possible he began helping Tiberius fill his pack. With Crispin's help, it wasn't long before the other pack was filled. The lanterns' woven handles were quickly looped through the packs' straps, and retied. Even though their cargo hadn't increased much in weight, it was swollen like an engorged tic and cumbersome. With each others help, the packs were maneuvered onto their backs and firmly secured.

Crispin glanced at the shaft opening and frowned. "There's no way we're going to return that way, especially with these bulky packs." He glanced at Tiberius with a cocked eyebrow. "Got any ideas?"

"I'm already on it," Tiberius reported quietly. "Haven't had much luck yet, but there's a rather large hidden area back in the shadows I haven't checked." He waved a leg towards a darkened recess beyond the vent cone. "I'm almost certain I saw an eddy of steam being sucked in that direction which indicates air move-ment." He moved on, still talking in a low voice as Crispin scurried alongside. "And, if air is flowing in, it has to be coming from somewhere. We just have to find it."

As if on cue, the vent cone released its pent up energy and the chamber thickened with fog.

"Here's our chance," Tiberius said batting at the misty curtain wrapped around his head. The steam cloud began to thin and spread along the floor but several wispy strands danced and spiraled upwards. The friends fluttered up to the ceiling chasing the eddies and immediately felt a current of air tugging on their bodies.

"There it is." Tiberius pointed as he spotted an opening where the rock had fractured. "Let's see if we can make it through."

Fortunately the fissure was roomy, and the pair had no trouble flying through. They continued on a level course until the fissure appeared to dead end. They landed and on closer inspection, found that it curved sharply and narrowed. "We'll have to go this way," Tiberius said as he thrust his head into the tunnel. "It might be a tight fit but," he withdrew his head, looked around and continued. "There doesn't seem to be any other way to go."

"I'll have to remove my pack and pull it behind me," he said. "You can leave yours on and follow. If I can make it through with my big wings, I'm sure you can."

"Okay, I hope you're right. Having my body parts rearranged isn't my idea of fun," Crispin replied. Even with the gravity of their situation, Tiberius couldn't help but smile at his young friend's quirky sense of humor.

Tiberius, his pack dragging from his rear leg, entered the next section with Crispin close behind. The pair ventured on and as expected, it was a tight fit becoming so narrow in several places they had to wiggle and contort their bodies to keep moving.

"I can hardly breathe," Crispin croaked pulling himself along on his stomach. "I should have taken my pack off too."

"Try to keep going," Tiberius coached. "I think we're almost out of this tunnel. The limestone rock is being replaced by another kind of stone."

"I hope you're right," Crispin moaned pushing a lose pebble from under his wing

Tiberius had been right. The amber veined knobby limestone ended and the pathway widened just enough for them to move on with ease.

The space they were now traveling through had oddly angled walls which were smooth as glass. The travelers ghostly faces stared back at them as they passed the reflective stone.

Startled, they began passing intriguing sections of wall which were softly illuminated from behind; their dark mirrored surfaces having been transformed into a translucent tapestry of wavy ringed circles. Some were very pale with folded layers of white and cream while others with hues of dark brown and amber resembled rings in a tree. Crispin and Tiberius, having grown suspicious of things glowing, moved on with a feeling of doom closing in.

A tiny black dot in the distance appeared and steadily expanded into an opening. They were glad to see a way out of the unsettling passageway but worried that something sinister lay beyond.

After studying their surroundings Tiberius was almost certain where they were but he wouldn't know for sure until they reached the opening. He wondered if Crispin had come to the same conclusion. Holding a leg out, he signaled for Crispin to halt. Their exit was close now and if he was right they would have to be prepared. Tiberius went ahead and drew alongside the opening. Holding his feelers down, he slowly stuck his head out, surveyed the surroundings then quickly pulled back in. His evaluation of the passageway had been right. The fissure in the crystal chamber had connected with the cliff wall. They had been traveling through one of the honeycomb pockets with Gorboos occupying the adjoining cells!

Crispin came near and pointed to the glowing walls around them then made a fierce face. Tiberius nodded smiling. He was right; Crispin had figured it out too. He peered out again to get their bearings. The chamber they were in was surrounded by glowing cells and the clusters of sleeping Gorboos were still snoozing and twitching on the canyon floor. Another group, directly below on the main thoroughfare was kicking a small pebble back and forth amidst periodic bursts of clicking and leg flailing.

'Hmm,' Tiberius mused. 'They're not paying very close attention to things.'

A movement below caught his eye and he glanced down just in time to see a moss carrier passing by. 'I wonder if it could work again,' he pondered; watching the carrier approach and then disappear from view. 'The Gorboos on watch might not even look up if we leave the way we came in, but two flying bugs would surely get their attention.'

Deciding on a strategy, he turned to Crispin and whispered instructions. After he finished, Crispin asked "If we get caught, then we fly right?"

Tiberius nodded; then added "Remember what I told you about getting away?"

Crispin gulped his eyes widening. "It won't come to that," he whispered emphatically.

"Just remember." Tiberius said sternly; then he paused, looked at the exit then added, "We need to leave before they start to wake up."

Tiberius untied the pack from his leg, brushed the dirt off, and re-secured it to his back. Crispin tightened his and after one last survey of the escape route they warily stuck their heads out. Tiberius stepped out first with Crispin close behind. As suspected, the Gorboos below were so absorbed with their rock kicking game that none of them even glanced up. The ledge was still unoccupied and the pair moved along in their Gorboo posture at a slow, nerve wracking speed. As the moss station drew near, they were feeling a bit easier at having made it this far when a carrier suddenly crawled from behind the station and started up the ledge. Alarmed, Tiberius searched for another alcove but finding none decided to chance the encounter and hope for the best. They pressed tight against the wall, still moving and the carrier passed, casting an uninterested glance in their direction. They couldn't believe the Gorboo hadn't noticed the bulky packs or their strangely shaped bodies. Maybe their eyesight really was bad! Their relief didn't last long. The carrier halted, turned and headed back. Crispin and Tiberius were almost to the ledges' foot when the trailing Gorboo started clicking. The pair moved on, trying not to show their panic.

The carrier paused and another flurry of clicks flew at their jangled nerves. It was obvious that the carrier wanted a reply. When none was received, it scurried closer and glared at them, tipping his head in curiosity.

Crispin and Tiberius jumped as it let out a menacing hiss followed by a rush of more urgent sounding clicks. Another Gorboo slithered from behind the moss station and jumped across their path hissing and spitting.

"I don't like t-h-i-s," Crispin spat out no longer seeing a need to stay silent.

Before Tiberius could reply, the two Gorboos rushed at them mouths open, teeth gnashing and front claws snapping.

"Fly," Tiberius yelled.

They took to the air not a second too soon. The Gorboos lunged into empty space crashing into each other in a shower of stringy spit and tangled claws. Crispin and Tiberius didn't even chance a look back. A loud piercing hiss, more like a scream rose from below, followed by sporadic clicks which rippled through the lair. The alarm had been sounded! A group of Gorboos just beginning their trek down the switch back were turning back towards the top.

'Oh no,' Crispin thought. 'They're going to head us off at the overlook.'

Crispin, having flown faster, was safely on the overlook edge. Tiberius motioned for him to go on. "Keep going! Run!" he yelled.

Crispin hesitated momentarily; then ran. Tiberius landed on the overlook, but the Gorboos were faster than expected. They were already there. Crispin glanced back just as the Gorboos swarmed toward Tiberius.

'He'll never make it,' Crispin gasped. 'I have to do something.' He searched frantically, and noticed a small stalactite overhead. 'It's in the right position.' he thought. 'My fire crackling will do the job'.

The Gorboos closed in on Tiberius, eyes seething, teeth gnashing and talons digging at the ground. Tiberius quickly glanced over at Crispin. A terrible sense of guilt rushed over him, 'I told him this wouldn't happen.' "Run, Run!" He yelled again.

Instead Crispin moved closer calling out, "Tiberius, move back and cover your eyes, **NOW**!"

Tiberius jumped back. 'What was he doing?' He thought. 'They'll get him too!' Suddenly a blinding orange spark shot upwards followed by a loud boom. A shock wave of dust filled Tiberius' throat.

"Run," Crispin screamed.

He plunged blindly through the lingering cloud fighting his way through a sea of writhing limbs toward Crispin's voice. He chanced a quick glance over his shoulder. The Gorboos were on their backs kicking at air or staggering around blindly. The stalactite which lay close by was completely blocking their path.

Tiberius saw Crispin dash over to the pool room tunnel entrance gesturing at the boulders perched over it, "I can zap these too...seal it off. It'll cut off their source of moss!"

"No!" Tiberius yelled, "You can't do that. Hurry," he waved impatiently, "I'll explain later. That roadblock won't hold them forever."

The pair ran faster now, trying to put distance between them and their predators. Not wanting to get lost, but with a sense of urgency they retraced their steps. They found the waterfall junction, and paused momentarily for a drink before entering the hidden crawl space. This time there were no complaints of the smelly glop, only silent relief they had made it this far. The arched bridge welcomed them and they paused long enough to wash in the water swirling underneath. Flying in pitch black, even with their body glow and lantern light it was difficult enough, but with glop stiffened wings and joints, it would be almost impossible.

"We look brighter," Crispin said waving a leg in the air.

"Our glow must have been re energized when we crawled back through the secret tunnel." Tiberius said; then added. "Although it's not much help now that we've been discovered."

"Maybe we lost them," Crispin said hopefully.

"We don't know that for sure," Tiberius replied, "We have to keep going."

They were drawing close to the bridges' opposite side when Tiberius halted and held up a leg. "Shh, I hear something."

In the distance they could hear faint but unmistakable sounds of scraping talons; then a Gorboo slid from behind the secret door to the waterfall. Crispin and Tiberius bolted, running in the more confined spaces, or gliding when they had room. A short time later, Tiberius slowed, and looked around puzzled.

"We're lost, aren't we?" Crispin said with a gasp.

"Sort of," Tiberius confessed. "The exit to the tunnel where we met the old cricket should be here but I don't see it." He hesitated then added. "Okay, we need to open our lanterns."

The area immediately flooded with light and Crispin pointed to a darkened area under an outcropping resembling a turtle.

"Maybe that's it," he pointed.

"We don't have any other choice. Let's take it." Tiberius ordered. "I think I hear them again."

It didn't take long for Tiberius to realize this wasn't the tunnel they had come through. He saw nothing familiar but remained silent not wanting to worry Crispin.

"I think we took a wrong turn," Crispin whispered. "Look at these strange knobby rocks on the floor. I would have remembered them."

'So much for keeping quiet,' Tiberius thought then said out loud, "I'm sure we're heading in the right direction. Remember the three tunnels just after Captain Jack's lake?"

"Do you think this is the one we didn't take," Crispin asked.

"That's what I'm hoping," Tiberius replied.

THE GORBOOS WERE noisy travelers and announced their arrival with muffled clicks and thumpings. "Come on," Tiberius coaxed with new urgency in his voice. "Captain Jack's lake is in a big chamber. We can fly through it if we're careful."

The few odd knobby projections soon spread into a continuous carpet causing them to slow and pick their way through. The ominous sounds and weak blue glow spilled into the darkness as the Gorboos raced to catch up. Crispin and Tiberius scrambled over the maddening obstacles; their pulse quickening when they caught a glimpse of the exit around a bend.

Moving at full steam, they scrambled out the exit and immediately lost their footing as the ground fell away. They began to slide down a smooth but bumpy course, using their wings as brakes. After a frightening but mercifully short trip, they skidded to a stop.

"Are you all right?" Tiberius asked.

Crispin sat moaning, moving his joints. "I'm okay - you?"

"I'm in one piece," he answered rubbing a wing, then standing slowly.

They swung their lanterns in a wide arc and the surrounding darkness jumped to life. They were in a large chamber at the bottom of a flowstone hill which poured like a frozen waterfall from a gaping hole above.

"That's the tunnel we were just in," Crispin pointed.

Tiberius scanned the room quickly; scratching an antenna then led Crispin farther into the chamber. "Look over there," he pointed.

"It's the amethyst tunnel," Crispin exclaimed. "And past that is the tunnel where we ran into the old cricket."

"We ended up coming out of the tunnel we didn't take." Tiberius said; then continued. "Remember, we didn't want to climb the steep hill."

"Then Captain Jacks' lake is not far away," Crispin said.

"We need to get moving," Tiberius ordered. "Undoubtedly, the Groboos aren't far behind."

As if on cue, a commotion above caught their attention. A group of Gorboos burst from the opening, and slithered down the flowstone in a blue wave.

Tiberius glanced upward then said tersely, "We can fly for a while." With a push of legs and flutter of wings, the pair became airborne but couldn't go very fast. Even with the extra lantern light they feared colliding with unseen obstacles. It was enough to give them the advantage they needed, and soon the pursuing horde disappeared from view.

They knew captain Jack's lake was drawing near because of the thickening forest of stalactites and stalagmites. Eventually, maneuvering between them became too difficult and they dropped down to continue on foot.

Their mood had lightened considerably thinking they had possibly shaken their pursuers. "I think we'll be seeing the light of day soon," Crispin stated; then crooned, "Ahh. I can feel the warmth on my wings already. Hey! Can we stop and see the blind fish again?"

"We'll see." Tiberius replied trying to remain objective.

Crispin was the first to spot the lake. "There it is he called out excitedly. I see the light reflecting off it. Can we please stop for a second?" Crispin begged.

Relenting, Tiberius agreed. "All right, but we can't stay long."

LATER, PERCHED OVER the pool's rim watching for the silver flash of darting fish, Tiberius noticed a momentary blue flicker on its surface. He flinched, but then relaxed, deciding it was their reflection. Then he heard a strange tap...tap coming from some-where close by. 'Probably just a drop of water hitting the floor,' he thought. But deep down he knew it didn't sound quite right. Another strange noise, more of a scratch, came from behind. A knot formed in his stomach, then tightened as a rustling sound followed.

Crispin heard it too. He turned to Tiberius, eyes bulging with alarm.

Tiberius leaned close and whispered, "Let's get out of here now!"

Before they could even stand, a bright blue wave flooded the chamber. A quick glance over their shoulders revealed the nightmarish hoard. They were pouring from behind every stalagmite and crevice, hissing, clicking, and snapping their claws in a murderous rampage. "Ambush!" Tiberius yelled. Several of the nearest Gorboos rushed in flinging their eel like tongues at their intended victims.

"Quick," Tiberius ordered, "Open your lantern."

Crispin froze for a moment faced with the onslaught then threw the cover open. Brilliant light hit the first wave of attackers. They screeched, jerked their claws over their eyes and stumbled backwards trampling those behind. Tiberius knew there would be no escape on the ground. Gorboos swarmed the exit to the next chamber. "Up! Up!" He yelled.

With a spring of legs and thrash of wings they buzzed over the Gorboos narrowly escaping the huge snapping claws. Crispin shot a few well aimed lightning bolts as he descended sending several swaths of Gorboos flying through the air. A storm of frustrated hisses and clicks erupted as the Gorboos realized that their prey had escaped once more.

Crispin and Tiberius fluttered erratically among the stalactites not knowing what to do. It had all happened so fast. For a few tense moments they lost sight of each other in the maze of frozen spears. Finally Crispin caught sight of Tiberius' wing and flew towards it. He found him hanging from a stalactite above the lake intently studying the ceiling.

"There you are," Tiberius gasped, "You scared me to death. I was about to come search for you."

"I lost you when I was aiming my fire cracklings. Some of those slime balls won't be walking for a while."

"You're amazing," Tiberius said then pointed down. "Look. They're trying to climb up the columns." Crispin looked down and saw the bugs crawling up, then with screeching talons, slipping back down. "Fortunately, they can't get a foothold." Tiberius added.

"Good," Crispin said breathlessly. "We could use a break. Jumping junebugs! Where did they all come from?"

"I don't know," Tiberius replied, "and right now I really don't care. We need to find a way out of this chamber and I think there might be one just beyond the stalactite scarred area." He swept his lantern beam along the ceiling, tracing a long fissure; then paused at the round jagged craters.

"Can you see it," Tiberius asked.

Crispin tilted his head, "Yes, there it is."

"Now, look at this spot." Tiberius moved the beam a bit. "See how the opening closes in on itself."

"Let's go check it out," Crispin piped up, already heading for it.

They inspected the spot where the fissure narrowed and discovered an opening which seemed promising. A small lip of brownish stained rock dripped from its entrance. Beyond that a dried and cracked deposit of mud carpeted the tunnel's floor. The pair entered and made their way along the passageway hoping to find an alternate route to the massive domed area. Just beyond would be the cave's entrance and freedom. What they found however was a dead end.

"This isn't good," Crispin said.

"Let's not give up yet," Tiberius reassured him, "We could have missed an opening. We'll work our way back through the tunnel slower this time."

Even with their lanterns fully opened, they found no other exit. The fissure was one long continuous path leading to nowhere. They returned to where the passageway opened into the cratered ceiling and decided to check on the Gorboos.

"Maybe they've given up and left," Crispin said hopefully.

"I guess they could have." Tiberius replied but deep inside, he feared that would never happen.

The Gorboos were too cunning and ruthless, not the type to give up so easily. They peered over the opening's edge, and surveyed the lake room. A large group of Gorboos were still milling about snapping at the water with their oversize claws or bathing their legs, clicking incessantly. Several lounged nearby propped against stalagmites, munching on the remains of an unfortunate fish.

"We might be able to fly over them and make it to the exit," Crispin whispered.

"We could try, but...look at the exit. It's crawling with Gorboos. They've piled on top of each other to block the entrance. We'd get snagged for sure."

They sat for a while, watching and hoping they would see some sign of retreat. To their dismay, there seemed to be more Gorboos than before. "Look at them," Crispin whispered. "I think they've decided to give up the chase, and have a pool party."

"They do seem to be enjoying themselves," Tiberius whispered back. "This could be to our advantage if we could only find our way into the domed chamber. Even if there are guards posted we could make a beeline for the cave's mouth."

"It would be even better if there were no guards at all," Crispin replied.

Tiberius nodded then suggested, "Well, we could wait for a while and see if they leave. We'll check again later." They returned to the dead end dusty, tired, and hungry.

"There must be another way out," Crispin said looking around the blocked tunnel.

"I'm sure we'll come up with a solution," Tiberius replied. "Right now, we need to get some rest. Maybe it will energize our brains."

Crispin sighed, "I think my brain would work better on a full stomach."

Tiberius chuckled, "We'll be out of here soon, and you can eat until you can't fold your wings."

Crispin looked at Tiberius, a glimmer of hope in his eyes. They removed their cumbersome packs, stretched out on the smooth tunnel floor and fell into a deep but disturbing dream-filled sleep. Tiberius dreamt of disembodied eel like tongues, slurping and tightening around his body. Crispin, spared from visions of nightmarish beasts, had tortured dreams of biscuit like stones magically changing into his mothers poppy seed cakes. They floated tantalizingly just beyond reach; then fell, bombarding his body.

Crispin woke with a start and a rumbling belly or was he still dreaming. Something hit his head: then his wing. He stirred and shook his head. More particles rained from above in a shower of 'ping pings' and 'tap taps'.

Tiberius; also awakened by the commotion, jumped up and threw a protective leg over his head.

"The Gorboos, they're digging in." Crispin cried. "They might cause a cave in. We will be eaten or buried alive. We have to get out of this tunnel. Hurry!"

Chapter 22
Help from Above

He was rushing to get his pack on when Tiberius opened his lantern and swept its beam above their heads. A chunk of the rocky ceiling accompanied by another shower of dirt fell to the floor. They jumped back. A hole opened followed by a dark brown pointed head, and two black shiny eyes. It caught sight of them and quickly jerked back.

Tiberius held his lantern higher. "If I'm not mistaken, that was an earthworm."

Crispin's pack fell to the ground with a dull slap. "We must have scared it," he said.

"Hey. Come back," Tiberius called. "We won't hurt you."

"Yes, we're friends," Crispin added.

A moment later, the worm peeked out; then spoke. "Why are you glowing like Cenrabs then?" Crispin and Tiberius shot puzzled looks at each other.

"Cenrabs?" Tiberius said. Then looking up repeated louder, "Cenrabs? You mean the blue glowing monster bugs that live down here."

The worm waggled his head. "Yep. Those are the guys." Then he went on, "Never seen the scum bugs myself, but heard some weird stories about them. Supposed to look like a cross between a centipede and crab all rolled into one freaky-droolin-eat-anything-they-can-get-their-claws-on-bugs. Don't ever want to run into those guys."

"Well," Tiberius said. "We're not them."

"I can see that now," the worm replied.

"I'm Tiberius, a luna moth. This is my friend Crispin. He's a lightning bug."

"That doesn't explain how you're glowing," the worm stated.

"Oh!" Tiberius began to explain. "It's because we're covered in this slimy stuff the Gorboo......I mean, the Cenrabs drop all over the place."

The worm cocked his head. "What the mole hill are you doing in this cave?"

They explained as quickly as possible about their quest, and narrow escape from the lair. "Then they chased us into this dead end," Crispin chimed in. "We can't go back. They're waiting below. Can you help us get out?" He added excitedly.

"All right you guys. You sound like you're on the up and up. I'm Mortimer McDigger, but my friends call me Mac. Pleased to make your acquaintance. I'd offer you a leg but," he chuckled, "as you can see, I don't have any legs."

"You guys have guts; I'll say that for you. I'm glad we don't have to tangle with those slimy maggots for crystals. We're not too crazy about light. In fact," he squinted, "Don't suppose you could dim those lanterns a bit?"

"No problem." Tiberius replied as they lowered the lids. "Are we close to the surface," he asked remembering the dried mud at the fissure's entrance.

Mac scrunched up his pointy face and replied. "Well now, that depends on your viewpoint."

"And what viewpoint would that be," Tiberius asked.

"It could be a long way for you guys, but for us worms, it could be closer. I guess it depends on how much you can stretch."

Tiberius thought he saw Mac wink, but the worm's eyes were so beady and heavily lidded he couldn't quite tell.

Mac chuckled again with a deep mellow voice. "Just teasin' you guys. Sorry you look like you've been through a hail storm. Me and my buddies from the AVA can dig you out."

"What's an AVA?" Crispin asked frowning.

"That's who me and the crew work for. It stands for Annelid Valley Authority. You're looking at the head digger for the department of excavation." A proud smile formed at the tiny slit under his pointed nose. "I'm also in charge of investigating possible new burrowing sites. That's how I dug into this chamber. Knew there was a cave system down here somewhere. Guess I misjudged my depth."

Tiberius cleared his throat to stop the worm's rambling. "Uh; not to be rude, but how long would it take to dig us out? We've been out of food for a while."

"Don't get your wings in a bunch. You guys sit tight. I'll go get my crew. We'll have you out of here faster than a bumble bee wing." He started to pull back; then stopped. "Hey, you guys want us to bring back some food? The department of waste and composting just found a mound of half rotted apples: mmm, mmm. Good stuff too."

Crispin and Tiberius glanced at each other and grimaced. "No thanks," Tiberius called up. "We can hold off a little longer." Mac disappeared and they sat down to wait.

"Yuck," Crispin spat. "Rotten fruit."

"That's not what bothered me," Tiberius said.

Crispin shot him a puzzled look.

"Think about it," Tiberius replied raising an eye then said, "Where would they carry it?" They sat for a while talking excitedly about their return trip home until they ran out of things to say and the dead end chamber fell quiet.

Crispin broke the silence. "Do you think they can really dig us out?"

"I think they can manage it," Tiberius replied. "Earthworms are renowned for their tunneling talents."

"Don't you think he was sort of peculiar," Crispin asked.

"No," Tiberius replied emphatically then went on, "Not compared to all the other unusual creatures we've met: gypsy moths, the stink bug boys, and Rock E. Crab."

"Especially Rock E. Crab," Crispin chortled.

They laughed heartily. It felt good after such a long time.

"HEY, WAKE UP down there," Mac called out some time later. He pushed further into the room, dangling. "I'm back with the crew. You thought I was going to be a no show; didn't you."

"No, we didn't," Tiberius said trying to sound convincing.

"We've been widening the tunnel so you guys can fit. Now, move out of the way, the dirt's going to fly when we open this hole."

They moved down the tunnel a short distance, and watched as a shower of dirt and pebbles rained to the floor. Then they heard Mac's voice ring out. "Coast is clear guys, we've busted through."

They stepped back into the dead end, waded through a pile of debris, and stared up at four worm faces dangling from the newly excavated opening.

"Hey, how's it going?" A thinner reddish brown worm spoke. I'm Ed Wiggler:" He thrust his head up against another worm of the same color, "And this is my twin, Red. We work on Mac's excavation crew." Red didn't say a word.

"What's the matta' with you Red?" Ed prompted. "Mind your manners. Say hello to these guys."

He squinted at Red; then laughed. "Sorry guys, he's turned himself around again. I was talking to the wrong end." Red's tail disappeared momentarily and then his other pointed end appeared.

"Oh, there you are," Ed said, exasperated. "I hate it when I'm talking to the wrong end."

"So do I," Red replied. "Sometimes I can't tell if I'm coming or going." Then, glancing down added, "Say, look at those guys down there, where did they come from? And glowing blue. Now I've seen everything."

"It's a long story," Mac cut in, "Don't have the time. We need to get them out. There's Cenrabs hanging around."

"Cenrabs!" Red and Ed spat in unison. "You didn't mention anything about those monsters when you volunteered us for this job."

"Don't get your segments out of joint." Mac said sternly. "We'll be out of here before those maggots can roll over."

Crispin noticed a worm hanging behind Red and Ed. "Who is that." he asked pointing to the fourth worm.

It wagged its head and squeezed closer. "Nice to meet you guys. I'm Brad Bait." Then he added quickly, "Yeah, yeah, I know, bummer of a name." He shot a warning glance at the other worms. "I've heard all the jokes before, so don't bother. I work for the department of waste management. It's my job to locate compostable materials. These guys would starve if it wasn't for me and my crew."

Crispin, puzzled, asked. "Compostable:" then added. "Like rotting apples?"

"You got it, kid." Brad said proudly then went on. "We follow these guys around trying to keep the tunnels free from worm castings." He chuckled, "You know; waste products."

"Yeah," Ed laughed. "He's a garbage mover."

"Hey," Brad yelled shoving Ed, "Waste engineers if you don't mind."

"Oh sorry, I forgot," Ed rolled his eyes trying to sound non apologetic.

"All right you dirt bags," Mac cut in , "that's enough jabbering. How about a little action."

He looked at Crispin and Tiberius and wagged his head, "What do you say we blow this joint?"

"We're more than ready." Tiberius said stretching his legs.

"Great, just follow me and the crew." Mac instructed then added. "We rigged up a root rope in case you need some help along the way. The walls of freshly dug tunnels can be a real problem, you know loose pebbles, landslides; that sort of thing. A nervous glance passed between Crispin and Tiberius as they adjusted their packs.

Mac noticed and quickly added. "Hey. Don't worry about it. You're with the master excavators."

"Yeah, that's right," Ed and Red chimed, "We're the masters."

"Hrumph," Brad mumbled.

Mac and Brad headed into the tunnel with Crispin and Tiberius following single file. The twins were bringing up the rear. The tunnel was tall and narrow but even with Tiberius' wings folded, they barely fit.

The worm crew; in pairs, squirmed through the tunnel while Crispin and Tiberius crept along its sides, clutching onto pebbles and deposits of clay. A short way up, the walls turned sandy and they began to loose their footing on the loosening grains. The twins below were being pelted.

"You guys having trouble?" Red shouted.

"It's this loose sand," Tiberius replied.

"Ahhh," Crispin cried out as he slipped.

He caught a small white root, and dangled until the twins caught up. They moved under him supporting his legs with their backs and shouted to Mac, "Hold up guys, got a problem down here."

Mac and brad halted and looked down. "I was afraid of that sandy area." Mac answered. "We're almost to the root rope. Can you carry Crispin for a short distance?"

"You got it." The twins called back. "Okay kid, hang on."

Crispin let go of the root, and dropped onto their backs. They weren't slippery, as he expected, just dry and sturdy like a mushroom cap. Tiberius with his stronger legs was able to keep going.

The twins slid along with Crispin hanging on, eyes shut tight against the shower of sand.

"Here comes the root rope." Mac announced.

Tiberius looked up and saw Mac and Brad shinny past a thick yellowish root. He scrambled onto the root's tapered end and began crawling up. Crispin grabbed on as the twins moved passed. Eventually, a forest of smaller roots sprang from the crumbly earthen walls, slowing their pace. Whitish roots as fine as a gnat's eyelash were easy to maneuver through, but the tougher pink fleshy ones snapped back as they tried to pass. The experienced worm crew wove their way through the roots with ease, but Crispin and Tiberius were smacked several times by the whip like pink tentacles.

Not one word of complaint was heard from Crispin and Tiberius. They knew the roots were a sign that the surface was near. The moist soil exhaled a sweet earthy aroma like the one which lingers in the air after a summer rain shower. Crispin and Tiberius scrambled upward as hard and as fast as their legs would go, spurred on by the expectation of fresh air filling their lungs.

The roots became shorter and tuft like; then a faint grayish glow, slowly brightening to a pale violet blue, seeped into the tunnel. The root rope angled sharply and disappeared through the wall. Tiberius looked up and lost sight of Mac and Brad. He scurried up the remainder of the tunnel and crawled out onto a welcome mat of early morning dew covered grass, then reaching down, he helped Crispin from the hole. The sun had just risen and was perched low on the eastern horizon splitting the waning night into a thousand golden shards. Crispin and Tiberius covered their weakened eyes, but felt its warm rays caress their bodies. They breathed deeply embracing the crisp heavily scented air like a long lost friend.

Tiberius' feelers vibrated furiously at the kaleidoscope of aromas floating on the air. Suddenly he felt ravenous. Crispin flopped on the ground rolling ecstatically through the sweet smelling grass while Tiberius flapped his wings and giddily glided around several rocks. The worm crew lay half buried in a huge dirt pile surrounding the tunnel's entrance, grinning as wide as their tiny mouths would spread.

"Great turtle tracks," Brad said. "How long have you guys been down there?"

"Too long," Tiberius replied.

"And we're starving," Crispin said jumping up from the grass. "I could eat a whole oak tree."

Mac thrust his head westward and said. "There's mostly grass and weeds around this neck of the woods, but there are some orchards and vegetable patches in that direction."

"That must be what my feelers are picking up," Tiberius exclaimed.

"I'll eat anything as long as it is not a honey cake," Crispin sang out.

Tiberius cocked an eye, "They tasted a little stale at the end; but at least we didn't starve to death."

The crew slithered from the dirt pile and surrounded the pair of insects.

"Me and my crew need to head for shelter. It's gonna' get hot soon, and we don't want to dry out."

"Yeah," the twins sang out. Let's head over to the compost pile, and slurp a few brews before going home."

"Sounds good to me," Brad said.

"Hey," Red snapped. "Who invited you," then chuckled. "Had you going; didn't I: just worming around with you." An annoyed look crossed Brad's face then their bodies all quivered in laughter.

"All right you dirt bags," Mac spat, "head over to the compost pile. I'll join you later."

The twins and Brad turned to go; then yelled back. "Hey you two, stay out of caves from now on! Sure you don't want to come and hang out with us for a while?"

"Maybe another time," they called out as they waved. "Thanks for all the help."

"Which way you headed?" Mac asked.

"Our home's that direction," Tiberius pointed. "But first we need food. Where did you say that orchard was?"

Mac turned and wagged his head. "Go that way. You'll pass a group of hills in a circle. That's Glen Burrows. That's where I live. After that, just follow the rock wall. The orchard's just on the other side."

Mac glanced up at the sun. "Slugs bugs, it's getting' hot. Sorry, got to get under cover. Have a nice trip and watch out for those birds. They'll snap you up quicker than a six legged mantis."

"Well we really appreciate what you did for us. We might have died in there." Tiberius said.

"Yeah or starve to death," Crispin added.

Tiberius gave Crispin a funny look. "I better feed the little one," Tiberius said with a wink.

"You'll fill your bellies in that orchard," Mac said. "That's where the composting crew found the rotten apples. There's ton's of 'em this time of year."

Tiberius sniffed the sweet morning air and noticed a crispness that hadn't been there before they entered the cave. Late summer had melted into early autumn. 'My goodness,' he mused, 'had it really been so long since they left Dragonfly Landing?'
They needed to hurry and return home before the cold wild winds of winter wrapped their icy fingers around the land and its inhabitants.

Mac's voice broke through his thoughts. "One of these nights, the crew might get brave enough to sneak into the cave and check out the Cenrabs."

"Believe me," Crispin replied. "You don't want to have anything to do with those scum bugs. Especially if you want to stay in one piece."

The worm thrust his head back and let loose a trill of chuckles. Tiberius caught sight of his soft toothless mouth and suddenly thought of Captain Jack. "Hey," Tiberius exclaimed. "How far are we away from the cave's entrance?"

"It's not far," Mac answered, "Why you're not considering going back in after all you have been through."

"No, No," Tiberius shot back, "We ran into a salamander named Captain Jack who helped us a lot. Do you know him?"

"Can't say I do," Mac replied.

"Well," Tiberius went on. "He lives just outside the cave."

"Yeah," Crispin jumped in, "and gave us a ride in his ship, past the bats."

Tiberius nodded then continued, "We promised to bring him a crystal back, and ...we wouldn't want him to think we're dead or that we break promises."

"I wouldn't want to get on the bad side of a salamander either," Mac said looking a little puzzled. "If I'm not mistaken, don't salamanders eat your kind?"

"Believe it or not, Captain Jack has only one tooth," Tiberius said. "He only eats plants now."

"He lost them in a fight," Crispin added. "And he has a treasure but a lot of it looks like junk to us."

Mac just stared, his mouth agape not knowing what to make of their bizarre story. Then he replied a bit skeptically, "Ohhhh Kayyyyy. A toothless salamander with a ship and junky treasure. I have heard stranger stories, but not many." Then he added, "I suppose you want the shortest route back to the cave?"

"Definitely." Tiberius answered.

Mac twisted around and jerked his head. "In that case, see that grove of pinion pine on that ridge?" They nodded.

"Just beyond is a large outcropping of balanced rocks that look like a jack rabbit. Just past that is the cave entrance."

"Wow. We're that close," Tiberius exclaimed.

"That's great," Crispin chimed in glancing at Tiberius. "Can we leave as soon as we eat?"

"What," Tiberius shouted, "I couldn't hear you over somebody's rumbling belly."

"You guys crack me up," Mac laughed; then added. "Have a safe trip home. I'm itching and twitching from the sun! Gotta go!" They were all still laughing as Mac slithered towards the compost pile and the two friends took off for the orchard.

THEY FOUND THE small apple orchard bordered by flowers and vegetables just beyond the stone fence. Crispin gorged on apple leaves and tender young tomato blossom's, while Tiberius sipped nectar from festively colored zinnias and white fuzzy capped Echinacea blooms.

After eating, they found a pool of fresh rainwater in an old wheelbarrow to bathe in. They laid their packs and Crispin's vest in a niche on the wheelbarrow, and collected several stiffened clumps of lichen from a nearby hawthorne tree. They jumped into the refreshing water and scrubbed with the lichen sponges until their glop stiffened bodies felt squeaky clean.

"Ah," Crispin sighed. "I feel like my old self again."

"It's amazing what a good bath can do." Tiberius said flapping his huge wings, sending a spray of water into the air. "Are you ready to go see Captain Jack?"

"Aye, for certain," Crispin quipped.

Tiberius threw his head back laughing loudly; then replied, "Tiberius'll be flyin' slower so me matey can catch up. You'll be needin' to exercise those wings."

"Aye aye," Crispin replied. He executed a crisp salute then slipped on the wet grass and rolled over. Still laughing, they collected their things, and zoomed skyward. It was good to be flying again after being in the confined spaces of the cave, and they made it to the pinion pine grove in record time.

"That was fast," Crispin yelled. "We're already at the pine trees. I can't believe how light these crystals are. I can barely tell I'm carrying any extra weight."

"You're right," Tiberius replied, "they're light as a feather. I'll have no trouble carrying you and your pack."

Not long after passing the bristled conifers, they spotted a strange rocky outcropping in the distance. "There it is!" Crispin pointed. "It does look like a jack rabbit. Those two thin rocks balanced on top of the larger boulder look like ears, and that ridge line forms a leg."

"The cave couldn't be much further," Tiberius shouted to Crispin as they navigated towards the unusual formation. They rounded the jack rabbit sculptured head and were startled to see the Triton River spread before them.

"Where did that come from?" Crispin shouted.

"It curved in from the east," Tiberius called back. "We couldn't see it because the pines and outcroppings were blocking the view. Last time, we followed the river. From that angle these boulders probably didn't look anything like a jack rabbit."

"Hey, there's the cave." Crispin pointed. "It looks different from here too, but I see the opening."

They dipped their wings altering their flight path, and glided in for a landing. Captain Jack was stretched out on a rocky ledge sunbathing when he heard shouting

"Captain Jack! Captain Jack! We're back."

"There he is!" Crispin shouted.

Captain Jack cracked an eyelid and rolled over when he heard the familiar voices. He caught a glimpse of the sun glinting off Tiberius' pale green wings and he jumped up waving his arms. "Ahoy mates, Captain Jack be here!" Crispin and Tiberius waved back, and fluttered to the ledge.

Captain Jack welcomed them with his huge toothless grin, and a gentle slap on the back. "Well now, Captain Jack be right glad to see you swabs. I was 'afearin those nasty beasties did you in."

"They almost did," Crispin said with a quick kick and jab to the air. "But we fought them off and got away."

Tiberius grasped the salamander's shoulder and gave it a firm but friendly shake. "It's good to see you again, we'll fill you in on our adventures in the cave later, but right now, we want to give you something."

Tiberius slipped his pack to the ground and un-cinched it a bit. A beam of golden light shot out and quickly fused with the sunlight. He reached in and retrieved several of the crystals. Captain Jack's eyes bulged and shone with delight as he presented them to him. "These are for sailing us past the bats."

He rolled them lovingly between his fingers. "Ahh these beauties be treasure for sure."

"They can help you steer the Chameleon in the dark," Crispin exclaimed.

"Right you are, lad: Captain Jack thanks you from the bottom of mi' heart."

"Wait," Crispin said looking at Tiberius, "What about the other one."

Tiberius' brow wrinkled momentarily, then his eyes widened. "I almost forgot," he said rummaging in his side pocket. "Ah, there it is," he exclaimed removing the purple amethyst shard. "We found the tunnel just past the pool room you told us about. It was covered in these. We thought you might like one."

"It was beautiful," Crispin added. "And we can tell you where it is if you want to go and get more."

Captain Jack held it up and the sunlight filtered through, illuminating its purple brilliance. He was practically drooling. "Captain Jack'll be guardin' these treasures with me life," he said reverently.

THEY SAT WITH Captain Jack relating their amazing discoveries and hair raising adventures in the cave until the sun was poised overhead. Captain Jack held the shard skyward again. "These be treasures for certain, but argh, these Gorboos beasties sound fearsome. Captain Jack'll think twice before goin' in for more of this treasure."

Crispin and Tiberius stood and stretched. "We hate to leave so soon," Tiberius began, "but we have a long trip ahead of us and the blustery winds will be blowing before long."

"Argh. Captain Jack knows." He touched a leg to his nose. "There's a different smell hanging about these days. You best be goin'. May favorable winds be followin' ye home."

"Thanks again for all the help you gave us," said Tiberius smiling graciously.

"Yes, we really loved riding in the Chameleon," Crispin said then added, "You watch out for old Davey Fang, okay?"

Captain Jack belted out a roaring laugh. "It'll be an ill wind for that scalawag if he blows into me port."

"That's for certain!" Crispin and Tiberius quipped in unison.

They lifted off and once airborne glanced back for a parting view of Captain Jack. He had slithered into the bushes along the river bank. There was a momentary sparkle of reflected sun as the shrubbery parted and they caught a glimpse of the Chameleon bobbing in the water.

Chapter 23
Homeward Bound

The two travelers retraced their route past Jack Rabbit Mountain and the pinion pine grove and soon, Annelid Valley's clustered brown furrows and velvety green cloak came into view. "I wonder where the compost pile could be," Crispin called out.

Tiberius searched the area and pointed to a large solitary hill of rich black soil. "Well I'm no expert on compost, but, I bet that's one of them."

"How can you tell," Crispin asked.

"Look, it has steam rising off it. When organic matter rots, it gives off heat."

"Wow," Crispin exclaimed, "Those worms must be having a great time inside."

Tiberius chuckled, "It's like a sun bath; except underground."

"I thought they didn't like heat," Crispin said.

"No," Tiberius replied, "it's the sun's drying rays that they can't tolerate. The heat in the compost pile is moist."

"And there's all those rotting things they can chew on," Crispin chimed in.

THE DAY PASSED quickly and soon the iridescent shores of Dancing Fish Lake drew nearer. Crispin wanted to stop and catch another performance of the talented fish, but Tiberius thought they should keep going. "We need to cover as much ground as possible," he said then added, "and last time we were there it was so relaxing we fell asleep."

"Maybe the fish hypnotized us," Crispin joked.

"I hardly think so," Tiberius stated, "but whatever it was put us in danger. We were totally vulnerable lying asleep in the open like that. It's a wonder that a bird or frog didn't pick us off."

"Moley mud puppies," Crispin gasped, "I guess we were really lucky."

"You can say that again," Tiberius replied.

After passing Dancing Fish Lake, Tiberius decided it would be out of their way to continue flying towards the fern forest, so they adjusted their course. They banked gently eastward leaving the Triton behind and headed into unknown territory. If his calculations were right, they would skirt the Woods of Forgetfulness and then make their way to the Centipede River.

As the day wore on, they passed several more stands of pinion pines springing up like green oasis along a dried river bed. Farther on it narrowed into a shallow scar like road which disappeared into a stand of shaggy Cyprus trees. Just beyond was a vast area of inland marshes bordered by clumps of reeds and rushes which swayed gracefully in the wind.

Crispin and Tiberius studied the myriad of activities as they glided overhead. Dragonflies, marsh flies, and other winged visitors danced and darted playfully amongst the foliage or floated serenely on the water's surface. Small white egrets and long legged gray herons waded and splashed along the marsh edge, fishing for their next meal.

They saw a heron plunge its sharp pointed beak into the brackish water and emerge with a fat, twitching crawfish clasped in its bill. Nearby a group of red and yellow spotted turtles floated motionless; chomping on stringy plants and lying in wait for unwary victims to swim past. A yellow striped garter snake slithering through the damp undergrowth caught their attention as it searched for frogs, salamanders or worms.

They approached the far edge of the marsh and watched as a family of minks slid from a sandbar into the water. Their sleek brown bodies and long bushy tails cruised expertly through the water on the prowl for fish and other small marsh creatures.

"Look at those strange animals," Crispin pointed. "Their heads and faces look like a mouse, but the rest of their body resembles an otter."

Tiberius started to say something about the minks but his voice was drowned out by an oncoming chorus of loud annoying honking. They glanced up just in time to see a large V pattern flock of Canadian geese coming straight at them! "Yikes!" Crispin shouted. "Not these guys again!"

"Quick, let's make a dash for that clump of reeds!" Tiberius yelled.

It was too late. The lead goose whizzed past followed by several others honking so loudly that Crispin and Tiberius were almost knocked out of the sky by the vibration. The startled pair bobbed and weaved among the gray and white mottled feathery bodies until the flock passed and touched down on the shallow marshy waters.

"Whew! That was close." Tiberius gasped.

"Yeah," Crispin retorted. "Silly geese! Think they own the airways just because they're so big and ....."

"Loud," Tiberius cut in.

After collecting their scattered wits, they journeyed on, passing more Cyprus groves, and several smaller swampy areas. The sun was sliding towards its nightly destination as they reached the edge of a heavier forested area of redwoods, and smaller under story trees of buckthorn and native redbuds. They spotted an opening in the dense canopy, and the sinking sun glinted off a body of water nestled among the congested trunks.

"How about a water break," Crispin suggested.

"I was thinking the same thing," Tiberius replied then went on, "Just a short one, we need to keep going."

"Are we going to fly for part of the night," Crispin asked.

"Yes," Tiberius replied, "but not too far. Just until I find a safe place for us to sleep. This forest looks like owl territory to me."

They glided into the forest and landed on the smooth pebbled shore of a narrow stream. Stringy pale green strands of mossy plants clung to the boulder lined bottom and swayed in the brisk current. After drinking their fill of the refreshing water, they sat for a moment resting and watching the waning rays of sun filter through the forest. Several huge girthed trees glowed a pale saffron hue but one in particular caught their eye. Its trunk, instead of being rough and stippled with greenish gray moss was clothed in a brilliant orange and black patterned cloak. A slow fluttery tremor arose from one side of the trunk and spread in a wave around its circumference. The pair sat transfixed: then out of sheer curiosity crept closer towards the tree.

"It's amazing," Tiberius whispered.

"And so beautiful." Crispin added. "I've never seen so many monarch butterflies in one place. What are they doing?"

"It's a monarch migration," Tiberius explained. "They're flying south to Mexico for the winter. They stopped here to rest."

"I bet they came for a drink, like us." Crispin said.

"You're probably right," Tiberius replied. "I hope they leave before the owls find them."

Just then, there was a rustling in the leaves and a hauntingly shrill 'Woooo, Whooo' pierced the still evening. The disturbed monarchs took to the air in a blur of tangerine wings and Crispin and Tiberius followed them through the canopy enjoying the rare spectacle. The fiery embers of the spent sun silhouetted the graceful flock as they rose into the dusky sky like a winged plume of smoke.

AN IVORY CRESCENT moon shone through the dark curtain which evening had pulled over the sky as the travelers flew onward. Tiberius wanted to cover as much distance as possible so Crispin and his pack were now firmly nestled onto his back. There was a noticeable difference in weight, but it wasn't enough to hamper his speed or the flapping of his powerful wings. It was well into the night when they came upon a grove of trees, lying at the base of a cluster of knobby hills.

They could tell from the flitting gold specks of fireflies and incessant chatter of crickets, cicadas, and frogs that they were flying over a forest with a thriving community. The familiar sights and sounds reminded Crispin of Dragonfly Landing, and a wave of homesickness washed over him. Then he remembered that they were on their way home and the sadness was replaced with excitement. Tiberius' thoughts flashed back to the beautiful monarchs and how they reminded him of Maleva. He dismissed the thought and glanced down; wondering if he should stop for the night. 'I think I can keep going for a while,' he thought to himself and pushed on.

A good portion of the night passed, and Tiberius hadn't heard a peep from Crispin for some time. Deciding he must be asleep, Tiberius started searching for a safe place to stop and rest. The area he was flying over at present unfortunately had the familiar stagnant rotting aroma of a bog, not to mention the chorus of thrum-thrum, peep-peep, and garoom-garoom's rising from its amphibian inhabitants.

'Not a good place to stop,' Tiberius mumbled as he flew on. A short time later, he spotted a rocky outcropping bordered by a small trickling creek.

'Maybe we could find a nice safe niche to snuggle into,' he thought. He dipped a wing and headed in for a closer look skimming a promising ledge. Several long tailed dark shapes skittered from under a nearby boulder. Tiberius, startled, flapped frantically upward. 'Yikes, too many lizards in this spot.' He was almost sorry he hadn't stopped earlier at the familiar sounding friendly forest.

Just beyond the outcroppings lay a meadow with a few gnarled trees, tall slender grasses and clumps of tangled underbrush. Best of all his sensitive feelers were vibrating from a wonderful berry smell. He slowed and surveyed the area. He heard no owl hoots or frog crooning, so he picked the closest tree, and landed on a branch. He climbed along the branch and realized to their good fortune that it was a mulberry tree, loaded with late season berries.

"Crispin wake up, I have a surprise." He said loudly, shaking his body to rouse him.

"Whaaat. Where are we?" he said groggily.

"I've stopped for the night and we're in a mulberry tree."

Crispin's head jerked up. "Ohhh I can smell the berries." He jumped from Tiberius back, and hopped around stretching. "Did I miss anything," he asked.

"Not much," Tiberius answered. "Just another froggy bog, and some lizards on the prowl."

"I'm glad I fell asleep then. Those are two things I can do without seeing."

"Hey, there's a cluster of mulberries on that limb. Let's go, I'm famished."

They slurped and munched on the tangy berries until they were satisfied; their legs and faces stained bright red. "Great grubs," Crispin moaned, "Why do berries have to stain so bad? We just got over being blue, and now we're red."

"Well," Tiberius replied glumly, "I don't see any water around so I guess we'll stay this way for a while."

Crispin glanced at his vest. "At least I didn't drip the juice on my vest. Mulberry stains are the worst."

They found a rotted out hole in the tree's trunk, and settled into it for the remainder of the night. "I hope this isn't an owl's home," Crispin said looking around peevishly.

"It's not." Tiberius reassured him, "If it was, I would be able to smell it. Those big eyed fellows have a very distinctive aroma."

Using their packs as pillows, they stretched out inside the spacious cavity and tried to sleep. Crispin, having slept already, had trouble falling asleep and chatted about their adventures in the cave. "What really stumps me is how the old cricket knew so much about us. Especially that part about 'help will come from above'. How could he know the earthworms were going to dig us out?"

"Beats me," Tiberius replied. "But there are some really bizarre creatures in that cave. And while we're on the subject of the cave: you probably want to know why I wouldn't let you block the pool room tunnel with your fire cracklings?"

Crispin perked up, "I'd forgotten about that. Why wouldn't you let me?"

"Because, if the Gorboos couldn't get to the plants in the pool room, the crystals would eventually run out."

"You'd better explain that one to me," Crispin said puzzled.

"Remember when we were in the crystal chamber," Tiberius began. "And I went to check on the crystals that weren't glowing much?" It was dark in the tree cavity, but Tiberius saw Crispin nod. "While I was standing by the steam vent, a drop fell from a crack in the ceiling and hit me. Then another fell, and landed close to the vent."

Tiberius yawned, and decided to get on with the explanation. "Here's the theory I came up with. The Gorboos in the nursery chew the moss, and some of the juice they spit runs down a crack in the floor; then drips into the crystal chamber. The drops land next to the hot vent, and after a time, a chemical change takes place inside, causing them to harden and eventually, to glow."

"That's a brilliant theory," Crispin gasped. "Now I see why you wouldn't let me seal up the pool room."

Tiberius nodded then replied. "The Gorboos, moss, and crystals are interconnected. If anything interferes with the cycle," he paused dramatically, "NO CRYSTALS!"

Chapter 24
Tiberius' Dilemma

A new day was dawning with a bite to the air hinting at the cooler weather to come. Crispin was the first to wake and he poked his head from the hole. A caterpillar with thick black bristly fur and bright red horns sat on a nearby branch munching a soft mulberry leaf. Crispin heard a loud buzzing and ducked inside as a yellow and black female wasp zoomed overhead. He knew that the wasp wasn't a danger to him but the caterpillar was definitely a target. The female wasp was looking for food to store in her hidden nest to feed her young which would soon hatch.

Crispin stepped out and called to the gorging caterpillar. "Hey caterpillar!"

It stopped chewing and turned towards him. "Are you talking to me," it asked in a grumpy voice.

"Yes, I am." Crispin replied. "There's a female wasp flying around. I suggest you make yourself scarce for a while."

The caterpillar glanced around the tree then said, "I don't hear anything."

"Well, she's here somewhere, and you're about to be picked off," Crispin replied impatiently.

"Okay, okay. I'll make myself scarce," the caterpillar groaned then disappeared into a thick patch of leaves.

"Stubborn worms. Don't know why I bothered warning it," he mumbled crawling back into the hole.

"Warning who?" Tiberius asked groggily.

"Ohh, just a silly caterpillar that was being stalked by a wasp."

"I could use a little food myself," Tiberius said stretching, then went on, "and I'm sure there are lots of berries left."

"Yum! Sounds like the perfect way to start the day," Crispin said excitedly.

They exited the hole and Crispin made his way to a branch tip where he noticed an exceptionally large plump berry. "Great grasshopper legs! Would you look at the size of this one," he exclaimed sinking his face into it.

Tiberius spied a cluster of small berries nestled among the tree's denser foliage, and in anticipation of the scrumptious banquet fluttered through the canopy. After choosing several of the ripest dark red fruits he whacked them with a foreleg and began sipping their sweet tart juice with gusto. Suddenly, remembering Crispin alone on the branch tip, he glanced quickly in his friend's direction. Crispin was still in the same spot devouring his breakfast. Reassured, Tiberius resumed his berry whacking. He was about to take another sip when an annoying earsplitting squawk and blur of blue swept through the branches. Panic tore through his body as he realized the spot where Crispin had been was empty.

Bolting from the tree, Tiberius chased the abductor watching helplessly as his friend struggled to get loose. He flapped his wings furiously, but Crispin and his captor shrank more as each devastating moment passed. A knot of despair gripped his stomach as he lost sight of the bird when it darted into a thick stand of scrub oaks. He pushed on gathering strength in hope of a rescue finally arriving at the spot where he thought that the jay had landed. He covered the area several times, but saw neither the jay nor Crispin. Finally he fluttered to a rock, and slumped onto it exhausted and in utter despair. "Oh No!" he moaned cradling his head. "I've lost Crispin. How could I have let this happen?" Tiberius knew deep down that it really wasn't his fault, but felt responsible anyway. 'I should have been watching him closer,' he thought shaking his head. The sinking sensation he felt while watching Crispin disappear only worsened with each sweep of the area, and he was afraid that the jay had eaten him. If so: how could he ever face Crispin's parents?

The village needs these crystals, and Crispin would want me to go back for their sake. He shook his head again glumly 'How can I bring myself to go back with such ill tidings?' With a heavy sigh he decided. 'I must put my feelings aside, and think about those kind creatures at Dragonfly Landing. It's my mission to get the crystals back, and I'll do it,' he nodded emphatically.

Then another possibility came to him. 'What if Crispin got free and is lost. Would he know which direction to fly? Or maybe, he's looking for me.' Tiberius decided to circle the area for a while longer, hoping they would find one another but as dusk approached, that hope began to dim.

He fluttered off the rock and perched on the topmost branch of the tallest oak tree for one last view of the area. Several birds fluttered by and he crawled under a leaf for protection. There were plenty of insect conversations and singing going on, but nothing which sounded like his friend. He stayed under cover for a while listening to the chattering of several robins lurking nearby; giving him time to think a few things through. 'I wonder what happened to Crispin's lantern and pack. Wouldn't a bird toss aside something that's inedible?' He didn't want to think about Crispin getting eaten and he shook his head to drive the image away.

'Wait a moment,' Tiberius mumbled as a thought struck him. 'If he's lying somewhere injured and still has his pack and lantern, I should be able to spot him after dark.' It was a long shot, but one he wanted to take before giving up.

The robins finally flew to another tree, but Tiberius cautiously stayed hidden, anxiously waiting for the sun to sink below the horizon. When it finally did, he opened his lantern, lifted off and began scanning the darkness for a familiar light. His heart skipped a beat when he saw a pair of fireflies darting and flashing through the tree tops. He followed them to a cedar tree and then inquired if they had seen an unusually dressed firefly. Neither had seen Crispin but promised to let him know that his friend was searching for him. He also spoke to several fidgety brown field mice, an extremely talkative squirrel and an opossum swinging from a tree branch. None of them had seen Crispin or any objects which might be his lantern or pack.

By now Tiberius decided that Crispin was either eaten or had left the area. He wanted to believe the latter was right and that Crispin had escaped and gone on ahead. 'I have to think positive,' he told himself. 'Crispin's alive; I can feel it in my gut. We'll find each other somehow. Maybe he'll see my lantern if I don't see his.'

Reluctantly, he flew northeast scanning the sky and earth for his tiny lost friend. Without his passenger and spurred on by the chance of catching up with Crispin, Tiberius felt as if he was racing the wind.

He wanted to cover a great distance before the moon stood overhead, but his hopes were dashed as great gusts of howling winds roared in on a bank of angry, dark streaked clouds. 'Oh great,' he muttered to himself, 'now it's bad winds. 'I was hoping they would hold off for a while.' Then he thought about Crispin, all alone, battered by the merciless winds. 'No,' he thought 'Crispin's too smart to keep flying in these conditions. He would land somewhere and wait it out.'

Just then a huge gale tossed him around like a dried autumn leaf, and he knew it was time to find shelter. He spotted a thick stand of trees, folded his wings, and plunged earthward. At the last moment, he opened his wings and glided into the swaying treetops. It was still too windy so he descended to a lower branch where the surrounding forest offered more protection. It was a nice smooth birch branch so he decided to rest and ride out the wind storm. With only a gentle breeze stirring the forest floor, Tiberius could hear the usual sounds of nocturnal creatures going about their business. Soon he began to doze and while slipping into a deeper sleep he mumbled, 'There sure are a lot of crickets around here.'

Sometime later, Tiberius woke from a fitful sleep having dreamt of Dragonfly Landing and the grief stricken looks on Crispin's parents' faces when he arrived alone. He pushed the unsettling thoughts aside and glanced at the fuzzy rimmed moon. 'Good,' he thought 'I haven't been asleep very long.' He stretched and then heard the unusually loud chirping below. Even with the murky moon he could see the dark shiny round backed bodies of camel crickets jumping and scurrying about on their nightly patrol for food. The wind had died down and the moon momentarily cleared sending shafts of silver through the canopy. A beam struck Tiberius' wings, and a green shimmer flashed in the darkness. Several of the crickets noticed and shouted. "Hey, we've got another UFO!"

'A what,' Tiberius wondered.

"It must be the wind storm bringing them in!" A raspy voice yelled from the darkness. "And this one is huge," another voice added as a group gathered under the tree. Tiberius moved closer and the raspy voice yelled out excitedly, "I think this could be the large green fella."

"Hey! Green fella," it continued. "Come down here. We need to talk to you."

"All right I'm coming: but my name is Tiberius."

"It's him. That's the name the firefly used." One of the crickets said jumping up and down. Tiberius landed and the group moved back to make room for his large body. An older cricket with a puckered face pushed through the crowd and said in a gruff voice.

"You haven't lost your little firefly friend by any chance have you?"

Tiberius' heart leapt; then he replied somewhat skeptically, remembering the old cricket in the cave. "Are you one of those crickets that knows things before they happen, or have you actually seen him?"

The old cricket threw a foreleg into the air. "Not only did we see him, but we fed the little guy. And he told us about your incredible journey."

A huge smile lit Tiberius' face and he thrust a foreleg into the air. "I just knew he had to be alive, and in one piece!" He shouted with relief and delight.

He began dancing around in jubilation; then his eyes grew wide and flicked around the area. "Is he still here?"

"I'm sorry," the raspy voiced cricket said. "He flew away some time ago, and oh; you should probably know, he has a broken leg."

"What!" Tiberius gasped. "How bad? It couldn't be too crippling if he could still fly. Oh well," he grinned, "He's alive. That's all that matters. Do you know which way he went?"

"He headed off that way." The old cricket pointed. "We tried to keep him here because my joints felt a storm brewing...he wouldn't hear of it....seemed really anxious to be on his way....said you might be looking for him. I hope the little guy made it through okay."

"I'm sure he did," Tiberius replied trying to piece together the old cricket's ramblings, "He does have a little common sense. I bet he's found shelter somewhere along the way."

The old cricket puckered his mouth and said thoughtfully, "He might have common sense, but there were some pretty nasty cross winds tonight....might have blown him off course."

A look of concern crossed Tiberius' face. "The storm was moving from east to west," he muttered. "Maybe I should expand my search further west." He glanced at the moon. "I'm not exactly sure where I am at the moment," he went on: then asked, "What lies west from here?" A haunted look filled the old cricket's eyes and a hushed nervous chirping went through the crowd. "Why, what's in that direction," Tiberius asked worriedly.

"The Woods of Forgetfulness," the raspy voice replied. "Stay out of there."

"Its bad news," another voice called out.

Tiberius held a foreleg up. "Unfortunately, we've already experienced that dreadful place."

"And you came out with your memory intact?" the raspy voice questioned.

"Yes, but we had a lot of help," Tiberius answered. Not wanting to take the time to explain, he went on, "Crispin and I learned our lesson last time. We would never eat anything in the woods. A murmur of approval rose from the crickets along with several shouts of, "the food's poisoned in there."

Tiberius suddenly remembered the puzzling remark one of the crickets shouted earlier. "By the way," he asked, "could someone please explain what a UFO is?"

"Unidentified flying objects," the whole cricket group yelled in unison. Then a wave of chirping chuckles rippled through the jumping crowd. The old cricket smiled crookedly, and winked.

Tiberius laughed loudly feeling as though a great weight had been lifted off his shoulders then quipped, "I'm glad you were watching for UFO's tonight. Well, I'd better be off. My deepest thanks to all you crickets for taking care of my little friend." Then, he went on. "If I'm lucky, I can catch up with him soon."

As Tiberius took off he heard a tiny voice call out, "crickets are lucky you know!" Tiberius was giddy as he sped through the air knowing now that Crispin was alive. He would fly to the moon if necessary to find his friend.

A HUGE SHADOW swooped overhead and before Crispin could even look up, or scream, he was torn from the branch and whipped through the air at a heart stopping speed. A fiery pain shot through a back leg as he dangled head down, watching the earth whiz by in a blur of green and brown. He could tell from the bright blue and white flash of feathers that his assailant was a blue jay, and if he didn't think of something quick, it would be the last thing he ever saw. Crispin kicked and squirmed, but the bird had his leg clasped in its beak like a vice. His pack strap had slipped loose and was caught around his neck, causing him to gasp painfully for air. A wave of panic stabbed at him like an icy thorn when his attacker slowed and glided towards a tree. It wanted to find a nice comfy limb to sit on and enjoy its snack. Another excruciating pain shot through his leg, and an odd notion flashed through his mind. 'At least I'll still have five good legs. What a stupid thing to ponder when I am about to die,' he thought. 'It would have been funny if it wasn't so tragic.'

Suddenly a tiny voice of reason broke through his fog of panic and he decided to take its advice. The jay settled onto a branch, and momentarily loosened its grip on Crispin's leg. Then a painful blinding orange spark seared its eye. It squawked in pain then shook its crested head, confused. With its one good eye, the jay searched the branch for its catch, but it was gone.

Once the jay dropped its prey; Crispin immediately dove to the ground to hide among a thicket of quack grass. He jerked the pack off his neck, and lay gasping in pain listening to his heart pound wildly. It had all happened so fast! It was only moments ago, but every gut wrenching detail seemed to creep by in slow motion. At the moment, he was hurting and disoriented; but most importantly, alive. 'Where was Tiberius,' he wondered, 'did he follow me?'

Suddenly a terrible thought punched him in the gut. Jays didn't hunt alone. Had Tiberius been picked off too? What if he hadn't gotten away or was lying somewhere wounded too. If they could find each other maybe together they could limp back home or find help. He peeked out of the grassy clump and looked around. There was no sign of the jay and he didn't hear anyone calling his name. Which way had the bird carried him? He wasn't sure. He gingerly touched the wounded leg. It was still there, thank goodness; but there was a jagged tear where it joined his body and moving it made a sickening grinding sound along with the white hot shooting pain. "Ahhh!" he screamed. It was definitely broken. Desperate to rest, he laid his pack down and stretched out for a moment. He was in a relatively safe place for the moment, but a weakened insect was an easy target. He would have to move on soon even if he was in terrible pain but the cool grass felt comforting to his injured body. 'I'll close my eyes for just a moment,' he sighed as a vortex of darkness pulled him into unconsciousness.

AN OMINOUS SHADOW lurked close by and then suddenly he found himself in the clutches of a faceless creature having his legs and wings pulled off. Another stabbing pain shot up Crispin's leg, and he woke in a cold sweat, his heart racing. He bolted upright and squinted overhead. There were no threatening shadows, only the languid midday sun and a scattering of wispy grayish clouds.

'Oh no, how long have I been out?' He groaned shaking the haze from his brain. He checked his leg again and noticed it was swollen, and purplish, with a yellowish fluid clotting around the injury. In his pain, he hadn't given much thought to the important cargo he was carrying so he quickly checked it, and to his relief, found the pack still tightly cinched and its contents unharmed. Even his lantern, still attached to the strap, was intact.

He sat cautiously and put his pack on, being careful not to jostle his leg then studying the sun to get his bearings decided to cruise the area in hopes of spotting Tiberius. 'If he is all right, I know he's searching for me too. Maybe we'll run into each other.' He flew in the direction he thought the mulberry trees were, but before long became completely lost. Also, his leg was causing so much pain that he could go on no longer. 'I need something for the pain,' he groaned as he searched the landscape for medicinal herbs. Soon he had collected small slices of willow bark, a piece of golden seal root and several sturdy comfrey leaves.

Spying a small stream nearby he landed on its bank and immediately began cleansing and soaking his battered leg. He found a sharp stone, and scraped a white pithy substance from the willow bark, and swallowed a handful for pain. Then he placed the rest in his vest for later.

Next, he pulverized the fleshy pink golden seal root into a pasty ointment and laid it next to the comfrey leaves. The cool water bath had relieved some of the swelling but he still grimaced as he worked the ointment into his wound. Finally, he secured several comfrey leaves around his leg with bits of sturdy trumpet vine to immobilize the break.

Crispin rested for a short time, propped against a cool rock along the stream bank.

The cold water bath, willow bark pain killer, and herb salve had done wonders. His pain was manageable now, and he gently positioned his leg so it wouldn't have pressure on it as he pushed for a take off. Flying back and forth several times, he searched again for Tiberius but had no luck. He wasn't even sure that he was looking in the right area, but knew the direction they were supposed to be heading. 'What if Tiberius thinks the bird ate me,' he pondered. 'He couldn't search for ever. Tiberius knows how important the crystals are and he would eventually continue the journey alone. If he's already on the way; and I follow the same route, we might run into each other.'

Crispin shook his head, 'No, I could never catch Tiberius, especially with a busted leg; but there is something I can do.' He glanced at the lantern. 'When it gets dark, I can fly with the lid open. It can be my beacon. Maybe Tiberius will see me. Of course, I will be a target for bats and owls. "Oh well," he sighed, "that's a chance I'm willing to take." He studied the afternoon sun using it as a compass and plotted a northeasterly course. Crispin lifted off and flew slowly, scanning the landscape one last time for his lost friend.

HE WAS WELL on his way by the time the sun dipped below the horizon and dusk was devoured by darkness. He opened his lantern and the crystal's brilliant beam spilled out and enveloped his body in a golden halo. The moon also had a fuzzy grayish blue halo encircling it and a bank of dark wispy stacked clouds sailed over its face. 'This doesn't look good,' he thought looking up at the sky. 'I might have to land if the weather gets rough.'

The breeze eventually died down and Crispin's fears of an impending storm eased. The long flight had taken its toll on his injured body, so he began searching for a safe resting place. He was flying past a lightly wooded area, when the raspy chirping of many crickets rose from below. 'Wow, I've never heard so many crickets in one place before. I wonder what's going on. Maybe it's a cricket festival, and it certainly sounds safe and friendly.'

He descended into the canopy and alighted on a branch above all the commotion. A swarm of camel crickets were hopping and scurrying about, poking their heads among the leaf littered forest floor, chatting and scrounging for food. Suddenly, one of the crickets noticed the bright glow in the tree and shouted. "Hey! Look up there."

"What is that," another of the crickets sang out. A cluster of dark, shiny, round backed crickets rushed over and gathered at the tree's base, looking up curiously and slightly frightened.

"I think it's a lightning bug," a raspy voice rang out.

"No, can't you tell. That's no lightning bug," another voice said. "They flash on and off, and aren't this bright. I think it's one of those glow worms."

"Don't be stupid," another cricket chimed in. "Glow worms crawl around in the dirt."

The group continued staring up circling the trunk several times, then one of them said in a low soft voice. "Maybe it's one of those UFO's."

"A what?" the raspy voiced cricket asked.

"You know; an unidentified flying object." The soft voice answered.

"Awww. There's no such thing," one of the other crickets retorted.

By this time Crispin had heard enough of the crickets funny ramblings and decided to put an end to it. He fluttered to a lower branch as the crickets scattered backwards, and disappeared under the leaf litter. "All right. You crickets can come out now. I'm not a UFO." After several silent moments had passed, a group of tiny black faces peeked from under the debris and several crept out and came closer.

"Ah ha!" the raspy voiced cricket shouted. "I was right – it's a firefly, but..." he came closer and blinked curiously at Crispin's lantern. "His glow light's in the wrong place. Wait just a ...." He came closer and touched the lantern and the bulging pack on Crispin's back. "This is the strangest get up I've ever seen. Hey you scaredy gnats, come check this out."

Soon, Crispin was surrounded by a swarm of camel crickets staring in disbelief and asking a never ending string of questions. They seemed especially interested, and quite concerned about his injured leg. Crispin was led to a honey mushroom which was sprouting from a rotting beech stump and urged to rest before going on. He removed his pack and stretched out on the soft golden wavy cap. Soon, several cricket servers appeared with nut shells filled with tasty roots and hollow stems of water.

"This will boost your energy," one said placing a soft leaf napkin next to Crispin.

"Thank you. I'm going to need it," he replied gratefully.

He dined on the delicate roots and another strip of willow bark for his pain; then washed it down with the straws of water. He was brushing crumbs from his vest when suddenly; a throng of inquisitive crickets closed in, begging for the story of his travels. There was much wide eyed shaking of heads and excited murmuring among the listeners as he spun the tale of the quest for the crystals.

Afterwards, he thought briefly about lingering in this congenial place, but decided that Tiberius would never see his lantern through the thick treetops. Before he left however, Crispin wanted to ask about the huge gathering of crickets. "You haven't told me what so many of you are doing here," Crispin asked.

One of the crickets, with an older sounding gruff voice spoke, "We were delivering material to a building crew up north. Some of our relatives are constructing a new tree house in an aspen grove. It has to be finished before winter sets in, so it was a rush job."

Crispin suddenly remembered the cricket caravan they had seen crossing the bridge after leaving the fern forest. "Hey! I've seen you guys before." He sang out. "It was near the Last Stop Sinkhole. You were crossing a bridge. We stopped and said 'Hello' to one of you."

Just then, a voice from the group called out, "Of course. I knew you looked familiar, but I didn't make the connection without your large green friend by your side."

Then the cricket with the raspy voice chimed in, "Hey! I have an idea. We'll keep an eye out for your friend. If we see him, we can tell him you're alive and heading northeast."

"That would be great," Crispin exclaimed. "I'd like to hang around for a while, but I need to get up in the sky in case Tiberius is cruising around."

"Sure you don't want to stay a bit longer," the older gruff cricket asked. "I think the weather's going to turn bad. I can feel it in my joints."

"I'd like to, but I really shouldn't. I'm sure my friend is looking for me and is quite worried. Thanks. You're a great bunch of crickets, and I really appreciate all your help."

"It's a good thing you stopped in," a voice rang out from the group. "We're supposed to be good luck ya know."

"I could use a little good luck right now," Crispin replied. They all laughed and several of them helped him into his pack. As he lifted off, he turned and waved. All the crickets waved back then sent him off with the loudest chirping serenade Crispin had ever heard.

Chapter 25
A Confusing Day

*I*t wasn't long before Crispin wished he had accepted the crickets' invitation to wait out the storm. The stiff breeze he encountered earlier had come back with a vengeance slapping his injured body with unexpected wracking gales. 'Next time I'll listen to old crickets when their joints are talking,' he scolded himself, 'Now I'm caught in this storm being tossed around like a mosquito in a dust devil.'

"Aiieee!" he screamed as a particularly strong gust sucked him into a spiraling down draft and he tumbled painfully towards the ground. The darkened silhouettes of tree tops were rushing at him with alarming speed, so he braced for a difficult landing. He folded his wings and tucked his legs tight; then with a rustling 'thunk', made a clumsy landing on a swaying branch. There wasn't even time for a sigh of relief. Another gust suddenly hit whipping the thin branch and catapulting him back into the air.

"Oh no! Not again!" he yelled, frantically grabbing for another branch.

The next thing he knew he was sprawled on the ground dazed and clutching his aching head. 'Ugggh. Must-have-hit-head' he groaned then quickly checking his leg added, 'At- least-didn't-fall-on-leg.'

He tried to stand, but groggily fell back to the ground. 'What's going to happen to me next,' he groaned. 'At this rate I'll never find Tiberius or get back home.' He lay on his back staring into the canopy for a short time and then said aloud. "All I need is a little rest and some food."

His vision was a bit blurry but he rolled over and immediately spotted a freshly cracked acorn. "Great grubs. I'm starved," he gasped. He crawled to the nut, and quickly devoured it, then found several wild strawberries dangling above his head, and wolfed them down.

"Mmmm." he smacked his mouth "Now for a little nap, and I'll be good as new." He was thinking about how lucky he was to find food so easily when suddenly an unnaturally heavy stupor drug him face down into a patch of yellow elf cup mushrooms.

Some time later, Crispin woke, rolled over, and pawed at the tiny goblet shaped mushroom stuck to his face, then sat.

He yelped as a pain shot through his leg and a puzzled look flashed through his eyes. What was wrong with his leg, and why was it wrapped in leaves. Then he noticed a strange pack with a nut shell attached to its strap. He crawled over and opened it. A blinding light shot out and he hurriedly closed it. 'What was that,' he mused 'and where did it come from?' Next he opened the nut shell and another beam of light spilled into the darkness. He left its lid opened. Somehow, it made him feel safe. It bothered him that he didn't know what the unfamiliar objects were, but what really gave him the willy-wollies was that he couldn't remember who he was, or how he came to be in these woods.

Crispin shook his head in frustration; then noticed the unusual garment on his body. He patted the vest and found a map and a seed pod box. He unrolled the map and stared at it. It was just a document with meaningless writing and funny symbols. He rolled it up and sat it on the ground, then opened the box. He let out a gasp as the brilliant blue stone twinkled back. 'These must be important,' he thought mater-of-factly and returned them to the vest pockets. Not knowing what to do next, he limped aimlessly through the nearby trees, but eventually ended up where he started. He flopped against the pack, realizing that he had forgotten about it while wandering about.

"I guess I was meant to stay with these things, although why is a mystery to me," he mumbled. The overpowering sleepiness returned later and he tried to fight it off, but finally gave in.

TIBERIUS HAD BEEN so worried that he had ignored his hunger; but now knowing that Crispin was alive, he felt ravenous. 'I won't be able to go much longer without food,' he thought. 'I hate to take time out to eat if Crispin's in trouble; but I wouldn't be much help lying in a heap, too exhausted to go on.' He began testing the air with his sensitive feelers and before long; he picked up a wonderful sweet smell. He followed it to a lush vine covered in dainty white jasmine blooms. It was twining its delicate green tendrils around a wild rose thicket growing in a roadside ditch. Unfortunately, the roses had long since stopped booming but Tiberius sipped a belly full of the scrumptious jasmine nectar.

'Ah, there's nothing like a vine in full bloom for quick energy,' he sighed as he lifted off and continued his search.

Sometime later, Tiberius approached the edge of a dense forest and wondered if it was the far boundaries of the Woods of Forgetfulness. In the darkness, it would be impossible to see the warning signs, but as he glided through the canopy a familiar chill crept through his body. There was no doubt in his mind that he was in the treacherous woods. Not a single bird song, owl hoot, or any other sounds of life greeted him. The eerie quiet was pierced only by the flapping of his wings. 'I wonder how far these woods go,' he pondered. 'If I can't find him tonight, I can get Sergeant Mudd, or who ever is on watch to help me search when it's light.'

He started at the edge of the woods and worked his way inward, covering one small area at a time. "Crispin, Crispin. Can you hear me," he shouted until his voice became raspy and sore.

The woods were huge and after searching for most of the night it seemed that all the trees and shrubs were beginning to look the same. Finally, tired from flitting among the trunks, he perched on a branch in an oak tree loaded with ripe acorns. The light filtering through the woods was turning from a dark gray to a deep lavender, and Tiberius realized that dawn was not far away. Suddenly, he thought he saw a tiny flicker of light below and headed in its direction, 'I hope it's not a lightning bug that's wandered in here by mistake,' he said hopefully. As he drew closer, his excitement mounted as the blinking light became steadier.

'Yes, it has to be him,' he almost shouted with joy. Then his heart began to pound as he fluttered to the ground and found Crispin's tiny battered body resting against his pack. He held his breath as he crept up, fearing the worst. To his relief, he saw Crispin's chest rise and fall.

'Good, he's just sleeping.' Then he saw the red stain on his face. He looked around and saw the remaining wild strawberry Crispin hadn't finished. 'Oh no,' Tiberius groaned. 'If the wind blew him off course he probably thought he was in an ordinary forest.'

Then he tried to remember what Rock E. Crab had told them about eating too much. "What was that about long term memory loss," Tiberius mumbled. Then his eyes widened, 'I need to get Crispin to the gypsy moths for the potion, and quick!'

'I'm sure he won't remember me,' Tiberius thought pacing around Crispin. 'If I wake him, it might scare him. He could go berserk.' Tiberius stopped pacing and stared at his friend puzzling about how to wake him when Crispin began to stir.

'Well,' Tiberius decided, 'I'll just sit peacefully a safe distance away and try to look non threatening.' He moved a short distance away, folded his wings and perched on a rotting log. Crispin cracked an eye and mumbled something then opened his other eye, stretched and yawned.

He sat, and winced as he moved his injured leg, then glanced around the woods. Tiberius was so still Crispin didn't see him at first; then he froze as his eyes landed on the unfamiliar pale green creature. Crispin sat straighter, an alarmed look crossing his face; then relaxed as he noticed that the creature didn't seem aggressive. Tiberius sat and waited. Then finally Crispin spoke. "Hello."

"How are you today?" Tiberius replied.

"My head and leg hurt."

"I expect so; your leg's bandaged. Do you know where you are?"

"No, I'm really confused."

"Would you be scared if I came over there," Tiberius asked.

Crispin stared suspiciously at the stranger for a few moments; then grabbed for his pack. "Are you here to steal these crystals?" Tiberius opened his pack, removed a crystal and held it into a shaft of light for Crispin to see. "Why would I want yours when I have a pack of my own?" Tiberius questioned.

"Ok. You're not here to steal my crystals, but I still don't know you."

Tiberius managed to creep up and sat opposite him. "Would you like to know why we both have a sack of crystals?"

"Yes."

"First, your name is Crispin and mine is Tiberius. We're good friends, but we got separated while traveling. Unfortunately, a wind storm blew you into these woods." Then he explained to Crispin why he couldn't remember anything.

"I'm really in a lot of trouble then," Crispin said with fear in his eyes.

"I'll get you out of these woods, and take you to some friends who have a potion that will restore your memory." Tiberius reassured him; then added. "They also have wonderful ointments which can heal your leg in no time."

"What about these glowing crystals?"

"I don't have time to tell you all the details," Tiberius answered, "but I can tell you that we're a long way from home and the crystals are very important. We need to get them back as soon as possible." He gave Crispin his most sincere smile and asked, "Do you trust me?"

"Yes, but I'm still really confused. It does makes sense though." He glanced at his pack and Tiberius'. "Why else would we both be carrying sacks of identical crystals if we weren't traveling together?"

"So, what do you say," Tiberius prompted. "Shall we get out of these stagnating woods and get you some help?"

"Yes. Please get me out of this place; I hate it. At least I think I hate it. I can't remember." Crispin said, flinching as he tried to raise himself off the ground.

"Great," Tiberius said with a broad grin, "let's get you mounted on my back."

"What?" Crispin shot back, "I have to ride on your back?"

"Don't worry; you do it all the time. It's perfectly safe."

"Oh-kay," he replied.

Tiberius helped Crispin put on his pack, then crouched low so his little passenger could easily move onto his mount. Crispin grimaced as he slid his injured leg up, but once he was situated, it actually felt quite comfortable. He held onto Tiberius' pack straps, and they lifted off.

Avoiding the impenetrable boundary above the canopy, Tiberius stayed low to the forest floor and headed back the way he entered. They exited the woods, just as the sun peeked over the eastern horizon.

Crispin stayed alert for a while watching the hazy morning landscape pass below but eventually, his painful leg and unfortunate ordeal in the woods drug him into a deep sleep.

Tiberius flew on, trying to keep his mind busy by calculating the remaining distance to the Centipede River. 'Okay. I need to think back. Gaylord ferried us to the far side of the river and we left when the sun was overhead. It was dusk when we reached the honeysuckle vine, then spent the night in the hawthorne tree.'

'The pitcher plant bog episode delayed us the next morning but we made it to the Woods of Forgetfulness by dusk...so...' He shook his head. 'We don't know the extent of the woods. It would be a miracle if we ended up at the same spot we were at the first time.'

His thoughts were distracted by a tantalizing honey like aroma traveling on the wind's currents. 'Ohhh! It smells like a butterfly bush. I'm sure Crispin's hungry too and we need to keep our strength up.' He zeroed in on the bush and landed gently on a branch. "Wake up Crispin. It's time for a snack."

There was no response. He shook his body several times and Crispin finally stirred. He glanced at Tiberius with a tired and puzzled expression on his face then asked expectantly. "Are we there yet?"

"No, I stopped so we could eat. You don't have to get off. Just lean over and grab something, while I sip some nectar."

A long gracefully arched stem bearing lance shaped leaves and several honey scented clusters of violet blossoms dangled over their heads. Crispin reached up and started nibbling on the closest leaves while Tiberius sipped the sugary juice from the long panicles of tiny flowers. A few foraging bumble bees buzzed in to dine but there was more than enough to go around and everyone minded their own business.

"Are you full yet," Tiberius asked later.

"Yes, it was delicious, but why do they call this a butterfly bush? It doesn't look a thing like a butterfly."

Tiberius chuckled. "That's because butterflies are crazy for its nectar, and flock to it. You can't beat a butterfly bush for a fast smorgasbord."

"I think there's a flock heading this way now," Crispin pointed.

"Let's get going before this bush gets too crowded," Tiberius suggested.

Crispin, too full and drowsy to answer laid his head back onto his riders pack and was asleep in no time. Later, as the sun marched across the sky, it warmed and a wet blanket of mugginess hung in the air like an invisible fog. The heavy moisture settling on Tiberius' wings: plus the extra load on his back was making it difficult to go on. His flapping became labored and soon his breath was coming in huffs and puffs. "Need-to rest!" he gasped making an exhausted, clumsy landing on a rock.

After catching his breath, he scanned the area and noticed a thick stand of maple trees crowning a small hill. It looked shady and misty, so he flew in to cool off.

To his delight, there was a gurgling stream winding its way through the reddish autumn tinged maples. 'This would be a good place to rest and clean Crispin's wound,' he decided landing on a patch of moss covered rocks on the stream's edge.

Tiberius noticed that it had drawn the usual crowd of water creatures. A festively colored painted turtle slid from his stone island down stream and disappeared with a plop. A moment later several expanding rings appeared on the surface followed by a yellow striped head and wrinkled neck. The turtle scanned the stream slowly as if debating which way to go; then disappeared again, leaving a churning wake in its path. Green and blue dragon-flies, midges, mosquitoes, caddis flies, and other skating, flying and diving creatures were busy going about their daily activities without taking notice of the newly arrived strangers.

Tiberius shook his body, and this time Crispin immediately woke. "Ohh. I nodded off again," he mumbled rubbing his eyes.

"You've been sound asleep for quite a while," Tiberius replied, then went on. "It was so hot and muggy I could hardly fly, so I decided this cool stream would be the perfect place to rest and clean your leg."

By this time, Crispin had slid from Tiberius' back and was laying on the rock. They removed their packs and stretched out for a while, enjoying the shady serene spot.

"Are you ready to clean your leg," he finally asked.

"Yes. These bandages have gotten quite stiff and are very uncomfortable."

The pair crept to the water's edge and gingerly submerged Crispin's wounded leg. "Ahh. That feels wonderful," he sighed.

Tiberius reached into the water and tested the brittle comfrey leaves. "They're beginning to soften up," he reported gently unwrapping the vines around the bandage. "We better save these vines," he went on setting them on a rock. "They're still usable, but I'll have to scrounge around for new bandages."

With Crispin's help, they peeled away the comfrey leaves and inspected the jagged tear. The yellow oozing had stopped but the crust it formed along the injury looked very fragile.

"Well," Tiberius began, "the break is trying to mend, but one wrong move might very well rip it back open. We need to wrap it as tight as possible so you can't move it too much. If it re-opens it might not ever heal right."

"I'm glad it's healing," Crispin said. "Don't worry. I'll be extra careful when I'm moving around."

"Okay," Tiberius replied. "I'll see what bandaging material I can find close by. I'm not going to let you out of my sight again."

He was about to leave when suddenly the turtle's large round head popped out of the water. It swam over to them and began talking. "You chaps moving into the area, or just passing through?"

"Just passing through." Tiberius replied as they suspiciously crawled back a bit. "Returning from a trip, and heading north," he added.

"Looks as if your traveling companion had a spot of trouble," the turtle said in a clipped voice.

"I have a broken leg, but it's healing," Crispin replied.

"Oh! How unfortunate," it replied then swam closer. "Had a crab nip off part of my tail once," then added. "What a bloody mess that was."

Tiberius cleared his throat and asked. "I don't suppose you know of any plants around here that would make a good sturdy bandage."

The turtle squinted his eyes for several moments then answered, "By Jove, I think I might have just the thing for you chaps...be back in a flash."

It swam off up stream and returned later with a mouth full of dark green arrow shaped leaves. The turtle dropped them next to them and said. "These are soft but strong. They should do the job nicely: if I may say so. Now," the turtle continued, "Where in the north might you be traveling to?"

"Have you ever heard of Dragonfly Landing," Tiberius asked.

"No: can't say that I have."

"Well. That's our final destination, but first we have to cross the Centipede River."

The turtle stuck his baggy neck higher and grinned, "Now THAT, I know about. Used to live there in fact: but uggh – there were too many crabs. I like it here much better. It's quieter and," he glanced at the water... "lots of fat juicy minnows."

"Do you know how far it is to the river," Tiberius asked expectantly.

"Not in insect distance," the turtle laughed, "but I can tell you, this stream widens not too far downstream and empties into a larger river east of here."

"That might be the one we're looking for," Crispin said hopefully.

"Good," Tiberius added. "We can follow this stream and maybe it will lead us to the Centipede River. Thanks. You've been a huge help."

"Anytime I can be of service," the turtle replied as he dived for a school of passing minnows.

"What a nice turtle," Crispin exclaimed as they watched its head bob out of sight. "Are all turtles this nice? If I've ever met one, I can't remember."

"Most of them are," Tiberius answered, "but they're like everyone else. Every now and then you run into a real stinker. You have to judge each turtle as it comes."

"Well, I'm glad this one was helpful," Crispin said.

"Me too," Tiberius replied; then went on. "I don't have to look for bandaging material and we found out there's a large river not far away."

"Do you think it's the one we're looking for," Crispin asked.

"I hope so. In your condition we need to find help as soon as possible." Tiberius grabbed one of the arrow shaped leaves. "Let's get this new bandage on so we can go."

He tore several thin strips from the fibrous leaves and began wrapping them around Crispin's wounded leg. He grimaced as the leaves were secured tightly with the vines.

"There now," Tiberius said, "how does that feel."

"My leg feels very stable," Crispin answered: then with a puzzled expression he asked. "Have we been friends for a long time?"

Tiberius thought for a moment then replied "After all we've been through, I would have to say: yes, we're old friends."

"Good," Crispin said smiling wistfully. "That makes me feel better. Sometimes I get really sad and frightened. It's as if I never existed."

"Oh don't worry," Tiberius reassured him. "You exist, and so do your parents, and all your friends at Dragonfly Landing. They care very deeply for you and I'm going to get you back to them safe and sound, with your memory intact!"

Crispin breathed a sigh of relief, then grinned, "Well, what are we waiting for, let's go find it!"

The pair lifted off and Tiberius followed the stream, watching expectantly for it to widen. The maple clothed hill eventually sloped into a broad goldenrod strewn field taking the stream with it. Later, the thick stands of maples reappeared shading the stream bank and they sighted several beaver families working diligently on their jumbled log homes. Upstream from the paddle tailed creatures the narrow ribbon of water widened.

"This must be the place the turtle told us about," Tiberius called to Crispin. "It's definitely getting wider."

"Wow," Crispin yelled. "Those beavers sure do build strong homes. Looks like most of the water flowing downstream is being choked off."

"That's why they're called dams," Tiberius replied.

The further they flew, the wider the stream became, and Tiberius felt that he was on the right course. With a sense of urgency he pushed onward, stopping only for quick nectar snacks and short rests. The afternoon sun was poised low in the western sky and Tiberius hoped that they would make the river by nightfall. Crispin spent much of the afternoon snoozing waking only when Tiberius stopped. A fiery sunset was building and Tiberius caught sight of a large flock of migrating geese silhouetting against the melting sun. They were flying very low to the horizon in the same direction. 'Those geese must be heading for a large body of water,' he thought, 'and it looks like they're getting ready to land. I hope it's the river they're aiming for and not a pond or marsh.'

The tributary curved abruptly and disappeared into a swath of thickly wooded vegetation. The geese arrived well before Tiberius and dropped just beyond the wood's edge, startling several white plumed egrets into the surrounding bushes. 'Was that a good sign?' he wondered. 'Egrets can be found fishing at various bodies of water. This could be anything, even another marsh.'

As he approached the wooded area he glanced down and saw the tributary cutting a dark shiny path through the trees and underbrush. He followed the ribbon of water, and soon it curved again, this time sharper. The vegetation eventually thinned and Tiberius caught a glimpse of red gold reflecting off a body of water in the distance. Later, he rounded a huge oak tree and breathed a great gasp of relief as the tributary merged with a large river. "This could be the Centipede River," Tiberius shouted.

Crispin woke and rubbed the sleep from his eyes; then stared spellbound at a vast lazily meandering body of water stretching towards the horizon. A rippling golden luminescence shimmered off its surface as the sun bid farewell to the day.

"Is this the Centipede River?" Crispin shouted excitedly.

"I sure hope so. It's going in the right direction, so we're following it." Tiberius answered. "I'm going to fly close to the river bank in case we need to stop and inquire for the gypsy moths. We'll need to stop and rest too."

"I can't see the banks. Where are they?" Crispin asked.

"According to my calculations from the sun, they should be that direction," Tiberius pointed as he dipped a wing to alter their course.

Crispin suddenly shouted and pointed below. "Look, at those loud honking birds. What are they: and oh, those white twig-legged birds are really strange."

"Those are geese and egrets fishing for food," Tiberius answered, "and migrating south for the winter."

They landed on a cattail for a short rest and then fluttered to the gently lapping water along the bank. Tiberius got a drink and then scooped some up in a leaf for Crispin. He gulped it greedily; then asked, "Do our kind migrate?"

"No," Tiberius answered, "Only monarch butterflies. Most of us find a cozy warm spot to crawl into and snooze the winter away. You and your parents live in a nice warm tunnel at the roots of an old oak tree."

"It sounds nice," Crispin replied.

"Yes, it is," Tiberius said. "Okay, we better move on and search for the river bank before it gets too dark."

Darkness fell all too soon, and the pair opened their lanterns as they skimmed along the river surface. 'I hope this doesn't go on much longer,' Tiberius thought. 'I'm getting tired.' He couldn't remember when he had slept last; then just as his energy was running out, he spotted dark shapes looming in the distance. As they neared, the objects took on form, and as Tiberius came in for a landing, he saw thin wispy branches dangling over the bank. They landed among a clump of horsetail leaves growing along the muddy bank and walked inland a short distance.

The pair stopped at the base of a gray mottled river birch, and sat on a pile of soft, newly fallen leaves. "We'll rest here for a while, I'm too tired to go on," Tiberius told Crispin. He leaned to one side and Crispin slid carefully onto the ground. "How does your leg feel?"

"It feels like I landed on a burr," Crispin reported. "But at least my headache is gone."

"Good," Tiberius replied. "You'll feel even better once you stretch out and rest."

"Do you know where we are," Crispin asked.

"Not really," Tiberius replied, "but those willow trees look familiar." He sighed then went on, "of course, willow trees are a very common sight near the water. Our best bet is to wait until morning; maybe then I can spot something which looks familiar. We'll also be on the lookout for our friend Gaylord."

"Gaylord," Crispin repeated. "Who's that?"

"He's an alligator who ferried us across the river."

"Why didn't we fly across?"

"My wing was hit during a lightning storm and it was still healing."

"Oh," Crispin replied. "By the way," he added. "What's an alligator?"

"You have forgotten everything, haven't you," Tiberius replied shaking his head. "Let's get some sleep, you'll learn all about alligators tomorrow."

Chapter 26
Searching for Gaylord

*T*iberius was awakened later by the bloodcurdling screech from a guinea fowl which was roosting in a nearby tree. He cracked an eye and threw a foreleg over his head. "What's a guinea doing here," he grumbled. "Must be a runaway from a nearby farm." It shrieked again and he sighed; then sat. "Now I'll never get back to sleep."

Fortunately, the heat of the afternoon had dissipated, but the mugginess still hung heavily in the air. He caught a glimpse of the river as a breeze parted the grasses. Patches of thick mist hovered over the surface like watery ghosts on a black glassy field.

He glanced at Crispin who was sleeping peacefully. 'Must be deaf' he thought.

Then he noticed the vines around Crispin's bandage. They were frayed and starting to disintegrate. 'Those will have to be changed.' He decided. 'I'll search for new tying material when Crispin wakes.' Finally the guinea moved on and Tiberius breathed a great sigh of relief. He shut his eyes and soon drifted back to sleep.

Sometime around dawn, Crispin awoke. He tapped Tiberius gingerly on the wing and his eyes flew open. "What time is it?" Tiberius gasped.

"Don't worry; the sun's barely up."

Tiberius stood and stretched. "Good. I was afraid of oversleeping. A runaway guinea kept me awake for a while."

"Guinea?" Crispin said puzzled.

"Never mind," Tiberius waved a foreleg. "Just some loud screaming chickens – not worth mentioning really....I need to find something new to tie your bandages with."

Crispin glanced at his leg. "Oh. You're right they're falling apart."

"Let's see if I can find something close by," Tiberius said scanning the area. "Hmm," he continued, "I don't see any vines."

Suddenly a movement in a nearby bush caught his eye. It was a golden orb spider dangling from his web; munching on his latest victim. "Of course," Tiberius exclaimed. "It's the strongest stuff around."

"What is," Crispin asked.

Tiberius pointed to the bush. "Spider web. And it's practically weightless too. Much lighter than the trumpet vine tendrils. Of course, I'll have to pull a fast one to get a thread away from that eight legged, fanged acrobat."

Crispin scratched an antenna and looked puzzled. "If it's so strong, how would you break off a piece?"

"Great," Tiberius groaned, "I hadn't considered that. Let me think about it for a moment." There was a long pause while Tiberius pondered the options, then shook his head glumly. "I give up. Let's move on to plan B."

"What's plan B," Crispin asked.

"We'll smear pine pitch over the vines. It's sticky and will hold them together. There might be a bad smell until it dries, but I won't have to fight that spider. They're not too smart, but they are lightning fast."

"Let's not press our luck then," Crispin suggested. "The pine stuff sounds a lot safer."

"All right," Tiberius announced, "I spotted a pine tree beyond that sumac thicket. I'll go collect some and be right back. You can hide under a leaf until I get back; and I promise not to be gone long."

"Okay." Crispin grinned. "It's like hide n' seek isn't it."

"Yes, but I'll know where to look because I'm going to watch where you hide."

"Oh, all right," Crispin said somewhat disappointed, then crawled under a large oak leaf.

Tiberius turned to leave, then glanced back and asked, "By the way; how is it you've forgotten what birds, turtles, and alligators are, but you can remember a game?"

"I have no idea!" his muffled voice called back.

Tiberius fluttered past the sumac and landed at the base of a longleaf pine. He circled the trunk and found a tiny wound in the bark with a clear yellowish liquid trickling from it. 'Ah haa! Pine sap. Just what I was looking for. Now all I need is a leaf.'

He scrounged around and found a Holly bush loaded with nice fat red berries and bowl shaped leaves. He collected a tiny leaf from the ground, returned to the tree, and scooped some of the pine sap into it. When he returned, there were so many leaves on the ground he wasn't exactly sure which one Crispin was under.

"Crispin! Come out; come out wherever you are."

He heard a small laugh, and a leaf trembled. Tiberius went over and moved the leaf.

"Oh there you are. Did you move while I was gone," he said in a teasing voice.

"Nope. Not with this bum leg."

"Well, I must have forgotten where you were."

Crispin grinned impishly, "Now who has the bad memory."

"Well that's too bad," Tiberius retorted, "I think I forgot where the juicy holly berries were too."

"No! No! Try to remember that," Crispin begged. "I'm hungry and I think I remember liking berries."

"Very well, I'll be thinking about it while I put this pine pitch on your leg." He reached in and retrieved a gob of the gluey substance then smeared it over the vines and in the gaps along the bandages. "That will be nice and strong once it dries," Tiberius said as he finished, "and it shouldn't take very long."

He looked at his forelegs. "That was a dumb thing to do. I should have used a stick to spread it on." he moaned. "Now I'll have to wash or everything I touch will be stuck to me."

"Over there," Crispin pointed. "I see a dried puff ball fungus, and its top has been knocked off. Maybe some rain water collected inside."

Tiberius fluttered to the shriveled white ball nestled among the grass and peered into the opening. "There's water in it all right," he called back, "and yuck: that's not all."

"Oh well," he grumbled, "can't be too choosy. If I wait any longer, my legs will be stuck to this puff ball." He leaned over the crusty edge, stuck his legs into the stagnant rain water and began scrubbing. He winced as tiny specks on the surface darted and dived in all directions. 'Yuck, I hate mosquito larvae. The little creeps like to swim in everything.' He braved the infested waters until every spot of sap had disappeared. "Ahhh! That feels much better," he sighed. He dried his forelegs on a soft patch of moss; then glanced over at Crispin who was touching the pine pitch to see if it had hardened. "Watch out," Tiberius scolded as he came nearer, "You don't want that stuff stuck on you."

"I think it's dried," Crispin said.

"Let me see," Tiberius replied running a soft leaf over it. "Yep. It's dry enough, so I guess it's safe for you to slide onto my back. We'll go get some of those holly berries." He went on; then chuckled, "I think I remember where they're at now." Tiberius made his way back to the green glossy leafed bush without getting lost, and the pair feasted on the tangy berries.

"I hope we don't have too much trouble finding Gaylord; sometimes alligators look like floating logs." Tiberius said as they continued to follow the river bank. Twice he spotted a long object cruising just below the surface and fluttered by for a closer look. The first one was an extremely long, big mouth buffalo fish and the other one turned out to be a piece of driftwood. He also paused now and then to ask the riverside creatures if they had seen a bespectacled alligator or a band of gypsy moths.

A soft furry water vole dining on waterside plants knew of no alligator along his stretch of the river and later, they talked to a huge mouse faced water shrew which was busy catching frogs. He hadn't seen any alligators either, but had recently conversed with a ruddy duck who had mentioned a close encounter with one further up river.

They continued on, and after more searching, stopped for a rest and a few tasty tidbits of bramble berries. They were about to leave when a rustling sound nearby caught their attention. A patch of leaf litter moved and a bright orange round headed lizard popped up. "It's a newt," Tiberius whispered. "Let's go talk to it. Maybe it's seen Gaylord or the gypsy moths."

They crept closer but kept a discrete distance. Tiberius knew that the bright coloration on some amphibian's skin was a warning to its predators that it could be poisonous. "Hello," Tiberius addressed the newt. "Sorry to bother you, but we were wondering if you've seen any alligators lately or gypsy moth caravans."

The newt poked its head out further followed by its vivid black speckled body, and gave them an amused look. "Now why would two insects be searching for an alligator? That's the strangest thing I've ever heard. The gypsy moth caravan I can understand, but..." He shook his head, "a 'gator?"

"His name is Gaylord, and he's a friend of ours." Tiberius explained. "He also wears gold rimmed glasses."

The newt whipped its extremely long tail back and forth and cracked a one sided smile. "Now that's even funnier. An alligator who wears glasses. Are you two sure that you haven't lost your cranium berries?"

"No," Tiberius said testily. "All our cranium berries are intact." He quickly glanced at Crispin, then mumbled, "Well, almost."

The newt held up a hand, "All right, all right, I believe you, let me think a minute."

They waited patiently while the newt pondered in silence, "Come to think of it," he finally spoke, "I heard tell of a strange alligator upstream not too long ago. Of course, I got the information from a mole. They're not very trustworthy, and like to make up stories."

"Did he mention where the alligator was spotted," Tiberius asked.

"Somewhere upstream. It couldn't have been too far. Moles don't stray too far from their tunnels."

"Great," he replied, "we'll check out the lead. Thanks a bunch."

"Glad to be of help, hope you find your friend." The newt said with a wave as he slunk back into the leaf litter.

Soon after, the travelers spotted several kingfishers landing on an outcropping midway across the river. As they drew nearer, Tiberius could make out a large strip of land jutting above the river's surface. It looked somewhat familiar, and the closer he flew, the more excited he became. "Hey, I see something familiar," he called to Crispin. "This looks like the sandbar Gaylord stopped at for the water bug races. I think we're back at the spot where we crossed."

"Hooray!" Crispin shouted. "Maybe that Gaylord fellow is still here."

It wasn't long before Tiberius caught sight of the rocky bank and trees where they had first met Gaylord. Now he knew for sure they were back. He landed on one of the small smooth stones and scanned the area for the gigantic reptile. Seeing no sign of Gaylord, Crispin suggested that they fly to the sand bar for a view of the opposite shore. When they arrived, the kingfishers had caught their meal and were lounging quietly in a nearby clump of reeds. There were far less bugs hanging around than on the race day, but mosquitoes, sand flies, and several damsel and dragonflies zoomed and darted about the sandbar's swampy edge.

Part of the announcer's stick tower was still there, and Tiberius perched on its top for an aerial view of the opposite shore. At first, he didn't see anything obvious, then he heard a curious slap-thunk sound, and a splash of water caught his eye. He zeroed in on the movement and saw a large tail thrashing back and forth. "That's definitely an alligator," he said to Crispin. "But I can't tell if it's Gaylord." 'Come on, turn around,' he mumbled swatting at a pesky mosquito. Suddenly, as if hearing Tiberius' voice, it turned its head sideways, and they saw a reflecting gold flash. "It's him," Tiberius shouted triumphantly. "I can see his glasses."

"Are we going to wait for him to come back this way," Crispin asked.

"No," Tiberius replied. "It might take too long and if we tried calling him, it's just too far. He would never hear us."

They left the sand bar, and headed for the opposite bank, but before long, they noticed Gaylord had left the bank, and was swimming back towards the sand bar.

'Good, here he comes,' Tiberius thought. 'Now we won't have to fly the extra distance.'

Gaylord noticed a winged creature coming towards him; and as it drew closer he shouted happily. "I'll be a four eyed muskrat. If it isn't my two little insect friends!"

Tiberius landed on Gaylord's head, leaned over, and gave him an extremely jubilant grin. "Hello Gaylord: are we glad to see you! We've been searching the river bank all day for you!"

"Land sakes, I didn't expect to see you critters back in these parts. And what's happened to Crispin. He looks a mite peeked."

"That's why we need your help," Tiberius explained. "He's been hurt. A blue jay tried to eat him. He managed to escape, but ended up with a broken leg."

"It really hurts too," Crispin groaned.

"Not only that," Tiberius went on. "He crashed in the Woods of Forgetfulness, and has amnesia."

"That's right," Crispin agreed. "I can't even remember you."

"Sounds like you two are in quite a fix. How can I help?"

"We need you to help us find the gypsy moths. They have a potion for amnesia, and medicine for Crispin's leg."

"Why, I'd be more than happy to help out," Gaylord said. "But it might be difficult to locate the gypsy moths. I've never seen such traveling fools and I haven't ferried them across recently. Do you have any ideas?"

"We thought since you're such a fast swimmer you could ferry us along the river bank. There might be some creatures along the way who might give us some leads."

"That's a dandy plan," Gaylord replied. "Grab a comfy seat, and we'll get a movin'."

They found a nice spot between two bumps just below Gaylord's neck and the trio returned to the far bank. Gaylord began the trek swimming parallel to the shoreline stopping occasionally for inquiries. They had no luck until they came upon a group of slider turtles piled on top of each other, sunbathing on a log barge. Gaylord, not wanting to frighten the turtles, kept his distance and camouflaged himself in the rushes along the bank. Tiberius fluttered to the heap of green and yellow striped reptiles hoping one of them might give him a good lead. He touched down on the log's tip, introduced himself, and inquired about the gypsy moths.

"We don't know nothin'," several of the turtles replied crankily, then with a splash-plop, slid off the barge. The pile of turtles collapsed and there was much grumbling among the remaining sunbathers as they scrambled for a new spot.

One of the turtles who remained was much friendlier and gave Tiberius the break he had been hoping for. "There's a raccoon which comes here every night to wash his food," the turtle reported in a sluggish voice. He yawned, blinked his wrinkled eyelids; and then continued. "Likes to talk too. Nearly wore my ears off a couple of nights ago. Don't rightly remember all he was saying, but seems he mentioned something about moths. He asked me if I heard the wild music at night."

Tiberius eyes widened as he realized the turtle actually knew something helpful. "Did this raccoon happen to mention his name?"

"Sure," the turtle answered, "but my memory's not what it used to be. Seems like it was Rocky, or Bosco, or something like that."

"Was it Roscoe," Tiberius asked hopefully.

"Yeah, that was it. Hey, you a mind reader or something?" The turtle said attempting to yawn and chuckle at the same time.

"No," Tiberius replied, "If I was a mind reader, I wouldn't have to ask where the gypsy moths are. We just happen to be their friends," he added.

"Weelll," the turtle said slowly then paused. Tiberius thought for a moment that the turtle had fallen asleep, but then it continued. "If I were you, and wanted to see this guy, I'd hang around here after nightfall. He'll eventually be by."

"Thanks," Tiberius replied glancing at the lengthening shadows. "I'm afraid that trying to find him during the day would be a waste of time."

"Yep, exactly what I was thinking," the turtle remarked.

Tiberius flapped his wings, readying to leave; then said. "I and my friends will wait on the river bank for him."

The turtle turned his red splotched head slowly as if it took great effort. "Where are they? I don't see anybody around."

Tiberius pointed to the rushes, "They're hiding in there."

"Why are they hiding," the turtle frowned. "We're not going to hurt them."

"Weeelll," Tiberius hesitated, "one of my friends is an alligator."

The turtle's eyes widened and his legs began to twitch. Several of the other sunbathers shrieked and slid off the barge. "A gator': for heaven's sakes! Why are you bringing one of those monsters around here for?"

"But he's friendly," Tiberius protested. "His name's Gaylord, and he's helped us a lot. He ferried us across the river, now he's helping us look for the gypsy moths. He really is very nice." Tiberius reiterated.

"Easy for you to say," the turtle replied, "You're not on the top of an alligators' dinner menu!"

"Don't worry then," Tiberius said reassuringly. "I'll be sure he keeps his distance."

"Okay, but don't expect to see me and my buddies hanging around here tonight."

"Sorry if we've caused any problems." Tiberius said apologetically.

"Oh it's okay, we'll be going on over to the other side of the river anyway, for a midnight raid on some grubs."

"Happy hunting, and thanks for the help," Tiberius said as he lifted off and headed back to relay the good news.

"I hope y'all don't mind if I soak my bones and snooze a bit while we're waitin'." Gaylord said later.

"Of course not," Tiberius replied. "But do me a favor, and leave the turtles alone. They're really skittish about you being here."

"Mmmm," Gaylord teased. "They're mighty tasty critters." He laughed in his gravely rumbling voice then added, "But since you're asking' nice, I'll try to restrain myself."

Tiberius smiled and waved a foreleg in the air. "Thank you, kind sir. That's very magnanimous of you."

"Well, I don't know about bein' magna what ever, but since I ate a whole duck just last week, I think those little crunchy guys are safe for tonight."

"But you said gators don't like eating ducks," Tiberius interrupted sounding perplexed.

"Yeah, well. I got desperate." Gaylord replied shaking his head. "Still trying to get the feathers out of my back teeth too. Serves me right."

"Great, then they're safe for the night, and let's not wake Crispin, he needs his rest. Can you watch him from the bank?"

"You can count on me," Gaylord answered. "I'll be sure to keep an eye above the surface."

"I'm going back to the turtle barge now," Tiberius announced. "Let's hope Roscoe shows up soon."

Tiberius sat on the log, and stood vigil for quite some time, almost giving up hope. Eventually his eyes grew heavy and he slumped sideways against a knot protruding from the log.

Later, he was jolted awake by a splashing noise nearby. He peered through the misty vale which had floated in with the darkness and saw a shadowy four legged form standing on the bank swishing a small object into the water.

He crawled off the log, and made his way to the animal. As he approached, he could tell that it was definitely a raccoon, and called Roscoe's name.

The raccoon glanced down and a look of amazement crossed his black masked face followed by a huge toothy grin. "Well, I'll be a son of a squirrel," he announced in his gruff voice. "Never expected to see you guys again." He quickly looked around. "Say, where is the little guy, what's his name. Oh yeah: Crispin." He laughed loudly, "and how could I forget a name like Tiberius.

What's up with you two anyway? Did you find those crystals you were after?"

Finally, when Tiberius was able to get a word in, he answered, "Crispin's in the rushes asleep, and has a broken leg."

"Sorry the kid's laid up," Roscoe said.

"And he has amnesia," Tiberius went on. "We were hoping you knew where the gypsy moths are. We need their medicine, and yes we found the crystals."

"Boy, are you guys in luck. Just so happens I do know the whereabouts of the gypsy moth camp, and it's not too far away." He stuck the small morsel of food he was washing into his mouth, swallowed it and grinned slyly. "Hey, don't suppose, I could get a look at those crystals some time?"

"Of course you can," Tiberius replied. "They're in our packs over by Crispin and Gaylord."

"Gaylord, Gaylord," he repeated somewhat perplexed. "That name sounds familiar. Oh yeah. Heard the gypsy moths talking about him once. Wears glasses or something weird like that, right."

"He's nearsighted so he wears glasses, and he's the one you helped rescue at 'Gator World," Tiberius informed him.

"Well great. Maybe he won't eat me right away," Roscoe chuckled.

"Of course he won't, besides, he said he wasn't hungry yet: ate a duck last week."

"Eeww; nasty," Roscoe grimaced and made a peculiar spitting sound. "All those feathers and hard bony pieces. No thank you. I'll stick to soft slimy things and loot from garbage cans."

"Come on then," Tiberius laughed, "let's go meet him."

Tiberius and Roscoe appeared from amongst the rushes, and Crispin stirred; rubbing his eyes.

"Hey kid," Roscoe waved. "Nice to see you again. Sorry to hear about your unfortunate accident." Crispin smiled faintly, but had a vacant look to his eyes. "Oh, I forgot," Roscoe groaned. "You've got that amnesia problem. Well kid, your worries are over, Roscoe's here to save the day. I'll get you guys to the gypsy moths pronto. They'll patch you right up with all those stinky magic elixirs and pasty salves they make."

Gaylord, who was camouflaged nearby in the grasses suddenly moved, and Roscoe tensed. "It's all right," Tiberius said. "Don't get jumpy on me now."

"Okay," Roscoe said, running a paw nervously across his brow.

Gaylord's huge head appeared through the rushes, and Roscoe sucked in a short breath as he caught sight of the sharp teeth overlapping the massive snout. "He-ll-oo," he stuttered, "I'm Roscoe."

"Now don't you be scared of me," Gaylord said in a low gentle voice. "I've never eaten a raccoon in all my born days, and don't plan on starting."

Roscoe calmed a little and moved closer. "You really do wear glasses," he said incredulously.

Gaylord chuckled, "Goodness gracious. Word sure does git around like wildfire. You'd think I was famous."

"Well maybe not famous," Roscoe replied, "but certainly much talked about."

Gaylord laughed louder, and Roscoe joined in, finally confident he wasn't going to end up in the beast's belly. The four unusual companions chatted and laughed for a short time until Tiberius suggested they needed to get Crispin to the gypsy moths as soon as possible.

Gaylord said his farewells, and they watched as he slipped silently below the river's surface. The pair snuggled into their old traveling spots amongst Roscoe's thick woolly back and the trio began their journey.

Chapter 27
The Crazy Moon Music Festival

*T*he soft warmth of Roscoe's fur coupled with the gentle swaying of his body soon lulled the tiny passengers into a deep sleep. Roscoe traveled away from the river through a swampy area populated by towering Tupelo trees. It was too dark to see the inferno of reddish orange their leaves had acquired from a touch of cooler days, but their gracefully flared, horizontal branches stood sentinel over the soggy forest floor.

As time passed, the terrain dried, and Roscoe made his way to a ridge line of tall buffalo grass. Beyond, the land sloped gently into a flat bottomed ravine sprinkled with clusters of low growing shrubbery and tall ash trees. He paused, and gazed down into the ravine. 'Lemon Springs is down there,' he thought. 'And that's where I heard the Crazy Moon Music Festival is being held. The gypsy moths always show up for that. I've never heard of them missing a music festival – especially this one. It's one of the largest, and the prizes are highly sought after.'

He proceeded into the ravine and began making his way past the ash trees, listening to their delicate leaves rustled in the soft night breezes. Roscoe had been here for the last music festival, but he wasn't sure of its location this time. He decided to check the previous site and moved in its direction. Soon, he thought he heard the faint strains of music floating through the air. He paused and listened carefully. 'Is that a lone cricket or katydid', he wondered. Then he heard other chirps, and raspings join in.

"Wonderful, I've found them," he mumbled. "I hope the gypsy moths are really here, Crispin didn't look very good last time I saw him, and his body feels way too hot. I can feel it through my fur. I bet he has a fever."

Feeling a greater sense of urgency, he quickened his pace and followed the musical sounds. Roscoe knew he had found the festival when he spotted a golden glow illuminating a clearing surrounded by a group of ash saplings. Several winged sentries darted from the surrounding treetops on his approach. They landed among a group of grasshoppers lounging in the clearing and began gesturing excitedly. One of the grasshoppers arose and in one gigantic jump landed next to Bela to convey the message.

Not wanting to frighten the small creatures, Roscoe crept towards the campfire and very slowly stuck his nose into the clearing. The first thing he saw was the gypsy moth's wagons arranged along one side of the clearing. 'What a break,' he thought as he stuck his head in further. 'Now Crispin we'll get help.'

When Bela and Latslov saw Roscoe, they flew over and landed on a branch close to his nose. "Welcome, welcome," Bela gestured grandly. "Our sentries tell of your coming. How is our old friend this fine evening? Has Roscoe come to enjoy music?"

"Yeah. Sure Bela; but later. Right now I've got a couple of your acquaintances on my back and the little one's been hurt...real bad. They seem to think you're their only hope."

"Who are these troubled souls," Latslov asked.

"It's the moth, Tiberius and his firefly buddy Crispin," Roscoe explained. "The little guy has amnesia and a broken leg."

The two moths threw each other an alarmed glance; then Bela turned, clapped his hands sharply and called to several others nearby. "Quickly, quickly. Bring the injured one to emergency hut....Pavl, get Maleva..."

"Please to follow me," Latslov gestured to Roscoe.

Tiberius awoke and stuck his head out of Roscoe's coat. He blinked in amazement at the sight of the huge campsite and large gathering of insects; then breathed a great sigh of relief when he heard his gypsy moth friend shouting orders.

Roscoe followed Latslov to a makeshift structure constructed of sticks and magnolia leaves. He lay down at the hut's entrance and several moths, along with Bela came rushing over.

Tiberius crawled through Roscoe's fur and shook Crispin. His eyes fluttered, but they didn't open. "I'm so c-o-l-d," he mumbled faintly. Tiberius touched his body: It was burning up. "Hurry," he shouted to the moths. "He's got a high fever." Then he called to Bela, "Can you stash these packs for me? I can't help with my hands full."

"Yes, Bela will find safe place." He let the packs drop to the ground, and Bela motioned to Pavl, "Take these to my wagon and guard them."

Three moths landed on Roscoe's back next to Crispin. "Looks very bad," one of the moths observed, then added, "Do not worry my friend, we will help."

Tiberius and two of the moths grabbed hold of Crispin and gently lowered him to the ground, where a sturdy leaf mat was waiting. Maleva and her two attendants, Maria and Nikki were waiting just inside the hut's door. They grabbed the leaf litter, pulled it inside and slid it onto a softer pile of lambs-ear leaves. Maleva and her two attendants took over in a flurry of urgent activity.

Tiberius stuck his face in the door and Maleva rushed over. She could see the concern on his face and spoke to him in a quiet reassuring voice. "Do not worry; your friend is in best of hands. We know you worry, but please wait outside. There is no room."

"All right," Tiberius replied reluctantly; then added quickly. "Did they tell you he has amnesia? Be sure to give him that potion right away."

"Of course," she replied then went on. "Maleva very glad to see you but no time to talk. There is hard work ahead." A faint smile played on her face.

Tiberius was able to muster a half smile in response then went to worry by the warm fire. He found a comfortable moss covered log to sit on and slowly let his eyes roam around the grounds taking in the colorful landscape. A huge campfire centered the clearing with the festival activities radiating from it like planets orbiting a sun. The first thing which caught his eye was a cluster of toadstool umbrella-d booths arranged along a meandering path, flanked by rock tables and moss cushion seats. Most of them were occupied by festival goers, eating, drinking, and chatting gaily. The booths were manned by insects sporting poofy white hats and aprons in a rainbow of colors. Each was offering a variety of food and drink that filled the air with a smoky kaleidoscope of delectable aromas. His antenna picked up sweet honey and roasted nuts mingled with savory spices and the unmistakable smell of gypsy moth brew. One booth however, stood farther down the pathway as if it had been isolated or thrown up as an afterthought. Just beyond it lay the gypsy moth wagons and the emergency hut. The other half of the fairgrounds consisted of a long crescent shaped grassy knoll with a stick built rectangular platform facing it.

On the knoll, clusters of snacking multi-legged creatures were lounging, enjoying the mild evening air. There seemed to be a large number of katydids, crickets, grasshoppers, bees and gypsy moths but he also saw mosquitoes, fireflies, junebugs, and too many beetles to count. Even an occasional squirrel, hedgehog or field mouse would stick its head through the surrounding brush for a glimpse of the unusual activity. Roscoe was the only large animal which seemed interested enough to hang around.

At the moment the raccoon was sprawled on a patch of soft newly fallen leaves behind Bella's caravan. Two other caravans were parked nearby, arranged in a circle around their own smaller campfires. Tiberius could hear the occasional faint sound of 'dongs, boinks, tinkles and plucks' as the gypsy moth musicians warmed up for the next competition.

Several other groups of insect musicians were assembled just beyond the main campfire and Tiberius watched mesmerized as they began practicing. The bright green katydids were closest to the fire, and he could see them clearly as they rubbed their knobby lined front legs against the sharp edge on their front wing. Their familiar 'katydid katydidn't katydid katydidn't' music blended in with the tunes from the spotted and striped grasshoppers who practiced nearby. The burly male hoppers were lined up on a log playing with great gusto and wearing broad confident grins. As the comb like scrapers on their back legs flew along their front wings, a flurry of raspy crackling notes were orchestrated into a cheerful melody.

Further away in the shadows, a cluster of crickets were practicing under an ash sapling. The conductor was standing on a toadstool waving a tiny stick baton. The choir began to chirp madly, then paused, changed pitch and began the refrain again.

Tiberius glanced back to the stick platform in front of the grassy knoll. It was decorated with garlands of colorful flowers and autumn leaves as brilliant as the roaring campfire. To one side of it were several rows of log seats and a flat topped toadstool. He decided that this was the stage and would be alive with performers very shortly. The gypsy moth band's unattended instruments lay nearby on a group of rocks. His eyes fell back on the emergency hut and the urge to check on Crispin was overpowering. He talked himself out of it and sat still.

INSIDE THE EMERGENCY hut Maleva and her attendants were assembling the small vials of potions and nut shell cups of salves they would need to treat Crispin. Maleva quickly mixed the amnesia antidote with powerful sleeping herbs and stirred it with a thin stick.

"Crispin must sleep and be still while we work on injured leg," she announced. "But first, he must drink it. Bring water to wake him." she ordered.

Maria brought a cup of cool water with a fuzzy leaf floating inside. Maleva twisted the leaf and wiped her patient's face.

Crispin felt a cold sensation on his face and it slowly brought him to consciousness. He groaned and his eyes fluttered open. Then he wished he hadn't. The burning pain rushed up his leg and spread like a fire along one side of his body. He was freezing and began shaking. Through the pain he was able to focus on a face hovering over him but it was unfamiliar. Suddenly the face began to change and he panicked as its eyes glowed red and two sharp fangs grew from its mouth. It spoke and a small forked snake like tongue flicked at him.

"Gorboos, Gorboos!" he cried out. He had to get away. He jerked and twisted, but the pain throbbed worse and he felt paralyzed. The monster spoke but Crispin couldn't understand what it was saying. Suddenly something wet trickled down his throat and he couldn't help but swallow it. 'That's it, the monster has poisoned me. I'm dead,' he thought as a deep sleep sucked him into a dark tunnel.

Maleva and Nikki tried to hold Crispin's legs still while he was hallucinating but he was strong. "The fever, it causes very bad dreams while awake," Maleva explained. "We must hurry and dress injury while he sleeps deeply. Nikki, go to fire and bring much hot water."

Maleva turned and grabbed a small wooden box and opened it. Inside was a ball of shimmering spider web. She unwound a length of it and cut it with a sharp piece of glass.

"We must make Crispin still or cleaning will be very difficult," she said. "Also, vest must be off."

They untied his vest and carefully moved his body enough to slip it off, then began to truss him with the spider thread. After he was immobilized Maleva gingerly pulled his wounded leg outwards.

"First, we must remove bandage. Please to bring cutting instrument, Maria."

She rushed away and came back holding two sharp edged pieces of shiny black stone. Cautiously, they sliced away the pitch covered vines and began stripping away the sticky leaf bandages.

Maleva sent Maria to help Nikki with the hot water and began inspecting the wound. There was a long jagged tear in Crispin's exoskeleton and instead of healthy ivory tissue inside; his leg was filled with foul smelling green pus.

"As I feared. Infection is very bad," she mumbled.

Maria and Nikki returned with the hot water and they went to work, flushing the wound until no more pus was seen. Maleva could now see the cleaned interior of the wound and found several areas of dead tissue.

With a shell scraper she removed as much of the infected flesh as possible then flushed the wound again. Next she sprinkled a yellow sulfurous powder in the wound followed by a vial of dark blue liquid and the concoction began to foam and give off a cloud of grayish smoke. After the air had cleared she instructed Maria and Nikki to bring the ointments. They rushed over and retrieved the bowls filled with various colored substances.

Maleva sniffed them and asked, "They are fresh...no?"

"Of course," Nikki answered. "We bring only best for Maleva's friend. Wild garlic and onion very strong and honey is finest around."

"Also, horsetail and yarrow, I picked myself two moons ago," Maria added proudly.

"Good," Maleva nodded; then grabbed an empty nutshell and a stick. She scooped generous portions from each bowl and mixed them together. Nikki dried the wound with pieces of soft fibrous cloth; then Maria packed the opening with the ointment mixture. Lastly, they wound strips of the cloth around the broken leg and tied it securely to his body.

"We are finished," Maleva said wiping her brow. She turned to her assistants and smiled. "If you please, stay with Crispin for short time. Maleva will go give news to friends."

Tiberius was almost frantic for any report on his small friend when he saw Maleva step out of the hut. He rushed to meet her, and she suggested that they go back to the campfire. They sat on a log bench and Maleva began describing all the procedures they had done to Crispin.

"It sounds like we got here just in time," Tiberius said shaking his head sadly.

"Yes, infection is very serious. Crispin must stay still and sleep for long time. You are tired...no?"

"I'm too worried to sleep," Tiberius sighed.

Maleva touched his foreleg. "Do not worry. Young one will be fine."

"I wish I knew that for certain."

"Maleva will bring you a warm drink. It will help you relax."

She left and returned a short time later with a cup of warm sweet liquid. "You like," she asked.

"Mmm! It's good. There's honey in it and something else I can't describe. What is it?"

"Rose hips and willow bark," she smiled. "It will also help headache."

Tiberius gave her a quizzical glance. "How could you tell I had a headache?"

Maleva touched his forehead and replied "The face tells many stories if one can read it." She stood to leave, "Maleva must take turn and sit by patient now."

Tiberius watched as she headed towards the emergency hut. As she passed the campfire, her wings flashed a brilliant gold. He shook his head and mumbled, "What a gal!"

To his astonishment, Maleva reappeared from the hut almost immediately, and headed in his direction. For some reason, his face felt very warm and the fact that his heart beat quickened as she approached had not escaped him either. 'What's wrong with me he wondered,' shaking his head trying to clear the strange feeling. He didn't have time to answer; she was already standing next to him speaking.

"You must be hungry after long journey there is much good food at festival."

"Yes, yes," he stammered trying to regain his composure. "It has been a while since I've eaten." Then he added. "I thought you were going to stay with Crispin."

"Nikki stays with him. She is very trustworthy and he sleeps deeply. I will take turn later so others can watch competition."

Tiberius nodded and they strolled towards the mushroom covered food booths where other festival goers were clustered around waiting to be served. A few of them were twitching or buzzing impatiently and occasionally a hungry grasshopper would bounce into the air to survey the line's progress.

"We need place to put food," Maleva said.

She left, but returned soon bearing bowls and plates. Before long, they had worked their way to the first food booth. It was being operated by an animated cluster of bumble bees who buzzed about feverishly manning a huge stone bowl nestled into a fire pit. Tiberius watched in amazement as grains of pollen were tossed into the bowl and stirred with a wooden paddle. He jumped slightly as a sharp popping sound began, and the grains erupted into puffy yellow balls. Maleva smiled, amused at his reaction. The bee servers quickly scooped the tidbits out and filled the hungry patron's outstretched bowls.

"Is popped pollen," she stated. "You will like."

He ate one and smiled. "It tastes like pollen, but it's light and crunchy. It's delicious; I've never tasted anything like it."

"The bumblebees are good cooks...no?" Tiberius' mouth was so full; all he could do was nod. "Come to next booth. You will enjoy this also," she suggested as they moved on. They wove through the onlookers and saw three red lady beetles sitting on a patch of clover handing out tiny balls and singing,

"Come one come all
Get your yummy fruity nut balls
They're absolutely the best around
None better will ever be found"

Behind them were more industrious lady beetles chopping nuts and berries with stones, and mixing mysterious ingredients in large bowls. It reminded Tiberius of the cake factory at Lady Bug Town. Tiberius and Maleva were each given several balls, and they wasted no time devouring the tasty treats as they strolled along.

At the next booth, they received a serving of mixed leaf salad tossed with wild mustard sauce. The servers were two bright yellow striped grasshoppers who ate as much as they served. The hoppers didn't say much, but managed an occasional green stringy smile. Tiberius accepted the small plate of salad and tasted a morsel.

"It's okay," he reported to Maleva, "but I bet Crispin would really love it."

She laughed and replied, "If young one wakes soon and is hungry, Maleva will take salad." They continued on and Tiberius set his salad plate on a table as they passed. Maleva took his front leg, smiled coyly and said, "Come now, Tiberius must see next booth. Chef Morrell is very famous and very entertaining."

They rounded a curve in the pathway and Tiberius heard the booth well before he saw it. A gruff voice was chanting very dramatically, "Git your fungus here folks. Nice chewy fungus." He paused then began again, "Fungus on a stick, folks. We got em all: earthballs, stinkhorn, bracket jelly, meadow puff balls, come and git it. Fresh picked fungus!" Tiberius could smell it too. A musty earthy odor seeped from the booth, waiting to entice or repulse passersby.

Tiberius and Maleva cracked up laughing when they heard the comical pitch but managed a straight face as they approached the booth. They joined a group of riveted spectators who were helplessly caught in the spellbinding web of showmanship.

"Ahhhh, good evening," a shiny black-red striped fungus beetle greeted the crowd. "Could I interest you in a delectable fungus tonight?" He waved a long stick towards a pile of rotting tree stumps arranged on the ground. "They couldn't be fresher if you picked them yourself! Why, look at those jelly fungus. Have you ever seen a brighter color?"

He turned and tapped the transparent yellow gelatinous blobs oozing from the side of a log, then pointed to a pile of white, tan, and pale yellow pitted balls. "And get a look at these puff balls." He paused and made a wet smacking sound with his mouth. "Picked this morning. They make your mouth water, don't they?"

He grabbed a potato-like earth ball, poked it on a stick, and resumed chanting; waving it in the air. "Fungus on a stick. Come and git it folks!"

Tiberius and Maleva doubled over in another fit of laughter as they left and continued to the next booth.

"Now comes yummy sweet food," Maleva said with a glint in her eye.

As they moved closer, a thick cloud of sweetness rushed up to meet them. Tiberius was not at all surprised to see that honeybees were operating the sweet foods booth and the main ingredient in most of the treats was honey. One of the dishes contained roasted pine nuts, and chopped acorns which explained the smell of roasting nuts he had picked up on his arrival. Several bees were stirring the ingredients in a stone carved cooking pot which resembled the one used at the popped pollen booth. After the nuts were toasty brown, they were transferred to a rock slab where honey was added. Other honeybees wearing bean pod mittens stretched and folded the mixture until it cooled into a soft sticky slab. Small wedges of the dough were then pulled off and dredged through a powdery mixture of finely crushed juniper berries. Other delicacies offered at the booth were thin strands of spun crystallized honey twisted around jasmine blooms, honey dipped wild berry crunch, and honey filled reed straws. The servers were very generous with their portions when they heard of Crispin's plight and the pair left with an extra bowl of goodies.

"We will have beverages now," Maleva suggested as she led him onward. They were welcomed at the beverage booth by the soft strains of a gypsy moth fiddler who was perched on a stone. A ring of blazing torches surrounded the parasol mushrooms.

"Welcome friends, it is most wonderful evening...no?" An old female gypsy moth with a red scarf headdress greeted them as they arrived. "We have many fine beverages tonight: brew, tasty nectars, and spring water." She gestured to a row of gourd pitchers lined up on a log table. "What will be your pleasure?"

Just then a group of junebugs and fireflies approached and two moth helpers hurried over in a whirlwind of tinkly colors, to assist them. Tiberius chose a cup of beard's tongue nectar which he sampled first, and found to be bold and full bodied. Maleva decided to play it safe and ordered passion flower juice. They sat at a vacant table nearby and chatted while enjoying the hypnotically beautiful music.

"What's over there?" Tiberius pointed to a booth far removed from the others.

Maleva turned to look and replied, "That is beverage booth for female mosquitoes. You do not care to go there. It is," she waved a foreleg through the air. "How you say it? Not our cup of tea."

"Well, they seem to be having a really good time," he remarked, as loud buzzing laughter erupted from the group, and several mosquito fell off their log stools. They laughed heartily at the mosquitoes' antics, then Maleva stated. "It is festival time, everyone is happy now." After finishing their drinks they reluctantly strolled back toward the competition arena.

"Maleva will take sweets to emergency hut. Crispin will need extra energy for healing."

"Can I see him when he wakes up," Tiberius said between bites of honey nut balls.

"Of course; but only for few moments," she replied seriously.

"I promise to be brief," Tiberius said; then added as he took another bite. "These are great. What are they called again?"

"Sweet and sour balls," she replied. "The sweet is from honey of course, and sour is from juniper berry dust."

"It's an intriguing combination," he said; then went on, "I've never seen this much food at a festival before. Is it like this every time?"

"Yes. Cooks volunteer to bring food. They like to compete, same as musicians."

Tiberius plucked another sweet and sour ball from the bowl; then chuckled, "I vote for these then!"

Maleva headed to the emergency hut and Tiberius returned to the bench by the campfire. He continued munching on the food feeling somewhat guilty at enjoying himself so much while Crispin lay close by fighting for his life. He looked at the emergency hut just as Maleva exited and motioned for him to come over.

"He asked to see you," she said. "Remember, do not be long. More sleeping herbs will be given soon."

Tiberius nodded, entered and crept slowly to the pallet. Crispin was very still and cocooned in bandages. His face was puffy and seemed off color. His eyes opened groggily but he managed a feeble smile.

"Don't try to talk," Tiberius said in a low voice. "You need to save your strength. The gypsy moths are taking very good care of you. They say you're going to be all right soon."

Crispin managed another smile and then replied hoarsely, "Good, lets get home.....miss parents."

"Yes, we'll be home soon, and you'll be a big hero."

"So will you," Crispin added.

"Shh. No more talking. There will be time for that later. Then you can jabber your fool head off."

Maleva came alongside holding a small cup of liquid. "Maleva must give sleeping herb now. Crispin need sleep."

"Okay, I'll see myself out," he replied. Crispin was still smiling as he drifted back to sleep.

Tiberius was returning to the campfire feeling relieved that Crispin was recovering when he stopped dead in his tracks. Something Crispin had said suddenly hit him. "He misses his parents!" he mumbled. A broad smile lit Tiberius' face as he realized that Crispin had gotten his memory back. With a lighter heart, he chose a seat close to the performing stage and waited for the next competition.

Nearby, a small group of mosquitoes sat, sharing a bowl of popped pollen. He wasn't that close, but with his excellent hearing; he couldn't help but catch some of their conversation. "I wish those girls would hurry and get back. They're going to miss the opening number!"

"Yeah," another mosquito griped, "We come to this festival for the music and half the time, the girls are hanging out at the beverage booth."

"You can't blame them really," a new voice interjected, "free food is hard to turn down."

The first mosquito voice groaned then added, "but we're the ones who have to listen to them complain about how bloated they feel afterwards."

Tiberius chuckled then thought, 'That must be the booth Maleva said we didn't want to visit.'

His pondering was interrupted by a voice calling his name. He turned towards the sound and saw Roscoe motioning to him. He was still lounging just beyond the gypsy moth caravan, and Tiberius hurried over.

"I finally got your attention," Roscoe blurted as Tiberius sat next to him. "Any news on Crispin?"

"Yes. Maleva says that they've done all they can for him, and he just needs rest now. She seems confident that he will recover."

"That's great. Glad to hear it," he replied. "The little guy sort of grows on you."

Tiberius nodded, "I know what you mean."

"The final competition should be starting soon," Roscoe informed him. "You'll have a front row seat too."

"Can you hear okay from this distance," Tiberius asked.

"I'll probably move a little closer: don't want to step on any festival goers." He pointed to the bandstand. "Do you see that grasshopper in the funny red feathered hat and green vest? That's Bugsy Muldoon. He's the master of ceremonies."

"Don't like him much," Roscoe went on. "A sort of pushy-boorish sort of guy. They elect a new master of ceremonies for each festival. The last time it was a firefly. What was his name?" He shut his eyes for a moment. "Sam something....had a strange last name...what was it....oh yes Piddlewing. That's it, Sam Piddlewing....nice guy too." He glanced at Tiberius and winked. "Maleva's nice too isn't she?"

Tiberius held his breath and thought, 'Oh no, here it comes.' "Well, yes of course she's very nice," he answered.

"I bet she's quite a looker too; for a moth." Roscoe went on. "Not that a raccoon such as myself would notice."

Tiberius knew where this was leading, and gave Roscoe a warning glance. "Yes, she is very pretty. Now, what's this all about?"

Roscoe held up a paw defensively and smiled. "Hey, not that it's any of my business, but saw you two cruisin' the food booths earlier. Looked like you were havin' a real good time."

Tiberius decided that it was time to change the conversation and asked. "By the way, why is this called the Crazy Moon Festival?"

Roscoe chuckled, well aware of Tiberius' strategy. "I'm not going to tell you. You'll find out soon enough."

"Hrumph," Tiberius snorted. "I'm in no mood to play games. Can't you just tell me now?"

"Nope. It would spoil the surprise," Roscoe grinned slightly. "But I'll give you a clue."

Tiberius sighed, "Okay, if that's all I can get from you, I'll take it."

Roscoe glanced at the moon. "It's because the moon goes crazy on the last night of the festival...and it always happens just like they plan."

"Oh for goodness sakes," Tiberius said impatiently, "that really explains a lot."

"Shh," Roscoe held a paw up. "I think the competition's about to start. You'd better hurry back if you want a good seat. Other-wise, you'll be watching from a tree."

Tiberius rose to leave and said, "I'll keep you posted on Crispin's condition. Now don't leave without saying good bye."

"Don't worry, I'll be hanging out for a while," he replied with a wave.

Chapter 28
The Entertainers

The competition began with a fanfare of 'da da da daah: da da da daah', boinging from the gypsy moth musician's keyboard. The master of ceremonies: Bugsy Mulddon, attired in his lime green vest and red feathered top hat jumped onto the stage and shouted into a bark cone megaphone. "Welcome everyone. Please gather around. The final competition of the festival is about to begin."

The competing groups were hanging about nervously to one side of the stage and all the log and rock seating around the campfire had been claimed earlier. The other festival goers rushed in from every direction and soon the competition arena, grassy knoll and surrounding bushes and trees were occupied with excited spectators.

Bugsy Muldoon gave the audience time to settle down, and then brought the megaphone to his mouth again. "Good evening everyone. You know, a funny thing happened to me on the way to the festival tonight. A fly stopped me on the path, and said he was so depressed about winter coming that he was thinking of committing insecticide."

Bugsy laughed loudly at his own joke. The tambourine player jangled a 'baramm-ching'. The crowd laughed, mostly out of politeness, but Tiberius saw several spectators roll their eyes.

"Okay, seriously folks," he went on hopping back and forth, "is everybody enjoying the festival?"

Some spectators waved vividly colored flags while others applauded with excited buzzing, clicking, chirping, and twittering. As the crowd began to calm, he went on. "How about that great food folks? Let's give a big thank you to all those volunteer chefs." Another rambunctious cheer rose from the spectators.

"Now, before we get started with the last competition of the festival, it's my pleasure to announce the winning chef of the food preparation competition. This award goes to the food booth voted

most popular." The head chef's from each booth were assembled
by the stage waiting anxiously.

"The envelope, please." Busgy announced as a ladybug
wearing a daisy head wreath flew onstage and handed him a small
document. "Thank you, Ginger. Isn't she a cutie folks?" She
curtsied daintily and flew off stage. He opened it slowly, read it:
then smiled broadly. There was another fanfare from the band.
"And the award for best food booth goes to," he hesitated momentarily then shouted, "The fungus booth headed by Chef Morrell!"

The beetle jumped excitedly and headed for the stage. Tiberius
recognized him as the one who was entertaining the crowd with his
feverish fungus pitch. The spectators quieted and a toad bug sitting
by Tiberius spoke up. "That was no surprise. Everybody knew that
he was going to win. The other chef's never had a chance. Person-
ally, I think he's obnoxious."

"Thank you folks, thank you," Chef Morrell shouted to the
audience waving his arms grandly. He made his way to Bugsy
straightening his floppy chef hat which had slipped over one eye.

Bugsy shook the winner's leg and placed a shiny medallion
around his neck. The chef turned back to the audience and shouted,
"Don't forget to come by after the competition we have lots of
great fungus left. It's still fresh too folks. Don't miss out. This is
fungus season, and it's really, really tasty."

As he kept talking, Bugsy motioned curtly to Ginger and
another attendant. They rushed over, took Chef Morrell by the leg
and led him off the stage.

Suddenly, Bugsy jumped across the stage in one big leap and
almost flew off the edge: then shouted breathlessly, "How about
that Chef Morrell. What a fun-gi!"

The audience laughed loudly this time, obviously finding this
joke funnier. Bugsy straightened his hat and vest and went on. "As
you know this is the last competition of the festival, and we saved
the best for last. Let's welcome our four competitors for the group
entertainment category." He waved a leg with great flourish
towards the entertainers waiting by the stage. A tremendous roar
rippled through the crowd and the competitors waved and bowed.

Bugsy motioned to the grasshopper group who had moved to
the stage entrance. "Our first competing group tonight will be 'The
Fiery Fiddlers and Happy Legs' quartet conducted by Leopold
Fuzwig." Bugsy rushed off the stage, and the crowd cheered again

as the grasshopper musicians bounded onto the stage. The Fiery Fiddlers had donned red and orange striped bow ties made of flax leaves and the quartet were outfitted with flat brimmed straw hats.

The conductor, wearing a long tailed blue jacket came forward, and announced that the quartet would sing an unaccompanied version of 'Autumn Time' followed by the Fiery Fiddlers who will be performing the 'Haystack Six Step'. The quartet moved forward and warmed up by humming a few notes while the others arranged themselves on the log seats. Conductor Fuzwig hopped onto the toadstool, faced the quartet, and readied his baton. When he brought it down, they began to sing in skilled harmony, their front legs outstretched and bodies swaying to the melody.

> In the good old autumn time
> When the leaves of gold are fine
> We'll hop and play all the livelong day
> In a land called moonlight bay
>
> At the end of autumn time
> Sweet memories will be mine
> It won't be long till winter time
> Takes away the leaves of lime
>
> We'll sleep in the hay till the snows' away
> Cozy and snug my dear
> Biding our time 'till the sun again shines
> And life does reappear
>
> So when spring comes round again
> It is time to renew and then
> We'll work all day
> In the evening play
> At our home in moonlight bay

At the end of the song, they removed their hats and executed a long bow then took a seat alongside the fiddlers. There was a thunderous applause from the audience and the quartet stood for another bow.

After the crowd had quieted Leopold Fuzwig turned back to the Fiery Fiddlers and with a rustle of legs and wings they poised to play. Leopold waved his conductor's stick and the raspy crackling notes began to fly. The group's talent was very obvious as the varying tones and pitches melded themselves into a leg tapping rendition of the 'Haystack Six Step'. The Fiery Fiddler's bodies moved with perfect coordination and became lost in a golden brown blur. After the last note had been played, the conductor and fiddlers took a bow as the audience cheered wildly.

When the roar of the crowd began to dim, the grasshopper group jumped off the stage, and Bugsy reappeared. "Wasn't that just great folks?" He shouted through his megaphone. "Those fiddlers sure were on fire tonight weren't they? And how about that Happy Legs Quartet? Have you ever heard such harmony?" He jabbed his free leg into the air emphatically and went on; "and without musical accompaniment. Just amazing."

His voice calmed, and he continued, "All right, moving right along. Our next competitors came all the way from Turtle Back Bend. Please give a warm welcome to the 'Stardust Chirpers' and their conductor, Cherry Moonbeam."

Bugsy flew off the stage and it immediately filled with dozens of black big headed crickets wearing shimmering golden vests. Hurriedly they arranged themselves in several lines. The ones farthest back standing on the log pedestals. Cherry Moonbeam, clad in a red cape and ivy leafed head wreath, faced the group and tapped two sticks together. The musicians became very still and then positioned their wings in the playing position. The conductor turned to the spectators, bowed, and announced that they would be performing an instrumental piece called, 'Cricket Road'.

She tapped the sticks again, and the 'Chirpers' struck up the opening chords to an old and famous song. As the tune floated through the air, the crowd hopped, flapped, and swayed with the melody. Several groups of rhythmically talented ladybug beetles who couldn't resist the beat jumped up and began dancing along the grassy knoll's edges. Tiberius even found himself tapping his legs and swaying to the music.

He glanced toward the emergency hut and thought 'Crispin would really love this music. I wish he could be by my side having fun too.' Tiberius promised himself he would go check on him as soon as the competition was over. All too soon, the last notes were played and the crickets' wings fell silent.

He joined the audience in a thunderous cheer as the crickets took a final bow and exited the stage in a storm of shiny black bodies.

Bugsy was back on the stage in a flash, as excited as the crowd. He bounded from one edge of the stage to the other, shouting "Wow. That was definitely an oldie but a goodie, wasn't it folks. They're gonna' be a tough group to beat."

"Now join me in another round of applause for those magnificent, 'Stardust Chirpers'." He set his megaphone down, rubbed his leg and wing together and the audience followed. The clicks, chirps, buzzing and raspings were even louder than before and the cricket group was coaxed into coming back for another bow.

Finally the crowd quieted and Bugsy continued. "Moving right along, our next competitors hail from Turkey Trot woods, just over the next hill. They're no strangers to this festival. They've been competing for a long time and have several medals to prove it. Let's give a great big Crazy Moon welcome to the Green Strummers who will accompany the popular singing duet, Kit and Kip Diddlefern. The renowned maestro, Leif Mossbuckle will conduct them in an old katydid ballad, 'You Beautiful Gal'."

The audience broke out in a cheer as the katydid group hopped to the stage. For the competition they had adorned their bright green heads with round caps made from orange Chinese lantern pods. As they converged on the stage, two of the group moved forward and jumped onto taller performing logs while the rest divided into two groups. One of the groups, carrying flute-like instruments, situated themselves on the log seats while the others remained standing and formed a ring around the flutists. Maestro Leif Mossbuckle took his place front and center of the musicians on the conductor's mushroom with Kit and Kip to one side. The maestro raised his arms into the air and the flutists brought their thin reed pipes to their mouths. He lowered his arms, and the strummers struck an introductory chord followed by the whistling high pitched notes of the flutists. He then signaled to Kit and Kip and they began to sing in a soulful blending of velvety voices and expressive leg gestures.

I met you by the garden gate
And chased you down the water well

I want you for my lifelong mate
Please slow down my heart's a-swell

I saw you in the moonlight haze
And chased you over hill and dale
Please be mine for all our days
Please slow down my heart's a-swell

I saw you shyly look my way
You were blushing, I could tell
It must be love so they say
Please slow down my heart's a-swell

You flew past me one early morn
And hid amongst the coral bell
Just come back, I'm so forlorn
Please slow down my heart's a-swell

As the singers finished, the notes from the musicians swelled and with a final flourish of melody the group jumped up and took a bow.

The audience applauded ecstatically until it rose to a deafening roar. The katydid group continued taking bows and finally left the stage and rejoined the cricket and grasshopper contestants.

Bugsy, reappeared clapping exuberantly and picked up his megaphone. "Great gooseberries, that's what I call talent. Those folks at Turkey Trot woods must be real proud!"

A smattering of cheers rose from the audience as he went on, "and it seems we have a few of them here tonight. But we have to move right along," he shouted louder. "Our next and final competing group is no stranger to anyone. Please put your legs and wings together in welcoming the multi-talented and very colorful, 'Bela and the Moonspinners'."

Bela, Latslov and the band stood and executed a dashing gypsy moth bow as the crowd went wild. Tiberius laughed as he noticed several female gypsy moth fans huddled around the bandstand swooning and throwing brightly colored scarves.

Accompanying Bela and Latslov, were a half dozen other fiddlers, four pipers, three tambourine players, and the cymballa musician who was sitting behind his square wooden stringed instrument. Tiberius recognized several of the group, especially the piper with twig-like legs and the wizened old fiddler. Instead of the usual hodge-podge of clothing, the 'Moonspinners' were wearing gold sashed purple tunic vests and matching scarf caps.

The noise of the crowd finally subsided and the cymballa musician tapped out a tinkly, bing-bonging fanfare with his nutshell mallets as a signal to begin. The fiddlers readied their bows in the air, the pipers steadied their reeds on their mouths; and the tambourine players gripped their festively decorated instruments. There was a nod from Bela and they struck up a fast paced pulse quickening gypsy tune.

Tiberius thought that they sounded great the first time he heard them play; but tonight they were mesmerizing. The fiddle bows bounced along the strings at lightning speed, the pipers along with the keyboard were enchanting and the tambourines jangled wildly in a whirlwind of brightly colored streamers. The audience jumped and tapped their legs, caught up in the feverish pitch and Tiberius couldn't help but join in too. The 'Moonspinners' abruptly stopped. After a moment of silence, Latslov laid his fiddle down and stepped onto a bright red mushroom. The audience fell silent as he began to sing; accompanied by Bela who fiddled softly in the background.

> Last night I awoke to the sound of rain
> But nere a care, we're a wagon train
> Pack up our load, and hit the road
> Wanderers that we be
> Its gotta be the life for me
> Ba deedle bee bee
> Ba deedle bee dah

> If thunder and lightning tear from the sky
> No need to fear, just say good bye
> Pick up our load and hit the road
> Wanderers that we be
> Its gotta be the life for me
> Ba deedle bee bee
> Ba deedle bee dah

> When the cold north wind begins to blow
> We won't be freezin or diggin snow

Pick up our load and hit the road
Wanderers that we be
Its gotta be the life for me
Ba deedle bee bee
Ba deedle bee dah

The sun's a burnin', and wind's too still
Its lookin' greener over the hill
Pack up our load and hit the road
Wanderers that we be
Its gotta be the life for me
Ba deedle bee bee
Ba deedle bee dah

Latslov and Bela bowed followed by the other band members and their fans again went wild. Tiberius covered his head as insects of all kinds jumped and buzzed around in a frenzy of excitement.

The commotion continued until Bugsy reappeared and shouted into the megaphone. "Aren't those guys magnificent? They're just out of this world, aren't they folks. Wow! What a competition." He paused and wiped his brow, "I'm glad I'm not one of the judges."

"Let's have another big round of applause for all of the fantastic musical groups!" Tiberius ducked again, but this time, it was only the usual cheering. "Okay folks," he went on, "there will be a short break to give our judges time to tally the votes after which the winners will be announced." He hopped into the air, and pointed to the food booths. "How about trying some award winning fungus while you're waiting?"

He flew off the stage, and landed at the judging stand. Some of the spectators headed to the food booths, but most stayed put. Tiberius watched as the judges huddled together, heads bobbing and legs gesturing in intense conversation.

Finally, the judges handed an envelope to Bugsy, and he returned to the stage. He ran along the length of the stage calling into his megaphone. "Gather around folks the big moment has arrived. It's time to announce the winners in the group entertainment category."

There was a flurry of activity as spectators returned and then silenced as anticipation mounted.

"Before I read the contents of this envelope," he began waving it around, "I'd like to remind everyone that we have several awards. Those categories are: best singer or singers, best instrumentals, and of course the grand prize, best overall group performance." Bugsy slowly opened the envelope then smiled. "And the winners are" - the keyboard and tambourine boinged and clanged out a drum roll.

"The award for best instrumental goes to the 'Stardust Chirpers'."

The audience cheered as the 'Chirpers' jumped into the air and rushed onto the stage. Cherry came forward, and Bugsy handed her a gold medallion on a woven purple rope. She bowed with a flip of her cape, and returned to the 'Chirpers' who immediately swarmed around her for a glimpse of their award.

As they exited the stage, Bugsy read the next winner. "The award for best singers goes to - looks like we have ourselves a tie folks, 'The Green Strummers', and 'The Fiery Fiddlers - Happy Legs Quartet' have both won an award."

Another cheer rose from the crowd as both groups squeezed onto the stage. The conductors rushed forward and accepted their medallions; bowed, and the ecstatic group left the stage hopping, waving, and cheering 'hurrahs'.

"And now for the grand prize winner!" Bugsy shouted.

There was another drum roll, and Bugsy paused to let the suspense build. "The grand prize of this year's Crazy Moon Festival goes to 'Bela and the Moonspinners'!"

The band fluttered excitedly into the air and flew to the stage. The spectators immediately sprang up waving, buzzing, chirping, clicking, rasping and twittering their approval of the judges' choice. Bugsy shook each of the band member's legs and handed Bela and each musician a medallion on a silver rope. The 'Moonspinners', holding their medals up triumphantly and grinning proudly, bowed to the audience and judges. Finally the crowd quieted and the group flew back to their instruments.

"What a show," Bugsy shouted, "but it's not over. The best performance is yet to come: and, if I'm not mistaken it's already begun!" Tiberius was confused. He didn't see anyone else on or around the stage waiting to entertain. Bugsy suddenly threw his arm skyward, and the crowd let out a collective gasp. Tiberius noticed that everyone was staring upwards and he followed along.

At first he couldn't figure out what was going on; then he spotted the moon. A dark shadow had settled over one side, but there wasn't a cloud in the sky. "What's going on," he asked a fat toad bug sitting nearby.

"The moon is going crazy. Haven't you been to a Crazy Moon Festival before," he asked flicking his antenna in disbelief.

"No, I haven't," Tiberius replied.

"Well," the bug continued, "before too long, the whole moon will be blacked out."

Tiberius smiled. Now he understood Roscoe's cryptic teasing. He had seen this phenomenon before, but hadn't connected it with the festival's name.

"Don't worry," the bug added. "It will come back before morning."

"Thanks. I know." Tiberius said as he stood and headed to the emergency hut.

On his way he noticed that the festival goers were starting to thin out. Some with youngsters in tow were beginning their trek home, but others lounged about in small groups chatting excitedly as they stared at the slowly disappearing moon. He glanced to the toadstool umbrellas and stopped a moment to watch the activities taking place.

To his amazement, several Rhinoceros beetles had appeared and were having cooking equipment and left over food containers tied onto their backs.

The only group who didn't seem to be in a hurry to leave was the gypsy moths who Tiberius could tell were in a celebratory mood. The ones clustered around the roaring campfire were singing and dancing merrily, refreshing themselves with large cups of brew. He even spotted Bugsy Muldoon, still clad in his outrageous hat and vest, hanging out at the fungus booth talking to Chef Morrell and munching on something hanging from a long stick.

Tiberius arrived and knocked lightly on the emergency hut's thin wooden door. Maleva opened it and stepped out.

"Crispin is resting well. Did you enjoy competition?"

"Yes," Tiberius replied. "It was very entertaining. The musical groups were fantastic."

"We hear Moonspinners won big prize." She smiled proudly and went on. "Is great honor for gypsy moths. Caravan will be traveling to play at many festivals now."

"Have you seen the moon? It's going crazy." Tiberius informed her. "Can you come and watch for a while?"

"Maleva must stay 'till Nikki or Maria come."

"Okay, I'll wait for you by the campfire." He replied hoping his disappointment wasn't apparent.

He was about to leave when Maleva pointed over his shoulder. "Nikki comes. Please wait. Maleva will get shawl: night air is chilled."

Nikki and Maleva went inside the hut and Maleva reappeared with a fringed shawl the color of blueberries draped over her wings. They strolled to an ivy covered bench and watched; transfixed as the black shadowy disc inched its way across the pale yellow moon. Occasionally, smoky gray clouds sailed across the orbs surface hiding the eerie phenomena.

Tiberius glanced at Maleva's upturned face and noted how lovely she looked in the shimmering moonlight. There was an awkward silence, and he racked his brain for something to talk about. Staring at the moon gave him an idea, and he asked. "By the way; I was wondering why Bela's band is called 'The Moonspinners'."

A smile played gently at the corners of her mouth, and she drew her eyes away from the moon to Tiberius. "It is very old folk tale the Moonspinners," she said. "This is not known to your people?"

"No, I've never heard of it," he smiled quizzically.

"Maleva will tell tale then." She pulled her shawl tighter against the growing chill then began. "Moonspinners are spider sisters who spin web so well they also spin moonlight to keep clean and bright. Sisters spin threads of light away from full moon then cast it upon river for washing; then threads carried by current to horizon where wind blows it back to thinning moon. As threads return moon grows fat again. Sisters never stop so moon stays bright and keeps changing." Maleva paused then smiled. "That is end of story. You like?"

"Yes....very much. It's a quaint tale, but..." he gestured to the moon and shrugged. "They must be spinning very fast tonight."

Maleva giggled and shrugged, "Perhaps when moon is all dark sisters have short rest."

"Well, it's about that time," Tiberius said pointing to the sky. "Look, the black disc has almost blotted out the moon."

They watched fascinated as the moon was finally transformed into a muddy brown ball. The evening marched on and before long, a sliver of brightness peeked out as the shadow receded from the orb's surface.

Eventually, the moon magically re-appeared, and the remaining festival goers slowly made their way into the forest. Tiberius scanned the almost abandoned site and caught sight of Bela and Roscoe coming their way.

"Hey, look who's coming," he said to Maleva. "It's your uncle Bela and his sidekick Roscoe."

"Definitely an odd couple," Maleva said laughingly.

Bela had changed from his flashy band tunic into a more comfortable looking dark green jacket which was tied loosely with a yellow sash.

As they approached Bela gestured skyward and proclaimed loudly. "Crazy moon gave good show tonight...yes?"

"It was fantastic," he replied as Bela sat next to Maleva and Roscoe sprawled on a nearby patch of lush grass.

"How you like music tonight," Bela asked grinning expectantly.

"I don't believe I've ever heard such fine music." Tiberius gushed. "And I think the gypsy moths were the best group. You definitely deserved the big prize."

"Many thanks. Our band practiced for long time. Is great honor to be named festival champion. Band will have much fame now."

"Yes," Tiberius interjected. "Maleva said you would be invited to play at many festivals."

"Niece is right. Much traveling is required." He gestured, "but; that is life of gypsy moth...no?"

There was a lull in the conversation; then Tiberius spoke up, "Maleva told me the tale of the Moonspinners."

Bela smiled at Maleva with a mirthful sparkle in his eye. "Maleva is good storyteller...no? And best healer among gypsy moths."

"Maleva thinks uncle brags much," she protested. "Young Maria has trained well and is good healer also."

"This is true," Bela nodded. "Niece is good teacher and Maria knows much now."

"The little one," he added. "How is injured leg?"

"Crispin rests very well," she answered, "but must stay still for leg to heal."

"You guys were obviously heading home," Roscoe chimed in. "This will definitely slow you down. How about a ride home? I can have you there in a jiffy."

"Dragonfly Landing is long way," Maleva said. "Crispin would have rough ride on Roscoe's back. Also, will need much help before leg is healed. Better for little one to stay with gypsy moths for short time."

Bela nodded; then his eyes widened as an idea came to him. "Wait. Bela has answer. Moonspinners must play at ant's harvest festival. Is not far from your home. Gypsy moths will stay here until Crispin well enough to travel, then take you with us."

"That's a great idea," Tiberius replied, "but we don't want to hold you up."

"Is okay," Maleva reassured him, "Crispin can be moved to wagon soon."

"That's great," Tiberius said excitedly, "I want everyone at Dragonfly Landing to meet you."

Bela frowned; then said glumly, "Is nice gesture; but some creatures only think bad of gypsy moths."

Tiberius shook his head stubbornly; reluctant to accept the unfair situation. "I'll tell them how you helped us when we were injured. They'll change their minds. I'm sure of it. They welcomed me, even with my gigantic wings."

"Tiberius is right," Maleva added. "Creatures are sometimes afraid of things unknown. Gypsy moths should give them chance."

There were a few moments of silence: then Bela slapped a leg and announced boldly "Gypsy moths will take Crispin and Tiberius home and try to make new friends!"

"Wonderful," Tiberius grinned. "Don't worry, you'll fit right in."

Roscoe stood and shook a few stray blades of grass off his fur. "I hate to break up the party," he began, "but I need to shake a leg and head back home. I'll stop in and see Crispin before I leave."

After a round of fond farewells, the raccoon made his way towards the emergency hut. He peered through the tiny door for a time, and then left. Later, they saw him amble up and over the grassy knoll and disappear into the darkness.

Chapter 29
A Gypsy's Life

*T*he night wore on and the three remaining friends chatted gaily about the festival and their travels. Finally Maleva yawned and excused herself, then headed to the emergency hut to check on Crispin. Tiberius remembered what she had said at their first meeting about having trouble staying up all night and decided she probably needed to get some sleep.

Bela studied Tiberius as he watched Maleva leave. He noted how Tiberius watched her all the way to the hut and the tinge of sadness in his eyes. Bela wanted to discuss something with his new friend, and this seemed like the best time. He cleared his throat not knowing how to start.

"Ahh...Bela wonders: do you have friends and family somewhere waiting your return?"

"Well," Tiberius began, "I've made quite a few new friends at Dragonfly Landing and on our journey: but," he hesitated thinking about the rest of his answer then continued, "I guess you could say that until now I've been a loner. Oh sure, there's several trees I'm fond of, but nothing like the tunnel homes at Dragonfly Landing or your nice cozy wagons."

"And you have plans on returning to Dragonfly Landing?"

"To be honest, I haven't given it much thought. We've been too busy trying to find the crystals and survive for me to dwell on what comes afterwards."

"Bela understands," he said with a firm nod. He decided to stop beating around the bush and just come out with it. "Gypsy moths would welcome Tiberius into caravan. You are also moth....not so different...no? Maleva would like also," he grinned and continued. "Yes, Bela thinks this make niece very happy."

Tiberius was quite stunned at Bela's proposal. The thought of him joining the caravan had never crossed his mind, but these creatures had proved to be very surprising. The notion wasn't all that far fetched having gotten to know and experience their warm hospitality and graciousness.

He looked at Bela in disbelief and replied. "That's a very generous offer, but," he hesitated. "Are you speaking for every one? Some of the others might not feel the same."

Bela let out a little chuckle. "Do not worry; there are no bad feelings among gypsy moths. Everyone welcomes the moth with large wings like glowing green moon."

Tiberius gave Bela a warm smile. "It's very tempting, I must admit. You do lead a very exciting life, but I' not so sure about all the traveling."

"Ha," Bela said with a wink, "Maleva thinks this also. Mother was monarch butterfly. Their kind only traveled south for winter."

"Yes, I know. Maleva told me about her parents."

A shadow passed over Bela's face. "Brother loved Maleva's mother very much. Flood was terrible. It was great loss to everyone....but life must continue...no?"

"Yes," Tiberius replied as a wave of sympathy washed though him. A few moments of awkward silence passed; then Tiberius spoke. "I would like to talk to Crispin first before deciding anything if you don't mind."

"Is okay," Bela gestured. "Big decisions need much thinking. There is time yet."

THE SUN ROSE and set several times before Crispin was out of danger and on the road to recovery. Tiberius spent the time living the colorful life of a gypsy moth. He had to admit that it was extremely interesting and exciting, but he wasn't sure if it was the right lifestyle for him. One thing however kept nagging at his mind. Would it still seem so inviting if Maleva wasn't part of the group? They had been spending a great deal of time together taking long strolls, chatting and going on exciting flights. Being with Maleva made him feel giddy and he was sure that they had become more than just friends. He went to sleep and awoke thinking about his choices but hadn't discussed them with anyone.

Crispin still thought that Tiberius would probably stay at Dragonfly Landing. He saw no need to disturb Crispin's peace of mind until he was stronger. He and Maleva had discussed at length his staying but she didn't want to pressure him.

It was early evening and Tiberius was napping on a rock still warm from the day's captured sun when an excited voice woke him. Maleva's delicate face stared back and smiled.

"Wake now. Maleva have surprise."

"What is it," he asked yawning.

"It is secret," she giggled. "Hurry." He followed Maleva towards her wagon and when they entered, Crispin was sitting on the soft pallet. "Wow," Tiberius exclaimed, "You're up."

"Wait," Maleva ordered.

"Yeah, watch this," Crispin said grinning.

Maleva handed him two smooth, straight sticks which were leaning against the wall and he tucked them under his two forelegs. He slowly stood and took several steps.

"Look! They made me a pair of crutches," he said beaming, "and Maleva says I won't need them very much longer because I'm healing so fast. We can go home now. Can't we?"

Tiberius was so elated at seeing his little friend happy and well on his way to recovery that he gave Maleva a big hug. "You are a true healer for sure," he gushed. "Where would we be without the help of our friends?"

"Yes, friends are important," she replied, "but don't forget you were the one who found Crispin in the woods."

"Yeah, that's right," Crispin blurted. "I would still be lying in that terrible place if it weren't for you." His eyes widened "Great grasshopper legs. Sergeant Mudd and Vinney would have found me and I would be in Rock E. Crab's care. Ohhh," He shivered. "He probably would have put a shell over my leg."

They laughed, and Maleva stared at them totally confused.

"I guess you didn't tell her about meeting Mr. Crab." Crispin said still chuckling.

Tiberius glanced at Maleva. "I'll tell you that part of our adventure later."

"Yes, Maleva would very much like to hear of this Rock person, but first Crispin should have fresh air."

They helped Crispin out of the wagon and he was greeted by Bela and a crowd of well wishers. With Tiberius and Maleva's help, he walked to the campfire and sat on a soft patch of clover. The female gypsy moths bustled back and forth lavishing much attention on the little patient. They brought food and drink and several of the older ones tried to place shawls around his body in fear he might catch cold. Crispin discovered that he had the appetite of a rhinoceros beetle and ate so much that he was afraid he would not be able to hoist himself onto his crutches.

Since Crispin had missed the festival, the Moonspinners gave a repeat performance, this time wearing their prize medals around their necks. Crispin was very close to the cymballa musician and inspected his medal very closely. Embossed on its surface was a smiling faced moon surrounded by a ring of ivy leaves. As the band dipped and gyrated to the music of their instruments, reflecting sparks of gold glinted from their medals and mingled with the dancing embers of the campfire. Even though Crispin was still weak from his ordeal he couldn't help swaying to the pulse quickening rhythm. Afterwards Maleva ordered Crispin back to bed and with a wave to the gypsy moths; he was reluctantly escorted back to the wagon.

Maleva returned later and reported to Bela that Crispin was well enough for the caravan to move on. On Bela's orders, the gypsy moths moved as a well oiled machine and before long, the entire camp had been struck, and the beetle wranglers who had disappeared into the woods earlier, reappeared with the beetle heard in tow. By this time Tiberius had become accustomed to the lumbering giants and helped the wranglers attached the harnesses around several of the giant beast's bellies. Before the night was half spent, the snorting, impatient beetles had been fed and the caravan began its journey.

Tiberius was invited to ride with Dimitri, a wagon driver to learn the tricks of the trade. Most of the time they chatted as the beetle followed the lead wagon, but every now and then their charge would hesitate snorting, and clawing at the ground; raising thick clouds of choking dust. A gentle flick of the reins however seemed to remedy the situation and they moved on.

Tiberius soon became sore and stiff as the wagon bounced and jostled its way over twigs and gravel. He shifted to different positions to alleviate the discomfort but being unaccustomed to sitting for long periods it did little good. Occasionally one of the beasts would pause to relieve itself and the rancid smell seemed to follow the caravan for an eternity.

Finally the wagons halted for a short rest and Tiberius excused himself, thanking Dimetri for the lesson, having gained more respect for the wagon drivers. After checking on Crispin and finding him resting well, he joined a group inside another wagon to continue the night's journey in more comfortable and hospitable surroundings. These gypsy moths however weren't lying about idle, but busied themselves weaving spider web and yucca filaments into sturdy rope. They showed him how to strip the tough thread-like strands from the yucca and weave it together tightly.

Laughter erupted as his first attempts at weaving resulted in a knotted mess. Eventually with more practice he produced something which loosely resembled a rope. Before long his forelegs felt blistered from the friction of the filaments, but not wanting to look lazy he kept working. By nights end he had decided that living the life of a gypsy moth was not only singing and dancing but a lot of hard work as well.

Sometime before dawn, the caravan stopped and formed a circle. The occupants of the wagons came out, stretched their legs and wings, and retrieved bulky sacks and gourd pitchers from the food wagon. They sat in the safety of the circle for a while chatting, eating and drinking.

The wranglers unhitched the beetles and led them into the woods so they could forage for food and rest until they were needed again. As the sky lightened to a deep blue the food and drink was stored away and the gypsy moths retreated to their wagons for a well deserved rest: however, a small group who had slept for part of the night remained awake. Several stood guard over the wagons while others flew away into the forest. A young female with a loud spotted scarf on her head gave Tiberius several brimming bowls of fruit, leaves and berries to share with Crispin and Maleva. He knocked on the wagon door and Maria answered.

"Welcome Tiberius," she said in a lilting voice. "Crispin is waking. Come visit. Maria would like to stay, but it is time for sleep." He entered as Maria flashed him a timid smile, grabbed her shawl and scooted passed on her way out.

Crispin was sitting propped on his downy pillows as Maleva retied his bandage. She smiled warmly when she saw Tiberius and reached for the bowls. "Good morning. Your friend is tired from being kept in wagon for so long. Maleva has trouble making him rest."

"Yeah," Crispin grumbled. "I'm going stir crazy. If I don't get outside soon, I'm going to scream."

"Now I know he's getting better," Tiberius said chuckling. "Eat something first and then we'll take you outside, okay?"

"All right," He gave in and reached for his food.

While they were eating, Tiberius asked Maleva about the moths he saw flying away. "Those are scouts," she began. "They search for safe route so wagon drivers will have smooth travel next night."

"I see," He replied. "What kind of things do they search for?"

She finished sipping on the wild blueberry and continued, "Mud holes, ditches, ant mounds, fallen trees and swamps with hungry frogs. She waved a foreleg casually, "The usual things which cause delays, wagons to break, or danger to gypsy moths."

"Ahh, of course," Tiberius nodded. "I hadn't thought about those things, but I can see how important it would be to know what lay ahead in the darkness. They have a very important job," he added.

"Everyone in group has important job," she replied with a cocked eyebrow.

Crispin finished his food in record time, and they helped him negotiate the wagon steps. Once on the ground however, he was able to hobble about easily without assistance. He made his way around the encampment with his escorts by his side until he was tired. The threesome found a cozy patch of purslane to rest in and passed the morning chatting and laughing. Crispin thought he was going to burst his wound open when they described Chef Morrell and his fungus pitch and the female mosquitoes falling off their log seats.

"Sounds like I really missed out on the fun - especially all that yummy food," Crispin complained then quickly added, "except the fungus of course. Yuck! I can't believe that anyone would like stinkhorn fungus. Phewee!"

This caused another round of chuckles and Tiberius was pleased to see that Crispin's color had returned and he was back to his chipper self. They were basking quietly in the early morning warmth when Crispin suddenly spoke. "I had a really bad dream when I was sick. There was a monster trying to poison me with some sort of potion."

Maleva smiled and patted Crispin's head. "Fever caused Crispin to hallucinate. Monster was Maleva and poison was sleeping and amnesia medicine."

"Ohh," Crispin exclaimed rolling his eyes. "You look a lot better now that I'm well."

"Maleva certainly hopes so!" She replied with a teasing smile.

They escorted Crispin on another walk around the encampment and he collected a wild rose leaf to munch on along the way. After eating, he stifled several yawns and when his head began to droop, they had no trouble coaxing him back to bed.

It wasn't long before Tiberius began to feel the effects of his long night of driving and rope making. Not wanting to disturb the sleeping moths in their wagons, he crawled into a safe and comfortable cleft between two branches in a sumac bush and fell asleep.

Later, he woke just as the sun was dipping below the horizon to the sound of Maleva's voice calling his name. He slipped from between the branches, stretched and made his way to the top of the bush. "I'm over here," he shouted. She fluttered to the bush and landed beside him, then planted a soft kiss on his cheek.
Tiberius felt himself blush and grin self consciously.

"Maleva worry when you not answer."

"I didn't want to waken anyone in the wagons," he explained.

On their way back, they passed a group of female gypsy moths and older children pulling their food laden carts through the surrounding woods. Back in the encampment, Bela and several of the wagon drivers were huddled around the scouts who were drawing in the soft sandy soil. Tiberius assumed that they were giving a report on the safest route to take for the next leg of the trip. Maleva left to see if Crispin was awake, and Tiberius strolled around the campsite watching the early evening activities. A group of females were busy feeding babies nectar water while another group of oldsters were cracking open seed pods and scraping out their contents with a strange hooked stick. The small black balls were collected in a larger nut shell and passed to another group who were mashing the pieces with a sharp rock.

"What are you making," Tiberius questioned the workers.

A wrinkled old moth smiled crookedly; then answered. "It is for brew. When nectar is added, pods improve flavor and makes better nutrition for seeing in dark."

"How very interesting," he said thanking them; then walked on.

A few wagon drivers and wranglers were busy cleaning and repairing their wagons. Tiberius stopped and asked if they needed help, and before long he had a stick in his forelegs scraping mud off the wheels. Some of it was very sticky, and smelt bad, but after a while, he got used to the odor. Sometime later, he looked up from his labors, and saw Maleva coming his way. She giggled and wiped a smudge of dirt from his face. "Tiberius' having fun...yes?"

"You bet! This is the most fun I've had in ages," he replied with a wink.

"Come," she coaxed leading him past the wagons. "There is spring for washing. Crispin wakes too," she added.

"I guess he's raring to get outside again," he said.

"Of course. Is good though. Little one needs fresh air for health," she replied.

Not far from the caravan a sparkling spring bubbled from a hole at the base of a granite outcropping. Tiberius took a long refreshing sip of the water; then scrubbed the thick mud from his legs and face. Maleva handed him a piece of the woven gypsy moth fabric which she had tucked into her shawl and he dried off. They paused for a few moments and sat by the gurgling springs to soak their legs in its churning waters.

"Ahh! Feels wonderful," Maleva cooed softly.

"Yes, it's very invigorating," Tiberius agreed.

"This is nice place," she said. "Maleva could stay here for a while." She looked questioningly at Tiberius then asked, "Tell Maleva of Dragonfly Landing."

"Well," he began, "I wasn't there very long, but it's very nice. There are lots of big beautiful old oak trees and green rolling hills. The Fish Hole River is close by and they even have a landing strip for everyone even though it's mainly for the dragonflies."

"It sounds wonderful," she sighed wistfully.

"It is; but hey - you'll get to see it when we get there," he replied excitedly. "I can hardly wait for everyone to meet you. Crispin's parents are extremely nice and there are some really interesting characters that live there. There's this old guy, Mr. Icherio: he's a Japanese beetle – tells wonderful stories."

Maleva's eyes crinkled with delight as he described the cozy tunnel homes and intricately decorated council chambers. "Maleva can hardly wait," she said breathlessly, "but now we have little patient to take on walk."

"I guess we better get going," he suggested. "Crispin might try to climb the steps by himself."

On the way back to the encampment, Tiberius realized that talking about Dragonfly Landing gave him a warm cozy feeling inside. 'Could this be the way everyone felt about their home no matter where it was?' he thought. He had to admit it was a nice feeling, one he had never experienced until now. Perhaps his future was at Dragonfly Landing and not with the caravan. He glanced at Maleva and an idea seized his heart, but for now, he couldn't bring himself to speak it.

Chapter 30
Tiberius Takes Charge

Several moonrises passed and the caravan had covered a large distance with only a few delays. At one point in the journey they made a sizable detour around a swampy area which the scouts reported was brimming with warty, pop-eyed frogs. Another small delay came when they encountered a lightning scarred, fallen pine tree which blocked their path. Luckily, the scouts discovered an opening below a branch with just enough clearance for the wagons to pass.

Crispin continued to recuperate at a remarkable speed and became so proficient at using his crutches that he now called them his 'other legs'.

Maleva changed his bandages several times and was so satisfied with his progress she declared that before long he would be doing the 'whirling weevil' dance.

Tiberius continued helping with the chores whenever he could. The wagon driving didn't seem as grueling now and he had almost mastered the rope weaving. Even the beetle stench clinging to the muddy wagon wheels seemed to mellow.

Bela had not pressed him for a decision about staying and he was glad. The truth was he simply couldn't make up his mind, and decided he might not until they returned to Dragonfly Landing. The one thing he knew for sure was how he and Maleva felt about each other. They decided that no matter what, they wanted to be together and he knew that he should discuss his idea with her very soon. Bela had told him last night that the village wasn't far off.

Tiberius was almost certain that the swamp full of frogs they had detoured around was the Milkweed Bog and the forest they passed through with the lightning damaged pine looked very familiar. Even Crispin who had taken to watching out the wagon window at night remarked that there was a familiar smell to the air.

THE WAGON SUDDENLY jerked violently as it navigated a rut. Tiberius and Maleva rushed to the window just in time to steady Crispin. "Wow!" He cried. "That was close!"

"Yes," Maleva replied, "Time to sit now."

"We can't have you damaged again," Tiberius added, "not with all the time and hard work Maleva and the others have gone to."

They situated Crispin on his bed, plumped his pillows and he began talking excitedly. "I'm almost sure we're passing through a birch forest. The tree trunks were glowing in the moonlight."

"Why are birch trees important?" Maleva said, looking perplexed.

"It's probably because we flew over a birch forest right after we left Dragonfly Landing," Tiberius explained.

"That's right," Crispin sang out, then glanced at Tiberius. "Do you think they could be the same ones?"

"We're so close, they probably are," he answered.

"I can't believe that we're almost home," Crispin exclaimed. "My parents are going to flip a feeler when they see me on crutches!"

"Your parents," Tiberius began emphatically; "will be so glad to see you alive it won't matter. Now, why don't you rest for a while," he suggested. "You'll need lots of energy. When we get home we'll have a celebration."

Crispin lay back, his forelegs under his head, daydreaming about their homecoming while Tiberius and Maleva sat in the corner on a pair of small wood carved stools talking quietly. Tiberius decided it was time to discuss their future and spring the idea he had been keeping to himself. He looked earnestly into her eyes and cleared his throat.

She touched his face softly. "There is something Tiberius wishes to say...no?"

"Yes, I've been..." he hesitated; then went on. "I've been thinking about something for a while and would like to discuss it with you."

"Oh," she smiled warmly, "Maleva thinks this very good time."

"Well," he began slowly, searching for the right words. "You know of course your uncle has asked me to join the caravan." She nodded as he continued. "And we've discussed it some: but I was just wondering..." he swallowed nervously, "Would you think me terribly selfish if I asked you to live with me somewhere else?

Maybe close to Dragonfly Landing. I don't have a real home but we could make one, I'm sure of it."

Maleva gave him a brilliant smile, and leaned closer as she spoke "Maleva would like that very, very much and have discussed this with uncle."

Tiberius looked a bit startled; then replied, "Oh, I didn't know you two had spoken about us."

"Maleva hopes this does not trouble Tiberius?"

"Of course not," he replied; then continued. "And what did he think? Did he seem upset that I might be taking you away?"

She tightened her shawl again. "Not so much. Uncle is very unselfish and wants only happiness for us."

"You know that I would stay if that is what you wanted," he quickly added.

"The traveling is very hard," she said thoughtfully. "Our lives should be not so troubled: uncle knows this also and understands."

"That's good, but they'll be loosing a good healer," he stated.

She nodded. "Is true, but Maria is good healer also."

Tiberius let out a relieved sigh "Well, that makes it a lot easier then."

"Maleva is excited to be settled."

Tiberius gave her a hug, and said "We'll be fine, I promise."

"Maleva not worried," she replied giving him a gentle kiss on the face.

Crispin was sleeping again and they decided to go outside for a stroll. The couple sat on a rock thinking and talking excitedly about their new life together, watching the sunrise as if it was the first one they had ever seen.

BELA SUDDENLY APPEARED from a nearby stand of sweet briars and when he noticed them he smiled broadly and hurried over. "It is beautiful new day...no?" his booming voice rang out.

"Yes, the day will be wonderful," she paused then continued. "Uncle, we have news."

Tiberius nodded; then added, "First, I'd like to say thanks to the gypsy moths for inviting me to join the caravan; but we've decided we would like to live closer to Dragonfly Landing."

Bela wrapped a wing around her tenderly and said, "gypsy moth life is not for every one. Niece will be happy...yes?"

She nodded, and wiped a tear from her eye then smiled, "Maleva will miss uncle Bela and friends, but caravan will come visit much, yes?"

"Of course," he said, waving a foreleg. "Caravan will need to travel north and stay a long time. Gypsy moths will visit Maleva and eat much food."

"Yes, caravan certainly will," she said with a giggle.

"Now," Bela went on, "There is another important matter to discuss." Tiberius antennas' pricked with interest as Bela continued. "Scouts are checking new trail, but one has returned early with interesting news."

"What is it," he asked anxiously.

"Scouts are reporting your village is through forest, only short distance from here."

Maleva jumped up excitedly and grabbed Tiberius foreleg, "It is wonderful...no? You are home."

"WE - are home," he corrected with a beaming face.

When they returned to the wagon, Crispin was awake and sitting on the wagon seat. When he saw them coming he waved a crutch frantically and yelled "Have you heard? We're almost home!"

"Yes. We know," Tiberius called as they approached. "Bela said it was just through the forest."

"I just knew it was close by," he declared. "Those birch trees looked so familiar; but I couldn't get my bearings. I'm usually flying over them."

Tiberius decided it was time to tell Crispin about Maleva, and settled on the seat next to him. "I have some news of my own that you might be interested in."

"And what might that be," Crispin replied with a crooked smile.

"Maleva's coming with me and we're going to get married," he blurted with a big grin. "We've talked with Bela, and it's okay with him."

Crispin threw a foreleg across his chest and feigned a swoon. "My goodness. You and Maleva. I never would have guessed." He rolled his eyes then added. "It's about time: that's all I can say."

Maleva and Tiberius glanced surprisingly at each other and she shrugged her shoulders. "I guess we weren't as clever as we thought," Tiberius chuckled.

"I'd have to be blind not to see what was happening between you two," Crispin stated with a self satisfied grin. "Anyway," he went on. "I definitely approve."

"We're so glad," Tiberius replied teasingly.

"Maleva is happy too!" She winked.

Crispin jabbed his crutch into the air and proclaimed, "Enough of this chit-chat. Let's find out exactly how close we are to home."

"Yes, let's!" Tiberius and Maleva agreed.

They tracked down the scout who had returned early and found out that the village was just over the next ridge line. Unfortunately, the news had come after the wagons had been unhitched for the day.

Crispin's face grew glum when he heard this. "If my leg wasn't messed up, we could fly."

"Would not be wise thing to do," Maleva said sympathetically. "Leg is healing well but still big risk in flying."

Later, as the threesome enjoyed a hearty breakfast of dried huckleberries Tiberius was struck with an idea. "Why don't we take Maleva's wagon," he began with a mischievous grin. "I feel confident in my driving skills now; so what do you think?"

"Is good idea, but need uncle's permission," Maleva said.

"Great grubs! What are we waiting for? Let's go see the king," Crispin sang out.

The group made their way to Bela's wagon and Maleva knocked on the door. He answered immediately wearing a small brown nightcap and simple matching tunic. Without his usual flashy clothes, Tiberius thought that he could have passed for an ordinary gypsy moth.

"Good morning uncle Bela."

"I hope we didn't wake you," Tiberius quickly added.

"No, Bela is having bed time snack."

"Good," Tiberius continued. "We have an idea but would like your permission to carry it out."

"Very good, very good." He gestured as a few crumbs flew off his leg. "Sit on wagon seat, and we talk."

They arranged themselves, and Tiberius began relating his plan. "We were wondering if it would be all right, since the village is so close, if we borrow Maleva's wagon and leave right now. That way, we could prepare them for your arrival tonight. I could even drive it myself." he added. "I've learned quite a lot from the drivers, and feel confident that I can do it."

Bela nodded thoughtfully, then replied. "Is good idea if beetle is willing."

"We'll offer one of them more food," Crispin spoke up impatiently.

"Yes, will work," Bela said. "Must be careful and go in right direction. Speak to scout first."

Maleva gave him a hug, and Crispin and Tiberius shook his foreleg vigorously. They made their way to a shadowy outcropping of rock where the scouts were resting and sipping brew. After getting directions, they headed into the woods. The black giants hadn't wandered far and they found them rooting their horned heads in a pile of composting logs and snoozing in the brush. They spotted a young, energetic beetle and decided that it would be the best one for the extra duty.

"Have you ever wrangled one of these beasties," Tiberius asked Maleva.

"Only watched few times but will need sticks for herding."

"Okay," he said taking charge, "First - Crispin you better stay out of the way. We don't want you to get kicked or trampled."

"Oh all right," he replied, disappointed at not being included in the escapade. He found a stump a safe distance away and plopped on it sullenly.

Tiberius and Maleva gathered two sticks each and approached the young beetle. They tapped its back legs lightly and it stood. "So far, so good," Tiberius reported. They then tapped a middle leg, imitating the wrangler moves but the beetle went in the opposite direction and kept going. When it finally halted to graze on something irresistible, they tried coaxing it back into action by tapping its other legs, but it kept eating.

Maleva stifled a laugh and suggested that they sit on a nearby rock and try again after it lost interest in the food. Tiberius watched Maleva wave her stick playfully in the air while he studied the hungry beetle. He suddenly jolted upright and asked. "Is there any fungus left in the food wagon?"

"Most likely. Why?" She answered.

"The beetles love it, maybe we can make a lure with it," he suggested.

"Ah. Good thinking," she praised him. "Maleva will go find so Tiberius can watch Crispin."

As she passed Crispin who was looking very bored, he called out teasingly, "Having a few problems, are we?"

"Is okay," she waved. "Tiberius has new plan."

Maleva returned very shortly with a bag and they lost no time impaling chunks of fungus onto the sticks. They approached the beetle, and dangled the lure just within its reach. It snuffled and snorted excitedly, then reached for it. They moved back, and it followed.

"It's working," Tiberius gasped.

They fluttered just beyond the beetle, pausing occasionally for it to get a fresh whiff of the bait, and after a few tense moments, led the beetle into camp. Tiberius dropped the fungus in front of Maleva's wagon and they placed more in a bowl. As the beast snuffled loudly consuming the delectable morsels, they slipped the harness around its body. After the beetles finished eating, Tiberius left to retrieve the crystals while Crispin and Maleva made themselves comfortable inside the wagon.

After he returned, Tiberius situated himself on the seat, grabbing the reins and driving stick. He flicked the reins, and tapped the beetle on its back. His charge stood, and moved slightly. He was grinning and congratulating himself when suddenly, the lumbering beast sat back down and yawned. "Oh great," he grumbled. "What now. Do I have to pull this wagon myself?"

There was a commotion nearby, and he noticed several scouts laughing as they strolled his way. The larger one of the group approached, patted the beetle's head and asked, "Tiberius could use help...no?"

"Yeess. Thank you," he stammered somewhat embarrassed.

The scout, whose name was Stephan turned out to be very helpful, showing Tiberius how to coax the beetle into action, and to use the driving stick correctly. After a practice turn around the campsite, Tiberius felt more confident of his driving abilities, and pulled into the woods. As time went on his driving mastery improved and soon they were rolling along smoothly.

Crispin was about to jump out of his skin with excitement and Maleva couldn't keep him away from the window. Before long, the ridge line of birch trees was behind them, and they began following a meandering moss coated stream. It snaked lazily through a grove of sun dappled beech trees which flashed an iridescent gold pattern on the wagon window as they passed.

Crispin noticed a long row of hills in the distance, and pointed them out to Maleva. "Hey," he almost shouted, "Look! We passed those on our way out of Dragonfly Landing. Now I know we're almost home."

A SHORT TIME later the languid stream and beech trees gave way to a forest of gigantic oaks. When Crispin saw the oaks, he cried out, "We're here. I can see the pathway to the village!"

The wagon suddenly halted. Tiberius appeared at the door and announced, "We're almost there, but I don't want to frighten anyone with the wagon." He glanced at Crispin.

"Can you walk from here?"

"Yippee," he yelled. "I feel like running."

Maleva, bustled about nervously grabbing a shawl and a small drawstring bag, then they stepped down from the wagon. They unhitched the beetle, leaving him with several bowls of food; then began walking down the path.

Maleva, breathless with expectation, smiled happily at Tiberius when she saw the Dragonfly Landing signs. They had to quicken their pace to keep up with Crispin; who, true to his words, was practically running along on his crutches. As they drew near to home, Tiberius stopped Crispin and asked if he wanted to carry his own pack of crystals. He did, and Tiberius placed it gently on his back. Crispin held his head high and entered his village.

Several young lightning bugs and bark gnawing beetles noticed the travelers and their eyes widened in disbelief. Some of them scampered away and dove into Crispin's tunnel while others ran about the village shouting "They're back, they're back! Crispin and Tiberius are home!"

Chapter 31
Homecoming

Almost immediately, Crispin's parents appeared from the opening, and other villagers began cheering and surrounding the trio. Katrina and Bertram rushed over, forelegs outstretched and faces beaming with relief and delight. They hugged Crispin and Tiberius tightly; then Tiberius quickly introduced his bride to be. Katrina was crying great sobs of happiness and Bertram explained. "We were beside ourselves with worry. Your mother was frantic at times."

She nodded blinking away tears, and gingerly touched his bandaged leg. "What happened? Is it bad...Oh you poor thing."

"Don't worry mother, Maleva took good care of me. I'm going to be fine."

Katrina glanced at her and sniffed, "Thank you so much for taking care of my son."

"Crispin is good patient," she replied with a warm smile.

Katrina looked a little confused at Maleva's accent, but returned the smile. They removed their backpacks, set them on the ground and untied them. Crispin's parents and the surrounding villagers gasped when the brilliant glow spilled out.

Shouts of 'It's the crystals', reverberated through the crowd, and a great cheer rose up. More villagers gathered and some took turns standing on each others back for a better view of the returning heroes.

By this time the whole village and the council elders had been alerted to their return. Mr. Icherio was the first to show up with the grasshoppers trailing behind in great excited leaps. They were followed by the old potato and junebugs who waddled up at an impressive and unprecedented speed. Lastly, the crowds parted giving the dung beetles a wide berth as they arrived in a great cloud of odiferous muck. The elders crowded around the returning travelers pumping their forelegs with amazed and ecstatically happy expressions.

"We can't tell you how glad we are to have you back safe and sound." Mr. Icherio began. "We were afraid some calamity had befallen you;" he glanced at their packs and added. "And with so many crystals – this is quite unexpected. It's better than we had hoped for, and just in time too. Our crystals are very dim now."

The other elders nodded and mumbled in agreement; then Mr. Icherio continued. "You shall have the honor of dispensing the crystals to the villagers, and we offer our services as well."

Crispin suddenly remembered the heart of the sky box and fished it from his vest. "We also brought this back. The Fern Queen refused to take it. She didn't think she deserved it. We tried giving it to her...we really did but," he hesitated handing it to him, "well, here it is." The elders and Crispin's parents stared in disbelief, not believing that anyone would turn down such a treasure.

"The Fern Queen must be quite a lady." Katrina quickly declared.

"Yes," Mr. Icheiro added. "It certainly is unexpected. Not a queenly behavior at all."

"She's really not a queen," Crispin spoke up.

"What: not a queen?" The elderly grasshopper said perplexed.

"Why does she have the title then?" The potato bug added.

"That's one of our stories for later," Tiberius said with a wink.

"You must have many fascinating stories to tell," the grasshopper said with a gleam in his eye.

"Of course they do," the potato bug snickered. "Do you think they've been laying about munching moss all this time?"

The group laughed at the funny remark; then Mr. Icherio held up a leg and proclaimed loudly, "There will be a celebration in honor of our returning heroes to be held beginning at dusk tomorrow night. Spread the word. Everyone is invited."

The villagers cheered excitedly and great numbers of them scampered or buzzed away to begin preparations and to spread the word.

"There are many things to discuss," one of the grasshoppers said; then continued excitedly. "Did you encounter the Gorboos? What did they look like? Was it a terrible ordeal getting the crystals away from them: and, oh by the way, what about the Fern Queen?"

Mr. Icherio cut in to save Crispin and Tiberius from the onslaught of questions. "There will be time for all these discussions later. Don't you think they should rest a spell after their long journey?"

"Yes," Bertram agreed, "They might be hungry too. Nobody can whip up a meal like my Katrina," he added beaming.

"Of course, of course. Where are my manners," the old grasshopper replied. "We will see you later."

"Actually," Tiberius spoke up. "There is a matter of some importance we need to discuss as soon as possible. It concerns some good friends of ours who are waiting in the forest, not far from here."

Mr. Icherio looked very puzzled; then asked, "If they're your friends, what are they doing in the woods. By all means, invite them into the village."

Crispin, Tiberius and Maleva glanced at each other nervously. "Well," Tiberius began. "We thought the village might need to be prepared for their arrival. I'm afraid they've gotten a bad reputation."

"Yeah," Crispin interjected, "and it's too bad because they're really nice and very interesting."

"They saved our lives when we were injured," Tiberius added, "and gave us rides to shorten our journey. I would trust them with my life any time. In fact that's where I met Maleva."

The rest of the group looked confused: then after studying Maleva's unusual accessories; made the connection. They looked shocked and somewhat nervous.

"Your new friends are gypsy moths," Mr. Icherio said with disbelief. "We've always been led to believe that they're..." he cleared his throat and said diplomatically, "A bit on the shady side."

Crispin and Tiberius were ready to defend the gypsy moths but Maleva spoke first. "This is great mistake. Gypsy moths are like everyone else. There are no shady ones among my people. Is only stories you hear, and pass on. Gypsy moths would like to be friends with Crispin's village."

"That's right," Crispin cut in. "Once everyone meets them, they will change their minds: and wow you should hear their music! They just won the biggest award at the Crazy Moon Music Festival."

The elders and Crispin's parents were speechless, having found out that their knowledge of the gypsy moths was completely wrong. "Well my goodness," Mr. Icherio stammered. "What a revelation." He glanced at the others and they all nodded. "I think its time for a change of attitude in this village," he stated. "I'll hold a meeting right away and inform everyone." He paused, scratched his head in thought, and then added, "We need to include your new friends in the celebration. It would be the perfect time for everyone to meet."

Tiberius nodded and said, "We will go deliver the good news to the caravan this evening."

"Very good," Mr. Icherio replied, "We will await their arrival with great anticipation."

"There's another bit of news you might be interested in," Tiberius began.

"Yes, what is it," Mr. Icherio asked.

"Maleva and I are getting married."

Mr. Icherio threw his foreleg up and called out, "There's going to be a wedding as well!"

MALEVA COULD HARDLY wait to see the tunnel homes so they followed Crispin and his parents through the opening in the gnarled roots of the oak tree.

On the way, Tiberius leaned close to Bertram and exclaimed, "Those gypsy moths make the most wonderful brew. Wait till you taste it!"

Maleva was fascinated by the tiny woven doors with hazel nut door knobs and a bit taken aback when they passed the spider filled chamber. The flower wreath on Crispin's door which had fallen into disrepair hung brown and listless.

"Oh my," Katrina exclaimed gleefully batting it with a leg. "Time to get rid of this old thing."

Crispin and his parents entered, but left the door open so Maleva could peek in and see the home. Crispin walked around quietly touching all his old things, then took his vest off and hung it on a stick hook.

He felt strange. Nothing had changed except for an accumulation of spider webs in one corner but it felt like he had been gone for an eternity. Everything was familiar, and at the same time, unfamiliar. The feeling was very confusing but he was overjoyed at being home.

While Katrina and Bertram cooked a gargantuan meal of pollen cakes, wild blackberry soup, nasturtium leaf sandwiches and honey sunflower seed bars, Crispin and Tiberius took Maleva on a tour of the village. She was delighted with the intricate carvings and portraits in the council chambers and amazed at the smooth lighted runway which was carved out of the oak forest. Several young dragonflies practicing barrel rolls landed and she clapped enthusiastically.

Everywhere they went the villagers smiled and nodded. The bolder ones rushed up to shake the heroes legs and express their gratitude. A group of young fireflies who seemed particularly enthralled with Crispin followed him around like a flock of ducklings. When he turned and looked, they would giggle and scamper into the brush. The group was on their way back when Bertram sighted them and waved.

"Oh good, there you are," he said breathlessly. "Katrina and I have the food ready and we've decided to have a picnic."

"Ohh," Maleva gushed. "Picnic is much fun."

"Great," Tiberius added. "I'm starved, and I bet Crispin is too."

"You're right about that," he said flipping a crutch into the air.

Bertram led them to a secluded spot behind their oak tree where the food was arranged on a low stick table. There were five plates made from thin strips of pine bark and five nut shell bowls and cups. In the middle of the table was an artistically arranged bouquet of autumn flowers and leaves. A gurgling stream in the distance completed the charming setting. They took their places and dove into the sumptuous fare, chatting about their travels between bites.

Katrina was curious about how Tiberius and Maleva met, so they took turns relating the story about his injured wing, and Crispin's broken leg.

Bertram and Katrina fidgeted anxiously as they told the part about Crsipin's abduction by the bluejay, his ordeal in the Woods of Forgetfulness, and the return trip on Roscoe's back.

"Oh, my-my," Katrina moaned. "I had no idea you went through so much. We owe the gypsy moths and Maleva a great big thank you. I can't believe we've misjudged them all this time."

Bertram suddenly interrupted, "I think I heard someone calling for the village meeting."

They rushed to the clearing where the council elders and many villagers were already gathered and were surprised when a brightly clad harlequin beetle escorted them to a log bench on the front row. Mr. Icherio surveyed the crowd and when he was satisfied everyone was in attendance, two other harlequin beetles helped him onto the speakers stump. A chorus of buzzing, chirping and rasping conversations filled the air as the curious villagers waited for the meeting to begin.

Mr. Icherio signaled to quiet the crowd then began speaking. "Thank you for coming on such short notice. I'm sure you're all wondering what this is all about. First, I'd like to say on everyone's behalf how wonderful it is to have Crispin and Tiberius back among us, and thank them for their unselfish service." There was a thunderous applause and the pair waved and nodded.

Mr. Icherio shifted his body and almost fell off the stump, but the harlequin beetles caught him. A gasp went up from the crowd, but he continued unfazed. "I'm sure that everyone knows by now about the celebration tomorrow evening to honor our returning heroes." Another round of cheers rose and died; then he continued. "Also, everyone please bring your lanterns and other receptacles to the village entrance after the meeting. The long awaited crystals will be dispensed."

The villagers roared with excitement at hearing the news, and Mr. Icherio had to wait for them to quiet before going on. "This brings me to the next matter for discussion. We're going to have some special guests who will arrive this evening to join us. They are good friends of Tiberius and Crispin and, as I understand it, are responsible for saving their lives. I hope everyone will be cordial and invite these guests into our village."

Several shouts of 'Who are they?' erupted from the crowd, and Mr. Icherio waved for silence. "Our special guests will be a band of gypsy moths, led by their king; Bela."

At first, there was stunned silence but soon scattered cheers rippled through the crowd and eventually everyone joined in, shouting approval. Crispin, Tiberius and Maleva smiled at each other relieved that the villagers seemed happy at the prospect of meeting the gypsy moths. Mr. Icherio signaled to the harlequin beetles that he was ready to get off the stump, but when they approached, he waved them off, and re-addressed the crowd. "There's one more thing I'd like to announce while we're all here," he said grinning and gesturing to the front row. "I'm sure you've all been wondering who Tiberius' lovely companion is. Her name is Maleva, the niece of the gypsy moth king. Their wedding ceremony will be taking place shortly before the celebration begins."

The somewhat embarrassed couple waved as the villagers applauded and several shouts of 'Good going old chum' were tossed out.

After the meeting, Tiberius and Crispin met the elders by the village entrance and choose a shady, ivy covered log to sit on while dispensing the crystals. They divided the crystals equally into bowls and passed them to the elders. The fat potato bug had been detained by celebration business so they placed his bowl on a vacant seat. When they were ready, Mr. Icherio sent a young grasshopper with an unusually loud voice to make the announcement.

He hopped from tree to tree calling in a booming raspy voice, "Hear ye, hear ye! New crystals for old. Come to the village entrance with your lanterns."

Soon the villagers emerged from the oak roots and tree canopies clutching their lanterns. Some, who were in charge of acquiring crystals for the tunnels were pushing carts filled with their receptacles. Before long, a disorganized throng of jumping, flitting and scurrying villagers had congregated around the group and the elders glanced at each other nervously. The fat potato bug finally appeared and seeing the dilemma jumped onto a tall stump and shouted, "Everyone please form lines in front of the dispensing stations. There are plenty of crystals so everyone will get what they need."

Wanting to say 'hello' to Crispin and Tiberius, most villagers quickly filed into their lines and the potato bug had to make another announcement. "Please, please. I know everyone wants to be in our heroes' lines, but this way will take forever. Some of you please try to fill the other stations."

The villagers politely cooperated and moved to the other lines. Before long each villager had been given enough crystals to supply their needs and they returned to their homes with relieved smiles. Extra crystals were given to the dragonflies for runway maintenance and to the ants who took care of the village pathway lighting. The common area and trees were conspicuously silent for a time as the villagers replaced their beacons and rejoiced in their brightened world. Back at the entrance, the group took stock of the remaining crystals.

"What should we do with the ones left over," Crispin asked.

"I think we should send them to Queenie along with our report on the Gorboos, but let's get Mr. Icherio's opinion also," Tiberius suggested as the pair sauntered in his direction.

All of the elders except for Mr. Icherio were lying on the ground sleeping peacefully, "I guess the crystal dispensing wore them out," the old beetle observed yawning; then went on. "I heartily agree. The Fern Queen has been of great service to us and should be rewarded, especially her unselfish refusal of the gemstone; and don't forget to take extra ones for yourselves as well. You never know when you need to light something up," he added trying to hide a mischievous smile.

"Thank you," Tiberius replied, "If we need some, we'll let you know."

Suddenly the old beetle's eyes flew wide and he pointed at Crispin. "I just had a magnificent idea."

"What? About me," Crispin asked.

"Yes. Come here," the beetle gestured, "I want to see something."

Crispin limped over and the old beetle retrieved a crystal from his bowl, and held it next to Crispin's back wing.

He grinned proudly then made a suggestion, "I bet that if you placed this in your empty tail light it would glow and then you would be like everyone else and very popular."

Tiberius looked at Crispin questioningly; then said "I'm sure it would work, but do you want to try it?"

Crispin was silent for a moment, his brow wrinkled in concentration, then stated, "It's a good idea, and I might use it for emergencies, but for now, I'm happy just being me...empty tail light and all. Just think about it. I went on a long, dangerous journey and did fine without it. Besides," he went on, "everyone seems to like me just the way I am."

Tiberius smiled and patted him on the back, then commented, "I do believe you have grown up some."

Mr. Icherio looked a bit disappointed at Crispin's response, but smiled anyway and said "I understand young man. Everyone would be better off if they accepted themselves the way you do."

AFTER DISPENSING THE crystals, Tiberius and Maleva returned to her wagon to check on the beetle, and continue on to deliver the invitation. Maleva, tired from the day's activities decided to stay and take a nap. Since Tiberius was flying the return trip he made better time and on arrival, found the gypsy moths still asleep. He was feeling a bit drowsy and knew there was a big night ahead, so he found a flat topped rock to rest on. It was still radiating the day's warmth and he soon fell into a cozy sleep.

Back at Dragonfly Landing some of the villagers were also napping, but others, too excited to sleep, were foraging for food, or making preparations for the big celebration. The council elders decided that there wasn't enough room to park the wagons in the common area to hold everyone, so the landing strip was being prepared for the caravan. A thick stand of kudzoo which had run rampant during the hot summer was threatening to overtake the runway so a group of hungry grasshoppers were hard at work munching the unruly vines.

Back in the common area, several families of fungus beetles were coming and going carrying, toadstools and mushrooms to be used as seating for honored guests. An army of ants had disappeared into the woods to collect firewood, and the first group was returning loaded with sticks and brush. Other villagers were roaming the surrounding fields and trees collecting nuts, seeds, leaves, berries, and bark for the snacks which would be served to the hungry guests.

The bees and butterflies were resting, waiting for morning and open blooms to collect the pollen, nectar, and honey that would be needed for sweet cakes and drinks. Katrina and some of her friends were gathering baskets of leaves and flowers to be woven into beautiful festive garlands and head wreaths. The prettiest ones were left on the plant to be picked fresh for Maleva's bridal outfit. Some villagers, especially the young ones, zoomed and skittered about excitedly at the trail's entrance, watching for signs of the caravan's arrival.

TIBERIUS FELT A tapping on his wing and he awoke to Bela's bristly haired face, haloed by the last weakened rays of dusk. "Tiberius, my old friend, wake now. Is there news? Maleva not come?"

"Y-e-s-s, I have news," he replied groggily. "Maleva is sleeping in her wagon, just outside the village."

"Come get brew, will help Tiberius wake up. We will talk of it then."

Tiberius fluttered from the rock and noticed the caravan was beginning their nightly rituals of food preparation and fire tending. The campfire blazed to life and the pair perched on a log close to it's warmth.

"I have great news," Tiberius began, taking a large gulp of the energizing liquid, "We had a talk with the council elders; and they held a meeting with all the villagers. I'm happy to report that everyone at Dragonfly Landing is anxious to meet the gypsy moths and you're welcome into the village anytime."

"This makes Bela and all gypsy moths very happy," he smiled expectantly. "When is good time to come? Tonight is okay?"

"Yes," Tiberius replied. "You should definitely come tonight. Everyone is expecting you. They're really very excited about meeting the gypsy moths - and oh yes," he continued, "tomorrow night there will be a big celebration and," He hesitated then grinned broadly. "Maleva and I are getting married before the celebration."

"What," Bela shouted happily, "So soon! This is greatest news. Bela will perform ceremony. Is okay?"

"Of course," Tiberius replied. "We wouldn't want anyone else."

Bela shook his head in disbelief. "Little Maleva, getting married. Does not seem possible."

"When would you like to leave," Tiberius asked.

"Caravan will eat first, then leave. Night is young, and everyone is hungry from long sleep."

"Of course: I can help the wranglers," Tiberius offered, "I've learned how to lure them with fungus on a stick."

Bela howled at Tiberius revelation, then stood on a high rock and clapped his hands loudly to gather the group. "There is good news," he began. "Caravan will leave after eating. Invitation is sent from Dragonfly Landing for all gypsy moths to visit and join celebration. Also there will be marriage of Tiberius and Maleva."

Everyone cheered and shouted 'Long life to both' and several in the group rushed forward to congratulate Tiberius. After the gypsy moths and Tiberius had filled their stomachs with food and brew, hitched the beetles, and doused the campfire, the wagons uncoiled, and began the short trek to Dragonfly Landing.

When they reached Maleva's wagon, Bela and Tiberius knocked on her door, and she answered sleepily then gave Bela and Tiberius a hug.

"Good, the caravan has arrived," she commented. "Villagers are very excited at meeting."

Bela glanced at Tiberius and asked. "Is place to park wagons at village?"

"Yes, the villagers have prepared a spot by the landing strip. You can follow Maleva's wagon. I'll show the drivers where to park. Are you ready to go?"

"Is good, but must speak with Latslov and drivers first." Bela took a deep breath and added, "This is big day for all gypsy moths."

"Yes. For everyone," Tiberius added.

Bella gave the order to move on and the chain of wagons pulled into the forest. Following Tiberius's orders the caravan arrived at the landing strip in no time and maneuvered their wagons into the grasshopper chewed area. The drivers immediately unhitched the beetles and fed them. Only Bela's wagon remained ready to carry him, Latslov, two scouts and the driver to the village.

The wagon doors slowly opened and the younger moths were the first to venture out. Some of the oldsters still wary of the meeting could not be coaxed outside and their pensive faces would appear now and then peeking suspiciously through the colorfully framed windows.

The villagers had heard the tinkling and crackling of wheels as the caravan neared. Inquisitive children and those not busy with celebration preparations rushed to meet them. On the way they met Bela's wagon making it's way down the pathway. They waved and shouted excitedly to the visitors and as the carriage passed Bela called "Good evening", in return. As the entourage drew closer to the village entrance they heard shouts of 'Here they come' and 'They're here' echoing through the woods. Bela and his driver scanned the darkness for the invisible voices but saw nothing until they came to the lantern lit village entrance.

Illuminated in the trees were the curious, expectant villagers who had been perched in the oaks for most of the afternoon waiting patiently for a glimpse of the surprise visitors. Once the wagon had passed there was a mad exodus as the curious spectators trailed them into the common area.

Tiberius and Maleva who had gone ahead on foot earlier saw the wagon enter and shouted "Hello! You can park right where you're at if you want."

"Many thanks," Bela called back as the wagon driver jumped down to attend the beetle. Latslov and Stephan, the head scout exited the wagon and joined Bela on the ground.

"Are any others coming," Maleva asked anxiously.

"Yes, others will follow when ready," he replied.

Tiberius cleared his throat and pointed to the path entrance. "I think a few are already here."

A group of gypsy moths with babes in tow were shyly hanging about the entrance taking in the festive village grounds. Several lady beetles and lightning bugs holding trays of cups approached them, offering beverages and snacks. The visitors accepted, took a sip and nibble then smiled.

"Good, some are mingling already," Bela remarked.

By this time the council elders had made their way to the king and Mr. Icherio, not sure of what to do; extended a foreleg; then quickly withdrew it and bowed. The other elders followed his lead and Bela bowed in return then shook everyone's foreleg.

After the introductions were made by both parties, Mr. Icherio stood on a log stool and spoke loudly. "On behalf of everyone at Dragonfly Landing, we welcome the gypsy moths and would like to take this time to thank you for the help and friendship you have shown to our returning heroes."

There was much cheering from the crowd as Mr. Icherio continued, "The village would be honored if you could stay and join our celebration tomorrow evening."

Bela smiled graciously and replied. "Gypsy moths thank great elders for hospitality and also desire friendship with village."

Mr. Icherio bowed again and said with a sweep of his foreleg, "Please make yourselves at home and enjoy the drinks and snacks." He gestured to the wagon then continued. "Do you mind if the villagers admire your beautiful traveling home?"

"This is good," Bela agreed, "but beetle is messy. Driver will escort guide to woods first."

After the formalities were over, Mr. Icherio readdressed the crowd. "Bela, King of gypsy moths and his subjects have expressed their happiness at our invitation and wishes the village to know his desire for friendship. Also, you're welcome to view the wagons after the beetle has been returned to the woods."

Everyone cheered and a curious group of villagers moved closer to observe the driver leading the gentle giant into the forest. The official party continued talking until they were interrupted by groups of eager villagers who were waiting to meet the king and his son.

Eventually, more gypsy moths from the caravan arrived and before long almost everyone was eating, drinking, and chatting. The village ladies were curious about the visitors beautiful accessories while the males asked many questions about the fascinating mode of travel. It wasn't long before the youngsters overcame their shyness and were dashing about playing kick-the-puffball and hide-and-seek together. The wagon drew spectators like a magnet. They studied its structure and brightly painted decorations with fascination and flattering comment.

Bela was very congenial and a good sport as almost everyone in the village wanted to be introduced and shake the leg of a king. He was most interested however, at meeting Crispin's parents. When Crispin introduced them, he shook their legs zealously then commented. "Finally, Bela meets parents. Son is very strong and brave: also highly regarded by gypsy moths."

His parents smiled proudly and replied, "It's a pleasure to make your acquaintance. We can't thank you enough for what you've done for Crispin and Tiberius and the village." Bertram presented Bela with a package wrapped in shiny maple leaves and continued. "We would like to give you this for saving our son's life."

Bela pulled on its woven string and the leaves fell away revealing a highly polished chestnut bowl. The outside was intricately carved in a fanciful design depicting fireflies and dragonflies dancing arm in arm. Bela gasped when he saw it. "It is most wonderful artistry. Bela thanks parents very much and will use it often and think of new friends."

As the night passed, the villagers began to retire to their homes, but several groups sat by the campfire and talked with the gypsy moths until the wee hours.

Tiberius escorted Maleva home then accepted an invitation to sleep in Bela's wagon. Crispin happily anticipating sleeping in his own bed after such a long time followed his parents with no reluctance. He laid his head on his pillow and heard the faint strains of a stringed instrument serenading the night. He drifted to sleep feeling safe and secure as visions of winged notes took flight and danced with the stars.

Chapter 32
New Beginnings

The golden rays of dawn broke from the horizon with the promise of a beautiful autumn day. A whirlwind of activities had already begun as preparations continued for the evening's event. The cooks and bakers were hard at work assembling the necessary items for their wares and the decorators were flitting about hanging the orange lantern pods and flower garlands.

Katrina and Bertram had prepared another meal behind their oak tree and sent Crispin to invite Tiberius and Maleva. He spotted them sitting on a log helping the decorators string purple asters and gold autumn daisies. "Good morning," they called out when they spotted him.

"How is leg today," Maleva asked.

"It's grand," Crispin reported. "It doesn't hurt any more, and I can put more weight on it now. Do you think I could try to walk or fly soon?"

"Is possible," she replied. "But only try little."

"Yes," Tiberius agreed, "you don't want to over do it."

"Good, I can hardly wait to fly again. I miss it. Oh yes," he went on. "My parents sent me to invite you to another picnic. Can you come?"

"Of course we can," Tiberius answered. "Anybody would be crazy to turn down your mother's cooking."

After their morning picnic, Maleva joined Katrina and several of her friends to work on the bride's wedding attire in the shade of a weeping willow tree. She was carrying a small wooden box which had been skillfully carved with wildflowers and honeysuckle vines. The ladies gasped in delight as she pulled out a beautiful shawl of shimmering gold flecked blue fabric and draped it around her wings.

Katrina left momentarily, and returned with woven baskets for the ladies and suggested they go gather flowers for the bridal head wreath. Luckily, since it was a sunny day there were many blooms to choose from and before long; their baskets were brimming with wild violets, blue cornflowers, white Queen Ann's lace and pale pink phlox. The group was returning, chatting and laughing in pre-wedding spirits when Maleva suggested that they collect special spider web sewing thread from her wagon.

The ladies looked around politely at her cozy home and Maleva could tell that they were fascinated by some of her things. She opened a few of the ointment containers and explained briefly what they were used for. Maleva laughed when they sniffed several of them and wrinkled up their faces. The wide eyed visitors cooed as they inspected her kaleidoscope of shawls and sparkly tinkley ornaments. Before they left, she gave each of them a small gift and the excitement grew as they took turns trying on the baubles. When they returned to the moss covered base of the willow tree, the flowers were sorted out and the sewing began.

TIBERIUS HAD FINISHED assisting the decorators, and went in search of Crispin. He looked for quite some time, and finally found him sitting quietly in a spice bush thicket.

"There you are," he exclaimed. "I've been looking all over for you. Whatever are you doing camouflaged in that bush?"

"I'm hiding," Crispin replied curtly.

"Hiding?" Tiberius chuckled. "What from?"

"It's those youngsters," he complained. "They won't leave me alone. Everywhere I go, they follow, asking question after question. I just wanted to be alone for a while."

"They'll eventually leave you alone once their curiosity is satisfied," Tiberius counseled. "Besides, you're their big hero now. They want to grow up and be brave and strong like you."

"A big hero?" Crispin asked with a crooked grin.

"Yes," Tiberius went on. "And it's important for them to have someone who sets a good example."

"Like answering questions, when they're curious," Crispin asked.

"Yes, and maybe being pestered for a while."

Crispin thought about his advice for a moment; then nodded. "I see your point. They won't learn things if they don't ask." He sighed and jumped out of the bush then grinned and winked, "Come to think of it there are a couple of young female fireflies hanging around who are kind of cute. It sure wouldn't be any trouble talking to them either."

They returned to the common area and Tiberius began helping a group of lady beetles grind mustard seed for nasturtium sandwiches. Later, he noticed Crispin talking animatedly with a group of spellbound youngsters. He smiled to himself, glad to know that Crispin had taken his advice. The lady beetles got a bit short with him for knocking over a bowl, so he decided to join Crispin and politely left.

By this time most of Crispin's audience had left but two very attentive fireflies wearing orange antenna bows were still chatting. Tiberius covered a fake cough to hide the grin which seized him as he approached. He quickly thought up a reason for his intrusion, and coughed again. "Ahh there you are," he said nodding to Crispin's companions. "I....was wondering if you had seen Maleva?"

"Why no, I don't believe so," Crispin answered suspiciously seeing Maleva in the distance.

"Okay, I'll just keep looking," Tiberius nodded slowly.

An awkward moment hung in the air while Crispin fidgeted. Finally he gestured to his companions. "Oh, I'd like you to meet some friends of mine. This is Shannon and her sister Molly. They live on the other side of the village under the oak tree surrounded by Irish moss."

"I'm pleased to make your acquaintance," he said with a low bow.

Shannon and Molly giggled shyly and replied in unison, "Thank you Mr. Tiberius."

He winked at Crispin and exclaimed, "Why my goodness, there's Maleva, sitting with your mother under that willow tree. I wonder how I could have missed her. I must rush over and speak with her right away." He glanced at Crispin's companions again and smiled warmly. "Will I be seeing you two at the festival later?"

"Oh yes! We'll be there for sure," Shannon replied. Molly just nodded and giggled again.

The gorgeous autumn day had melted into a magical evening alight with the softly glowing orange lanterns that dotted the common area like a roof of floating suns. Below, a circle of bamboo pole torches connected with wildflower ropes and silverleaf bows had been erected at the wood's edge. Several lightning bugs were still busy strewing flower petals along the pathway where the wedding party would soon march.

On the other side of the village common a stick built speaker's stand, draped in ceremonial decorations, stood lookout over rows of log benches and flat topped rock tables. A group of industrious ants were unloading tinder onto a smoldering campfire centering the celebration area and soon a blazing dance of flames would welcome the party goers. The flower ringed tunnel entrances twinkled invitingly from their re energized lanterns, and nearby a food and beverage buffet was being arranged along a rocky outcropping. The air hung heavy with the sweet scent of wild-flowers mingled with the lingering tantalizing aroma of the day's baking. Even Bela's wagon had been adorned with brightly colored gypsy moth lanterns and their finest harnesses.

The villagers, dressed in their festive clothing and hats, began to arrive in large groups and soon the common area was awash in a sea of colorful bobbing hats. The gypsy moths also dressed in their fanciest finery strolled through the village entrance in smaller groups.

Bela and the Moonspinners were the first to arrive sporting blue tunics and their prized silver medals. They made their way to Bela's wagon, unloaded the instruments, then arranged them by the campfire. The activity drew a curious crowd, and Pavl, one of the fiddlers patiently explained the name and use of each instrument as the others assembled the cymballa.

Bela scanned the common area and noted to his delight most of the oldsters had been persuaded to come along and seemed to be relaxed and enjoying themselves.

Inside Crispin's tunnel, Katrina was helping Maleva position her head wreath, and attending to last minute details. "Oh look. Uncle comes," Maleva suddenly announced. Katrina glanced up from her work, and saw the swarthy king making his way through the tunnel.

"Ahh! How beautiful niece looks," he cried out giving her a hug. "There is gift Bela needs to give for ceremony." He pulled a small beautifully wrapped package from his jacket and handed it to her.

She untied the shimmering gold ribbon, opened the glossy leafed wrapping then gasped in delight. Nestled inside was a necklace of translucent red gemstones. She held them up to the tunnel lights and admired their fiery sparkle.

"Ohhh, so beautiful," she exclaimed. "It is most wonderful gift. Thank you." She gave him a big hug and blinked away a tear.

"Jewels belong to Maleva's mother," he said softly. "Bela was saving for niece's wedding."

Maleva smiled lovingly at the gift and replied. "Necklace is more special then; will cherish always. Help to put on please?" She asked handing it to him. He tied the strand around her neck; then she stepped back. He grinned proudly and remarked, "Maleva is lovely as mother."

Meanwhile, Crispin and Tiberius were in the council chamber tunnel waiting for the ceremony to begin. Crispin stifled a laugh as Tiberius groomed his feathery feelers for the tenth time and paced around the room. "You're going to wear your antennas to a nub if you don't calm down," he said.

Tiberius stopped and sat. "I know, but it's just so hard waiting. I wish it was over." He started to grab his feelers again but stopped. "What if I trip coming down the aisle or say something stupid. I don't want to embarrass Maleva."

"Don't worry," Crispin reassured him, "You'll be fine. I'll be there right next to you. Well, for a while anyway." Silence fell between them, then Crispin glanced at Tiberius with a melancholy look and remarked. "I guess things will be different once you're married."

"Well yes," he replied, "I guess they will now that you mention it, but...," he paused realizing what was bothering Crispin. "Oh, don't worry, we'll still be friends, and hang out together."

"I know," Crispin said with a skeptical glance, "but you might not have time to go on any other adventures. Maleva's going to keep you busy with chores, and all that stuff the ladies like to do. You know...walks in the woods and gazing at sunsets that sort of thing."

"I probably will do those things with Maleva," he replied. "I want her to be happy, but I'm sure there will be plenty of time left for my friends." He gave him a wink and went on. "Why, I bet we can find all kinds of mischief to get into around here."

Crispin's face brightened for a moment, then fell again. "But, will you and Maleva be living close by?"

"Of course we will," Tiberius reassured him. "I'm thinking of enlisting the earthworms help to dig us a tunnel home under one of the oak trees."

This really cheered Crispin and he finally smiled. "I think that's a great idea. We'll have to get busy and collect some really good compost to offer them. They don't work for free you know, and the sentries will need to be warned otherwise they might run them off."

Tiberius was chuckling at Crispin's newfound enthusiasm when Bertram appeared from the shadows and announced, "It's time to go. Bela and the wedding guests are all assembled."

Tiberius took a big breath and stood up. "Well, what are we waiting for? If I'm getting married, I'd better not keep the bride waiting."

"Wait," Crispin exclaimed rushing to a small woven basket on a chair. He opened it and pulled out a garland of brilliant hued autumn leaves. "You're supposed to drape these around your neck. It has something to do with the ceremony. Maleva had my mother make it for you."

"Well, if Maleva wants me to wear it, I guess I'd better do it," he replied with a wink.

The threesome made their way to the ceremony site and stood in the shadows of a beautyberry bush, watching for Bela's signal to start. Crispin remarked about how nice everything looked and Tiberius began to admire the ceremony area to take his mind off his nervousness. The path of wildflower petals led from the woods into the torch rimmed circle and the flower decorations filled the night air with sweet perfume.

The gypsy moths, Crispin's parents, the elders, and other villagers were crowded around the torch lit areas with expectant looks on their illuminated faces. The other villagers who wanted a better view filled the surrounding trees. Most of the guests were holding carefully leaf wrapped and beautifully decorated wedding gifts to be presented during the toasts after the ceremony.

Tiberius was awakened from his observations by a tap on his wing. "It's almost time," Bertram said; then instructed them. "After Latslov finishes his song and leaves, you will hear Pavl start playing again. This is your signal to walk slowly down the path and stop in front of Bela."

"Sounds easy enough," Crispin said.

"Okay," Tiberius nodded. His throat felt like it was closing up, and he swallowed hard; then willed himself to calm down.

A few moments later, Bela, Latslov and Pavl appeared from the sidelines and took their positions in the fire lighted enclosure. Pavl swept his bow and the introductory notes of a sweet melody tumbled out followed by the velvety voice of Latslov who sang a tender gypsy moth love ballad. There was a long silence as Latslov left and disappeared into the shrubbery.

Crispin glanced at Tiberius and said with a crooked smile, "There's still time to make an escape."

Tiberius gave him a sly grin, then replied, "Now why would I want to do that. I'd loose the most wonderful lady on earth."

"Just thought it was my duty to mention it," he replied sheepishly.

Pavl began another tune, and Crispin nudged Tiberius. "That's our cue," he whispered. "Here we go."

The groom and his best friend began their slow promenade down the flowered carpet and fortunately with no stumbling incidents, stopped in front of Bela. Tiberius shifted his legs nervously feeling the crowd's eyes on him, then Bela grinned warmly and it made him relax.

Pavl's fiddle went silent for a time and then he began to play a fanfare melody. Tiberius noticed the crowds' eyes leave him and he turned to look just as Maleva, on the arm of Latslov, started down the trail. His heart skipped a beat when he saw his bride and knew he would never see anything as beautiful again.

Her wings were draped in the shimmering blue and gold wrap, and her delicate head was encircled by a ring of vibrant wild-flowers. In her hands was a bouquet of delicate white Queen Ann's lace and pink honeysuckle tied with a bow of rainbow grass. Tiberius thought the most beautiful thing on her however was the dazzling smile she wore. The bride and her escort finally arrived and she took Tiberius' foreleg, then Latslov and Crispin left to join the crowd.

As the couple faced Bela, they smiled expectantly at each other and he began the ceremony. "Marriage is most important decision in life. If Tiberius and Maleva are still willing, the ceremony will continue."

The bride and groom both nodded and Bela went on. "Tiberius, would like to marry with Maleva?"

"Yes I would," he replied firmly.

Then Bela nodded to Maleva, "Would Maleva be pleased to marry with Tiberius?"

"Yes. Very much," she replied softly.

Bela paused then rambled for several moments in a strange tongue. Maleva removed her shawl revealing a garland of flowers around her neck. In his nervousness, Tiberius had almost forgotten about his and he glanced at the rope of autumn leaves. Bela stepped forward and tied the bride and groom's garland ends together then said, "With the joining of these garlands, so be the hearts of Tiberius and Maleva." He stepped back and spoke several more phrases in the strange dialect and then announced, "With power of gypsy moth king, you are now married. Please to kiss." The happy couple kissed tenderly then turned to greet their well wishers who immediately showered them with congratulations and gifts. Katrina and several of the gypsy moth ladies, took charge of the packages and placed them in bow decorated carts while acorn cups of wedding nectar were served to everyone.

"To the newlyweds!" Bela's merry voice boomed as he thrust his drink high in the air for a toast.

The crowd followed suit and returned a toast of 'To the happy couple'. They took a sip and Latslov made the next toast in his native tongue. The gypsy moths repeated it, then shouted the translation, 'Long life and prosperity to both'.

After the toast the servers returned with small soft nectar cakes and everyone indulged in the delicate pastries while chatting gaily. A short time later, Pavl struck up a traditional wedding tune, and the newlyweds stepped forward for the bride and groom's solo dance. The guests watched enraptured as the couple executed a graceful wing fluttering gliding dance which ended with Maleva enfolded under Tiberius' wing. After the newlyweds caught their breath, Bela joined Maleva for an uncle-niece dance.

After it was over, Bela and Latslov joined Pavl with their fiddles, and the dance floor began to fill with swaying twirling couples. The music became louder and livelier as time passed, and soon more villagers crowded in to watch the frivolity. Soon, Maleva became dizzy from being twirled and dipped by her admirers and Tiberius found himself tiring from the blur of ladies he had led around the dance floor. Finally the music fell silent, and Tiberius and Maleva plopped exhausted but giddy on their bench.

"Time for opening of gifts," an old gypsy moth with a scratchy voice announced.

Katrina and the two ladies wheeled the gift laden carts to the newlyweds, and they began unwrapping the packages. Before long, the carts were filled with eating and cooking utensils, several of which were duplicates, brightly colored fabric, decorative lanterns, miscellaneous tinkley ornaments, stone and wood carved boxes, and an exquisitely carved sign which said 'Home Sweet Home'.

After the gifts were opened, Bela and the Moonspinners struck up a fast paced tune. Large groups of party goers drifted towards the hypnotic music and began to dance. The newlyweds moved to a table by the band, and were finally able to catch their breath and be alone. They had a good laugh at the dancers who were trying out every step they knew to the strange gypsy moth rhythm. It resulted in a chaotic ballet of jumping, twisting and spinning bodies. Some of the more uncoordinated dancers finally fell to the ground dizzy and exhausted. The food and drink kept flowing in a seemingly never ending stream of serving trays laden with nasturtium sandwiches and mountains of sweet cakes. The gypsy moths not being the kind of guests who come empty handed brought ample vessels of their special brew. Several of the ladies were circulating amongst the villagers offering a taste of their unfamiliar drink.

Mr. Icherio and the elders were some of the first to take a wary sip and finding it very delicious, grinned and called out, "It's wonderful!"

Crispin came by offering Tiberius and Maleva food, and asked, "Can I join you?"

"Of course, you need no invitation," she told him.

"Especially if you bring food," Tiberius teased then went on. "Were you watching the dancing? It was hilarious. They were trying really hard, but it's a hard beat to dance to."

"I saw a little bit of it," he chuckled; then went on, "Oh, speaking of funny things. I was running an errand for my mother this afternoon and passed an old Japanese beetle who was wearing an unusual yellow hat. He signaled to me, and I thought he looked harmless, so I went over. Then he said the strangest thing."

"And what did he say," Tiberius asked.

Crispin scratched an antenna for a minute then replied, "Oh yes," he said, "'Ah grasshopper, tell me what wisdom you learned from your many travels'."

"I don't know why he called me a grasshopper unless he has really bad eyesight, and I'm not quite sure but I thought he wanted me to tell him a story about our adventures."

"Hmm," Tiberius said scrunching up his brow. "And did you tell him a tale?"

"Yes, but only a short one, I didn't have much time. On our way back I looked for him again, but the old guy had vanished."

"It is most interesting story," Maleva said. "Maybe Mr. Icherio knows him."

Their conversation was cut short when Mr. Icherio's voice rose over the din of party goers. "If I can please have everyone's attention!" The crowd quieted and he continued. "The time has come for the reason of this celebration and that is the honoring of our two heroes Crispin and Tiberius," he gestured a foreleg towards their table and a group of dragonflies carrying lanterns hovered overhead spotlighting them.

The crowd applauded enthusiastically; then Mr. Icherio announced, "Would the heroes please come forward?"

Tiberius turned to his bride and urged her to join them.

"Yes," Crispin added, "You saved my life."

She shook her head, "No, this is honor for only two. Maleva is happy here."

Reluctantly, the pair made their way to the speaker's stand and took their places next to Mr. Icherio. They waved and bowed to their still cheering admirers. Then Mr. Icherio went on. "First I would like to thank the gypsy moths for being our special guests and providing us with their fabulous music and wonderful home made brew. There was another round of applause from the villagers as the gypsy moths waved and the band took a bow.

Mr. Icherio cleared his throat and continued. "On behalf of everyone from Dragonfly Landing I would like to express our undying gratitude for the selfless deed you performed; not to mention," he gestured toward Crispin, "at great risk of life and limb." The pair smiled and nodded humbly as he went on.

"That is why it is my great privilege to honor you with a gift from our village."

The Moonspinners played a drum roll as the spotlighting dragonflies hovered over a lush oak on the wood's edge. All eyes turned to the brightly illuminated tree and a group of wasps flew overhead and landed in the canopy. Crispin and Tiberius looked at each other in puzzled anticipation.

"Tiberius," Mr. Icherio began in an emotional voice. "It was with great happiness that everyone at Dragonfly Landing joined together to build this for you...in hopes that you would return and make our fair village your home."

The wasps grabbed hold of a tightly woven leaf net camouflaging part of the oak's canopy and lifted it up. On Mr. Icherio's signal, they let it slide to the ground revealing a magnificent and sturdy built stick tree house.

The two friends gasped in surprise but before Tiberius could express his thanks, Mr. Icherio stepped over and patted Crispin's shoulder. "And for our own brave hero the village also wanted to express our admiration by providing you with this."

The spotlighting dragonflies flew to a nearby oak followed by the wasps who unveiled a similar but smaller tree house. Crispin jumped off the bench and shouted, "Great beetle bazookers. My own place!" The crowd went wild with cheering and applause as Mr. Icherio and the elders shook the beaming heroes' forelegs.

The spectators finally calmed down and Tiberius addressed them, "On behalf of myself and my new wife," he gestured to Maleva and she came to join him. "We can't thank you enough for the beautiful home and would be honored to become members of your fine community."

The villagers showed their appreciation with a round of generous applause; then Crispin moved forward to speak. "I would also like to thank everyone for the great tree house, and say what a privilege it is to live in such a great place with wonderful friends and family. If I had it to do all over again, I would; because you're all the greatest." He paused then said exuberantly, "And you're all invited to come visit me in my tree house."

On Mr. Icherio's signal, the Moonspsinners began playing the village song, 'Dragonfly Landing Forever', and Crispin, Tiberius, and Maleva bowed and waved to the singing, swaying villagers.

After the ceremony, the celebration continued and many of the party-goers, especially the younger ones and Mr. Icherio, persuaded Tiberius and Crispin to recount the trials and tribulations of their adventures. The wide eyed children and expectant older faces glowed in the firelight around the story tellers, as they began, "Let me tell you about my terrifying ordeal in the carnivorous bog," Crispin started in a slow creepy voice.

As the ants kept the fire going, the pair related one adventure after another. Some of them caused the crowd to laugh hysterically, while others; especially their escape from the Gorboos elicited horrified gasps. Many of the villagers sighed in relief when they learned that the crystals were of no value to the Gorboos. In the wee hours they came to the end of their tales and the celebration finally came to an end.

Just as a few purple streaks of dawn appeared on the horizon, the Moonspinners packed their instruments into Bela's wagon and the remaining gypsy moths flew into the darkness or strolled back along the trail to their caravan. The villagers, too tired from the night's festivities, gathered only their lanterns and slowly disappeared into their safe and cozy tunnels.

Tiberius and Maleva flew to their new home, and after excitedly inspecting its every nook and cranny sat on the balcony to watch the sunrise and toast their new life together.

Crispin was also anxious to try out his new abode, and made his way through the post celebration remains to the village edge. On the way he paused and decided to test the strength of his injured leg. He laid one of his crutches against a sweet gum sapling and gently stood on his injured leg. It felt strong, and didn't hurt so he applied more pressure. There was still no pain and it held his weight with ease. Next he moved it and took a few slow steps. 'I think it's healed,' he said happily to himself. Just to be certain he walked a bit faster, and then did a little skip. "Hurrah, my leg's good as new." He almost shouted, "No more crutches and Ooh...I can fly again!"

He stretched his wings and zoomed into the air turning somersaults and reveling in the cool air rushing past his face. He got so excited he couldn't help but do a celebratory fire crackling in mid air.

"Oh a strange light," Maleva said pointing into the woods.

"I missed it," Tiberius said disappointingly. "What did it look like?"

"Was not firefly," she said shaking her head. "But more like tiny lightning bolt."

"Hmm," Tiberius replied grinning to himself knowingly.

Crispin perched on the balcony of his new home and watched the first golden beams of morning struggle to escape the earth's bonds. Moments later there was a brilliant flash as it broke free and spread its rays to hug the horizon. In the distance, the landing strip and gypsy moth caravan slowly emerged from the darkened forest. As the sun climbed higher it illuminated the runway and glinted off the wings of a lone dragonfly. The runway lights twinkled for an instant; then faded into the beginning of a new day.

THE END

About the Author

HELEN L. O'REILLY, left her native Texas after marrying an Army officer and spent the next 30 years living, working and traveling in Europe, Hawaii, and the continental U.S.A. When not writing, she can be found at Dragonfly Landing, tending her garden, and observing the resident insects.